Helen Jacey is the founder of ███ ██████ Productions which creates original stories with a ██████████████ ▐▐ media. A screenwriter and st▐ expertise on feminism and worked with internationa companies and leading bra *Story: Creating Memorable Female* ████ published in 2017, was the first creative writing guide to focus on female representation on screen. Previously Helen worked in the international aid sector in Eastern Europe, to reform the orphanage system and provide services for vulnerable women and children. She was awarded a BA by the University of Manchester, an MA by the London Institute and a PhD by the University of the Arts London.

Jailbird Detective

Elvira Slate Investigations Book One

By Helen Jacey

Shedunnit Productions

To Jack, with love

1

Coachella Valley, September 1945

Dust lacquered the windscreen like cheap hair spray. The cop couldn't see anymore so he pulled up. We were deep in the desert but he seemed to know his way around fine. I glanced out of the window. Prickly pear cacti stood between dried-out grasses, flat-faced and pockmarked freaky spectators. In the distance, a bird of prey scanned the horizon. A female, needing to feed her chicks?

The cop got out. His shoes crunched on the dry earth, as he came around to fling the passenger door open. 'Get out.' His pistol hung down loosely in his hand.

I tipped myself out of the car onto the clumpy terrain. Not so easy with cuffs on. Not so elegant, either. My hat, the one Alberta had lent me, and my only protection against the sun's inferno, tumbled off and rolled onto its side. One section of the rim was coated in dirt. The dipped-in-breadcrumbs look.

A shame.

I wouldn't be giving it back.

Without it, I would fry in seconds.

The cop made no move to pick the hat up. That he didn't spelt it out loud and clear.

Execution was imminent.

2

London, four months earlier

The wardress is new here, the nervous type, trying to tick all the boxes. Her neat little head with its mousy bun is in dire need of a good wash and set. At least we inmates have an excuse for looking like what the cat dragged in.

She is escorting me back to my cell. A battered copy of *Luminous Honeymoon* is tucked under my arm, a reward for chatting to do-gooders the week before and telling them how reformed I was. A safe bet the most romantic pages have been long ripped out by other women. Still, I can use my imagination. You have to, inside – or go barking mad.

I am miles away and don't pay much attention to the huddle of screws heading in our direction. After all, they get everywhere. Bossy cow Doodlebag, screw queen bee, is at the front, leading the way.

'Stand back!' the wardress hisses, pushing me around to face the wall. Something's up, something a prisoner shouldn't see. I'm four inches taller than her, and with a slight shift of my head I can easily watch.

Behind the screws, two men, older gents as usual, lug a stretcher.

On the stretcher is a sheet, and under the sheet, a stiff.

That's a turn-up. Somebody snuffing it – and in Block F, too. Women don't die in our block; we're all playing the long game. Who has actually gone through with what we all think about, but would never do? Faces race through my mind. Maybe it's natural causes. There are a few old biddies – Georgina, Millicent. Tough old birds, but this place is a strain on anybody's heart.

Death and I go back a long way. I've seen my fair share of the departed – life on the street and with Billy made sure of that – but the wardress is shaking. So, her first encounter with the Reaper, then.

Deal with it, sweetie.

I could comfort her but a screw is a screw. Another bluebottle feeding off the Holloway shit of our existence. I just hope she won't throw up.

The funeral party approaches. The wardress has recovered herself sufficiently to ram me further into the wall. Unexpectedly hard. Damn the bitch. My nose scrapes the cold brick wall, just as I meet Doodlebag's eyes.

Keep your mouth shut, her look demands.

I look down, taking a peek at the stretcher. A sheet covers the corpse. It's a slight frame, a tall body. Pointless guessing who it is. There's a peace and calm to the body under its gray shroud, almost a grace, a defiant grace.

You can't touch me now.

A gray cell blanket has been thrown over the woman's legs. A strange touch, she hardly needs it now. Maybe one of the screws did it, in a warped act of compassion.

They trudge past us. One of the older gents staggers a little. His face is emaciated, his arms like spindles. Definitely not cut out for this work. I'm not cut out to be a long-term inmate of His Majesty's Prison Holloway either, but that's war for you. We all end up somewhere we'd rather not be.

Something catches my eye. A blonde curl suddenly springs from under the side of the sheet. A pale ivory curl, perfectly formed.

My stomach lurches.

Only one person has curls like that.

Lena.

3

Lena is dead.

My only friend in this dump. *Why? Who has got to her?*
Someone in Block F.

So much for security.

Now this extended lockup. Shock has swallowed time and
I'm curled up on my excuse for a bed facing the wall. Staring at
the same old dents in the brickwork. Any other position gives
me a view of my '*chamber pot*', as the banged-up toffs who make
up the majority of the real fascists and communists, call them.

I don't want to watch whichever fly has popped by today to
crawl across the rim of the toilet, to circle over the bowl below.

Lena was laughing and singing only yesterday, one of the few
people inside who makes a point of staying chipper. She could
adorn a land girl poster, or be Hitler's perfect woman with her
model looks. A universal blonde. Up close, she is victim to the
Holloway beauty regime like the rest of us. Broken veins for
rouge, ingrained mud for hand cream. It was her hair that
defied jail. Naturally pale golden locks that we all envied. Mine
is mouse and I swear it looks green on a bad day, and there are
plenty of those. Dead straight, too. Lena's long fingers wound
it around strips of torn pillowcases to force it into shape; I
would look glamorous for a few days.

She'd only done it last night.

All dressed up, nowhere to go.

And last night she repeated her plans on release. She would
breed horses on her Tasmanian farm. Part-Arabs or something.

5

But she had seemed wistful, more so than usual. I'd asked her what was wrong. 'Other than this shithole?' Then she'd sniggered.

Lena and I shared a made-up joke that my father, the unknown American GI who was on his way home from the battlefields of Europe and who had left my mother Violet up the duff, had also taken a pop at Lena's mother Gwen, an Aussie nurse on leave at the time. Whoever the father really was, Gwen had retired with her pregnant belly full of baby Lena to Melbourne. She made up some cock-and-bull story about a fiancé who was shot down; Gwen was embraced with open arms. One day, her luck ran out – she was bitten by a red spider on her calf on the beach and died on the spot. When she was only two years old, Lena's rich aunt took her on.

'What's the point of a hot country if sunbathing costs your life?' I jibed.

'Come on down and you'll see for yourself,' she'd counter.

'I'll take your word for it, then. Think I'm going to spend months in some ship's berth after this joint? I'll only do that once more in my life and it won't be to get to Tasmania.'

'You're making a big mistake. I'll set you up with a dinkum cockie. Pop out a couple of brats. We can pretend we were nurses together.'

Now that was funny. We weren't the caring types. And so we'd banter away, locked up in dreary old Holloway, as the bombs and the rain poured down.

Recent events, impressions, race through my mind, searching for oddities, any kind of clue. Dirty looks in the washroom, raised voices, Lena being distracted once too often.

What have I missed?

She has been carted off to meet the Governor a few times recently. I didn't probe, but it was odd.

The Secret Service could be behind the whole thing. They had already done me over. Rubbing out a girl? *Fair dinkum*, as Lena would say. Being banged up on 18Bs makes us easy targets and all the more hated by the screws. Traitors, working for the enemy. Of course, some of the women in here are the genuine article and proud of it, self-declared Hitler-lovers now eating their words, especially the toffs. They don't exactly rough it inside, after their friends in high places intervene. Hypocrites. That's England for you. A country where we all shit the same shit, where we all breathe the same air, but where a posh accent and the right surname secures an early release and a pat on the back.

Darling! You've just been a little silly! Of course you didn't know he'd turn out to be a madman. Of course you didn't!

Others are like me. Petty criminals, call girls, or just plain idiots, doing the bidding of some man under the misguided belief he loved her; sleeping with a handsome foreign fellow. Seeking love with the wrong types, in the wrong places.

Fools for love.

Lena has never defended herself, she has never complained about her incarceration.

The times she came closest to grumbling were at breakfast, faced with dismal prison sludge each morning, pining for golden Tasmanian honey.

I never bothered to ask why a country girl from Australia was running around wartime Europe. And other than mentioning to Lena that I was betrayed by the man I thought loved me, I have never dwelt on who, what, where and why.

7

If it was all a bluff, she was a natural. Who knows what anybody really is inside? Who cares? We all lie, playing a twisted game of chums one day, surly bitches the next.

There has been the odd fuck-up. Like me not hearing Lena call out 'Jem' across the yard, the name the authorities know me by. 'Too young to go deaf, Jem,' She grinned, her blue eyes trying to read me. 'Just miles away,' I lied.

I haven't been Jem for years. Lena didn't need to know I'd gone by the name Ida Boyd before October '41, so I never told her. Just as I was never interested in her real name.

Inside, you need a friend, not the truth.

No way has she topped herself.

If the screws haven't done it, who else?

Muriel Sainte. No secret she and Lena can't stand the sight of each other. Muriel tends to be whimpering and pathetic. She moans and protests her innocence every second breath. Fainting fits, the vapors, but always with endearing manners. Toughie Lena has no time for such self-pitying antics and Muriel considers Lena a brute. But I quite like Muriel. She's almost theatrical, which can provide a bit of fun. Over the years, she's been a chum of sorts, singing *La Marseillaise* and teaching me French.

Je m'appelle Jemima Day, ça va?

And behind that weak veneer, there's steel in her veins. It's clever how she gets everyone to run around for her, even the screws.

Muriel is detested by her nation and is probably facing the chop, French-style, after a long marinade in Resistance rage. Her terror of her looming death has eaten her away. She can't

8

be more than five stone now. Her hair is thinning on top, all her eyebrows have gone and her top lip is puckered like somebody pulled a thread tight. At least the guillotine is instant, not like noose.

The noose. I try to think about something else. The thought of the noose always triggers the same panic in me. An uncontrollable tightness, a constriction of my neck that feels physical. Lena once joked about being hung and in seconds I was gasping, full of terrors, followed by waves of nausea. She'd laughed before she saw the state I was in.

I never comfort Muriel with the fact that if I am executed I will face a worse fate. 'It's going to be all right,' I tell her often. Is it? For any of us? While others have been released, there's a hard core of us left. We're the ones they don't trust an inch. We're the ones who will face the music later.

Muriel's clinging to the hope that peace will make her compatriots see sense, persuade them of her innocence. She's kidding herself; France will need scapegoats.

Shame and anger make a habit of landing someone else in it.

I know Muriel didn't kill Lena. She's always stayed out of trouble.

Her life depends on good behavior.

Now there's Jenny O'Mullins, a real oddball. Her wartime activities seem plain idiotic. The gossip is she'd been a secretary in the War Office but forgot documents on a train one evening. *As if!* She is creepy, with her long face and gray, watery eyes that stare for too long. I avoid her.

Then there's Bertha Fazekas, a Hungarian writer, who suffers manic spells and should really be in an asylum. One of the few ladies who stays fat on the Holloway ration. Extra dripping on her slice of National Loaf, in return for what? What can she bribe the canteen staff with? Once you get on Bertha's radar, you never get off it and she has had a crush on Lena from day one. Love and hate shared a very fine line in crazy ladies, perhaps even more so in Block F. Bertha could have done it. But, as with Muriel, I doubt it.

The obvious contenders are, well, just too obviously suspect. Austrian and German émigrés, clinging to each other like barnacles on a dry rock. Lena has intense debates with them in the yard, in German. She's fluent, her grandparents hailed from Frankfurt before moving to Australia. Sometimes they bicker. Once it erupted into a brawl. Lena got a fat eye before the screws broke it up.

'Let the fascists kill each other.' Muriel carted me away, arm-in-arm, preventing me from jumping in.

I don't speak a word of German, just a smattering of Italian. Even that is fading fast.

I stand up, and pace the cell. I feel the pangs in my stiff hip. My lasting gift from Holloway... if I ever get out. Giving this place my best years is bad enough. Now it is invading my bones.

Now it has taken my friend.

I will find the bitch that did it and get her.

My eyes fill, hot and fluid. Tears of rage. Tears for the stupidity. Tears for my powerlessness. Tears for my imprisonment.

Who am I fooling?

I rub my eyes with a corner of the grimy sheet.

You don't cry for strangers.

4

By late afternoon, I am on gardening duty with a couple of the others. The warders are acting normal; everything Holloway humdrum.

I could have imagined the whole thing.

Muriel, Bertha and Emilia, a jolly Italian who indignantly claims some of her dodgy clientele landed her inside, are gathered around, busy trying to work out the reason behind the extended lockup.

I won't breathe a word.

The ground is brittle; digging with the hand fork thankless and painful. Sturdy potato plants wave at me in the breeze. I want to trample them into pulp. I am sick of the place, and hate everything and everyone in it. Why the hell hasn't a V-2 flattened us by now?

To make matters worse, Doodlebag waddles out into the vegetable garden, craning her fat neck around. She looks like a pantomime dame, even down to the brass buttons straining against the buttonholes of her jacket. I continue to squat, scratching aimlessly at the surface of the mud.

Her large shadow looms over me. She literally growls at me. 'Governor wants to see you, Day. Now. Leave your tools here.'

I put down the fork, stand up and follow her, my mind racing. No secret to anyone that Lena and I were friends, but why this?

The others just stand there, leaning against shovels and forks. Women who have seen it all and probably done far worse outside, now reduced to schoolgirl gossip about who is in trouble with the headmistress and why.

To brighten their day, I mimic Doodlebag's fat backside as I follow her. A tribute to Lena. It's the kind of thing she'd do.

'Mamma mia!' Emilia roars with mirth.

Doodlebag spins around, eyes bulging in fury. I pull a blank face. Emilia's expression is an equally bad attempt at looking innocent and I stifle a laugh, sucking in my cheeks, looking down.

Doodlebag grunts, decides it isn't worth her while, and shoves me on, in front of her this time.

Near the entrance, Muriel yanks aimlessly at the bindweed, watching the proceedings. As I pass, she gives me a sneaky wink.

I shoot her a quick smile.

In reply, she silently mouths, *bonne chance*.

5

'I am aware you know a prisoner has died.' The governor, Lucinda Seldon, sits opposite me. Steam from cups of tea forms a protective veil between us.

The small table has a white lacy cloth and there's a pretty plate with fruitcake on it.

A very civilized inquisition.

Seldon is as immaculate as ever. I envy her the plum suit of the finest wool, and the ivory silk blouse with its elegant tie and creamy pearl buttons. But she's exhausted. Her skin has a yellow pallor like lampshade parchment and, unusually for her, dark rings under her eyes.

Dealing with Lena's killing must be a nightmare. Seldon is a by-the-book type. A defender of the faith, a rampart of decency.

Murder under her watch must be intolerable, especially if she has to turn a blind eye.

'I know it was Lena,' I blurt out. 'Who killed her?'

Is this the right card to play? I am out of practice, dulled by years of inertia – thinking on my feet is difficult.

Seldon arches her brows, incredulous. 'What? Lena took her own life. I'm very sorry. I know you were friendly.'

So this is the line. But she's a bad liar. Ordered to keep mum, but her features scream the truth.

A manufactured tear rolls down my cheek. I sniff. 'I can't believe it! She was happy last night.'

Seldon surveys me. She's buying the act, and hands me a starched white handkerchief from her own jacket pocket. Pure white, with embroidered dark violets adorning each corner. The prettiest thing I've seen in years. I dab my nose and a breeze of fresh lavender water fills my nostrils. Maybe a French brand. *Eau de Provence.*

When I lower it, it is smeared with dirt.

Eau de Hell.

Seldon gestures for me to keep it. She carefully puts her teacup down, her gaze all frosty officialdom. 'We will hold a small service in Lena's memory, in the Chapel. I'm afraid you won't be able to attend. We're releasing you.'

Released?

Lena is dead, and I am *free?*

The rotten stench of a cover-up fills the room. 'Is this something to do with Lena?' I ask.

'Of course not.' Seldon's eyes flick to the left.

Liar's left.

She goes on, all reason. 'The war's almost over. You are no longer deemed a risk to national security. Just like the others that have already been released.'

Is someone after me, too? Is she protecting me? I know I am one of Seldon's favorites. I was caught in '41 and dreaded another institution run by a bully. She seemed then, and still is, reasonable. And to give Seldon her due, she has changed things slightly for the better over the years. A rare creature, a woman who actually gives a shit about doomed women.

I must look stunned. Seldon allows herself a small smile. 'You will be free, subject to a short period of rehabilitation in the community.' She produces a white letter from her lap but she doesn't hand it to me, instead just waving it around for effect. It could be a shopping list for all I know. 'You are being

14

transferred to the South West. You will work on a Land Army farm in Torridge, Devon, for three months. Victory doesn't mean food shortages are over, so it's a chance to do your bit. You will go today, by train from Waterloo. With an escort.'

Land girl? Devon? The furthest west out of London I've ever been is Stonehenge, marveling at the stones while Billy and his gang looted a country house.

A farm in Torridge? Three months of rain and digging cow shit.

Another sentence.

Worst of all, more women. No, thanks. I am sick of the sight of women.

Seldon rattles on, gaining confidence in her bluff. 'Quite lovely countryside. Perhaps a bit more rain than London. You will have to report to a probation officer every week.'

'Probation? Aren't I free?'

Her eyes flash with irritated pity. I keep on saying the wrong thing. Seldon meets my eye. 'You will be free in three months. In cases like yours, where your innocence remains in doubt, probation is a test. Do not fail it. If you choose to break the terms, you will be returned here, no doubt branded a traitor. Women who leave here often fall back into their old ways. Don't be one of them. You must avoid the criminals who put you inside in the first place, the ones I suspect you have protected. Take this opportunity for change.'

The face of her handsome husband taunts me from its frame on her desk. He has an Errol Flynn moustache and spectacles. Bookish, but sexy. Next to the one of the husband, a family portrait; Seldon, the hubby and three little girls. Proud and happy. I look away but not in time. She caught me peeking.

Your husband would never betray you, Dr. Seldon. But the man I loved did and he was all I had. And I won't be getting on that train.

'I understand.'

Seldon offers the plate with the cake. I take it, reluctantly, but I don't eat it. She goes on. 'You have no family. If you could find a good man, marry and become a mother, it would give you more contentment than you have ever known.'

Contentment? A hot bath with rose-scented salts, a new silk dress, is more like it. Throw in a bottle of scotch or two, a snort of cocaine and some bubbly. Instead, I hear my voice sounding idiotic. 'A husband? I should be so lucky!'

At last, she gives me an encouraging smile.

We make small talk for a few more minutes about whatever a soon-to-be-released convict and a prison governor have in common. The conversation dries up fast enough and finally, Seldon rises.

She's done her duty and has got me out of the way.

Now it is all up to me.

At the door, she hovers. 'Stay in touch, Jemima. Write to let me know how you get on. I would very much like to hear about your new life.'

6

I quickly dress in the icebox of a changing room. My hands are shaking and I know it's not the cold.

It's the thrill of freedom.

Almost five years of my life down the drain because the higher-ups of society have decreed me a danger to the state. More fool them. They credit me with believing in something beyond looking out for myself.

I did, once. I believed in love. But Holloway put that right. In that respect, the nick's education beat a few years of grammar school.

Seldon thinks I'm protecting people. No, it's not love or loyalty that has kept me quiet for almost five years of lockup. I have been simply sticking to a pledge I made years ago. No pledge of honor among thieves, nothing like that. Just a pledge between two lowlifes, me and Billy, to keep the other safe if one got caught. But then he set me up, and I've still stuck to it. Why? Not to protect the bastard. Simple. Grassing on Billy will drastically cut my options when I get out. I have had no choice but to play a silent long game, which comes arm-in-arm with the high price of endless incarceration, and the authorities' unshakable belief that I'm loyal to some cause.

I've had no defense solicitor, no appeals, no attempts to shorten my stretch. All I could do, as the weeks turned into months, was let Holloway's stale blanket smother me.

Hush, hush, child. I'll wake you up when it's all over.

17

Then Lena arrived with all her big-mouthed Aussie brilliance and dragged it off me.

Like Muriel, I've lost weight. Turns out dread and paranoia is the best diet regime. The clothes they handed back are the same ones I wore when I was picked up, that rainy day in October '41. Now they are strangers from the past. The burgundy crepe dress hangs shapelessly, and the hem is coming down. The stockings are definitely not mine, vile rayon affairs in flat beige. One is laddered at the heel and as I slip it on, the ladder runs all the way up my leg. My seamed French ones have long gone, no doubt nicked by some magpie wardresses. Bloody cheek.

My black suede peep-toe shoes were brand new in '41. Not Utility. Now the heels are ground down and scuffed, the once velvety suede stretched and scratched. My feet slide around in them. Then it hits me what could be going on. The screws could have a weekend rota, pilfering the inmates' clobber as and when it takes their fancy.

My tilt hat, a faux fur little number, has seen better days. The ribbon at the back is bent and frayed. It whiffs, musty, or ripe with the stale odor of somebody else's head. My brown faux fox jacket has lost its shine. The only thing that has got off lightly is my green and red silk scarf. Crumpled and smelling of damp.

Like me, but the scarf is redeemable.

I've shared worse inside so grit my teeth and pin the hat on. Before I went down, I was a stickler for hygiene. Billy used to put it down to early teenage years on the street, never knowing when the next bath would come. *'Making up for lost time, sweetheart.'* I blame my neurosis on the children's home I lived

18

in after Violet, my mother, disappeared. Dead, the nun with the black eyes said. Black eyes that matched her habit. Pneumonia, she said. But she never let me say goodbye.

The home was a filthy place, only cleaned up when inspectors or visitors came. Us kids slept in sheets that stank of dried piss for weeks on end. Sometimes, the way we smelt was an excuse for some nun or other to give us a thrashing – teaching us that the system was rigged from the start. We ate bread with inky mold, stale biscuits that crumbled.

The only item as I remember it is my black handbag. Bedraggled, crumpled, dusty and ageless. Violet's old bag. The nun had given it to me. My heirloom. She said would look after it for me. But she hid it from me at the orphanage. It dangled from her arm when she went into town. When I escaped from the shithole, I broke into her room and pinched it back. She'd even kept my mother's unposted love letters and my birth certificate inside. I used to wonder if the letters gave the nun a cheap thrill or were some kind of validation of her choice.

I open the bag. Empty. Unused. The warders hadn't been interested in this. I pop Dr. Seldon's hanky into it. An unlikely prison souvenir.

There is no mirror, of course, nothing to help us pass as normal on the outside.

Don't get ahead of yourselves.

Looking down at myself, one word comes to mind. Dowdy. The outfit would be ditched – and fast.

I notice something. Words that someone else has scratched into the wall.

Truth is the slowest torture.

My truth? Billy was behind my stretch. Torture? Not really,

it didn't eat me up. Just a sad fact I didn't count for him anymore. Hardly worse than anything the Secret Service bastards did, with their bullyboy tactics.

Another truth – Lena's murder is something I can't do a thing about. I can't let it torture me. I'll let it go. Forget I know her.

And the final truth, one that has defined my whole life – Violet's disappearing act. A crushing blow when I was six, but the nuns instilled enough hatred in me as a distraction. Now the memory of Violet is a nuisance, like my Holloway hip. Hardly torture.

Don't cry over spilt milk.

I look at the writing again. The inmate must have used her nails to write it. Silly cow. Torturing herself, more like.

I leave the cubicle, bracing myself for life on the outside.

Goodbye, Holloway, you old bitch.

7

London.

The city is a tragic, pathetic heap. A gangster's girl after one too many thrashings. Blacked-out windows for kohl, bomb dust for powder. Jerry has beaten her good and proper – but she fought back. Defended herself and saw the back of him. And she will recover.

I won't be around to see her rise from the ashes. I'll be long gone.

I gaze out of the prison car at the alleys, side streets and parades of shops. People in heavy coats, queuing outside bakeries, grocers, fishmongers.

It's all unknown to me. I never spent much time north of the River, or in the East End. South London is my manor and by the time I went down I prayed it had been through the worst of the Blitz.

Bolting from the car is risky. I'll soon get lost, hurtling into likely dead ends. These loose shoes won't help either. Waterloo Station offers the only real shot to run for it. It could be busy and crowds mean cover. Caught, I'm as good as dead. That was Seldon's threat.

Don't confirm our suspicions.

After the tiny cells and narrow corridors, the vast height of the station is overwhelming, the noise disorientating. Engines, whistles, rowdy groups hanging around, the laughter of women. Eager newspaper boys shout out about victory, that Winnie's declaration is imminent.

21

Excitement sparks the atmosphere. Everywhere, men and women in uniform. All sorts, far more than I remember. I'll need a uniform to blend in. Red Cross nurse? WAAF? Sally Army, even? I'm not feeling choosy.

Doodlebag bustles through the throng to the ticket office. I follow dutifully but she barely looks back to check. The cow is willing me to bolt. She wants to be the hero, save the day and be the one to prove to Seldon I was a waste of trust.

Well, dearie, you've underestimated the dull little inmate. I'll bolt all right, but you'll have egg on your face. I escape on your watch.

A mass of khaki catches my eye. Returning heroes, swamped by their families. Family gatherings always sickened me and they still do. I look away. Against a far wall, a long row of injured men, slumped in wheelchairs. Some without legs, others without arms. Their ashen faces are barely visible behind luggage stands, casting shadows like prison bars. These chaps have to endure the odd member of the public shaking their hands, kissing them, like they own them. They have to smile, and nod.

Piss off, I lost my legs for you and I don't even know you.

I feel the first feeble flicker of patriotism in a very long time. Compared to the soldiers, we've had it easy inside.

At the ticket office, Doodlebag pushes the door. A long queue. Handy, but for what I don't quite know. I hover, coughing. 'Could I wait here? I just want to...watch the world go by.' I simper. 'Won't do anything silly. Free as a bird in three months.'

She glances at her watch and back at me with her fish eyes. 'Wait on that bench. Stay where I can see you.'

A very funny game of chess. I nod. 'Thank you.' I wander over to the wooden bench and sit, aware she's watching from the ticket office door. Satisfied, she waddles back in. The bench offers a good vantage point to scan the scene, and my mind is racing. Through the window, Doodlebag has joined the queue. She regularly looks up to glare at me.

You won't see me when I run. You won't have a clue.

But how? Should I just do it, go now? No. I don't have long enough. I've got to wait until she's being served, her attention off me. I fidget with the bag, noticing something trapped in the lining.

Yes!

Five years ago, I hid my engagement ring from my captors' eyes. Carted off in the back of the van, I'd quickly slipped it from my finger, shoving it through a split in the lining. All this time, it's stayed hidden. I bet if they had found it, the wardresses wouldn't have returned it.

My finger feels for the same split in the crumpled lining, as I look up and watch the passersby. There. I stick my finger in and poke around until I hook the ring.

I hold it low in the bag, buffing it slightly. The garnets and pearls glimmer back at me. *Blood and bandages*, Billy had joked, slipping it on my finger. *Devil and angel*, I'd answered. He had the final word as usual.

Love and hope.

Billy. He had his romantic moments. Knew how to treat a lady. Furs, pearls and the rest.

Pawnbrokers would be doing a roaring trade now, and surely the ring should fetch a few bob? Billy's meaningless proposal could finance my freedom, or at least pay for a new getup.

A girl saunters over to the bench, her head stuck in a women's magazine. She is about seventeen, with mousy blonde hair. It's longer than mine but the curls are limp. She looks careless and free. The war hasn't ground youth out of her. She's enthralled by the fashion pages.

She sits down next to me. I glance at the pages of her magazine. Haughty models in evening gowns glare out. Untouchable goddesses, the world at their feet. Features like *'Ration Recipes'* and *'Winning your war against wrinkles'* are new to me. They will stay that way.

The girl is pretty, with a snub nose. A baby-faced look. I feel like an old prune next to her.

It's her clothes that interest me. Her hat is dove gray, with a wide rim, blue ribbon, and a fake blue rose with silky petals. Her jacket is dark gray ribbed wool, with matching gray buttons up the front, and curved side pockets, matching a curved collar. Very different to my getup; she blends in, while I stand out. Nobody else is wearing in fur in May.

The conwoman's rush of adrenaline surges up. She's the mark, surely? If I let this one go, I'm stuck in Devon, digging cow shit in the cold and wet.

'Do you like this?' I say, my voice low, displaying the ring in my palm.

She glances down, then up again at me. 'Give over. I ain't got a penny.' The accent is pure South London.

'It's your lucky day, then.'

'Says who?'

'Says me. You can have it for nothing. Well, for a swap.'

'Swap what? This?' She raises her magazine, incredulous, but keeps her voice low, too. Instantly game, instantly on the make.

My type.

'Your hat and coat for mine. Hardly been worn.' I lied. 'But you have to put them on and sit here.'

'You having me on? What do you want my clothes for?'

'I know it sounds mad. I'm just in a bit of a pickle.'

The girl surveys my downbeat clothes and my gaunt face. She bristles and leans away from me. 'You in trouble?'

I make my voice slightly posher in compensation. The elocution lessons from a well-meaning foster mother come in handy yet again. 'Love trouble. You see the queue in there?'

The girl follows my eyes, nodding. There's an older man in the queue, reading a newspaper. 'See the gent at the end, with the paper? That's Cecil, my boyfriend. He bought me the ring. Cost a bob or two.'

'You're jilting him?' She's sucked into the drama.

I roll my eyes. 'No. I'm actually married. My husband, Henry, has been missing in action for years. I assumed the worst. Only took up with Cecil because he cheered me up. But I got a telegram today. They found Henry. Not only that, he's arriving today. Cecil thinks he's taking me to his cousin's in Sussex but I have to give him the slip. I simply can't face telling him!' I lowered my voice, whispering frantically. 'Henry's military train has just come in. The poor fellows are lined up over there on Platform One. Henry's completely lost his memory, trapped in a POW camp for years. Worst of all, he's lost a leg. I would have never have started anything with Cecil had I known. I've got to shake him off somehow.'

The girl's eyes widen. Is she taking the bait? I say, 'Look, take the ring. Sit here in my coat and hat. It will give me time to collect Henry and just go. If Cecil comes over, just say you noticed a woman had a very similar coat as you and you think that she headed towards Platform Eight. He'll go off, while I slip away to get Henry. For your sterling efforts, you get the ring and my eternal gratitude! I'll write to Cecil, and explain. He's a decent fellow, but I just can't do it now. Please help me, but we have to be quick. I can't leave Henry waiting a moment longer.'

I'm rusty as hell. It's fifty-fifty. In the ticket office, Doodlebag is about to be served. Sod this! I should just run. I will have to if she hesitates a moment more. One last-ditch attempt. 'Cecil's loaded, the type that likes to show a girl a good time. You're a pretty girl. Let him. Just don't show him the ring!' I wink. 'Here, try it on. The pearls are real.'

She glances at the ring, then to the chap inside, and then to me. 'All right.'

'Here you are.' I sound as calm as I can. I pass the ring to her.

The way she admires her finger, there's a good chance it's not coming off again. 'Suits you,' I say. Time is running out.

Make up your mind, goddamn you!

'All right. I'll keep it.'

It's too soon to let relief take over, but I want to kiss her. 'You're a doing a very good deed. Quickly, now! Stand up, keep your back to me. That's right. Eyes on Cecil and take your jacket and hat off.'

The codger remains completely engrossed in his paper. Doodlebag is at the counter. The girl moves fast, slipping off her jacket. I pass her my coat. 'Too warm for May, but it's quality.' She can chuck it in the bin for all I care. We finish up with our hats. She keeps her gold hatpin, though, with a pearl end. It was her granny's, she says. 'What's your name?' I ask.

'Elvira. Everyone calls me Ellie.'

'Thank you, Ellie.

She is still entranced by her finger. 'I got the better end of the deal. Should be thanking you, more like.'

Ellie will be picked up, questioned. They will do their best to brand her my accomplice. But how can they? Hopefully her total ignorance about me will help.

Say you just felt sorry for me. Repeat my sob story.

She'd be an idiot to mention the ring. They don't know it exists. I have a feeling she won't and will stick to the pity angle.

Looking like just like Jemima Day, newly released convict, Ellie sits on the bench.

Looking like somebody else I have yet to discover, I speed towards the large stone archway, through the crowds. Pigeons amassing for commuters' crumbs scatter in my wake.

I am running and have no regrets.

I will find Billy. I will demand compensation.

Then I will go back to the only place I have memories of sunshine, of playing, of friends, of something that could have been happiness.

America.

8

Once a fraud, always a fraud.

Seldon's face haunts me; my determined criminality, reverting to old habits at the first chance I have, will sting her.

Wise up, lady.

The side streets winding away from the Waterloo Road are safer. Bomb craters are everywhere, creating a bizarre and ugly landscape. If Doodlebag is quick off the mark, details of my escape and my mugshot could make tomorrow's papers. *Prisoner absconds.* Somebody might recognize my face and put two and two together.

Isn't that Ida Boyd, Billy Martin's girl?

I am a wanted woman.

Running confirms their stupid belief I'm a fascist. If I'm caught, they won't go as easy on me as before. A few cigarette burns could be replaced by the noose. Seldon didn't say it, but that was what she meant.

The noose. I can't think about it now. A seizure of panic won't do me any favors.

Predictably, the shoes don't help. The high heels, now caked in dust, wobble and slide over the cobbles. Taking them off would be faster, but looking like a tramp, or like a lunatic, is out of the question. I have to blend in. I belong out here. I am normal.

The authorities do not know I lived for five long years as Ida Boyd, gangster's moll. When they caught me, I gave my real name, Jemima Day. Telling them I was Ida Boyd could have led them to Billy if they'd put enough effort into it, and he'd have gone down, or even worse. Even in my shock at being caught, the pledge of silence held, Billy had drilled it in that good. It didn't take my captors long to check that Jemima Day was one and the same as the orphan, the street urchin, the juvenile offender, the reform school girl, the foster kid. Jemima Day's troubled life suited the Secret Service agents' most likely final conclusion: that a common piece of muck like me would do anything for money, even some fascist's bidding.

But they couldn't be sure, could they?

So down I went. Down the Holloway rabbit hole.

Now my pledge with Billy is just an insurance policy I can claim on.

Everywhere, people are getting ready for victory parties. Spirits are high, lonely old ladies hover in their doorways, smiling and waving. Their hallways look inviting and homely. I could talk my way into any of these. Get a decent cuppa, a cheese sandwich. From some open window, the crackly, happy sounds of a big band. I'm transported back to our dance hall days, me and Billy all dressed up, stars of the dance floor.

Screw him.

I pass the back-to-back slums. Some rows turn into wastelands, boarded-up fences with *Danger* sloshed on them in paint. Behind, bare structures of houses somehow stand erect, their innards ripped out, chimneys dangling like ripped windpipes, whole sides blasted off. Birds have claimed these as safe havens, their nests gather in nooks.

Fucking Hun. Why pick on us? People here aren't rich; they will take years to get back on their feet.

29

Raging inwardly, I suddenly trip over a bloody sandbag hanging over what was left of a gutter. As I fall, something catches me.

Two uniformed arms. A man's arms.

A copper?

'Somebody's not looking where she's going.'

An ARP warden, fifty-odd. His blunt fuse wire for hair juts out from beneath his cap. Breathing into my face, holding me tight. The smell is man, pungent with pipe smoke and sweat.

I grin. 'Oops-a-daisy! Miles away.' My guts churn.

He smiles. His eyes are as hard as the screws' but they are hungry, too, roaming over my breasts. 'Watch your step, poppet. Be a shame to twist your ankle on a night like this. We're all going to be dancing tomorrow.'

I bounce into dumb blonde mode. It's been five years, but it is like riding a bicycle.

'Ta very much. I will.'

Let the hell go of me.

'You all right? He peers at me. 'Nothing broken? Want me to check?' His hand slides down my backside.

I tense. 'Right as rain. In a hurry, if you don't mind.'

'Where to?'

'A friend's house. I don't have a wireless. Want to listen.'

'Where does your friend live?'

Any minute now he will be asking for my papers. 'Camberwell Road,' I reply, without thinking.

'Camberwell Road,' He repeats. 'It's a long road. Whereabouts?'

I want to say 598. Why? The only number that comes to mind. Betty's dress shop. But it would be stupid to say where

I'm really heading. I say 72. Let's hope 72 isn't known to have been obliterated. I pray to the god of lies.

'Give us a kiss, ducky.'

A *kiss?* He doesn't care where I'm going. Welcome back to the world of men and their liberties. His face looms over mine, his beard glinting.

Suddenly, a yell smashes through the darkness. A man's voice, loud and belligerent. A woman screams back. A pair of drunks having a ding-dong.

The warden reluctantly releases his pressure on my arm. He shouts out, 'Oi! What's all that racket about, then? Pipe down!'

The woman tells him to piss off. Wrong move, lady. Right for me. The ARP warden bristles. His ego and the uniform won't allow him to ignore the insult. 'Like that, is it?'

He struts off, full of self-importance. I relax. So my lucky streak still runs.

I dart down the first alley I come to, and collapse against the wall. It's only then I heave, throwing up. Nothing but bile comes out.

You're fine. Don't waste time. Move!

I reach the Walworth Road, a blister the size of a gobstopper on my heel.

Suffield Road is a minute away. My last known address. I can just look, can't I? I won't go as far as my house, just take a peek. My house. Our home. The place Billy would lay his hat when he felt like it. After my arrest, he'd have made sure nothing was left lying around the house linking me to him. The authorities must have ransacked the place.

But what about Kettle? If Billy has left the cat to fend for himself, it's a double betrayal.

I brace myself, approaching the corner of Manor Place. I stop. Disorientated, I don't know where I am. Another rubble meadow replaces most of the road where the terrace of brick houses once stood. All gone. It must have been one of Jerry's monsters. All those people, those families. Faces I haven't thought about for years come back to me.

I venture to the empty space where Number 37 should have been.

A crater for a home.

Icing on the cake.

The realization suddenly hits me that Billy could be dead. All this effort, and it hadn't occurred to me he could be gone. Billy was a born survivor.

Takes one to know one.

I stand still, frozen to the spot. He wouldn't have gone here, to the house. He wouldn't have been in the vicinity when Jerry hit. After they caught me, he wouldn't risk it. He would assume I would talk, break the pledge. He'd have laid low. Until the weeks turned into months, and he put two and two together, realized that I wasn't going to grass on him. The pledge stayed firm. Billy would laugh, he'd work out my reasoning, too. He would know I'd expect a payout on my release.

He cannot be fucking dead!

Dusk is falling, but not fast enough. I limp through the shadows, away from the dead space, away from the ghosts.

Billy used to limp, lame from childhood polio, so he dodged the conscription bullet. Even if they have tried to put him to use in the Home Guard, filing or something ridiculous, he will have wriggled out of that, too. I never saw him put himself at anyone's mercy. Not even thank anybody. Not for lack of manners, the occasion just never demanded his gratitude. 'Fetch us a pot of tea, love,' delivered as if he was doing you a favor. 'Marvelous,' he'd smile. But never a '*thank you*'.

Billy was boss, simple as that.

When I met him at sixteen, I believed the world owed me a living. I'd roughed it long enough, thank you very much, and here was my own sugar daddy to make everything all right. I'd happily spend his money, doll myself up, hang on his arm in return for my life of Riley. He was indulgent, but later my more frivolous moments would annoy him. He couldn't hide it. And when the money dried up, war was declared, and he and all the other Italians we knew were banged up, he came out different. Changed. Bitter. Reserved. They all did. Even smiling Betty. They all took offence at being made to feel like the enemy by the country they called home. Billy had new friends, a new set of spivs. He'd go off for days. To Little Italy, people said, when I called at his club at the Elephant. Then he'd return, with new men in tow. Men with black hair, sharp suits, teeth as sallow as their skin, chain-smokers the lot. They didn't smile at me, and I didn't smile back. I nicknamed them the Sour Grapes. Billy didn't like that.

Sugar daddy, lover, fiancé, cad, liar. If what Billy and I had was love, it was the type that bites you in the ankle, leaving you to bleed out. Plain and simple. He set me up and left me to rot.

But Billy a fascist traitor? I can't see it. Like me, South London blood ran through his veins. Like me, his political convictions didn't run deep.

But you don't know him anymore. You haven't known him for years.

33

Inside, other inmates got correspondence, even if words had been blacked out. Billy could have written in code with a false address or identification. 'Auntie Prudence' or suchlike. But he hadn't. Not a dicky bird. I wondered what he was saying to the few people who knew we were still an item, how he explained my disappearance. 'Took off in a huff, stupid bitch.' Is there a new woman? He can have a few on the go for all I care.

He'll have plenty of money stashed now, I can bet on that. *I have to find him.*

I shudder, from cold, from hunger, from fear of capture. From the new winds of change.

He has to be alive.

9

Betty Pizzi's dress shop, called *Betty's,* sits in a small parade on the Camberwell Road. She never cared what her customers got up to so long as they paid up every quarter and liked a bit of glamour to their dresses. Which was a good thing, as most of her clientele were South East London crooks' floozies, dressed to the nines on tick, bankrolled by boyfriends who ran with the Elephant Boys or the Messina Brothers. Betty worked hard and never mentioned her hometown of Naples. Rumor had it she ran away from a husband and child there when she was sixteen. A busy sparrow of a woman, a needle in her mouth, and a twinkle in her eye until they interred her.

If she is still around, she'll know Billy's whereabouts. She was one of the few people who knew we were an item because he settled my account with her. And until she catches sight of my mugshot in the papers, Betty Pizzi is my only chance.

The familiar mannequins in the shop window stare into space, posing in dreary dresses gathering dust. The fabric looks cheap. I never wore a Utility number. All my dresses and gowns were expensive leftovers from the late Thirties, or off the ration when Billy felt like treating me. Less and less often in the later years.

The blackout curtains are wide open, and several window panes replaced with painted black wood. There are small signs pinned to these, but I can't make them out. The glow of a weak light bulb is visible in the upstairs window. Somebody's home.

I knock on the door. Silence. The kind when someone inside is debating if they should open the door.

The creak of an internal door and the reluctant scrape of the chain.

Betty's familiar eyes. The lids more papery, hanging lower over her dark irises. The same pale gold crucifix around her neck. Faded hair with strands of pure white, thick like cotton. She must be late fifties now and her sallow face has a collapsed look about it.

'It's me, Betty. Ida Boyd.'

I get a blank expression in return. 'Billy's girl.' I hate the words. 'Can I come in? Just for a minute?'

She thinks about it, giving nothing away. 'I thought you were dead.'

Dead. Not *sent down*.

I have to play it safe. 'So what blighter says I'm dead? Billy? That's a bloody cheek, considering he sent me packing.' I do my best to look indignant.

It's a gamble. But a gamble that tallies up with whatever she knows. Betty Pizzi opens the door.

A tiny fire burns in the small grate. Betty stands in the door, gesturing for me to sit down. I obey, grateful to get the weight off the blister. Her old sofa is a billowy cloud and I fight off a wave of exhaustion.

'You never come here, nobody sees you in years. Are you sick?' She looks me up and down. If she knows about prison, she's doing a good job of pretending otherwise.

Yes, I've changed. And so have you. But we won't share war stories, will we?

I smile, shaking my head. 'Right as rain.' Now for the real test. 'I split with Billy. Been on a Land Army farm, up North. Wrecked my nails.' I grimace, waving my dirty fingertips around.

'A farm? You?' Betty's brows dance into her forehead.

'Not much choice. Didn't want to stick around here, did I?'

She takes it in and leaves the room. So far, so good.

I call out, 'How are things with you?'

'Business is terrible. Nobody has a penny,' she calls back. I can hear her clattering around in her kitchen. She returns, like Mother Christmas, with a box of ciggies and a bottle of French brandy. 'A blast from a very big bomb broke all my windows. My big shop window. My glasses. Everything. The only thing not broken? This bottle. It's a miracle. So I save it for peace. I do not like to drink alone, and you are here, the night before peace. Maybe you are a miracle.' She smiles, and I get a flash of the old Betty.

Brandy and ciggies. My kind of tea party, Dr. Seldon.

Betty doesn't stint, pouring the amber liquid to the top of the cup. 'When all this is over, maybe I sell up. Go somewhere else. Somewhere there is sunshine.'

She waves the cigarettes at me and I nod. The box flies through the air and I catch it. There's an old bent matchbook on the edge of the sofa. Faded print advertises *Lonnie's Cabaret Club* in Beak Street. I'd been there. Seventeen years old, and wild with it. I remember opium smoke swirling into my brain in a back room. Billy finding me at it, furious, dragging me home.

Betty hands me a cup. My official reunion with alcohol.

Betty sits down on a small stool, studying me. To toast or not to toast? She takes the plunge. 'To a better life.' Not *to victory*. I wonder what it means to her, one who has been branded an untrustworthy Eyetie.

I raise the cup and then sip. It is hot and sharp on my throat like a blade slicing my tonsils. The only cure is a bigger glug.

She is saying, 'You know about the bomb in your street?'

I nod. 'How many?'

'Thirty, forty? It's a tragedy.' She makes the sign of the cross, briefly closing her eyes.

I light up, praying Kettle was far away at the time. The nicotine hits the back of my throat and I splutter like a kid.

'You know where Billy is?' I bluff, attempting another drag. 'I'm not here to cause a scene. He owes me dosh from a long time ago. I need it.'

I wait for it. *Dead, alive, near or far.*

Betty surveys me. 'You don't know?'

'No. What?' I exhale, better this time, but now I just feel sick. I meet her eyes, arching my brows. 'Not gone and snuffed it, has he?'

'No, Billy isn't dead! He has rooms, above the Jack & Jill. Don't say I tell you this.'

'Fair enough,' I somehow say. He's alive. He's nearby. I'm one step closer to running. 'Has he got a girl?'

'Maybe. One or two. I do not see him so often.' Betty spins her tumbler in her hand, avoiding eye contact.

'I feel like a tramp. Could I buy a dress? Perhaps lipstick and rouge? I can settle up with you tomorrow once he's coughed up.'

Betty looks me up and down. 'You do not have to pay me.' She gets up and leaves the room again.

After a while, she returns, saying she's put some things out on the bed and that she is running me a bath. It's unexpected. Do I look that dirty? She reads my thoughts and explains travelling by train is unpleasant. She either pities me, the half-starved filthy wreck in from the cold, or suspects I'm on a mission to get Billy back and she's on my side. Those few warm inches of water are like a bath in paradise after the gray scum in Holloway. Betty has left an old razor and coal tar soap on a towel. I use the razor on my leg stubble, skinning my ankle at once. The blood floats into the water, forming dancing scarlet ribbons.

Drying myself, I catch my reflection in a broken piece of mirror left nailed to the wall. Skin and bone. My face is darker than my body, thanks to the spell of recent Spring sunshine in the prison garden. One weak ray and I tan faster and deeper than everybody else. Mulatto blood, I'd been told by the nuns. Mulatto had sounded exotic to my childish imagination. Vagabonds, brigands and pirates on the Seven Seas – like me, free spirits. Violet had been white as daisy petals and I inherited her mousy hair. It was only when I saw Jean Harlow and Ida Lupino in the picture house that I yearned for ivory skin and platinum hair, cursing my unknown ancestry. My face was plastered in white powder, my eyes daubed in kohl, and my hair a cheap bottle blonde by seventeen.

I dollop some cold cream on my cheeks. It is waxy and smells of freesia, but feels like an oil slick on my face after years of nothing.

A pale blue dress lies stretched out on the counterpane on the bed, with some nylons and garters. I examine the dress's label. A Loretta Model, Mayfair.

I hold it against me. Nothing fancy but well made, with pleats on the bodice and pale blue buttons up to a pretty collar edged with blue lace. The lace is repeated on the three-quarter length sleeves. A bit simple for my taste, but then again, what is my taste now? At least the dress goes with Ellie's dove gray hat.

Betty has left out some old makeup. Powder in a gold compact, and waxy mascara. I pat creamy powder over my face, restoring paleness. The lipstick is dry and stiff, but red enough. It tastes slightly rancid. There is no rouge, so I use a crumb of lipstick and rub it hard onto my now oily cheekbones. I fluff up the curls Lena gave me. It's as if she knew I'd be having an outing.

I finish with the red nail lacquer, making a bad job of it after five years' without practice. Then I sit on the edge of the bathtub, blowing on my nails.

In the mirror, I admire my reflection. Somebody fresh and innocent looks back.

Not bad for an old lag.

I return to the sitting room to stuff my clothes into the bag. I use Dr. Seldon's hanky to wipe the teacup I'd held before Betty comes in. There can be no trace of my presence here, even if she later talks.

'You look like Lauren Bacall,' Betty says, at the doorway. I have no idea who that is. I slip the gray jacket over the dress.

'Ta-ta, Betty. Thanks.' I mean it. She's given me a fighting chance. Maybe likes me more than I remember.

It is dark now, and a violet sky hangs low on the Camberwell Road. The air is thick from smoke, the smell of celebration, not V-2 carnage. Teenage boys drag broken bannisters, ripped floorboards and doors towards huge blazing bonfires that spit orange flecks into the night sky. People huddle around them. New shrines to the god of victory.

I reach the Jack & Jill, a big pub with two bars. The double doors of the saloon bar are open and people spill out like entrails of humanity onto the street, drunk and emotional.

I stick to the shadows, head down, dreading familiar faces. I'm in Billy's territory, I'm the interloper. Someone drops a glass and everyone cheers. Another group holler a song I don't know. The din of the singing swells as more join in.

Around the side, a drunk takes a piss against the wall. He can barely stand, spraying everywhere. He hears me and turns, smiling toothlessly.

A dark exterior stone staircase leads up to the three flats, one on each level. The first two flats are boarded up. I keep going, my legs now like lead.

On the top floor, a dark wooden door shuts the world out, its two glass panels painted in the usual thick bitumen. No bell, no knocker. To the side, a cracked stone planter decorates the entrance. Was it ours? From outside my front door in Suffield Road? I used to grow pansies and marigolds in it in summer. This escaped the bomb? Odd if Billy lugged the thing here.

I put my ear to the door.

Run back down the stairs, forget this. Pick up a stranger. Anything but this!

My mouth is sandpaper, I have a leaping frog for a heart. My knuckles give a short rap. I stand back, shocked I've actually done it. Mindlessly, I bend down and feel the dry earth in the planter. I crumple the dried leaves of a dead geranium plant. Underneath, moist shoots trying to sprout. Fragile things, seeking out the light. They are probably doomed to die before they've had a chance.

The door opens. Billy's eyes. Two pools of blackness.

Dark as the barrel of the gun he points in my face.

10

'In accordance with arrangements between the three great powers, tomorrow, Tuesday, will be treated as Victory in Europe Day and will be regarded as a holiday'.

We both ignore the announcement. Billy hobbles over to a drinks cabinet. His limp is more pronounced.

Watch yourself. He didn't offer you any pity.

'How did you find me?'

'Betty.'

If he is annoyed, he doesn't show it. 'Not in a good way, Betty. Lost her boyfriend.'

She hadn't mentioned a boyfriend. But I hadn't asked. I'm just a freeloader from the past.

Billy and I look at each other. Long gone, the sharp-suited spiv with the boyish smile of my memory. His skin is an unhealthy putty color and his black hair has thick strands of gray. He's unshaven, a field of black and white stubble replacing the thin moustache he previously sported. The red and green silk dressing gown, a well-preserved Jermyn Street number, is the one constant. He always dressed well. And he always liked the finer things in life.

In turn, his eyes glance at my made-up face, over the blue dress. The whole look could be having some kind of effect. But I'm not his Ida anymore. I am too thin, and maybe I look a little fast.

I look around. Antiques and a large Chinese rug dominate the sitting room floor, lending the place a sense of luxury. 'War's been good to you,' I say, pointlessly.

He is pouring a large amount of scotch into two cut glass tumblers. On top of Betty's brandy, I'd better go easy.

'Can't complain.' He nods to the large, velvet sofa. I shake my head. 'I don't have long. Going out.'

'Suit yourself. What do you want?'

I lean against the wall. 'That's nice, after all these years. Where's Kettle?'

'Hit by a car near the Green. Couple of weeks after you were sent down. Think he was looking for you.'

So my cat is dead. The last tie.

Don't show it hurts.

'You bury him?'

'Yeah, under the crab apple. Now he's under the rubble. Have a butcher's at Suffield? Evil bastards.'

The crab apple. With its endless fruit that rotted and made the backyard smell like a brewery. Nothing could kill that shrub, not even a bomb. I bet it is pushing up the rubble even now. But Billy's referred to the Jerries as evil, and he means it.

'He didn't like being left alone,' I state, as uncritically as possible.

Billy walks over with the drinks and hands me a glass. I carefully avoid his fingertips and his gaze. 'He wasn't left alone. Maudie took him in.'

Maudie. I remember her. The old lady two doors down.

'Yeah, she snuffed it, too, when the bomb dropped. Loads got it.' Billy answers my thoughts. 'Turns out you were better off inside.'

He lifts his glass. 'To victory.' He sounds like he means it but it could be sarcasm. I say nothing. Victory so far is just a means of escape.

43

To Kettle.

Billy raises his glass again. 'And to your freedom.' He's really going to town. Provocative. He wants me to get mad, storm out. He wants to avoid coughing up.

He limps over to an armchair and lowers himself stiffly into it. 'When did you get out?'

Be cool. You need him.

'What's it to you? I'm out. That's all that matters.'

He utters a grunt that is hard to read. I don't let it bother me. I examine my red nails. They are rather lumpy. I'll do better next time. Buy some top-notch polish.

Billy picks up a cigar, biting the end off. He spits it out into a glass ashtray before lighting it. I open the pack of cigarettes Betty gave me and light up.

A wall of smoke divides us. 'So. Out in the big wide world.'

'Yes. Offered me probation, but I didn't fancy it.'

He is incredulous. 'What? Nick addled your brains?'

I exhale. 'Obviously I never talked. Today I gave them the slip and I won't be sticking around. Give me what you owe me and I'll be gone.'

I get up and pick up an ashtray from a side table. Cigarette butts lie at the bottom, like dead fish. A couple are ringed with red lipstick, vibrant and recent. I don't care. I take the ashtray with me and return to leaning against the wall.

'Where are you staying?' He's staring at me, trying to make sense of me without showing it.

'A hotel in Piccadilly.'

He snorts but plays along. 'Very nice. So you want lolly?'

'Yes. And a new passport.'

He blows out a smoke ring, another old habit. It floats

upwards before dissipating. 'The country's a fortress. You'd be mad to try it.'

Coming from the man who broke every rule in the book, this is rich. I quip back at him. 'Nothing ventured, eh?'

He waves his cigar. 'How much do you reckon I owe you?'

'Let me see. Loss of liberty. Keeping my mouth shut. I'm going away and I can't very well get a job. Something for Betty, for the frock. All adds up.'

Another half-smile. He is unreadable, a black leather book with the pages bound. Good thing I haven't come for any answers.

'Where are you going? America?'

'I was only over the River if you wanted to ask me anything.'

Another shrug. His black eyes absorb me.

I am on the verge of snapping but somehow keep my voice level. 'I gave up wondering a long time ago what went on, what you knew, what you didn't. You were happy to leave me to rot. Maybe you'd just got bored. We weren't exactly getting on. Still, might have been kinder to just jilt me than set me up as a gunrunner.' I give a sarcastic smirk. 'If you must know, I'm going to Devon.'

'A country girl? Come off it.'

'People change.'

'They don't. Ever.'

'So you were always a Judas?' Is it my imagination or does that sting him?

Too late for guilt, Billy. Far too late.

A sudden pain in my left temple. Tension, exhaustion, booze and hunger impacting like a bullet.

'You always wanted to go to back to America, until life with me got in your way, remember? Wasn't that what you used to fling at me? That you only stayed in this dump for me?'

'Forget the history lesson. It's tedious. Just give me what you owe me. If you need time, I can lie low. Just don't dilly-dally.'

He sees right through the bluff and sniggers. 'Oh, yes. Lie low. You've got nowhere to go.'

'That's *my* problem. Cough up and you'll never have to see me again!'

The singing from the pub downstairs is at top volume, a braying medley of *The Lambeth Walk* and *Jerusalem*. Our standoff while the whole world outside celebrates is silly, really. My life is inconsequential in the bigger scheme of things. The soldiers' faces at the station come back to me. They have a reason to hate, but do I? I'd been fed and watered, never had to kill anyone, never had anyone die in my arms, never had a foot cut off because of gangrene. This fear of a bomb falling compared to dying in combat? A piece of cake.

Our little tiff is just a storm in a teacup in comparison.

Never mind. Let's have a drink, let bygones be bygones.

Billy exhales another gray plume of smoke. 'Things aren't always as they seem. You of all people should know that. As for your stretch? Unlucky.'

Unlucky.

All the apology and explanation I'll get.

Billy stands up, leaning heavily on his cane. 'I've got a place where you can wait. I need to sort a few things out. We'll go now. That racket outside should help.'

Billy goes over to a bureau and pulls out a brown paper bag. 'Yours.' To save him limping over, I walk over and take it from him.

He doesn't stand back as I peer inside the bag. Papers. My birth certificate, a photo of Kettle and another of me at seventeen. And letters, a whole bundle of them. The pathetic, pleading letters that my mother Violet had written to a cad who had rejected us both but that she had never sent. Why had she lugged them around her whole life? Pathetic. I wouldn't be like her. And had Billy seriously poked about a smoldering bombsite to save these? Or had he taken them with him on the same day he set me up?

In a flash of anger, I toss the lot in the fire. 'Good riddance.'

'Ida!' he snaps. 'What the hell you do that for?'

He said my name. It's too intimate. It changes things. 'You think I want them on me?'

Out of nowhere, his arm reaches out. Impulsive. Possessive. I spin around. 'Don't touch me. And don't pretend to give a damn,' I hiss.

It must be the booze, but I feel a surge of desire. Irrational, uncontrollable, a chemical reaction to his presence. My body is fickle, with a very short memory for betrayal. Maybe bodies can love forever. Muscle memory. Our eyes meet. I say, 'Want to fuck?'

He doesn't flinch. 'Nick improved your manners. Thought you might prefer the ladies now.'

'Well, make do and mend, and all that.'

'Anyone special?'

'There was a beautiful Australian blonde called Lena.'

'Lena, eh?

If the thought excites him, fine by me. Billy instantly drops his cane. He pulls me towards him, crushing me, his mouth devouring mine. His stubble scratches, his cologne smells of lemons. New cologne, one I don't remember.

Then he pulls away, serious. 'We should leave now.'

'Why? Lady friend coming?'

'Not that.'

'I'm in no hurry.' I whisper. I want him now, this minute.

Billy's desire is debating with reason. Maybe I'm forbidden fruit, or he is disappointed my anger had been so quickly replaced by lust. Catholic boy that he is, desire wins. His hand reaches out for me, but I pull away. 'Give me five minutes.'

I head to the hall and find the bedroom.

The room is oddly similar to our old one. A bottle of tablets sit on a bedside table. I quickly open the drawer. Another gun. A dark and well-polished revolver. No change there, Billy is still well stocked. I check the barrel piece.

Six fat eggs, itching to hatch.

Instinctively I slip the gun under the pillow on the other side of the bed.

You don't know him.

I throw off the dress and shoes, leaving my stockings and garters on and slip between the chilly sheets. The thick eiderdown is heavy and comforting.

A silver light flashes outside the window. I sit up, breathing fast. A bomb? Then an almighty crack of thunder splits the sky.

Billy is at the door. 'Just a storm,' he says.

11

Dawn. My mouth is dry as toast, my head groggy. London sparrows chirp outside. In the distance, bells. The bells of every church in London, ringing triumphantly.

So here we are. Not entwined as we once would have been; now there are at least four inches between us, a polite distance.

The sex was a frantic truce, like a game of football in no-man's-land. Efficient, a temporary fix.

In the night, I woke, aware of a smell of burning, just cigarette smoke. I didn't turn, pretended to be asleep. I felt his finger trace the puce ridges of the scars on my arm. His breathing was shallow as he examined it.

All that and I still kept my mouth shut.

I pretended to stir, to shake him off me. It was only sex, and I would be leaving.

Next he slid his hand under the pillow, feeling for the gun. He didn't remove it. Who is this man who doesn't care if the woman next to him shoots his brains out while he sleeps?

Now the strangeness hangs heavy between us, like dirty tulle curtains. Breakfast could be awkward.

I haven't forgiven him, not a bit, and now I am completely at his mercy. If Billy is right, and people don't change, then sex should make him honor the deal. He must know I need him as much as I'm using him. I'm pitiable.

Where will he stash me away while he sorts things out? Hopefully somewhere empty, hopefully somewhere with a fire.

A rum situation indeed. Funny what peace brings.

The knocking is loud and insistent. I must have dropped off again. Billy's girl? He is already up, in his dressing gown. He shoots me a fierce look. 'Nobody knows you're here? Just Betty?'

I shake my head. So he trusts Betty, but not me. I never talked, so no one will look here. His fear is irrational.

Billy hesitates. He clearly wants the gun under the pillow but won't say. Is he expecting trouble? I say nothing, clutching the eiderdown. He limps out, closing the bedroom door after him. I jump up, stark naked, straining to listen at the door. Billy's footsteps head to the living room first.

He is getting the other gun.

A minute later he shuffles back along the hall. The chain scrapes off the lock, opening onto a volley of loud Italian voices. Two, maybe three men? They are speaking too fast, with harsh and insistent words – this is no victory party. Billy says, 'No, sono solo.' He says it loud enough for the neighbors to hear. It is only meant for me.

Don't leave the room.

They are persistent, entering the flat. The front door slams shut. Billy sounds placatory. It isn't working. The voice that answers him is flat, unimpressed, repressing anger.

As they move down the hall, Billy's voice becomes more indignant, denying something with good humor. Bluffing. Suddenly, one of the men chuckles. Then there's embracing, kissing, and Italian backslapping all round. I sigh with relief.

Billy says, 'Caffè?' and the others enthusiastically assent.

I can slip under the bed or wriggle through the window and cling to the ledge while the social call plays itself out. My clothes are strewn over the floor. The blue dress lies crumpled, the color not as fresh as I thought. In the cold light of day, it's a dull blue. Porcelain blue with mud slung in the glaze. I fling it on.

A muffled sound outside the bedroom. I freeze. *A shot?*

I go back to the door, straining to listen. No. It can't be. Damn those church bells!

I snatch the gun from under the pillow and tiptoe back to the door. The clock ticks in competition with my pounding heart. My hand shakes over the door handle but I gently twist it an inch open.

Someone groans. Billy? One of the men yells, 'Dov'è...?'

This is followed by a thud, a sharp kick in the ribs? More shouting. Billy groans again. He's shot, I know it. Pure instinct takes over. Forget payback. Billy is dying. I have to help him. Without thinking, I push the door wider and creep out into the hall, shoeless and pistol poised. The door to the living room is wide open. A man's voice growls low, repeating itself.

I peer in.

Billy lies on his front, his head yanked up in the vicelike grip of a young Italian man. He's got a pistol with a silencer pressed against Billy's temple! Billy's face ashen, his eyes rolling around and his mouth dangling open – a huge bloodstain spreading over his back – sodden silk – *he's dying!* The killer's face – mean, determined. He's a baby, really, all of eighteen years? He's dapper. Very.

An older guy, surely the muscle, larger, a mess... No, he's the killer! He's aiming, ready to fire again – a cold-blooded execution!

They haven't seen me. Should I hide? No, find me, they'll kill me. Can I force them to leave? A warning shot? Kill them? I don't want to! I just can't.

But the boy sees me. He shouts, and raises his gun. Who fires first? The guns are loud, and I'm thrown back. The bullet instantly drives though his forehead, his head flying back, cracking the wall. I spin around. The other man lurches at me, eyes bulging, firing! I lunge out of the way, safe. Breathless, I shoot again, hitting his leg. He collapses, his gun falling on the rug. He clutches his thigh, screaming.

Thank God for the church bells.

Panting, I keep my gun on him, glancing at the younger man. His body has crumpled and lies at an angle, sagging and lifeless. I've killed him. A boy. I feel sick. The larger man flounders in agony. What should I do? Help him? The blood oozes through his fingers under the ripped flannel trouser. He whimpers, his eyes are manically rolling with pain. I go over, kick his gun out of his reach, yelling, '*Uscire o ti ammazzo*!' The language was always in me, just buried.

He heaves himself up, lumbering. His skin is sickly white but he gets the message, all right. He lollops towards the door. Will I regret this? He knows my face. He's a mobster. I've killed one of their own. Billy's dying. They'll be back.

Yes, I will regret it.

Fuck him!

I fire at his back. He crumples, heavily. As he hits the floor, a bone cracks.

His body lies slumped on its side, his head at an angle upwards.

Billy! I run to him. He is motionless, face down, his cheek against the rug. His eyes flickering at me, his breath shallow and fast. His irises roll, as he tries to focus.

'Don't move. I'll get help.' I can tell the publican and flee. There is no other choice.

Billy's hand gropes for mine, fingers pressing into mine. His mouth opens slowly, trying to form words. A fractured whisper comes out. I bend my head closer. 'I can't hear you.'

'Bedroom... Go... They will...' His face flushes, his grip loosens. His eyes go blank.

'Billy!' I feel for a pulse.

He is gone.

12

I have killed only once before in my life. At least, I may have. I will never know for sure. I was thirteen. I'd knifed him in the belly with a small penknife, and scarpered. I never found out what happened to him. Maureen O'Reilly, who had taken me under her wing, said he got what he deserved, but we never saw him again.

Several years later, I told Billy about it. He'd taken me to Ashdown Forest every weekend for three weeks and taught me how to shoot. I was a good shot. Billy had been impressed and I liked the fact he was pleased with me.

Billy's head now lies on my lap. It's heavy and cold. Great shudders take me over every few minutes. It's so cold after the storm, after the killings.

Below, a rowdy street party is in full swing. The only sound inside is the ticking clock.

Move it. Get the hell out if you want to live.

The bells and the boozing below must have prevented anyone realizing a shootout was taking place in the top flat. I lower his head to the floor. I can't move fast, my limbs are so weak. The puddle of blood on the carpet has dried at the edges. The air is rancid with the odor of fresh shit.

I somehow manage to stand up with jelly legs. Hands shaking, I find Betty's packet of smokes, and pull out a cigarette, staring at the bodies. Sunshine illuminates the boy's pallid face, making the tramlines of rusty blood running down his face appear to glitter. His eyes are still open, the whites

54

flushed with scarlet, clashing with the amber of his irises. God, he's young. That it was him or me is not much comfort.

What did Billy want to tell me?

In the bedroom, the bedside tables have nothing else of interest. I already have the gun.

I open the big wardrobe. Lurking behind some men's suits, a large suitcase lies against the back. I pull it out. Inside, it is stuffed full with women's clothes. Several summer dresses and two lightweight suits, one cream, one dark blue. A few silk blouses, some plain, some printed. All tailored, all expensive fabrics. No ration jobs here. The suitcase's side pocket contains packets of silk stockings, and satin underwear.

Billy's girl's?

Underneath the lot, there's a deep indigo satin evening gown adorned with sequins, beads and tiny seed pearls. I pull it out. The words *Jacques Faliere, Paris* are embroidered on an ivory silky label. Next to the suitcase, two shoeboxes and a hatbox. I lift the lids of each. Unworn women's leather shoes. A brown pair for daytime, and satin ones for evening. Top quality.

In the hatbox, a woman's stylish hat. It's never been worn. I put it on, and it fits.

Billy's girl has class and now she is helping me escape. I'll take it with me. Expensive wardrobe, ironic that I don't have a penny but maybe the former will fix the latter.

Wait. Billy would hide things under the floor. Money, weapons, anything he didn't want other people to find. I will him to have kept to his habits as I pull up the rug and kneel down, using my nails to test the give of each board. Finally, one gives.

My fingers grope around the dark cavern. Dusty rubble and broken laths. Hard balls of crumbling plaster.

But something else.

It's smooth. Paper? Pinching a corner, I manage to lift a brown envelope, thickly coated in dust. Inside, there are several notes in different currencies – dollars, pounds, and francs. Fresh off the press and, knowing Billy, probably counterfeit. And a passport, a US passport. I flick it open.

What the hell?

My face stares back at me.

The name, *Constance Evangelina Muriel Sharpe.*

Why on earth hadn't Billy just given it to me? Why the charade of hiding me away for a day? It was here the whole time. Waiting for a good moment to give it to me? Waiting for sex? What game was he playing, if he'd already come good?

The clothes, too.

He got these for you?

I fling myself back on the bed, in turmoil. Why the silence? Why the game?

Even dead, he is one step ahead.

Time to run. Somebody, somewhere, will miss the dead. If they come looking now, that's it for me. Wipe everything down. I drag the bottom sheet from the bed and bundle it up. The bottle of tablets I noticed the night before still sits on the bedside table. I examine it. Practically empty. Morphine hydrochloride tablets. I stuff the bottle into my bag.

Back in the living room, I rummage through the younger man's pockets, my hands shaking, pulling out a wad of handwritten letters, all in Italian. A creased Ministry of War document states he was Paolo Salvatore, a registered POW. He must be older than eighteen, then. There's a lighter, engraved with *PS,* and a roll of pound notes. An Italian POW in fine clothes? Maybe his stretch ran for the same years as mine. Our new lives colliding on VE Day, but I'm the one with freedom.

Seldon was right. *Avoid the people you were protecting.* Now look. But I'm not responsible for Billy and his dealings. This is just bad timing, right? The Italians can't have come here looking for me. I am of no consequence to anybody; I know nobody, I have nothing they want.

I move over to the larger man. He carries no papers, just a large knife sheathed under his belt. His clothes are old, and stink of stale cigar smoke. Young Paolo must have come higher in the pecking order. A boss's son?

I find the scotch and glug from the bottle. I quickly wipe everything else down. Glasses, the door, the side tables. The fat one's prints on the gun might usefully confuse matters if and when the coppers arrive. Soon the bodies will stink. The carnage cannot go undiscovered for long.

As I work, I run a mental checklist.

One, Billy was in hot water and it is nothing to do with me. They had come to mow him down. Somebody wanted him dead, and they were after something.

Two, Billy had arranged papers and money, maybe even a whole wardrobe of top notch clothes, but he was in no hurry to tell me. Not even after sex. Why bide his time? Did he think I'd throw it all back in his face?

Yes, you would have.

Maybe after the long separation, he still knows me better than I know myself.

Three. It is only a matter of time before the shooting and my face are splattered all over the newspapers. Only Betty can link the two – Jemima Day, missing convict, and Ida Boyd, former girlfriend to the dead Billy. The old Betty would stay out of it, minding her own business as ever, but this one is a stranger. Even if she knew Billy was in hot water with this gang, would she have the guts to point the finger at them? No. I'm a stranger to her, after all.

If Betty implicates me, and I'm caught, I'll have a triple murder pinned on me, and the hangman will be curling his noose around my neck in no time.

Four, if I don't move now, the Mob could bust in and kill me before any of that happens.

Five… Five, a question. How does the sophisticated Yankee Mrs. Connie Sharpe jump on a boat back home before someone mistakes her for a wanted spy, or a parole jumper, or a former moll, or a Mob killer? I need to lie low. How? And where?

Bloody good questions.

I will have to work them out as I run.

Six. It is time to say goodbye.

Billy's mouth, bluish now, is partly open. I close it, for decency's sake.

He always observed the niceties of life. Sunny smiles and goodbyes.

You never know what might happen out there, he used to say. *Never go to sleep after a barney, in case you die in your sleep.*

Once upon a time, he'd been mine. Today I couldn't save him or stay to bury him. I am leaving him as I found him. A stranger, for whom other strangers will give whatever send-off they think he deserves.

Maybe Betty will see him off all right.

Please, Betty. Have a heart.

I kneel down and lightly kiss him goodbye on the cheek.

'Thanks for sorting me out.'

I feel warm tears filling my eyes.

Real tears.

Outside, the sunlight dazzles and the air is crisp after the storm. The revelers have exhausted themselves, some sprawling on the pavement, next to vomit pools and Union Jacks strewn like patriotic litter. Others sit in huddles, arms draped around each other. Nobody notices me.

Ahead, blue smoke billows from a fire on the Green. I pass a man up a ladder. He's tying a string of ancient and moldy bunting to a drainpipe. He waves at me. I wave back brightly, doing my best to act as if I haven't just committed a double killing and witnessed a third.

I head towards the smoke.

Nobody is tending the biggest of the bonfires. Couples lie in each other's arms, bathed in the dying heat. I edge nearer, and toss the sheet into the embers. The linen catches quickly, the cotton yellowing then blackening, before it frays into fragments of ash. They float gently up and away from the ravenous flames.

Gray confetti, for a marriage that never was.

RIP Billy.

A steady and growing stream of people flock towards central London. I slip in amongst them.

Only the mannequins in Betty's window watch me leave.

Victory protects me, and I am finally grateful for it.

13

Los Angeles, September 1945

'Like the joint?' The female cab driver pulled up on the other side of the street.

I glanced out of the window up at the hotel building, solid and bland brick, with a couple of squat palms on a front terrace. 'Sure, looks fine,' I said, without thinking about it.

The name *The Miracle Mile Hotel* was elegantly coiled in unlit neon tubes adorning the top of the solid deco building, a tiara on an elephant. It was hardly up there with the luxury hotels, places that tempted me but which would soon gobble up my remaining fake dollars.

I had to pace myself, and I was hot, hungry and tired from the journey here on the Super Chief. In less than ten minutes, I could be lying in a hot bath, knocking back a glass of something cold and bubbly. Shopping around for hotels with this chatterbox of a driver was not top of the to-do list.

'Classy place, not full of wannabes. Say Sal told you about it.'

I got out and paid Sal, adding a big tip for the fact she saw me as classy. She touched her cap and flew off.

The L.A. heat rolled over me like lava. I was dressed in a black suit, and I quickly put on my sunglasses. Months on the run and I still felt like an Albino rat, scared of the light, scurrying off to hide in dark holes.

'No vacancies.' Mrs. Loeb, as her name badge announced, didn't even bother looking up from behind her heavy gold spectacles. She was engrossed in the crossword. Her dyed auburn hair and the lavish amount of costume jewelry dangling from her ears and neck reminded me of a Christmas tree.

I dropped Sal's name. 'Sal, huh? I don't care if Eleanor Roosevelt sent you. If we're full, we're full.' A woman who flexed her muscles any time of day and I was fresh meat to pummel. She still didn't bother to look up. I wouldn't give this bitch the satisfaction of pleading with her.

I picked up the suitcase and hatbox, rather disappointed. It felt like a false start and I was too exhausted to shop around. A money-guzzling hotel it would have to be.

It was a pity. The joint was cool, literally, with the purr of air conditioning units. The lobby was buzzy and cheerful. Pale yellow walls, luscious palms in large Egyptian pots surrounding a busy tobacconist stand, and a lounge area where elegant girls chatted.

I felt eyes on me. A maid was busy polishing a large brass lamp at the end of the large desk, a distinctly unimpressed look on her face as she glanced at me. She had velvet brown skin and her brow furrowed a little as she attacked the brass.

'Here to make it in the movies?'

I turned. Mrs. Loeb glassy bug eyes were now giving me the onceover, taking in my fashionable and stylish suit.

'I beg your pardon?'

'The *movies*? Seeking fame?' She barked as if I was deaf.

I knew a trick question when I heard one. 'Not at all. I'm a personal secretary.'

'Where you hail from?'

'New York, originally. I've been living in London for ten years.' That would explain any remnants of the accent.

Mrs. Loeb glanced my ringless hand. 'Good. So you ain't married?'

'Widow.'

She had the last word. 'So long as you're no divorcee. They're trouble, too.'

The maid smirked at her boss' rudeness to me as if it was a familiar comedy routine, and I was the latest sucker.

Mrs. Loeb tapped her long nails on the glass counter. 'My friend runs a boarding house in The Palms. Jasmine Street. Lower rent than here, ain't so fancy, but respectable and clean. She don't take actresses, or models, or dancing girls. More trouble than they're worth. Want me to call Pearl or not?'

Maybe a suspected spy, probation bunker, and wanted murderess would make the grade.

I nodded. 'Sure.'

I noted the name. *Pearl.* If a plush hotel got too expensive, a boarding house run by Pearl in Jasmine Street would stretch out the money before I had to find some means of income.

'Take a seat.' Mrs. Loeb nodded at a seating area in the lobby, lifting the heavy receiver.

I headed for a couple empty armchairs near the front doors. More young women breezed in. They were stylishly dressed, red lipstick and shoulder pads and laughing at a private joke. They shot me a quick glance. Curious. Not unfriendly. One of them caught my eye and nodded.

They took me for one of their kind.

I gave a slight nod back.

Mrs. Loeb called out to me across the lobby. 'Hey, lady from London, what's your name?'

'Constance Sharpe, Mrs.'

'Oh, my God! Are you British?' A sweet, girlish voice squealed, from the direction of the palms.

A chubby bundle of pink and white gingham appeared behind me. She had a pleasant face with freckles that no powder would ever conceal. Her hair was an unnatural strawberry blonde, on the garish side, with dried ends. She was carrying a large sketch pad, but she didn't strike me as the artistic type, more like a dumpy girl from the typing pool. The kind who would settle down with an insurance salesman, raising a brood of kids and baking apple pies.

'No. My husband was English. The accent rubbed off.' In no mood for chatting, I looked away. She didn't take the hint, parking herself opposite me. She crossed her plump legs, getting comfy. 'I love England. I mean, I've never been there, but I am sure I was meant to live there. Now the war's over, I'm saving up to go. Shakespeare's my hero.'

Who cares?

'I'm June Conway. How do you do?' She leant across the brass coffee table dividing us and extended a hand. Her grip was steely and warm at the same time.

'Connie Sharpe.'

'Connie and Conway! We were meant to meet! You're staying here? You'll love it!'

'Full up. I'm being fixed up someplace else.'

I nodded my head towards Mrs. Loeb who was obviously catching up on gossip.

June Conway frowned.

'Leave it to me.'

She marched over to the desk, butting in. I could hear her interrupting the call. 'Connie Sharpe can room with me until Stella leaves on Saturday. Then she can take her room.'

63

What! I hadn't seen that coming. Three days with this cutie-pie would drive me insane. I stood up.

'Hey, no, it's quite all right.'

Ignoring June Conway, Mrs. Loeb held the telephone and called over to me. 'Got a single. Shared bathroom. Or are you happy to double up with June here?'

'I'll take the single.'

Conway's face crumpled. 'It's no trouble. Please!'

I wanted to swat her away like a mosquito. I headed over to the front desk, but she intercepted me, hands on considerable hips. 'Los Angeles is a very big city and I can show you around. It'll be fun!'

'You're sweet. But I like my own company.'

'It's only for three days.'

I hesitated. I was tired. I liked the scene here. Just how annoying could she be?

June leant in conspiratorially. ' "Hell is empty and all the devils are here." Shakespeare said that in *The Tempest*. He could be talking about L.A.'

I held back a snigger but I was impressed. Maybe this June Conway could be useful. I was starting again. I'd fled the law and got away with it. I could be anyone I damn well wanted. Being Connie Sharpe was my route back to the sunny dreams of my childhood. My start-over point. I could start straight and stay straight here. June, the sweet chump, was offering something for nothing. Maybe I could even be gracious about it.

Connie Sharpe would be, wouldn't she?

I put down my case. 'Sure. Why not?'

14

We'd seen the highlights of Hollywood from the Yellow Car and were now sitting in a French-style cafe, with cakes and pies heaped up with cream in the window. I would have preferred a drink but June didn't indulge in anything and had never even smoked. She only had a baby deer ashtray in her room for guests. 'You don't know who this is?' She'd squealed, when I said, 'Pass the ashtray with the baby deer.'

My 'bereavement' – fighter pilot hubby Leonard being shot down over France – had also served as the reason why I hadn't seen any movies in the last few years. June had been mortified and made it her mission to put this right, planning a daily schedule of the best of the latest pictures.

Over milkshakes, June told me her lifelong dream was to be a costume designer to the stars – ideally Rita Hayworth, of course – but disillusionment was clearly setting in after two years of being stuck on the bottom rung as junior wardrobe assistant at some studio. She spent her days just darning holes, measuring the armies of extras, replacing buttons, bent over for hours at the sewing machine.

June slurped through her straw, complaining. 'Estelle brought a new assistant in last week, and she's giving her better jobs already. Like assisting the designer for Ann Drake's new picture. I've been here a year and I'm still fitting pirates' pantaloons.'

'Some people would pay good money to do that.'

June didn't get it, now wiping up the last crumbs of her

lemon meringue pie with her finger. 'She hates me. Why? I've never been late, sick, anything.'

'We've ascertained she's a first-rate bitch,' I offered, unhelpfully.

'Oh, I shouldn't complain. I'm lucky, really.'

'Offer your services to a theatre group or an independent producer. Say they don't have to pay you, just supply the fabric, whatever. Then at least you could put 'costume designer' on your resume. After a while, maybe you could jump ship to another studio. Get in somewhere else at a higher level.'

She looked at me like I'd suggested she kidnap a baby. 'Oh, I couldn't do that. False claims.'

'Where's the lie? You would have designed, wouldn't you?'

'I'm just an assistant.'

'Sweetie, if you wait for the outside world to give you permission to breathe, I can personally guarantee you'll be ironing pirates' pantaloons for the rest of your career.'

'Dede said the same thing! But I'm not like you two.' She looked away, sad.

'Dede?'

'Dede Dedeaux. She has a suite on the top floor. The entire top floor! Wait, maybe she could throw a party for you!' June looked thrilled at this. 'There's always buckets of champagne. If you like drinking.'

'What about the no booze rules?'

June waved a hand in dismissal. 'Dede can do what she wants.' June didn't seem too troubled by the blatant double standards.

I got the old, familiar feeling of being trapped, so I changed the subject. 'Look. Take me as an example. I'm going Downtown tomorrow and telling all the agencies I've been a secretary, because I was, even if it was just for Leonard. It's not lying. It's being…creative with the truth.' I was beginning to like being Connie Sharpe with her can-do approach to life.

June's face flushed with shame. 'I'm just not sure I'm good enough.'

'Of course you are. I've seen your designs. One of them is as good as a Paris gown I've got.'

Her face brightened. 'Really?'

'Sure it is. I'll show you.'

Back in the room, June held the purple gown up, awestruck. When she saw the label itself, she squealed. 'Jacques Faliere! My absolute hero!' So Shakespeare had been replaced. 'What was he like? Did you go to Paris?' She sat down on the bed and turned the skirt inside out, her expert eye getting down to the serious business of examining the inside of the fabric, the darts, the seams, the tiny stitches.

'This is top secret. Leonard was a spy.' I was lying on my bed, pillows up against the headboard, craving a drink. While I bet most of the other girls had secret stashes in their rooms, I didn't want to push it with June.

June gasped. I laughed. 'I'm kidding.' I said. 'Seriously, a Free French aristocrat we met in London brought it over with her. We got friendly. We were the same size and did a trade. I had a gown she liked better.'

June loved stories from my invented respectable English life so I didn't hold back. It appealed to her love of the dramatic. And in a funny way, I enjoyed them, too. Connie Sharpe's glamorous life in London was a tiny bit of compensation for years of incarceration.

Later, I tried to drift off. Outside the open window, cicadas hummed in the rear yard and the air was like a warm blanket. Relief was slowly but surely seeping into my muscles and bones, dissolving the stiffness and damp I had thought I would just have to live with. I was finally uncoiling. I was safe. Now I could let myself remember what living was like. And I had my plans. Swimming in the sparkling Pacific, downing pina coladas on Hollywood terraces, and laughing like the starlets Mrs. Loeb disapproved of, next to some hunk in his convertible as we sped along the Pacific Coast. Maybe I would even hang out with this Dedeaux woman. I bet she knew the hottest clubs in town.

Then it hit me. Could this new life be worth the risk of running? Where would I be now if I hadn't? Probation would be over. Potatoes would have been harvested. There would still be mud ingrained in my fingertips and someone's hand-me-downs to wear. Billy would no doubt have been done in anyway. Would I have stuck it out in Devon and married a farmer? As if! No, I'd have returned to London after Devon, and what? Waited tables in a teashop? Become a librarian, with a cat for company?

Whatever his motives, Billy had made this all possible. He had loved the sun, and maybe he would have loved it here. But it was fitting he'd lived and died in South London, his Sicilian blood never even making it back. The Elephant and Castle was his true home.

I rolled over, trying to free my mind of the image of his dead face.

My eyes met the proverb embroidered onto one of June's many cushions that her granny would send her. '*Wherever you go, go with all your heart.*'

15

Downtown was heaving with people, high buildings and traffic. After the empty streets of London, the huge snake of cars was thrilling. Everything was vast here. I felt small, inconspicuous and very hidden.

It would be fun to drive again. I made a mental note of the models that really struck me. A cream dream. A nifty gray convertible. I could see myself whizzing around in any of those, but my dough wouldn't stretch to buying a car. There were the green rental cars but driving one of those would feel a bit like dancing with the ugly guy.

I passed a department store. Even the mannequins were better here. Stylishly sculpted, expertly painted to look like movie stars frozen in time. There was a movie theater or fancy restaurant on every corner. Sharply suited women overtook me on the sidewalk. Career girls with places to go and bosses to serve.

And I looked like one of their breed, in my navy suit and silky polka dot shirt, topped with a tilt hat in the latest style. As soon as I'd landed in New York I'd swanned up and down Fifth Avenue and blown a chunk of Billy's dollars on new clothes. Crisp blouses with floral prints and covered buttons, a pantsuit, and new evening gowns. I indulged in a faux fox fur jacket to replace the one Elvira had taken at Waterloo, and a white stole, faux fur also, to go with the evening gown. I bought a few more hats and pairs of shoes. And, of course, a bigger suitcase to cram it all in. My final indulgence was having my hair dyed. Should I return to the ivory blonde of the previous decade, when I ran around with a spiv? The hair stylist thought I could carry it off. But no, I was somebody new now. And deep down, I didn't want my hair to remind me of Lena. So I opted for a nice caramel blonde. Sunset Blonde, it was called. It wasn't showy and neither would it show up my mousy roots too fast.

As I didn't have a clue how to type, I could at least sign up for classes. Once I could bash my fingers in sequence on a keyboard, how hard could filing be? I'd had a relatively paperless existence up till now, Billy had taken care of that side of life. I couldn't remember the last time I'd had to write anything down, let alone type it.

It was just too hot. Sweat trickled down the front of my neck as I looked up at the tall building where De Lane's Secretarial School was. 'Learn shorthand, typing and stenography here,' a sign declared. 'Acquire new skills and find the career you always dreamed of.' Exactly opposite, on the other side of the street, a blue neon sign for *Mikey's*, a bar.

It wasn't a difficult choice. One drink, and then I'd face the secretarial school.

Stenography for beginners. Drunk beginners, even better.

The door was heavy, with thick frosted glass panels. Inside, murky smoke hung around the wide bar like fog. Groups of men had congregated like buffalo at a waterhole. Swing music blared out from a large jukebox in the corner.

I stopped in my tracks, halfway in and halfway out.

All eyes turned on me. The men were shabbily suited, most with the jaded look of the overworked and underpaid. I knew their type immediately.

Cops.

I'd stumbled upon the police department's Friday afternoon watering hole. Nice one, Connie.

Turn around and walk straight back out!

Most of the men looked away, uninterested, went back to their conversations. The eyes of a few lingered on me. Looks of appreciation? I looked serious in the suit. Wait, if Connie Sharpe could hold her head up high and order a drink surrounded by the law, I could relax. I didn't have a choice, anyway; walking straight out would generate suspicion. Putting a confident look on my face, I headed straight for the bar.

The barman was a wiry pixie of around sixty, wearing a striped apron. He came straight over and I ordered a gimlet. 'One gimlet for the lady in blue coming up.' He spoke with remnants of an Irish accent. In a second, I remembered Maureen O'Reilly, and her singsong Irish accent. Maureen, always plausible, even when she was stitching me up, her eleven-year-old protégé.

The semi-naked mermaid tattoo on his forearm seemed to writhe as the barman reached for a glass.

The Los Angeles Chronicle lay on the stained marble bar top. The front page was about the atomic bomb on Nagasaki. Another universe. Absentmindedly, I flicked past the front page, to be confronted with the face of a black man. An Arnold Moss, on death row. I didn't read on. His blank stare leapt out amidst the blurry words, and it made my stomach lurch. I knew that feeling when they shove a camera in your face to capture the moment of quicksand swallowing your life. That's how you'll forever be known, whatever you did, guilty or innocent. My gut instinct for the guy was pity. I had no reason for it other than I'd been there. I quickly closed the pages.

Sorry, Arnold, I don't want your bad news. Don't take me back to jail with you. Not today.

I closed the pages, pushed the paper away and downed the gimlet.

'He's gonna fry, then burn in hell.' A growl in my ear. I turned. One of the cops, a sweaty bull in a brown suit, breathed whisky fumes into my face. His eyes were glazed and bloodshot. 'That's what a cop killer gets.'

'Is that so?' My voice was frail. Was he hitting on me? His voice was heavy with menace rather than lust. He leaned forward and whispered in my ear. 'Come out back to my car I'll tell you everything. You be nice to me, you'll find out sure enough everything you want to know.'

'What?' I *didn't* want to know. The penny dropped. It could mean only one thing. He thought I was eavesdropping. I smiled, hiding fear. 'I'm not a reporter, sir.'

'Yeah, right. Ain't the first to try it in here, and you sure won't be the last to sashay up to the bar and play dumb.' He snarled at me before turning to his buddies. 'Hey, guys. Reckons she ain't no reporter.'

Someone laughed, but somebody else shouted, 'Let the lady drink in peace, Jim.'

I had no choice but to open the paper again. Concentrate hard. Pray that this Jim, if that was his name, would forget me.

No chance. 'Who you working for?'

'Nobody, sir. I'm just a secretary. Well, learning to be one.' Damn! It just came out. I could not get into anything with this jerk. It was a funny time to notice dried egg yolk on his lapel.

'Yeah, where?'

'De Lane's. The secretarial college, across the street. I'm new in town.'

The bartender, polishing glasses, watched the situation, but his eyes viewed me with distrust. Simple. If I was snooping, he didn't want to antagonize his core clientele. I finished my drink, opened Violet's bag and grabbed some coins.

'Going someplace?'

'Gotta make tracks,' I grinned.

As I stood up, he stood up, blocking my way. 'Not so fast. I want to see what's in that purse, newsgirl.'

I froze. What did I have on me? My passport. Not helpful, as Connie Sharpe had absolutely no other record of existence in America. On the boat over, I'd concocted the story of Connie Sharpe's staid life to the random sailors and wounded GIs, but it wouldn't stack up under any serious scrutiny. I also had a few of Billy's dollars. Pristine and authentic-looking but no doubt as bogus as hell. These alone could sink me, never mind the phony identity.

Only got yourself to blame. You picked the gamble.

'All right, Jim. Leave her alone.'

The voice came from behind. I looked up to see a pair of bright turquoise eyes, fixed on my assailant. His hair was dark, slicked back, his skin very pale. His nose was prominent, marring what could have been film star looks. The tie was loud, with bright geometric patterns. His long, pale fingers clasped Jim's shoulder, rather like the talons of an eagle.

Was it my imagination or did he jerk his head in the direction of the door? A subtle signal to me to leave?

You don't look a gift horse in the mouth, so I didn't. I slipped past, lowering my eyes.

73

Time to scram.

Out on the street, I took a deep breath, walking fast, my heart pounding. Forget stenography classes. I headed for the bustle on Broadway. Idiot! And what a creep. If a real Connie Sharpe had wandered in, needing a drink, what kind of treatment was that from Jim the jerk?

Career girl? I was in no hurry to take orders from a man behind a desk, doing the same thing day in, day out, fixing on a smile with my makeup each morning and bringing him coffee, and all for a miserable wage. I'd managed to avoid it all my life so far, and I wasn't about to start now. I hadn't jumped bail and risked hanging for that. I hadn't made a lifelong enemy of Little Italy for that.

No, sirree.

16

The rippling Pacific shimmered against the widest strip of pale sand I'd ever seen. Palm trees swayed on the esplanade, their shadows dancing across Pacific Drive. There were more open-tops down here, cruising along the coast road. People looked relaxed and happy – even the drunken sailors asleep on the hot sand, killing time before their trains back home, their skin already tanned from long tours. Some played volleyball, stripped off to their shorts.

I kept walking to find an emptier section of the beach. The palms were unkempt, like leggy dancing girls with dried grass skirts. I kicked off my shoes and peeled down my stockings, stuffing them in my bag. The sand felt hot, the tiny grains massaging my soles. I ran to the frothy surf. The icy water lapped my feet and calves.

Pure bliss.

I paddled along the edge of the water for about half a mile.

Finally, I found a patch of sand, sat down and had a cigarette.

Something splashed my cheek. I sat bolt upright. Rain. I must have slept for hours as purple clouds had smothered the setting sun. The beach was deserted. A storm threatened and the wind was up, blowing up sand. I ran under a wooden shelter, watching raindrops lash the sea, and stayed there, smoking, until the rain turned to a light mist. My skin prickled, slightly sunburnt. Even if it hurt later, it had been worth it.

Soon the dark sky and the sea merged into one, the reflection of the moon became a giant double brooch pinned on inky velvet.

When I got back to the Miracle Mile, the place almost felt like home. I was even looking forward to seeing June and catching up on the latest in the wardrobe department.

I tiptoed into the room, only to trip on the pink rug. I giggled. 'Oops-a-daisy!'

June was on the bed, sitting up, a book in her lap. She must have dozed off.

I peeled off my damp jacket. I wouldn't tuck her in; she could sort herself out when she woke up, as she no doubt would in that position.

As I was undressing, I heard a loud sniff.

'Oh. You awake? Sorry. I was trying to be quiet.'

I took my cigarettes out of my pocket. They were damp and I inwardly cursed. Then a loud sob came out of the darkness. I inwardly groaned.

'Hey! What's up?' Some boy had probably jilted her. I was in no mood to play agony aunt. The night before I got my own room, as well.

June whimpered and turned on her side, curling her knees up to her chest. The book, a Bible, slipped into her lap.

'Boy trouble? Take my advice. Fuck them all. Not literally.' I laughed at my bad joke. I knew June was a virgin.

'No.' Her voice was hoarse.

An odd chemical smell wafted by. Antiseptic? I knew it from somewhere. A distant memory. A painful operation. Another prison experience I'd blocked out.

'Are you hurt?' I went over to the space that divided our beds and looked down at June. Her eyes stared at me, glassy orbs in the dark, like marbles. Her cheeks were puffy from crying. Her hand clutched her wrist. Some kind of cloth was wrapped around it.

'What's happened? June. What have you done?'

June's voice was hoarse. 'I tried to finish it all...I couldn't do it.' She burst into tears.

17

In the low light, the gold words *THE BIBLE* shone like a bad joke. Calmly, I took the book from her lap and placed it on the bedside table. Then I flicked on the lamp to inspect the damage, sitting down on the edge of the bed. I picked up her wrist. A white hanky was roughly tied around it and the blood had seeped through but hadn't drenched it. No torrential flood, then.

'You really tried to kill yourself?'

I unpeeled the sodden hanky to see a small surface cut in the flesh. A cry for help kind of cut, not a real '*I can't take it anymore*'. Her wound could do with a stitch but it wasn't going to get one, at least not by me taking her to the Emergency Room. I remembered there were bandages in the bathroom cabinet. 'I'm going to fix this up.'

In the basin, I found a roll of cotton wool and the bottle of antiseptic, lying on its side, most of its contents down the plughole. That explained the smell, and I could take it as assurance June had already regretted her decision. A brand-new box of adhesive bandages sat in the cabinet.

I used the bandages to push the skin together. June stared ahead with puffy eyes. At one point, she winced. Saliva dripped from the side of her mouth. A magenta shade of lipstick was smeared over her face. I'd never seen her wearing any make-up before and now she was plastered in the stuff. She'd done a useless job of it.

What comfort could I give to her? Sorry you've got no boyfriends? Sorry you feel like a failure? If she was such a mush she could pack up and take the first bus to wherever and run back to Mommy.

For lack of something more consoling to do, I found a tumbler and filled it from the pitcher of water on her bedside table. 'Here. Drink. Need a painkiller?' I remembered the rest of Billy's morphine tablets. One of those would knock her out and spare me having to deal with this, but she shook her head. I held the glass to her mouth and she guzzled, her hand clutching mine like an invalid would. Even this irritated me. I hadn't come to L.A. to play nurse.

June lay back. 'I sometimes pose...for portraits.'

'What do you mean? For artists? Painters?' Was she a life model? I could see June's Rubenesque physique being the type artists like to draw.

She looked down, unable to meet my eyes. 'No. For private... magazines.'

'What? You mean...nude?'

Her eyes filled with shame. 'Just topless. Some guys like chubby girls. And the pictures, they make me feel pretty. And it pays good. How else can I afford this place?' June's salary was a pittance. I had assumed family somewhere was helping her to make ends meet.

'So what's the matter?' I acted blasé, but I was stunned. This was a side to June that, frankly, amazed me.

'He wanted me to do...total nudity. I said no. Said he didn't want to pressure me into anything. He was being real nice to me. Said I could go home, and he'd pay me anyway this time. He gave me a drink to make up for it. I felt bad for wasting his time. I don't touch liquor but a drop, to make things better. Next think I know, I wake up, groggy. I must have passed out.'

June's hand grabbed my arm. 'When I get back here, I see that one of my stockings wasn't fixed like I do it.'

'You think he stripped you? While you were unconscious?'

June looked at me. She nodded. 'I don't know what else he did.'

'So he has a make-up girl?'

June shook her head. 'Why?'

'You haven't seen your face?'

Another shake. My mind was now busy picturing all kinds of scenarios. 'Anything hurt, other than your wrist?'

She knew what I meant. 'No. Not down there. I just feel sick.'

Since June was a virgin, surely she'd be feeling it now if he had raped her. So she could have got off lightly. She'd stooped low to pay for a Beverly Hills life, and got burned. Surely she'd seen enough in this town to know who and what to avoid? It was not my problem if she couldn't tell a sadist from a church mouse, couldn't look out for herself in the big bad city, and flashed her titties at creeps.

I spoke calmly. 'So he could have taken advantage of you and drugged you. Maybe's he's taken some nudie snapshots. Plenty of perverts out there, but consider it a lesson learned, right? Don't hurt yourself over a jerk like that. A case of spilt milk.' My voice was ugly and terse. Maybe move out to a cheaper boarding house, I wanted to say, but didn't. This was not my problem.

In answer, June suddenly lurched over the bed and vomited all over the carpet. I grabbed her hair and held it up as she retched. It was like returning the favor to all those inmates who had done the same for me over the years. After, she lay back, sobbing. 'I'm sorry, Connie.'

'Don't worry about it.' There was nothing else to say. I got some tissues from the bathroom and began to mop up the mess. Now I just wanted out. I said, 'Did you know this creep?'

'A while. Some extra...Shiralee...something...told me he was looking for girls. Big girls...like me.'

'So he's taken your picture before?'

She nodded. 'A few times. What if...?' She burst into tears. 'I can't show my face in town! What am I gonna do?'

I sat down on the edge of my bed and lit a damp cigarette. It smoldered weakly. I stubbed it out in the baby deer ashtray. Its dark eyes loomed up at me, equally pathetic.

What if June really was suicidal? How could I really know? What would Dr. Lucinda Seldon do, for instance, the only role model I had for something like this? It was pointless to conjecture. I was no do-gooding, sensible Seldon. I went over to the window, watching the rain lash against the pane. 'You can tell the police.' I said. 'Do it in the morning. Go down to the nearest precinct and make a statement. You've got the guy's address. They can deal with it.'

Do it when I've gone, and gone for good.

And then came the predictable plea. 'Will you come with me?'

'Sure,' I lied. 'Now go to sleep.' I walked back to the lamp and gave her a smile. 'You'll be fine. I promise.' But the police wouldn't get very far. Even if they busted the place, he'd have a system for hiding his pornographic material. Nothing illegal in nude photos, if the model consented. I assumed. I didn't know the laws here.

June curled up. 'Thank you, Connie. You're a real pal.'
A real pal.

No. Somebody else would have to be that. Somebody else could go with her, pick up the pieces, be a decent friend.

Dede Dedeaux, June's wealthy pal on the Fourth floor. June seemed to like her enough.

After a few minutes, I heard her breathing slow down. I quietly packed my things into my case.

On an impulse, I left the Jacques Faliere gown behind. She needed it more than I did.

As I went to turn off the lamp, another embroidered motto on a cushion caught my eye. 'A fair-weather friend leaves holes to mend.'

18

I left my suitcase by the fire escape and slipped upstairs to the fourth floor. It was a little like entering heaven, another world. Everything was white and pearly. The floor was solid white marble inlaid with some kind of gold mosaic tiles. There was a silky runner with an emerald swirling design and gold edges. The brass rail was brighter than the ones downstairs. One thing stood out immediately – there were hardly any doors up here. Just two.

Dede Dedeaux must be one rich bitch to rent out the entire floor.

I rapped on the one door that had a brass knob and a peephole. I did my best to look anxious, knowing somebody on the outside was giving me the onceover. Then the door opened a crack.

I recognized the dark eyes immediately. The maid. The one that had stared at me in the lobby on the first day. Now she was busily tying up the belt of a simple plaid dressing gown over what looked like a rather nice piece of French lace edging her nightgown. Her wide arched brows framed her luminous dark brown pools of eyes.

I said, 'Is Dede Dedeaux in?'

'She's asleep, ma'am. It's one in the morning.'

'All right. Hey, could she look in on June in the morning? She's not doing so well.'

'Our Miss June, downstairs? What's the matter?' Her voice had a husky softness to it. It matched the expensive silvery flock paper that lined the walls.

'She's kind of low. Boy trouble, I think. She said something like that. Think she got tipsy. Could somebody check on her in the morning? I've got to rush.'

'Oh, yeah. You're the one rooming with her? Mrs. Sharpe, right?' Her eyes roved over my face. 'Saw you the day you checked in.' *You looked like trouble then*, she could have said. Her eyes certainly did. 'So you're just leaving her? After she shared her room with you and all?'

'The thing is, one of my relatives is sick so I'm leaving for good tonight. I won't be needing my own room after all.'

If this got back to June, it would be a surprise to her – I'd never mentioned family.

'Thought your husband was dead.' Damn! Of course, the maid had heard the whole interaction when I arrived. 'Now you found some family all of a sudden?'

'Turns out I do.'

'All right. So what's really up with June? Considering she don't date or drink.' Her eyes bored into mine and I squirmed.

'I said, I don't know exactly. She's asleep now. She'll probably be fine.'

The maid opened the door wider. 'You know, I think Miss Dedeaux would like a word after all. Shouldn't take long.'

'I can't. Listen, the room's unlocked if you want to go down. I'm sorry I've got to dash but I got no choice.'

I'm a fair-weather friend. Can't you take a hint?

I avoided her eyes and hurried back the way I came.

I sneaked out of the Miracle Mile in the dead of night. The rain pelted my face. June had joked that Hollywood raindrops were the tears of all the starlets in L.A. crying with disappointment at once. It was a line I suspected she'd overheard at the studio and thought it smart to repeat.

Life had taught me one rule about survival. If you grew up around Bad Things, you could handle the inevitable blows better. People like June, with cosseted, overprotected lives, who hadn't been starved, beaten or abandoned, they were the ones that fell the hardest. No scar tissue equaled zero protection. The trauma cut deeper. Now June would live with a fault line right through her. A fault line of shame.

It wasn't fair, but neither was life.

Sooner anyone learned that the better.

19

There were no taxis. I'd have to walk a few blocks and see if things improved. It was raining again, and soon I was drenched through and cold.

A distant, lonely car swooshed through the night streets. I crossed the wide boulevard, deciding on a hotel. Somewhere, the bar was still open where I could forget all about my failed attempt at playing the grieving widow turned wannabe career girl.

I passed an elegant fur shop and stopped under its hard canopy. A security grill formed a diamond-shaped black lattice cage, behind which were mannequins draped in sable and mink. No fakes here, just the real deal. I didn't buy real fur, like I didn't eat meat. Animals had no say. Kids don't, either. At least I could fight back now. Animals didn't have a chance.

I remembered Ellie, the girl at Waterloo Station with dreams in her eyes, staring at fox furs. What had they done with her?

Forget it, not your problem!

I found a late-night bar. A skinny barman, barely twenty, wiped the bar top. He couldn't hide his irritation. 'I'm closing, ma'am.'

I tried to sound pleading. 'It's cats and dogs out there.' I shook the rain off my suitcase. 'Just the one, just while it passes?'

He shrugged. I took it as a yes. 'Scotch on the rocks. Make it a double.'

I sat at a table as he brought the drink and a clean ashtray.

I lit up, pondering. I had done the right thing by going. I needed to look out for me. I was no career girl, no wife, no best friend. Going straight had got too old and too complicated fast. Wrong move, Connie. Connie? I hated the name anyway. Sounded like the name you'd give a pet rabbit. Now it meant nothing to me except a false start.

Time to think big. I had landed in a glittering city where I had no baggage, no duty, no obligations. A Garden of Eden. All those rich kid dumb Adam and Eves could be mine for the taking. I could swallow them whole, relieving them of their gems, their dollars, their gold, even their cars. I'd feather my nest. I would infiltrate high society, go to the swankiest place and blow my money on the con of my life. I'd come out rich and laughing. I'd retire in style. Not on some stupid porch in some sad neighborhood, lying low.

That was the fresh start I really needed. This is who I really was. Someone who could turn the game to her advantage.

I peered out of the window. The rain was much lighter. I stood up, leaving a small tip. 'So long.'

The barman grunted something back, without looking up from his paper.

Outside, I heard the roar of an engine. A yellow taxi with its light on. I flagged it down. It pulled up, narrowly avoiding the large puddle.

The cabbie looked out. A familiar face. The driver that brought me here. Sal.

'Hello, again. Where to?'

I couldn't speak.

'Something up? Late-night rendezvous?' She winked. I stared at her but only saw June's face. I tried to blink her away. Sal took my suitcase.

'Quitting the hotel already? Not good enough?'

The fault line. It would divide June from success. Thirty years from now, June would still be at the bottom rung of the wardrobe department, still darning holes and fixing hems, being barked at by her younger bosses. She hadn't got a hope in hell. June had done more for me in three days than hard nut Lena had managed in years.

But you don't owe her anything. Get in the taxi.

I looked at Sal. Her face was thin, her eyes shrunken. She was masking her impatience. 'I got five hungry mouths to feed. Can't sit here all night waiting for you to make up your mind. Not unless the meter's running.'

'I'm sorry. I made a mistake.'

I handed her a five dollar bill. She pocketed it and grinned. 'My kind of ride. Have a good evening!'

The taxi sped off into the night.

What had another of June's cushions declared? *A friend in need is a friend indeed.*

A born crook could do something for a lame dog.

20

'So you're the roommate?' The southern drawl was laced with disdain.

Dede Dedeaux leant against the wall in June's room, with a distinctly unimpressed look in her eye. She was in her thirties, with the confidence of the born rich, wearing an ivory satin silk dressing gown, with quilted lapels embroidered with scallop shapes, and edged with tiny pearls. The belt had the same embroidered pattern. The buttons were large pearls, edged in gilt. Her long black hair had a dramatic effect, coiling around her neck and over the ivory. One in the morning and she looked like a movie star.

That's what money can buy, and you'll be looking like that soon.

I hovered by the door, still in my damp coat, disheveled. June was still dead to the world, lying on her side in bed, in the fetal position. Dede's maid was tending to her.

'June said you were pals. But Alberta says you ran out on her.'

The maid looked up with another unimpressed look. I'd had enough of those for one night. I didn't have to explain myself to them. 'False alarm.'

Dede took a silver cigarette case out of her dressing gown's side pocket. She lifted it open with a scarlet nail and offered me one. 'Smoke?'

I nodded. The cigarettes were thin, and pale cream. 'Mentholated,' she added, as if it made a difference.

Dede's eyes met mine as she held up a heavily engraved lighter. I inhaled. The drag of menthol was soothing on the throat like liquid silk. We both puffed away, watching as Alberta tenderly mopped June's brow. I asked, 'Did she tell you what happened?'

'Alberta got the gist.' Dede picked up the baby deer ashtray, cradling it in her hand and holding her cigarette over it. 'The creep is a Mr. Elmore Caziel. I got the address out of her, but there's little point in going there. He'll deny it. I know these types. Sub-Poverty Row. June could have asked me for money if she was that broke.' She looked a little pained. 'No point in going to the cops either. Fat lot of good that will do.'

'I can help,' I said.

Dede eyed me, raising a brow, puffing on her cigarette. 'Yeah?'

'I could pay the scumbag a visit. If he took pictures, maybe I could destroy them.'

'Oh, you're just going to walk right in and get him to hand them over?'

'I can try.'

She almost laughed. 'Porno merchants aren't pushovers. He might have muscle.'

'Maybe. Maybe I could trick him.'

Alberta looked around and met Dede's eyes. Dede said, 'Trick? Sounds like you've done this before?'

I addressed them both. 'I've met my fair share of slimeballs. I know how to play them.'

'We don't want any more trouble than what we're dealing with now.'

It was an intriguing remark. A cough interrupted us. A

middle-aged woman and a younger woman entered the room. The older one reminded me of a beetle in a black rain mac, graying blonde hair messily pulled back in a bun, heavy tortoiseshell spectacles. Her skin was leathery from too many night shifts. The younger woman wore a nurse's uniform and was skinny.

'Dr. Rosenberg. Thanks for coming so late.' Dede greeted the woman warmly, shaking her hand.

The doctor headed straight over to June, giving me a look. 'Who's this?'

'Connie Sharpe.' Dede lowered her voice even more. The fact she knew my surname surprised me.

The doctor kneeled to take June's pulse and examined the wrist, pulling off my hastily applied plasters. 'We'll put a stitch in that and I'll check her over,' she announced.

Dede suggested we retired to her apartment. 'I want to hear more about your little plan.'

What looked like a Picasso sat on the wall next to a grand piano. On the opposite wall hung a collection of African masks. They took me back to my homeless days as a kid when I'd lurk in the British Museum to keep warm, gazing in cabinets at exotic wonders. A large dagger was mounted on the wall near the masks. The blade was pale, tapering to a lethal point. The handle was carved bone. A real tough guy of a knife.

'The Abarambo tribe, Congo.' said Dede, standing at her corner bar which was fatly upholstered in white leather. She sloshed two stiff brandies into the finest cut glass tumblers, and brought one over to me.

'A weapon would help. It would be more persuasive.' Now

this tainted the grieving widow image as much as running out on June did, but something told me if anyone had a gun, it would be Dede Dedeaux.

'Know how to use a gun, or just to wave it around?' She eyed me. I didn't see her hand flying for my throat. In seconds, she had pinned me against the wall, my head squashed between two masks. She was strong as an ox.

I dropped the glass, which shattered at our feet. I felt lumps of lead crystal pelting my ankles. She didn't seem to care, yelling, 'You working for that creep? You spyin' on us?'

Us? Spying? What the hell? I managed to gasp. 'Who? I don't know what you're talking about!'

Her breath was hot and furious against my face. 'He sent you here didn't he? Don't deny it!'

'Nobody sent me here! Please, I can't breathe!' *What the hell?*

'Too bad! Talk!'

Dede squeezed even tighter. I tried to think while the oxygen lasted. Did she have her own set of problems and think I was some kind of snoop? Bizarre. Everyone was mistaking me for something else. A newsgirl. A snoop.

But Dede's suspicion of my true identity had a silver lining. I could use it to meet her in the middle, and if I was going to continue living here, then loosening up the Connie Sharpe act would help.

I gasped, trying to wave an arm. 'All right. You got me. No dead husband. My real husband was a louse. A swindler and a cheat. I had enough and took off with some of his money. I'm just lying low. I only came to the Miracle Mile because a taxi driver suggested it. I never heard of the place, or you, until June told me about you.'

'So it's all been an act? You been living in England?'

'Years ago, I went for a vacation.'

'So what do you know about me?'

'What's there to know? You got a flashy apartment? If you've got trouble, sorry about that, but I know nothing. I've got enough on my own plate.'

Dede's grip relaxed. She took a step back. 'All right. Say I believe you. Why walk out in the dead of night?'

'I'm not the kind of person who holds anyone's hand, while they get over bad things. Anyway, I can't be around if the cops come calling.'

'So why the change of heart?'

'June was good to me. If I can destroy any pictures, I pay back the favor.'

Dede looked at me for several seconds. 'Had to ask.' She spun around, her dressing gown spiraling out behind her, leaving me standing among the crystal fragments and brandy.

I rubbed my neck and picked my way out of the mess.

Dede returned with a gun, a dustpan and brush and some rags. She handed me the gun and squatted, to start cleaning up the mess. Odd. Maybe she didn't want Alberta to see. Her ivory gown was soon sodden at the hem but she didn't seem to care.

I examined the gun, a small pistol, a neat piece with a cream pearly handle that matched her gown. Definitely pricey, judging by the detail and the weight.

Dede looked up at me. 'I want that back.'

21

Always carry a lighter. You never know when you'll need to start a fire.

Fire hadn't been on my mind but when I saw the tatty frame houses lining one side of Gordon Grove, it was clear they, and any smutty pictures of June, would all go up fast. It was mess of a street, caught between times, sad and neglected. Opposite the houses, a few ugly, squat warehouses lined the road, with large gated front yards dividing them. They must have replaced similar frame houses.

The place was too near Hollywood's main arteries to escape the greedy developers for much longer. Even the straggly palm trees looked like they knew their time was up. The trunks were blackened, the leaves yellowing and brittle, as if they'd made up their minds to die before being felled.

The house occupied a corner plot, with a long high wall around the side and rear. Three large cars, old models, sat in the drive leading to the timber house. Two of these were coated in grime. Wooden shutters on the ground floor windows kept the light – and people – out. The upstairs windows were festooned with curtains of heavy lace. The paintwork was peeling in great patches. Nobody cared, and nobody would.

I casually ambled around the corner so I could check out the back of Caziel's place. The adjacent street was similarly depressing, except dotted with cheap-looking bungalows with signs of life like washing lines and a dog barking. In the backyard was some kind of double-story guesthouse next to the high rear wall. The whole thing was covered in a flowering climber.

I turned back. Time to face the music.

Strolling into the front yard with a pronounced wiggle, I hoped I came over as gaudy and fast to anyone on the other side of the nets. I had plastered on the make-up and was wearing the blue summer dress that Betty had given me. I wondered why I was still holding on to it, this last vestige of my former life. I was sure the designer in Mayfair hadn't had this jaunt in mind when they sketched the frock.

I'd met perverts over the years. Men fueled by sex addiction, or a desire to denigrate others, particularly women. But their addiction is a bite in their own ankle, and if I had any kind of a game plan today, it was to kick the self-inflicted wound even harder.

I wasn't chubby like June so I hoped this Caziel creep catered for wider tastes. Besides, I'd have to offer something else if he was going to let me through the door. My talent for reading people fast would have to be sharp today.

With a cough and butterflies in my stomach, I rang the bell. I turned away, feeling the heat on my skin. Alberta had lent me one of her hats, a woven downbeat affair with a checked trim.

After a while, the door opened a crack. Two dark, suspicious eyes flickered at me. A woman's eyes in a sallow and tired face. I could glimpse a green uniform.

I beamed. 'Is Mr. Caziel at home?'

'Que?' *What?* She didn't speak English.

'Mr. Caziel? I need to see him.'

The woman shook her head.

I pulled out a five dollar note. 'I want five minutes with him.'

I held out five fingers, sounding a little desperate with it. She opened the door wider, snatching the note and slipping it into the apron pocket.

'You wait 'ere.' Funny how her English had improved so fast.

I quickly decided on a name. Minnie Groader. What seemed a lifetime ago now, I had owned a chipped teapot by Groader, all worn gilt, pink and yellow flowers and gold handles on the pot and lid. It must be forever part of the Suffield Road smithereens now. If they ever built gardens again, maybe fragments of my teapot would be discovered. In Holloway, gardening duty was made more fun by the pretty bits of china or glass we'd unearth when digging. Till Doodlebag cottoned on and decided to take them away from us, for fear we would use them on others or ourselves.

Footsteps. The maid returned. ''Ee see you. Two *mee-noo-tes*.' She opened the door wider and I stepped inside.

Caziel reminded me of a baggy, evil, scarecrow. How the hell did June trust this guy? But she saw the good only, was blind to the devil and his many forms. Caziel's head was buried in a paper, his greasy hair was almost mushroom-colored, with all the uniform lifelessness of a toupee. His feet rested on his wide desk, next to a coffee pot on a tray. His white and blue shoes were immaculately polished, and he wore purple silk socks that almost matched his tie, loosened at the neck. The baggy suit may have been stylish in 1930.

I pressed my handbag closer to me, glad that I'd slipped the pistol inside the garter around my thigh.

I coughed. 'Mr. Caziel? I'm Minnie Groader.'

Caziel slowly raised his head, keeping one eye on the

newspaper to rub in the point I was insignificant. His thin nose leant to the left of his face. The irregular look was unnerving.

'If you've come for the shoot, you're too late. Job's over.' His eyes roved up and down my body like I was a piece of meat. 'And you're too skinny. No meat on the bone. Wasting your time.'

'A pal said you needed girls.'

'Who said?' He put paper down.

'Someone at the studio. Shiralee? I'll pose nude.'

'Like I said, you've wasted your time. Get out.' He raised his paper.

I gave my best crestfallen expression and didn't budge. 'Sir, can't you just help me out? I got nothing.'

Beyond the lacy curtains and the grime on the pane I could just make out a man in a dark suit with a brown hat, smoking a cigarette. The muscle, on look-out duty. My eyes reverted to Caziel. 'Please?'

'*Please*! *Please*!' He whined back at me, mocking. 'Do I look like a goddamned job agency? Beat it!'

I feigned bursting into tears. 'I'm staying in a fleapit, ain't even got my bus ticket home. I'm down to my last couple of cents!'

He laughed. 'Those crocodile tears don't fool me. Scram.'

I slipped off my jacket and began unbuttoning the top of the dress. I flashed a sensual smile at him.

'What the hell do you think you're doing?'

'Showing you my talents.'

My brassiere was on show, with the pathetic little cleavage I had managed to gain since Holloway. His eyes were fixed on my bust, waiting to see what lay beneath the lace and the buttons. Hooked! I shot him a sneaky grin. 'Show you more, if you like?'

'Brazen little hussy, aren't you? Minnie Groader, huh?' He stood up. The bulge was visible in his crumpled pants.

'I could do with some better pictures. Help me get more work. I figured you could take some, give me copies.'

I needed to find the camera, expose the celluloid, anything. He'd tell me to pose but I'd pull out the gun, threaten him, and get to work.

Caziel's hand slipped under the open top of the dress and cupped my breast. His body gave off an odor that was a fusion of onions and cheap aftershave, a sickening mix. He whispered in my ear. 'Take it from me, Minnie Groader. You won't get far with a name like that.'

'You got any suggestions, sir? I appreciate your advice.'

Somehow I kept my idiotic smile fixed the whole time, willing myself not to kick him. Out of nowhere, he grabbed my arm and jerked it around my back, tight in an arm lock.

I gasped. 'What are you doing, sir? That hurts!'

He tightened the twist. 'Who told you about me?'

'I told you, Shiralee. Why would I lie? I gotta work!'

Screw this asshole. If I could trap him in the joint and burn him I would. 'Please! I'll do anything you want.' I pleaded, as pitifully as I could manage. 'Pay me anything!' I began to sob.

I could feel his erection on the back of my thigh. So he thought he was getting sex. *Sorry, mister.*

He pushed me hard away from him, kicked my foot from under me, and I stumbled, undignified, onto the floor. Caziel towered over me. 'OK, Minnie Groader. Get up. Plenty of time to go crawling around on all fours. You'll like that, won't you, a whore like you?'

The fact he'd treated June well made sense. She would have been nervous, guilty. He'd have liked the role of persuader. Pushy but desperate little Minnie Groader ignited his misogyny and disgust. To him, she was bottom of the barrel.

Caziel grabbed my elbow and strong-armed me out through the French doors. These led to a rear porch with dried, splintery wooden steps down to the backyard. A rickety wooden table had been pushed against the wall, with a few empty beer bottles. Tumbleweed had done a good job of suffocating a forgotten and rusty child's swing.

The muscle was finishing his cigarette and lumbered to his feet as soon as he saw Caziel. He was younger than his cheap suit and grimy fedora hat suggested. He gave a deferential nod to Caziel, then snuck a look at me, as if I was off limits.

'This piece of pussy wants to show us what she's got. Maybe you can help her, Jose.'

'Si, boss.' Jose grinned. He practically licked his thick lips. *Don't get too excited, Jose.*

22

Caziel pushed me into the lobby and slammed the door behind us. So here we were, at the heart of his seedy empire. I glanced around the tiny lobby with two doors off it, and a narrow wooden staircase.

I smiled. 'Any place I can make myself pretty?'

'Bathroom's upstairs on the left. Strip, then go in there. Make it quick.' He pointed to an open door.

'All right.'

His eyes stayed on me as I moved towards the staircase. As I passed him, I glanced inside the room he'd pointed at. It was creepy and gothic, some remnant of a movie set. The walls and window were roughly blacked out with paint and black canvas. Gold candles adorned a slab of marble, on a table base. A piece of satin was flung over it. Where the hell was the camera?

He laughed. 'If you're having second thoughts, too late! Make it snappy.'

'All right,' I whimpered. As I climbed up the rickety staircase, I could hear him shout out something in Spanish.

Time to get to work.

Upstairs there were another two small doors and a patch of landing with tired linoleum, lifted at the edges by years' worth of grime. The door on the left was slightly open and led to the bathroom, a dingy affair with a small tub coated in a thick layer of mineral deposit. A small window, covered by the purple petals of one of the climbers, was above the lavatory. I peered out. The bougainvillea wound around the building, forming a floral barricade. This was the climber I'd seen when casing the place at ground level.

I checked the other room, quietly opening the door. *Bingo!*

The dark room. Translucent amber strips of celluloid were pegged to a washing line stretched from wall to wall. I crept in and opened the curtains. I quickly examined the strips. Plenty of Minnies, but larger girls, in provocative poses. Perhaps it was just a matter of luck I hadn't gone down the same path.

I looked at the last few strips. There she was. June. I didn't want to look, so I yanked them all down and created a mound of celluloid on the floor.

But if a reel with another girl's pictures was left in the camera, it wouldn't really be payback for June, would it? True vengeance demanded I got rid of all the pictures.

With the help of a little lighter fuel, I could try to burn the dump down from this level alone. That could destroy the contents of the dark room, and I could run, but the risk was the fire might be put out before it consumed the rest of the place. I would have to go back downstairs, as Caziel had instructed. The camera had to be in that ornate room, maybe just out of sight from the stairs. I'd go down and light a fire in there, then I'd race back up and escape out of the tiny window in the bathroom.

Back in the bathroom, I picked up the gown Caziel had instructed me to put on. It was stained and practically see-through. It reeked of the same stale smell as the rest of the place. Fear and desperation, mingled with cheap fragrance.

Eau de Smutte by Caziel.

But I would put it on, just in case I needed to keep the act going a while longer. I kept my shoes on, the heels might help

101

me get down the purple bush; bare scraped feet wouldn't. I took my matches and lighter fluid from my bag, stuffed the dress back in the bag, and left Alberta's hat in the basin. I felt bad; she wouldn't get it back. I wondered what wages rich bitch Dede gave her hard-working maid.

I pushed the window wide open. I tiptoed to the dark room, and lit the celluloid.

I crept out and tiptoed downstairs. Some old ragtime music was playing. I caught a whiff of marijuana. The creeps were getting high, laughing from the backyard.

I slipped into the altar room.

The camera, on a tripod, stood at an angle behind the door, staring out like an accusing aunt. I opened the back of it and yanked the film out, leaving it dangling down.

I shook lighter fluid on the bottom of the strip of celluloid, lit a match and threw it down. The fire quickly caught its fuel. I jumped back as tiny green flames swarmed like water snakes over the Persian rug. The black satin draping would catch light next.

Job done, Minnie.

Thick blue smoke filled the room. I dashed back upstairs. On the landing, flames were spilling out of the dark room, stretching to the railings around the stairs. Smoke filled the landing and I gasped for air. The heat was so powerful. I dived into the bathroom and slammed the door.

In seconds, Caziel would smell it. If greed came first, he might die to save his work. Or force his muscle to risk it. Too bad. Minnie never existed. If anyone survived, they could identify me, but chances are nobody in this racket would stick around to be questioned by anybody.

102

Below, doors were opening and voices were raised – Caziel and Jose trying to work out what the hell was going on. The smoke was making them cough and splutter.

The bathroom bolt was flimsy and my hands shook as I slid it home. One kick could bust the door open. But would they risk the smoke and the fire?

Out of nowhere, a bullet bored the door. *Shit!* I darted to the side. Then another volley of bullets followed, hitting in random places. They had to still be downstairs, shooting up at me blindly through the smoke. The men were hoarse, coughing and shouting, torn between salvaging their precious images, saving their lives and drilling me with holes.

I crawled up onto the window ledge, scraping my shin badly, flinging the purse with my dress and the gun over the mass of climbers onto the sidewalk below. A branch caught the bag and the whole lot slipped down, out of my sight. I cursed, praying it was hidden. I'd have to retrieve it when I hit the ground. I crawled out onto the wall, quickly wriggling into reverse position, ass in the air, the branches prodding me. I grabbed thick branches in the hope they'd support me. Fat chance. They collapsed under my weight. Crying out, I was flung down, clutching at spindly leaves and branches. I found myself dangling a few feet above a patch of turf around the house, my hands scratched to bits.

Thank God the street was quiet. I let go, wincing, ready to be grated like a slab of cheddar.

The rough wall raked my skin. I winced again. The heels were a bad idea after all – I twisted my ankle as I crumpled onto the grass.

I stood up and brushed myself down. Nothing that wouldn't heal in time. There was a small path in the distance, an alley between houses. I'd hunt for the bag and dress, then run for it. I'd find a spot, like someone's yard, where I could just slip my dress on and limp calmly away. I stepped backwards.

But I couldn't move. What the hell?

Two arms around my waist. 'Easy,' a voice hissed.

I twisted, furious, kicking the shin, struggling, adrenaline killing the pain of my wounds. The arms tightened. I couldn't breathe. The arms were in navy blue, the rough fabric of workmen's overalls. 'Let me go!'

'Shut up.' The voice hissed, urgent. It was an odd command. I tried to turn.

Two cold turquoise eyes stared back at mine. He was tall, with very dark hair that looked almost navy in the light. His skin was ivory, stretched tightly over a prominent nose.

An unforgettable face. One I'd seen before only yesterday in Mikey's bar.

But did he recognize me?

'This is a police operation.' He spoke low and firm. 'You're okay. Keep quiet.'

I panted heavily, my mind racing. The cop kept my arms behind my back. My eyes darted around.

Another man was up a ladder propped against a lamppost. He was silhouetted against the sun, and signaling furiously to my captor.

I hadn't seen either of them on my arrival. They must have arrived when I was busy working on Caziel.

Talk about bad timing.

Survival instinct shoved me fast into Minnie mode. 'Let me go! It's a furnace in there! You gotta help them get out!' I yelled, trying to turn.

'What?' The cop spun me around. He looked up at the building. On cue, a plume of blue smoke billowed out of an upstairs window. His eyes got even colder. He spat at me, 'It's burning?'

'That's what I'm tryin' to tell ya!' yelled Minnie.

'Jesus Christ!'

The cop looked sickened, devastated even. He shouted to the other one. 'Place is on fire.'

Another huge cloud of slate-gray smoke billowed out of the small rear window. The whole dive was going up fast. He turned around. 'You did this?'

'What? No! I just got out in time. That guy's a creep! Professional photographer, my ass! Pervert! I had to get away.'

He studied my face. Intently. Coldly.

An engine suddenly roared from the front yard. The man up the ladder shouted, 'On the move!'

He bounded down the ladder. Turquoise Eyes dropped my arms and ran to meet him. They were shooting furious looks at me, locked in some kind of debate. They were the same height, but my captor was white and the other was black. They reminded me of two knights on the chessboard, head to head.

While they debated, I'd be on my merry way. I edged back towards the wall to find my bag and began to poke around the bushes.

'Lost something?'

I turned around, indignant. Turquoise headed towards me, furious. The other guy was running towards a car.

Damn! Dede's gun was in the bag. 'Yeah, a ring. Had it in my hand as I got out. Must have dropped it. That weirdo didn't want me wearing nothing. That's when I got the creeps.' I pretended to scan the grassy area. 'Look, I can't help. I gotta run.'

Turquoise Eyes studied me, hands on hips. 'What's your name?'

'Groader, Minnie.' I stood proudly, as righteous as a girl in a stained dressing gown and stockings can be. I prayed he would see his error and let me go. Instead, he flung my arms behind my back and cuffed me. 'What are you doing, sir? Let me go!'

'You're a material witness, or a suspect. Till I make up my mind which, you're going nowhere.'

'You got it all wrong! I'm a nobody!'

A muscle pounded in his cheek. He dragged me towards the truck and flung me inside and locked the door. At least he had the decency to avert his eyes.

I watched as he did the unthinkable and ran towards the building. Like a fool he scrambled up the bougainvillea, going in the same way I'd fled. Then he was gone, hidden in the cloud of smoke. He'd die in there. But that might be my only hope.

Cuffs still on, I sat on my hands, watching my handiwork. The guesthouse was a raging inferno. Odd they hadn't called the fire brigade. It would be a matter of seconds before somebody did.

Mission accomplished for June.

Now I just had to get myself out of this jam.

23

Cigarettes littered the floor. An interview room. Not a cell. *Not a cell.* I had to remember that.

And now I'd been in here for quite some time.

Relax, he's probably catching up on other cases. You're small fry.

Turquoise Eyes had driven me here without saying a word. In a way, I had been kind of relieved he had got out of the fire, sooty but unscathed. I hadn't had to wait for hours in that truck with the cuffs on. At least a cop didn't die thanks to my efforts.

He'd had the decency to uncuff me, before driving us off.

I'd kept the Minnie act up the whole journey. How I was in a hurry, how I could tell him anything he wanted to know right there and then, I had no idea and the rest.

He had growled, 'You can make your statement later, now shut the fuck up.'

I was giving a statement. That was all.

I glanced out of the window as we shot through Wilshire Boulevard, staring wistfully at the passing glimpse of the Miracle Mile Hotel off the main drag. Minnie certainly didn't belong there, but I wanted to.

Eventually, as the streets got busier, he turned into a public lot and parked the truck. 'Put this on.' He produced a rolled-up trench coat. I wouldn't have to walk the streets in the negligee. He was giving me *some* dignity, then. Except when I stepped out of the cabin I almost tripped over the hem, like a bad silent movie comedienne.

We'd walked around the block to Precinct. I gazed down. My ankle was swollen, red and shiny. He caught me looking but didn't drop his pace to take into account my obvious limp.

Nice guy.

I ran through the cards I had to play. They had nothing on me. He looked like the thorough type and would grill me, that's all. He had no idea I'd bungled his surveillance on purpose, and would see Minnie was just an idiot on the make. I'd soon be free.

I could do this.

I could relax.

I wanted to throw up.

There was a jug of water and a small glass on the table. I took a sip. It was lukewarm and tasted stale.

The door opened. A gray-haired secretary popped her head around the door and said, 'Won't be too long now.'

'Ma'am, could you tell the detective I'm in a hurry?'

She nodded and shut the door. Like hell she would.

My stomach grumbled with hunger. A fly buzzed around the room, flaunting its freedom in my face.

There's always a fly. Nosey Parkers of the insect variety.

You stupid bitch. You did a favor, you got soft, now look!

I had been a first-rate idiot to let soft-heartedness eat at my conscience. Why hadn't I left June in Dede's hands and got the hell out? Who had I been kidding? I was not a nice person and never had been.

I'd had a chance to run and I'd blown it.

Idiot! When would I learn?

The world screwed you, you don't have to repay anyone.

I slumped with my head on my arms and closed my eyes.

'Wakey-wakey,' a voice said, followed by a slight cough. I lurched upright in my seat, rubbing my eyes.

Turquoise Eyes had freshened up, changed into a dark suit and a jazzy necktie. He held a file, a pen and a witness statement triplicate form.

I said, 'Don't you look as fresh as a daisy? All right for some I guess.' I had to stay in role. Indignant, hassled, a girl down on her luck.

No smile. Instead, he just eyed me with cold curiosity.

'Your partner okay? He catch that creep Caziel?'

'Leave the questions to me, Miss.'

I had my work cut out. 'Don't suppose anybody found my ring?'

He ignored this. 'I'm Detective Randall Lauder. Now, how do you spell Groader? G-R-O-A-D-E-R, right?' Randall Lauder opened his notebook. I could see scrawled notes in illegible handwriting.

I nodded. 'Groader rhymes with toad, that was the teasing I got in junior high.'

Lauder finished writing on the form. He looked up at me. 'Start from the beginning. What exactly were you doing in Gordon Grove?'

I exhaled dramatically, as if it was a relief to finally offload. 'Only went for some portraits for my book. What a joke. I just want to forget the whole thing,' I sniffed.

Detective Lauder didn't offer a tissue so I dabbed my eyes with a sleeve of the raincoat.

Time for the sob story.

'Things ain't been exactly easy since I got here. I came here to act – start as an extra, work my way up. But all the agencies, the ones that bothered to see me, took one look at my book and said my pictures didn't make the grade. Now, I sure ain't no dummy! I'd been warned by pals to avoid the studio guys who sign a girl up and promise her castings, getting her hopes up over dinner, and next thing you know she's doing things she'd never do, all for a movie role that never existed in the first place! Mr. Caziel looked pretty neat, nice suit, serious-looking kind of guy. Met him at some hotel bar, can't remember where exactly. And he had fancy shoes. Mama always said, you can tell a gentleman from his shoes. He said he did portraits for girls' books, and did I need help in that department? I told him I was flat broke. Our deal was he'd keep some of my shots in case I made it big, then he'd make his dough back like that. Sounded fair enough to me.'

Detective Randall Lauder lit a cigarette, writing and smoking at once.

Not once looking up at me.

'So I called him up. Made an appointment for today. When I got to the house, I was surprised it was so, you know, shabby. But Mr. Caziel was being real friendly. He gives me an old-fashioned ball gown to wear. A real big skirt, one of those with all the hoops. And a huge wig. Black, glossy with ringlets. Like old-fashioned times. So I laugh and say, I don't wanna look like some Southern Belle. Don't get me wrong, I dig Vivien Leigh but how is that gonna help? Anyways, then Mr. Caziel gets a little snappy with me, ordering me to put it on! Now I *know* something ain't right. Then he pushes me into this real strange room.'

'Strange? In what way?' He was still scribbling.

'In a this ain't no portrait studio kinda way. Black velvet

everywhere, some kind of table thing. I just know next moment he's gonna be forcing me to strip and asking me to do things. So I made an excuse I needed the bathroom and got out through the little window. You caught me, here I am. Can I go now?'

'You escaped, in the big dress?' Now those eyes locked on mine. He'd caught me out.

'No! Ripped it off, didn't even have time to put my own clothes back on. Left 'em inside. Guess they're ashes now.' I gestured dramatically.

Lauder's eyes moved too, observing my every move. I started to relax.

'He must have dropped his cigarette or something, for that fire to start. Nothing to do with me. Can't tell you nothing else, wish I could.' I hoped he wouldn't ask for my details. I couldn't mention the Miracle Mile. Then where? *Think, idiot!* It came to me. Mrs. Loeb's friend Pearl with her boarding house.

I announced it, sure of myself. 'If you need to find me, I'm staying at Jasmine Street,' I bluffed. 'Shoot! I don't know the telephone number.'

Slowly, Lauder got up, keeping his eyes on me the whole time he walked around the table. 'How old are you?'

'Twenty-six. Why?'

'How tall are you?'

'What's that got to do with anything?'

'Just answer the question.'

I tutted. 'About five feet and six.'

He jotted this down, too.

'Dark blue eyes.' He barely looked up. 'Blonde, out of a bottle. On the bony side.'

111

I laughed. 'You auditioning me, Officer?'

'Any distinguishing features? Birthmarks, moles? I saw a scar on your arm earlier. How did you get it?'

'A burn. Foolin' around in the kitchen. Accident when I was fifteen.'

'Nasty. Looks like cigarette burns to me.'

I pulled a blank expression, hiding the new wave of tension. 'What's my scar got to do with anything?'

'Smoke?'

'Not much.' This felt like a prison medical checkup. I stood up. 'Can I go? I'm half starved. There ain't nothing more I can tell you. Give me your card. I'll call you if I remember anything else!'

'Sit down, Miss Groader.' That cold voice again. Lauder stood up. 'We'll get you something to eat.'

'Thank you, much appreciated,' I said. Then he left the room.

Where the hell was this going? Ten minutes later, the same secretary came in with a black coffee and a bread roll. Her eyes glared with disapproval over my negligee, poking out from under Lauder's mac, before leaving again. She could go to hell. I didn't care about her opinion and devoured the roll. What I had thought was cheese turned out to be dried turkey. I spat it out. I ate the rest with its soggy slice of tomato.

About twenty minutes later, Lauder returned, carrying a box. I couldn't see inside. He put it on the table and sat down, leaning back.

'You sure know how to treat a lady.' I glowered.

'Not up to your usual standards? May I apologize, Miss Groader, on behalf of the Los Angeles Police Department.'

I picked at a painted nail, ignoring him.

'Okay, so we found some items, but no ring.'

I shrugged. 'Finders keepers, I guess.'

'Guess this is yours?' My smile froze as he produced Violet's purse from the box. I watched as his graceful fingers took out an item one by one.

The blue dress.

My lipstick.

Dede's gun.

A pack of cigarettes.

A lighter.

Alberta's hat.

I hid my gulp. 'Not mine. Sorry.'

'So you don't buy hats from Janine's Millinery in Compton? And no frocks from Mayfair, London?'

The bread roll did a somersault in my belly. 'I never been to Compton. Or to London, for that matter. Never saw them before in my life.'

'Dress looks your size, but I'm no expert. And a nice little gun. Bet that piece of metal cost more than I make in half a year.'

'I wouldn't know about that. Ain't mine.'

'You know the thing about mother of pearl? Got a nice smooth surface. Ideal for prints. Lucky for us, we got a clear set off it.' He leant over and carefully took the coffee cup from my grasp. 'Good. Like I'm sure we'll get a match from this cup, too. But that's okay, isn't it, Minnie? They won't match because the gun isn't yours.' He leant back, grinning.

'You can't take my prints, just like that. I know my rights.' Minnie squealed.

He leant forward, menacing.

'I'm sure you do, Jemima Day.'

24

Nine lives gone, nothing to lose.

The English countryside would still be green now. There would be gentle downpours on muggy days. Block F would be empty now, save for a few of the hardcore cases. I wondered if Muriel had gone to the guillotine. The porridge would still be sludge and the bread still cardboard.

I could see Doodlebag's smug, fat face. Lucinda Seldon's disappointment. She would be civil at my hanging, but frosty. The noose. Eleven seconds of restraint and tightening suffocation, then to dangle in space, choking to death. Could this asshole spare me that? A quick bullet, a quicker death. If it came to it, I would beg for that.

I stood hatless and roasting under the afternoon sun. We were in the desert, seventy miles outside Palm Springs. Another place on my list when I entertained dreams of my glamorous new life.

A bird of prey asserted itself as number one in the pecking order, hovering patiently on a dead tree. Another bird was circling above. Soon there would a quite a queue for desert-cured female.

It was too bright to keep my eyes open. The asshole could just shoot me if he took it as insolence. Closing my eyes could get the whole thing over with.

The journey to this no-woman's-land had passed in silence. Questions had swirled around my head. Detective Randall Lauder from the LAPD must have called Scotland Yard as soon as he'd seen a dress from London and heard my weak attempt at the accent. He must have asked about missing female felons matching my description.

Jemima Day must have been high up on the list.

It was all down to the dress. The one I'd stupidly worn.

The British had my fingerprints. But what else did *they* tell him? Had they made me for the slaughter above the pub? Had Betty grassed me up?

Lauder only had to shove me on the first boat back to Blighty to face the music. But instead he'd dragged me to the back of beyond. He hadn't even taken my picture against the yardstick.

Why?

Instead, he'd pushed my blue dress over the table to me and hissed, 'Get changed.' He turned away while I slipped the dress on and shoved Alberta's hat on my messed-up hair.

'Keep your mouth shut. Take your purse.' Lauder had risen, without batting an eyelid.

He had opened the door. 'Thank you for your help, Miss Groader. I'll run you home.' And then, in plain sight of the other detectives at their desks, he'd led the way out of the stuffy office. A bunch of guys in shabby suits and loose neckties gawped at me. One was familiar – my drunken accuser at Mikey's bar. I avoided his eyes and lowered my head.

I walked out exactly as I'd come in – Minnie Groader, a witness. No more, no less. Then Lauder led me down to the basement car park, avoiding the elevator. He nodded at the attendant and headed for a black car. He opened the passenger door. 'Get in.'

And now I was frying to death. He was cool as a cucumber,

watching me shrivel up before his eyes. Was he a sadist? A pervert? This cop could be anyone if duping his work chums was such a piece of cake. Sleazier than his swanky veneer, playing the part of the Vice Squad dick whilst up to no good. Maybe he'd let Caziel escape, he hadn't exactly been in a hurry to race after him. Maybe I was about to be reunited with the creep, the pair of them with some kind of sick plan. Or maybe he killed for thrills and the LAPD didn't know they had a raving psycho in their midst. Someone who got his kicks from killing a desperate girl nobody would miss.

I braced myself for anything.

I was a goner and I deserved it. I'd had a good innings, considering the lousy start in life. Bowled out. I didn't belong here or anywhere. Never had, never would. I'd never done anything of note for anybody. I'd made my own way in life. Every time I'd relied on somebody else, I'd quickly learnt that was a fool's game. I didn't even know if Violet, my mother, was dead or alive. If alive, she'd happily rid herself of me a long time ago, in a very sophisticated scam.

Violet. She had saved all her pennies to take the first liner to America, but she couldn't find her GI lover. After five years of searching for him, palm trees in paradise must have become a living hell. She earned our keep as a live-in housekeeper in various grand Hollywood homes, our home a series of attic rooms. Then, one day, she told me we were going back home. As soon as she'd saved up enough to bring us both back to Blighty, we would leave. Home? I *was* home.

I remembered the cold deck and a gray sky. Where had my friends gone? Why was she doing this?

And then, halfway across the Atlantic, Violet took ill. A nun who was on board took charge of me. They never let me see her. They said she had died. Even then, I didn't believe her.

I disembarked an orphan and was carted off to some convent. It was all a haze. I later found out that Violet's relatives didn't want me, preferring to remain scandalized about my existence. They knew what I'd always suspected. I was as bastard as they come.

I prayed every night, down on my knees on cold stone floors, that someone kind would soon take me back to sunny America where I would find my old friends, the kids of the maids who worked in the houses. Fat lot of good that did me. I was done with praying by the time my seventh birthday came around. Done with asking anyone for anything. And as soon as I'd stolen enough pennies from the nuns, I'd be doing my very own disappearing act.

Like mother, like daughter.

Now my eyes strayed beyond Lauder's silhouette to the dancing waves of heat blurring the line between the mountains and the sky. Violet's face, or my hazy memory of it, appeared. Would I be reunited with her, finally? With Lena, and Billy? A good old knees-up at the Pearly Gates, with the few who passed as my family? Billy would be laughing. 'See, sweetheart, you just can't make it on your own. I made it all simple for you. You just had to lie low and keep your mouth shut. Pretending you're a smart-aleck, now look where you ended up!'

I let out an involuntary laugh.

Lauder pushed the gun into my temple. 'Something funny, huh?'

I said nothing, closing my eyes. Everything went red, the sun penetrating my eyelids.

Just do it, bastard.

The gun was pushed harder, scorching hot against my skin, burning. My breathing was shallow, the cuff of his jacket brushing my cheek. What was he waiting for?

Shoot, goddamn you!

The pressure of the metal against my temple suddenly eased. Going for my heart? I braced myself for impact.

No. The crunch of gravel. His feet, moving further back? My eyes flickered open, barely able to make out his silhouette against the raging sun.

'Jemima Day. You've got a rap sheet as long as your arm. Born on the Lusitania in 1920, to Violet Turner, an English seamstress. Father Montague Day, a GI.' He raised his brow. 'So, could be a US citizen by rights. Back in England by six, dumped in an orphanage. You ran away and had quite a spree of juvenile misdemeanors. Known associates – The Forty Elephants. The law caught up and by eleven stuck you in a correctional facility, a reformatory school for girls. Then you were fostered. Now, this is where it gets interesting. Your foster mother died and her relatives suspect you of a major theft of the family valuables in 1936. Couldn't pin a thing on you though, you had an alibi. Then Scotland Yard's got no record for five whole years. Try to go straight? In '41, you're up to no good again, picked up with a cache of weapons. Gunrunning. You were banged up for quite a stretch, the rest of the war, right? You jump parole the same day the war in Europe ends. Now here you are, jumping out of Elmore Caziel's window as the place goes up in flames. Looks to me like you're up to your old tricks.'

My tongue was dry, and it was hard to speak. 'Wouldn't it be easier just to send me back to England? Cheaper on gas.'

I didn't see him dart forward, his hand strike. He was that fast. A stinging, searing pain threw me. I lost my balance, twisting my ankle as I fell. My ears rang. Then he grabbed my ear, twisting me up. I yelled in pain. He said, 'Talk, smartass.'

What did he want, my fucking life story? Where to start? Just tell him about June? Or going on the run? Surely Betty can't have talked, as Lauder hadn't mentioned three dead bodies in rooms above the Jack & Jill. Had nobody discovered the bodies yet? Impossible. Billy was dead and so was our pledge of secrecy. Should I tell Lauder about my life as Ida Boyd? Would this buy me time?

Never give it all up.

'You seem to have the whole story.'

'No. Why did you run from England?'

'I don't know. Guess I should have done my time, the probation.'

Slap! He struck me again. Harder, this time. Stars danced before my eyes, and in the blackness, I lost my footing again. This time he didn't pull me up. I glared up at him. 'Just fucking shoot me, goddamn you!' I yelled, hoarse. No point in getting up again, just for another blow to the head.

'Oh, like that is it? You want me to put you out of your misery? If dying's a better deal, you must have done something real bad. What was it, Jemima? What did you do?'

'Nothing!'

'A jailbird, five years, saying nothing the whole time. The well-behaved inmate. And then you run? Somebody owe you something? Or did you grab your chance to serve up a little vengeance? Hell hath no fury, right? Who made going on the lam worth it?'

'My cat. I wanted to see him.' I spat the words out. Beating me to death would be better than the noose. I waited for the blow. None came. Lauder was swaying in front of my eyes. Was he bending down? I couldn't form words any more. I tried to meet his eyes but now there were two pairs. Four blurred saucers of vibrant turquoise.

An intense wave of dark red rose up over my eyes. Comforting. Soothingly soft. A warm blanket under which I could sleep forever.

If he meant to kill me, the sun got there first.

25

My head, or rather, the block of wood somebody was boring holes into with a red-hot drill, lolled forwards heavily. My mouth hung open, my lower jaw a dead weight.

My neck was painfully stiff as I raised my head.

Alberta's dusty hat lay at my feet.

I groaned, trying to see. It was dusk.

I was in Lauder's car, but we weren't in the desert anymore. The car was stationary and I was alone. Cuffed. I twisted around. Outside, the only lights were neon, illuminating a hamburger drive-in walking distance from the car. In the distance, lights shone from a scattering of buildings. Were we closer to the city? Or another town?

The thin silhouette of my captor approached the car, carrying two bottles of something and a paper bag. Somehow I managed to sit up. I could do nothing about the dribble from my chin before he got in. He nodded at the cuffs, indicating for me to turn around and he unlocked them. Then he dumped one of the bottles and a hamburger carton from the bag in my lap. The bottle was icy to the touch. Lemonade.

No point in pride. I downed it in one.

Lauder started tucking in. He noticed me holding the burger.

'Eat.'

'I don't eat meat.'

He stared at me as if I was speaking a foreign language.

'Eat the fucking roll, then.'

I looked out of the window, picking at the bread with my fingers, nibbling it. To anyone else looking in, we'd look like a date gone wrong. I wondered if he had a wife to get back to. Maybe he'd called her up.

'I'll be late for dinner, honey. Just bumping off some Brit ex-con.'

She'd be a bookish type, a dupe who pressed his shirts before she went off to her mundane job, unaware of his other life. He would like young women to be sweet, smiling and innocent. Anyone that fell outside of his narrow ideals of femininity would be scum. He'd even distrust Lucinda Seldon, despite her achievements. She'd be a ballbreaker to him. As a criminal, I was repellent...

Lauder interrupted my thoughts. 'How did you get into the country?'

'I volunteered, became a nurse. I travelled with injured soldiers coming back home.'

He guffawed. 'You? A nurse? Then what, got bored of playing Florence Nightingale?'

'I was actually good at it. They liked me. When we disembarked, I spent a few weeks in New York. Then I moved down to L.A. I booked into a hotel, the Miracle Mile. I roomed with a girl who Elmore Caziel drugged. He took pictures of her. Ones she didn't want him to take.' I met his eyes. 'She'd been sweet to me. So I burned the joint down.'

And all your evidence, I could have said. But he hadn't killed me and was feeding me, so I left that part out.

Lauder processed this, looking out into the night. After a while he said, 'The girl's name?'

'Can't you leave her out of it?'

'No.'

'June. June Conway.'

He grunted. 'How did you get the weapon?'

I hoped for Dede's sake it wasn't registered. 'I stole it in a New York nightclub. I forget the name of the place.'

He took another bite of burger. He was letting this lie go. I watched as he chewed fast, and then swallowed. The skin on his neck was marble white in the dark, and his Adam's apple jumped about, sharp and bony. 'What about your father? Montague Day? Been in contact since you arrived?'

'I got no plans to find him.'

'Good. You'll be pleased to hear he doesn't exist. Well, *a* Montague Day does, but I doubt he's your relative.'

I glanced at him.

'Deceased movie star. GIs in the First World War would sleep with foreign ladies and borrow actors' names. So you're probably not the only wretch in town with a fake name on your birth certificate.'

Exhaustion prevented me from laughing. Talk about a tragicomedy. Violet never had a hope in hell, chasing after a ghost. When did she finally cotton on to the fact she'd been hoodwinked? Was that why she finally decided to up sticks and go back to England? Now, thanks to Lauder, I knew even his name wasn't real and I was definitely illegitimate.

Dumping me with the nun on the boat could have been Violet's fresh start.

'What are you going to do with me?' I ventured. 'Hand me over?'

'Depends. We could come to an arrangement.'

I stared at him.

'I want the whole truth. You passed out before you got to the punch line. What were you doing before your arrest? And why did you jump probation?'

'All right. I had a quiet life in the years before prison. Then the war came, everyone was broke and hungry. Somebody approached me and asked me to pick up something, a quick job, nicely paid. Easy money on the side. Everything I told the Secret Service was true. I didn't talk because there was nothing else to say!'

Lauder watched me, then he burst out laughing. It was a hearty chuckle. 'Got to hand it to you. You don't know when to stop, do you? So the triple mobster killing in a London pub on the same day you ran is nothing to do with you?'

His words hung in the air. He'd known the whole time about the killings.

Betty! It had to be Betty.

It was dark and his eyes were now as jet black as his hair. I looked away and out of the window. Grasses were swaying in a gentle breeze.

The truth could burn or save me. But it was the only card left to play. I looked down.

'I didn't do it.'

He turned to me. 'Out with it, Jemima. The whole enchilada.'

Sitting in the dark, staring out into the windy night, I told a strange vice cop everything. About my missing years as Ida Boyd, Billy's girl. About our doomed relationship. About Billy's incarceration, about his secretive Italian friends. About the night he sent me out. The fact I never heard from him again while I rotted in jail, keeping my mouth shut. About Betty, who only knew me as Ida, who had seen me just before I saw Billy. I described the shootout above the pub with the Italian henchmen, and Billy dying in my arms. How I found a fake passport Billy had got ready for me, I had no idea why. I finished by saying Betty must have named me to the police. And Betty would have been able to point out the woman she knew, Ida Boyd, was one and the same as prison absconder Jemima Day.

By the time I finished, Detective Randall Lauder knew more about me than anyone else in the world.

The whole time, he had listened impassively, without eating. Now, he munched on his burger until he finished it, and screwed up the box. 'These hamburgers used to be the best in town. Personally, I think they make them too salty.'

He turned to me. 'One of the guys you killed was a certain Paolo Salvatore. Son of Don Giuseppe Salvatore. Mean anything to you?'

I shook my head. 'I didn't know any of them. I told you that already.'

'Big shot. A boss. The Mob has tentacles that stretch across the Atlantic. Scotland Yard likes you for the mobster killing. So you're right. Your seamstress must have squealed.'

Lauder lit up. 'We're talking about the heir to the Salvatore empire, right. You saw, the Mob don't mess around.'

'It was self-defense!'

'That's your story. Facts remain unproven.'

He was right but I could only shrug.

'Here's the deal. You've got no connections, no obligations, no friends, no family. But you do have debts.'

'Debts? What debts?'

'To society. Born criminal. Gangster's girl. You lived the life. Don't kid yourself you want a fresh start. People like you don't ever change, so we're talking more of a change of direction.'

I looked down. 'I never wanted anybody to die.'

'Scotland Yard has been informed that a corpse matching Jemima Day's description was found in the desert. I guess the word will get out to the Secret Service or anybody else who you've aggravated. Hopefully to the Mob too, if they now know Jemima Day and Ida Boyd are the same person.'

He had lied to Scotland Yard? 'What? You told them I'm dead?'

'Doesn't matter what I said, or to who. You can relax, for now.'

'Won't they ask for evidence? Pictures of the body?'

'Is that your problem? No. You're only problem is to do what I want, when I want, how I want.'

I didn't get it. 'What? Doing what exactly?'

'Odd jobs, on the Q.T. Things a girl can do. You can ease in and out, blend in. Like you did in Mikey's that day. Don't pretend it wasn't you. Funny thing is, I thought you *were* a reporter. I just thought I'd give you a break. Turns out you're a lot more trouble.'

We met each other's eyes. I looked away first, into the night sky.

'What do I have to do?'

'For instance, our mutual friend Caziel. Word gets out Minnie Groader's around, maybe he wants some payback. You could lure him out.'

'To kill me.'

'Could be. We'll handle that.'

126

He leant over and growled at me. I could smell burger on his breath, mixed with his aftershave. 'Try any escape artist larks, you'll be sorry. Sure you could probably trick some dope in the sticks into marrying you, hole up in Kentucky or some place, but you'll always be looking over your shoulder. That body in the desert? Turns out we got it wrong. Not Jemima Day. The Mob then gets an anonymous tip-off that precious little Salvatore's killer is alive and kicking this side of the pond. They get their hands on you, you'll regret I didn't send you back to face justice.'

Was he bent, out on his own? I had no idea why he was doing any of this. He could soon be climbing up the greasy pole with my high-risk work pushing him up it. This was permanent servitude and dangerous as hell. But if he had any hunch at all I was telling the truth, this was a form of protection. I was dead meat in England. Wanted for triple murder, my identities now rumbled. Lauder was my only chance. He was saving my life, at least extending it.

He looked at me. 'What's the name on your fake passport?'

'Constance Sharpe, from New York.'

He whistled. 'Sophisticated. That's what the people at the hotel know you as?'

'A few. Yes.'

He told me that the next time I met him I had to hand over the passport and think up a new name. And to clear out of the hotel that night.

'I've got nowhere else to go.'

Lauder had that covered. He got out his notebook and scrawled something, before passing it to me. *Astral Motel, S. Figueroa.* He said, 'Your new flophouse. Take a cab. Don't stray far, because I'll be visiting when I need you.'

127

I was now officially his slave. 'I'm flat broke. Down to my last couple of hundred bucks.'

Lauder stared, incredulous. 'I throw you a lifeline and you're *hustling*?'

'I got to eat! And how long does this arrangement go on for?'

'As long as I think you're useful. Till then, this is how it'll work. I'll leave word when I need you, when and where to meet. You do not ever try to contact me. Ever. Remember that. I'll brief you in person. And you might need to dress the part on occasions. Won't be a problem for a killer-diller like you.'

Lauder plucked my burger carton from my lap. He got out of the car and threw the cartons the trashcan, then meticulously wiped his hands on a napkin he'd tucked under his arm. He tossed that, too, and got back in the car.

He started the engine, putting it into reverse. 'This June Conway...'

'Yes?'

'She in a bad way?'

I had no idea. I hoped she was better. I had ended up here for her sake. Something good had better come out of my disaster.

'She know you put your neck on the line for her?' He said, unwittingly rubbing it in.

'Nobody knows what I did.' June would find out in time, because Dede Dedeaux would tell her. But Lauder didn't need to know about Dede. There was no point dragging her into my mess.

Lauder grunted, moving forward over potholes. 'If we bust Caziel, Conway can't take the stand.'

'She'll want to forget the whole thing anyhow.'

He turned to me. 'You don't get it, do you?'

'What?'

'She told her friend *Connie Sharpe* about her ordeal, right? Not Minnie Groader. On the stand, Conway would have to recall her dealings with Caziel without saying she told you. Good girls make bad liars, even if we prepped her. If she blurts out you found her, any half-assed defense attorney would prick up their ears if we avoided calling a key witness. Who's this Connie Sharpe? Now you get it? She can no longer exist.'

Suddenly I saw how it could all backfire on him. Harboring a fugitive. He'd go down for that, lose everything. Worse, he could become a target for the Mob if things really unraveled. But I wasn't going to thank him anytime soon.

Lauder grunted, turning out onto the deserted road. Suddenly I saw how high up we were. The L.A. basin spread out below. A thousand twinkling lights appeared like scattered sequins. Lauder said, 'Do what I want, when I want and you won't have a problem. Do anything else, you will.'

With that pleasantry, we started the long drive back to the city.

26

It was Herman, one of the soldiers I nursed. He was holding my hand, terrified. We stood on a listing boat, rapidly taking on water. A ragged hole split the deck. Bombs rained down all around us, missing the boat. Suddenly the soldier became Kettle, my cat, lying in my arms. He was thin, ragged-looking. He didn't know me anymore and he was dying. I had to keep him alive. Desperation and guilt consumed me. It was all my fault! I'd be punished for it, hung if he died. I felt sick with anxiety. I tried to escape, holding the dying cat and rushing around the deck begging for help. Soldiers with wasted bodies and haunted eyes stared through me. The liner was now burning, and sirens pierced the air. There was nowhere to run and Kettle struggled, flying out of my arms. The soldiers wouldn't move. I screamed at them to jump overboard. I had to find the cat, and searched through the ship's bowels. He would die, all alone. I hadn't held on to him! I screamed out his name. I ran to the edge of the deck. Ahead, a tidal wave of the darkest slate gray began growing, tall as a skyscraper. I was frozen, terrified, waiting for the dark curtain of water to roll over and crash...

Somebody was rapping at the door.

I gasped for air, splashing water everywhere. I was in the bath, back in June's room. It was dark and the water had gone cold. The twist of events, Lauder, it all flooded back. I sat up, dripping, collecting my foggy thoughts.

When I had got back to the hotel, it was late. Lauder had

dropped me off a few blocks away and I'd walked the rest of the way, in the crumpled dress, sticking out like a sore thumb amidst the slick residents. A group of them were buzzing around, dressed to the nines for a night on the town. A happy scene. They gathered around some newly arrived blonde bombshell who was handing out gifts for her friends. They didn't notice me but I couldn't take my eyes off them. A life closed to me, forever.

June's room had been tidied up. Dede had left a note to say June had gone, and I should come upstairs when I got back. Her handwriting was a spidery, elegant sprawl in blue-gray ink. The expensive paper, a paler gray, was adorned with an elaborately monogrammed *DD* in gold.

I had decided against it and tore up her note. Then I had downed the last of Billy's morphine tablets, and drifted off to sleep in a hot bath.

I hadn't drowned, if that had been my unconscious intention. Judging by the cold water and my goose pimples, I'd soaked in it for hours.

I prayed the person would go away. But there was another rap. I knew exactly who it was.

Dede's yellow eyes peered at me through the barely opened door. 'Thank God. Didn't you see my message?'

Nodding, I opened the door an inch wider. 'Had to crash. Busy day.' She ignored my sarcasm, pushing the door open and breezing past me. I closed the door behind her.

She was immaculate in a coral silk shirt with long sleeves and elegant cuffs, and pants of deep lavender. Her belt was a woven affair, cream with a purple and orange geometric design,

131

and a brass clasp. She wore a chunky gold and coral bangle, and gold dangly earrings with coral baubles set in each. Her eyelids and lips were a darker shade of red, her dark hair pushed up with a mass of immaculate shiny pin curls on top.

I envied her. That look took time and money.

Dede stood with her hands on her hips. 'You okay?'

'Sure.' I lied. Shivering, and wrapped in a towel, I wasn't convincing.

She nodded, focusing on my eyes.

'Get something on before you tell me all about it. You look half frozen.'

I obeyed, grabbing one of June's dressing gowns. It drowned me. 'Coffee?'

'No, thanks.'

I walked barefoot to the kitchenette, wanting to avoid a serious conversation. 'How's June?'

Dede called out. 'In good hands. Tougher than she looks.'

I searched through the cupboards. Not much, just a strawberry milkshake powder. Yuck. I returned to the living area, my head still muzzy. Dede perched on June's bed, lighting up a menthol cigarette in lilac paper that matched her outfit. I said, 'Everything went to plan. He bought my desperate act, fondled the merchandise but got no further. I managed to find his dark room in the back, and lit a match. Whole place went up but I think he got away. I got out through a rear window. I meant to pop up straightaway but I just crashed.'

She studied me. 'Simple as that?'

'Uh-huh. Place must be charcoal by now.'

'Yeah. It is.'

'You saw it?' She had *checked* on me?

Dede exhaled. 'When you didn't show up, I got a little worried. So I cruised past. The house was burnt to a cinder. Firemen, cops, press, you name it – crawling all over it like woodlice.'

'You stopped?' I was aghast. Had she talked to anybody? I didn't ask. Even more perplexing is what she'd have actually done to help me. Brandished her African dagger? Or maybe she had a more extensive personal armory.

Dede raised her brows. 'Is that a serious question? You did good and here you are, safe and sound. No more to say about it.'

I hid my relief. 'Make sure you tell June she's got nothing to worry about.'

'Tell her yourself. She'll be up to visitors in a few days.'

I leant against the wall, doing my best to look relaxed. 'Sure. I'll go see her.' It was a lie. I wouldn't see either of them again.

'I lost Alberta's hat.' Another lie. I'd forgotten to pick it up from the floor of the car when Lauder dropped me off. 'I can leave her something for it.'

'Don't worry about it.' Dede was decisive.

'About your gun...' I explained it had fallen as I escaped and that it was probably stuck in a bush, hidden. She seemed to be taking it calmly. 'I'd wiped it down. No prints. So no trace to anyone...if...'

No prints except from dumb old me.

Dede butted in. 'If I have a record? I don't.' She smirked. 'Anyway, you think I'd have given a total stranger a registered gun?'

27

The taxi crawled through a sleazy-looking district, a good few miles west of Downtown. A mixed area with clothing factories, cheap apartment blocks going up behind big hoardings, cemented wastelands between plots, and a main drag with some bars, a club or two, a snooker hall, a coffee shop or four, all draining each other's profits. South London had similar parts. Once in, you never got out. I remembered Seldon's caution to avoid lowlife. Lauder clearly had a very different approach to ex-offenders.

We drove on. Now we were in a black neighborhood. Guys in zoot suits hung around late-night barber shops. Jazz wailed from clubs. People were spilling out, having a good time, and the night felt electric.

The Astral Motel was no Miracle Mile. No uniformed doormen here. Just a low-rent establishment that wouldn't know the meaning of *full occupancy*. It was a flimsy-looking two-story affair, shaped like a U around a courtyard. It had probably been hurriedly erected to cater for the swarms of midwestern actors who traded the Dust Bowl for a sprinkling of stardust. A flaking paint sign declared the empty swimming pool was empty 'for repairs'.

As I entered the front office, a young man looked up. He couldn't have been more than eighteen. His mouth was full, his hand in a bag of candy. He stopped himself, caught in the act, with soft, childlike eyes. Swing music came from a radio behind the desk. He turned the wireless down and shuffled up.

'Can I help you, ma'am?' He was too polite to say, 'What's a haggard white lady doing in here?'

'I think I've got a reservation.'

'Oh, right. Mr. Clarence said you'd be arriving tonight, ma'am.'

Mr. Clarence? Who was he? I stopped myself from asking questions and played along. 'That's right. How much?'

'Oh, your room's paid up, ma'am.'

What?

'Name, please, ma'am?' Shit! I remembered Lauder's command to rename myself. I must have been staring because he smiled patiently. 'For the register.'

I blurted the one thing to come to me. 'Elvira.' Elvira had given me hope. Maybe she could again.

'I'm Malvin. You need anything, I'll do my best to be of service.' He smiled, all amiability. Malvin began to write in a column, with large handwriting. There were a few other names of guests. Fake, to dupe me? I had no idea.

I needed a surname. Favorite color? Purple. Ridiculous. Worst color? Gray? No. Far too depressing. Too Holloway Prison. Slate. Slate gray, like the smoke that had engulfed my dreams and got me into this trouble.

I would never forget the lesson in that.

Elvira Slate. Help and hindrance. That about summed my new identity up.

'Elvira Slate.'

Malvin studied the keys, hanging in a box, deciding which room. His fingers grabbed one and passed it to me. Number five. 'Miss Slate, room five's nice and near to the office, so you ain't got far to walk if you need anything. I go to lunch by noon most days. We've got a coffee shop around the corner – Tina's – and a grocery store, Ebenezer's. Do you have a car, ma'am?'

'Not right now.'

'You can take the Yellow Car Downtown. Takes about twenty minutes.'

'Thanks.'

Malvin smiled sweetly. 'Oh, Mr. Clarence left something for you.' Malvin bent down and came back up holding an envelope. I thanked him and took it.

I ventured into my room, a mustard affair. The worn carpet was probably once gold, now dulled from the drunken shuffling of too many travelling salesmen. The decorators had been sloppy and yellow paint drips had dried into the carpet.

I ripped the envelope open. Twenty bucks. Enough to feed myself for a week or so, without dipping into the last of my fake currency that Lauder didn't know about.

There was a rudimentary kitchen area, with a dented kettle and a small ring for cooking. The fridge was clean but made a buzzing noise as if it was about to keel over. The previous occupant had left a bottle of root beer inside. It was half empty. I picked it up and drained the smelly brown ale in the sink. It didn't flow away as fast as it should. I ran the faucet and brown water spluttered over me.

A pair of dice sat next to chipped china salt and pepper pots in the shape of pineapples. Pineapples with cute faces. One had the word *Aloha*. The other, *Hawaii*.

'Aloha,' I said, to nobody in particular.

Alcohol, and a lot of it, would be the trick to surviving here.

I pulled down the wall bed. The bed linen looked fresh and recently starched. I made a mental note to tip the maid. Next to the bed a worn copy of the Bible was propped on a low table. My life was somebody up there's joke, so I slid it under the bed.

I lay back, risking the invisible germs of the headboard and lit a cigarette to contemplate life. I was alive and had a kind of liberty. I could come and go, but not too far. Besides, Malvin could be Lauder's eyes. I had no idea who Mr. Clarence was. Maybe Lauder's partner on the ladder at Caziel's? There had been no sight or sound of him, and I hadn't asked. But I was in a black neighborhood, so there could be some connection. It was a clever move, but dumb, too. Nobody would look for me here, but I'd stand out like a sore thumb. I couldn't make sense of it. Other than the name change, the being at Lauder's beck and call, and the order not to call the LAPD, there were no other rules and regulations.

Lauder's orders.

Glamour and crime were off the table, unless I ran. I was in no hurry to do that, not until I had a game plan that had a chance of working.

The truce was fragile, but would hold.

For now.

I got back up and unpacked, hanging up my clothes in the wardrobe. Laughable, to blow all those bucks the moment I'd stepped on dry land. The black evening dress. The silk shirts. The fine wool suits. The few hats I had. And then the older garments I'd lugged all the way from Blighty – the clothes Billy had probably picked out for me. None of these suited Elvira Slate. But who the hell was she?

My stomach lurched at the thought of something. Betty. Why hadn't I put two and two together earlier? Had *she* supplied the outfits for Billy? She knew my size better than anyone. She would also know girls lost pounds inside. Betty probably believed I just wanted vengeance for the jail time and after that ran for my life. It made sense she told the cops. And it made sense if she named me to the Mob to protect herself.

I needed a drink, no matter what the locals made of me. I'd find a bar, and hope that any paying customer was a good customer. Lauder hadn't expressly forbidden anything like having a drink. In the dimly lit bathroom, the shadows under my eyes were more pronounced than usual. I threw on the skirt of one of the suits and a polka dot lawn shirt. Inoffensive enough.

I slipped out of the cabin, walking quickly away, not wanting to be seen by Malvin through the blinds.

Back on the main drag, there were quite a few late-night bars and a liquor store. I was the only white person around and got a lot of sideways glances. Curiosity, mainly. But nobody would meet my eyes. An older woman in a housekeeper's coat looked at me as she got off the bus. A '*what are* you *doing* here?' look.

I nearly offered her a drink, for the company. My criteria for a watering hole were basic; cheap liquor, no nuisances, and near to the Astral. Swing music would lift my mood, but I couldn't attract attention by jitterbugging the night away on the dance floor.

Suddenly, I stopped. This was crazy. Anything could get back to Clarence and Lauder, via Malvin.

I headed back to the Astral, feeling tired and very alone. Curling up in the crummy wall bed suddenly held all the appeal of a top dollar hotel.

The clock said two am. The room was stuffy and hot. I twisted and turned in the sheet, which felt sticky. I made a mental to-do list.

One. Get some basic forms of entertainment for the room. A novel, a pack of cards, a book of crosswords. Prison entertainment.

Two. Take the Yellow Car to a movie theater. Resume June's movie program.

Three. Ask Malvin for a fan that worked.

Four. Longer term, and the most important task. Get leverage on Lauder by being pals with Malvin. Find out who the hell Clarence is.

I switched on the lamp. Two roaches scuttled away across the carpet.

Five. Complain about the roaches.

28

'Well, look what the cat dragged in.'

Lauder loomed over me. I was sitting on the sidewalk, around eleven, having a coffee at Tina's. The sun was too bright, and I hid behind a cheap pair of sunglasses. I'd made sure Malvin knew where I was going and sure enough, he'd relayed the information.

'I've had better nights' sleep.' I muttered, not bothering to look up.

'Don't like the Astral? Could be worse.' He sat down, and leant forward, lowering his voice. 'Could be jail.'

I ignored this. Lauder pulled out a cigarette, called out, 'Coffee, Sandy' to a pretty waitress with two black buns on either side of her head, and shot me a fake smile. 'Getting to know the neighborhood?'

Probably that was a trick question. 'Not really.'

Lauder leant over the table and briefly sniffed the red carnation flower in the vase on the table.

'Who's Clarence? Is he the one who you were with? He left twenty bucks for me. Thank him for me, will you?' The sarcastic edge in my voice wasn't lost on him and Lauder almost laughed. 'I will. Got a name yet? Something to go by?'

'Elvira. Elvira Slate.'

He thought about it for less than a second. 'Elvira, sure. Neat. Could be you, at a push. If you clean up your act. Why Slate?'

'Good idea at the time.'

Because it reminds me of how I met you. It reminds me of my stupidity.

'Middle name?'

I gawped at him. 'Do I need one?'

'You do. Got the other passport?'

I slipped it out of my pocket and handed it to him. He examined the back and the front, flicking through the pages. 'See, even Constance Sharpe has a middle name. Two, in fact.' He looked at me, waving the passport. 'Nice job. Not that you'd operate with amateurs.' Lauder slid the passport into the inside pocket of his jacket. He'd burn it or keep it as part of his little Jemima Day collection.

'I was in jail for almost five years. I didn't operate with anyone and I have no idea who Billy ordered it from, as I already said.'

'Grouchy this morning, aren't we? All right. Susan.'

'What?'

'Your middle name. Susan.'

This was like naming a baby. 'No. Susan's dull.'

Lauder smirked. 'See, you do care.'

'Charlotte.' I said.

'That works. Elvira Charlotte Slate. Sounds educated. Something to aspire to.'

'I am educated. Could I have my purse back, the black one?'

'No.' He lit a cigarette, let it dangle between his lips as he ripped a sheet out of his notebook. 'Memorize this.'

A handwritten scrawl spelt out an address. *403 Fauness Avenue.*

'Got it?'

I nodded. Lauder plucked it from my hand and tore it up.

He placed the pieces in an ashtray and lit them. The flames quickly turned them to black.

'Malvin can give you a street map. Take the Car, then it's a short walk. You'll have a nice cozy chat with a couple of girls. Don't say I sent you, or mention my name. You're just delivering a message, short and snappy. They have to go back and pay back what they took by tomorrow, midday. They know where and what. Make it clear it's for their own good.' He viewed me quizzically. 'What?'

'I'm delivering a threat?'

'A message. Be convincing about it.'

I sipped the dregs of my coffee. Sandy, the waitress, came out with Lauder's, and gave him a smile. She had a wide gap in her front teeth that made her look young and cute. But she could be my captor's eyes and ears and I shouldn't judge books by covers. 'There you go, Mr. Lauder.'

'Thanks.'

When Sandy moved away, I said, 'Convincing? How? I don't know anything.'

'They'll be crapping themselves they've been tracked down.' Lauder drank his coffee fast.

'A couple of girls? Can I know their names?'

He weighed up the pros and cons of this. 'Shimmer and Rhonda.' Lauder looked at his watch. 'Go around four. Don't get into anything with Shimmer.'

'This has to be a gimmick,' I uttered. It stank. 'So who am I supposed to be? I mean, what should I, you know, look like?'

'Go as yourself. A crook on the make.'

'I'm trying to clean up my act, remember?'

He raised a '*why bother*' brow.

'What if they don't go back to wherever they're supposed to? What will happen then?'

'Not your problem.'

'I meant, to me?'

'Oh, yeah. I forgot – you don't give a rat's ass about anyone else. Then you will have a problem.'

Actually, I did once, and look where it got me. Stuck with you.

'What's to stop them lying to me to get rid of me? Then, what?' My voice wavered. Fear had nowhere to hide.

Standing up, he pulled out a couple of dollar bills and left them on the table. He leant over the table, whispering into my ear. 'Just don't fuck up.'

29

'No. Wrong place.' Through the small crack of the door, a pair of tired eyes with dark bags gave me the onceover. Shimmer went to close the door but I got there first, ramming my foot into the gap. She immediately pushed harder.

'Fuck!' I cried out. I lowered my voice, growling. 'Open the goddamn door or I'll make a scene and that old crow next door will call the cops.'

Moments before ringing the bell, I'd spied the neighbor in the next house peeking at me from behind her net curtains. A bona fide Nosey Parker. I had caught her eye and she dropped the lace. But I knew she was still there, having a good old snoop. It definitely looked like her regular pastime, watching the comings and goings of the bad girls next door.

My threat didn't make a jot of difference. Shimmer kept pushing and I pushed back. Her wiry arms were strong. Shimmer hissed, 'Scram, bitch!'

I panted my words out. 'Look, I got a very short message for you.'

Her eyes flashed with anger. 'Spit it out.'

'Get back by tomorrow, midday. And give back what you took.'

'Who says?'

I panted, pushing hard. 'You know who. I'm just the messenger.'

'Got it. Bye, messenger.'

I stopped pushing and the door slammed shut.

Short and snappy, as ordered. Convincing? Hardly.

I walked back through the front yard, aware of the old biddy's net curtains swaying.

'Hey, messenger.' Shimmer's voice was thick and sarcastic.

I turned around to see her standing in the doorway, hands on hips, cigarette in her mouth. Puffed up and dolled up. The pale mauve suit was a cheap copy from the expensive numbers in the fancy dress shops, but suited her. Underneath, she wore a frilly high-necked blouse that buttoned up the back. She had to be the same age as me, give or take a couple of years. Her brown hair looked recently dyed, a solid bronze color that jarred with her ruddy skin tone. I'd known plenty of Shimmers in London. Maureen O'Reilly was a Shimmer, and she had practically raised me. She taught me how to shoplift, how to fleece men and how to drink away the profits. A woman like Shimmer had educated me all the way to reformatory school.

She sneered, 'I got a message, too. One for you to give back...' She waved her finger, signaling me to come inside.

Don't get into anything with Shimmer.

I wouldn't cross the threshold. The orders had been clear. Even so, I was curious.

My eyes on her, I limped back.

Up close, I could see she'd been through the wringer of life all right, a faint scar across her cheek. Her tough veneer masked a once-pretty face that had dark rings under the eyes, and prematurely deep lines around her mouth. I could smell violet eau de cologne.

'Well, come on in,' Shimmer said, opening the door wider.

I hovered. Bad idea.

No. *Good* idea. Play it well, I might get something on Lauder.

I stepped into a gloomy room. The blinds were pulled down, and a side lamp with a lacy shade provided a glimmer of light. A small velvet sofa pushed into the corner near a fireplace had seen better days. A cheaply framed portrait of a young Mexican girl in traditional costume and a mini-sombrero, the type of picture a tourist might buy, hung on the wall. Three suitcases were lined up near the door. Somebody was coming or going.

Shimmer stood with her back to the door, scanning my outfit. I'd ignored Lauder's insult and put on a silk shirt with a tie neck, a mushroom skirt and espadrilles. Making an effort would get her on my side because she wouldn't respect me if I looked like a tramp or a lowlife.

I stood in the middle of the room. 'So what's the message?'

'Who the hell are you?'

'Nobody who counts. Just the messenger.' I was as solid as a waxwork under a hot sun.

Shimmer opened her purse and calmly took out a gun. She brandished it at me. 'I said, who the fuck are you?' She jerked the gun like a finger, beckoning me to the sofa. I put my hands up, walking backwards. 'Nobody, I swear.'

I sat down on the distinctly saggy cushion, cursing myself. Was she crazy? Was this the plan? Shoot the messenger? She wouldn't exactly have shot me in the street, not in front of Old Nosey Parker. I said, 'My name's Gina.'

'Gina who?'

'Gina Jones.'

'Gina fucking Jones. Think I'm dumb? You just made that up.' Shimmer blinked a few times as if she had a twitch. 'Tell Kaye she can stick it up her fat rat ass.'

Kaye. I played along.

'All right. I'll see her later.'

Shimmer stepped forward. She pushed the gun to my temple. 'I can make things up, too. There ain't no Kaye, so who the hell sent you, bitch?'

The gun felt cold and hard. The barrel could be empty, but maybe not. They'd packed their bags and were running. Leaving my rotting body as a 'fuck you' message to whoever – it wasn't outside the realms of possibility. Lauder and his demands suddenly didn't seem as pressing as the barrel against my temple.

The game was up. I croaked hoarsely. 'Randall Lauder.'

Shimmer froze for a few seconds. 'I knew it! Fucking Randy Lauder? How the hell did he find us here?' Then she craned her neck. 'Hey, Rhondie! Get down here. We got a visitor.'

At least she lowered the gun. We stood facing each other, about a foot between us. I didn't move an inch.

Footsteps, slow and deliberate, were coming down stairs beyond the inner hall.

A wisp of a young woman appeared at the door. I recognized her immediately – the girl in the portrait, a decade older. She wore a pinafore dress in a faded tangerine, soft from too many washes, and a smocked gray blouse underneath. Clothes that said she didn't go out much, or plan to. Her hair was concealed in a faded floral headscarf, tied up with a bow on top.

Her one luxury item was a gold bangle, engraved. I bet she never took it off.

Shimmer's voice went really soft, her hard eyes following suit. 'You tell anyone about this place, honey?' She jumped up and helped Rhonda over to a chair.

'No, why would I?' Rhonda spoke rather slowly as if it was

an effort getting the words out. She sat down. She was obviously sick, a gray pallor to her skin. Her dark eyes rested on me with muted suspicion.

'This is Gina, or so she reckons,' said Shimmer. She stroked Rhonda's head, turning to me. 'That sonofabitch.' Shimmer glared at me. 'How did that shady asshole find us?'

I shook my head. 'You said it. Guy moves in mysterious ways.'

'Must have tailed us here.' Shimmer glanced at Rhonda. 'Hear that, Rhondie? Fucking Lauder. Jeez!' Worry crumpled her features for an instant. It didn't last long before she sneered at me. 'So who the fuck are you?'

'I'm his personal errand-girl, in return for him turning a blind eye. Fact is, I know nothing about you girls. Never knew you existed till yesterday.'

This perked Shimmer up slightly. She and Rhonda exchanged a glance. 'What's he got over you?'

'Something to do with bogus lettuce.'

'So, you're a copycat.' Shimmer looked impressed. 'Where you from?' My accent was letting me down again. I hoped I could sound more convincing. Sailors, both black and white, on the boat over, got a kick out of a well-to-do widow getting down and dirty with Yank lingo. Little did they know I had spent my formative years in the gutter, a South London one. I swallowed the American equivalents like gravy. 'Don't stay in any place too long. I was up in New York, but cops busted me so I blew. Month ago. I was sniffing the air down here, Lauder made me, simple as that.' It was a loose interpretation of the truth.

Shimmer took it all in but gave nothing away. Rhonda folded her arms and leant her head back. Even sitting down looked like it wiped her out.

I continued. 'Lauder was clear. Don't pay back whoever by midday tomorrow, you're in big trouble, and so am I.' I pulled a really worried face. It wasn't hard.

'Then you got a problem. We ain't ever payin' anyone back. Cos we don't owe nobody nothing!'

Checkmate.

I looked at her. 'You know what? Maybe we can help each other.'

Shimmer's eyes narrowed. 'You listening? *You're* the only one who's screwed.'

'Just hear me out.'

30

For all his sharpness on the job, Lauder had yet to learn women could form strange alliances when necessity demanded. It wasn't exactly sisterhood, more like pragmatism. Lauder would never have seen it coming that an ex-con like me and a hard nut like Shimmer would collaborate to work the system to our advantage. He had either underrated me, overrated his power or just didn't know women. I figured the latter. Otherwise, I wouldn't be sitting here now, in the little dining room of the house, smoking Shimmer's grass.

The dining room had a little more going for it, with a heavy mahogany armoire stuffed with china ornaments and crockery, everything cloaked in a layer or two of dust. Some of the furniture was covered in white sheets, lending the place a weird Miss Havisham eeriness. A chessboard with an active game lay at the edge of the dining table. Shimmer and I sat at the other end. I peered at it. The queen was vulnerable, but I wouldn't point it out.

'You play?' Shimmer asked. 'Course you do. I've done time and I know a jailbird when I see one. How long?'

'Long enough.'

'I wasn't going to shoot you or nothing. Just needed to know. You ain't bluffin'. I know when someone's scared shitless, too.' She laughed pitilessly.

'I didn't know then we were birds of a feather,' I said. Shimmer seemed to like this and smiled at me.

Rhonda entered holding a tray with a coffee pot and china

cups and saucers. A very dainty load. Three streetwise ladies sitting down to tea.

We watched as Rhonda lowered the tray onto the table. Shimmer gave her a reassuring look. 'Thank you, angel. How about some of those peanut cookies for our visitor?'

'You want cookies?' Rhonda asked me, doubtfully.

'I'm good...' I began to say, but Shimmer's sharp look silenced me.

Rhonda shuffled out of the room. Shimmer frowned. 'Might seem like I'm bossing her around but Doc says small errands and stuff will help.'

'What's wrong?' I passed Shimmer the reefer.

'Brain tumor. Quacks say they can cure it but the operation and all the care is gonna set us back.' She began to explain how they needed to raise the money for the operation which would take place in another city. But my mind was already elsewhere, remembering Gwendoline, my foster mother, who had died of a brain tumor. She had been loaded but all the money in the world couldn't save her life.

Shimmer was going on. The house was sold, which would help pay the medical bills and for the relocation. 'We got tight margins, but we'll do it. I worked it all out.' She went on to say the house had belonged to Rhonda's granny and she had given it to her. Then after the operation, Rhonda would be able to study law, and Shimmer would set up her own accountancy business. 'We'll be straight as a die.'

She was equally forthcoming about their present predicament. They had fled the clutches of a tyrant of a boss, a mean bitch called Reba T., who ran a string of nightclubs. Shimmer had been the bookkeeper and Rhonda was a waitress at one of the clubs. They'd fallen in love. Lauder was a regular at the same club, a strip club with poker tables. The problem was Shimmer had fallen out numerous times with the boss lady over money; she had a habit of underpaying her staff with dubious deductions every month for so-called misdemeanors. So Shimmer took it upon herself to pay herself and Rhonda back. 'Cooked her books, all right.'

'Does Lauder know about Rhonda?'

Shimmer nodded. 'Yeah, heartless asshole.'

'How much you skim?'

'Two thousand bucks.' She said this with defiant pride. 'Everything she owed me plus interest, and a little hush money on top. Knew she'd catch on, just as soon as we didn't show up again.'

'Hush money?'

She nodded, putting a finger to her lips. I whistled, taking mental note of the name Reba T. 'Well, she's sure got her talons out for you now.'

Shimmer mused, looking dreamy. 'Reba T. wasn't always bad, not until her husband became a she.'

That, I had not expected.

'Reba T. got bitter, after Joyce has got her own nightclub. Dyke club.'

'Joyce?'

'Yeah, that's his...*her* name now.'

'So Joyce digs the girls?' Maybe that was why Reba T. got miffed. Husband turns woman turns lesbian? Maybe she'd been traded in for a younger model.

'That's Joyce's business.' Shimmer was surprisingly loyal.

'So Lauder works for your boss?' I puffed again.

'Ex-boss. Who knows who's in whose pocket? She's got her fingers in all kinds of pies. Lauder could get a slice of the action to keep his mouth shut. Reba T.'s place was never busted in the five years I worked there. Maybe thanks to you-know-who.'

I whistled again, sucked into the intrigue. I wanted her to ramble on but at that moment Rhonda returned with a plate heaped with chunky golden cookies. They smelled delicious. Shimmer smiled. 'That's my girl.' She took the plate and gave Rhonda a kiss on the cheek. It wasn't just a kiss. Rhonda broke into a sunny, open smile, as she plucked the joint dangling from Shimmer's mouth. She spoke slowly. 'Quit partying. Got your meeting, remember? Need all your smarts with that guy.' Rhonda carefully handed the joint to me. 'Don't give it back to her.'

Shimmer laughed. 'OK, you know what's good for me.'

At the door, Rhonda turned to address me. 'She takes care of me real good and it ain't easy for her.'

Shimmer pulled a hangdog expression, looking up at Rhonda with big eyes, and a pouty mouth. 'Ooh. Nothing's too much for my Rhondie. I love takin' care of you, honey.' They blew each other kisses.

That's what love must be, then. Being able to make a fool of yourself without feeling like a fool.

I'd never been like that with anyone, and the odds were I never would. Billy and I had never doted on each other. No canoodling and silly fun. He never let his guard down, never looked like a fool for love. I would get drunk and have a good time, but he never joined in. He'd just stand there with that expression that I later decided was indulgent, like a protective daddy. As the years went by, he didn't even show that.

Shimmer got up and dug a bottle out of the dresser. 'Want a chaser with your cookie while you tell me your proposition?'

'Sure.' The whole errand had gone to pot and liquor on top wouldn't hurt.

She pulled out two tumblers and a bottle of scotch, pouring it generously into each glass. Shimmer handed me a glass and sat down opposite me. I took a long slug. I said, 'When you don't return tomorrow, I can throw him off your scent.'

'How?'

'I'll say you're real sorry. You messed up. You'll pay all the dough back. You want to come back but it has to be the weekend. You'll be out of town for a wedding, a funeral, whatever. Important family business. I can say some place far away you'll never go to. I can buy you two days like that.'

Shimmer considered this. 'Okay. Here's the thing. We *are* leaving this dump tomorrow. Like I said, sold up – lock, stock and barrel. We'll be renting someplace else Randall Lauder don't know about.'

The smoke created a thick aromatic haze between us.

I said, 'Lauder is a sly rat. Found you once, he can find you again. Best you leave it to me to throw him off the trail.'

The cookies looked more enticing by the minute. I picked one up and bit into it. It was crisp on the outside and buttery. The chopped peanuts gave a good crunch. Now I was buzzing and I could eat the whole plate.

Shimmer's voice burst through my cookie reverie. She was saying, 'Don't see how any of this helps you.'

I swallowed. 'You can return the favor. I want dirt on Lauder.'

Shimmer sniggered. 'Something for a rainy day, huh? All

154

right. Well, his fiancée is some high-class piece of ass, lives in Hancock Park. Society pages type. Rich daddy, who owns the city water board or something like that. Now, Lauder wants to go up in the world, so he's got the right girl. But some things he just can't give up. Like one of the girls at Reba T.'s club. He's been with her for years. Now, the fiancée is a virgin and saving herself.'

'Who said?'

'His girl at the club, Lauder must have told her.'

'What's her name?'

Shimmer raised a brow. 'Don't be greedy. I just gave you a real juicy morsel.'

Her gossip rang true. Lauder and his desire to rise through the ranks, dressed up with his nice tailored suits and snazzy silk ties. A top job, a perfect wife, leagues above him on the society ladder. She was just a step up to the top of the promotion ladder in the LAPD. One word to the grand family about the mistress would scupper his plans, but without a name it was hardly rock-solid leverage. Getting her name would be next on my to-do list.

I said, 'Let's stay in touch. I'd like to find out how Rhonda's doing.' Shimmer could be a slow burner. Eventually she'd give up more if I really earned her trust.

'You're sweet, but no dice. This is where it ends, cookie.'

I'd pushed it too far. But I was glad she was doing her own thing, helping her lover get medical help. Their new life was their business.

Then she surprised me. 'You know what? I dig you, bird of a feather. Leave a message with Joyce, with your number. Maybe I'll call you.' She suddenly looked at her watch. 'Shoot.

155

I gotta run. She opened her purse, took out a lipstick and applied some without a mirror. She fluffed her curls and batted her eyelashes. 'How do I look?'

'Elegant.'

She grinned, ruining the look with a coy pose that didn't suit her. 'That's the big idea.'

'What's the gig?' I asked.

Shimmer looked at me. 'Why do you want to know?'

I laughed. 'Guess I don't, really.'

I had a card up my sleeve for sure, but one wasn't enough.

The booze and the smoke were working their magic, emboldening me. I could handle that creep Lauder till I got more. I would have to bluff my way out of failing my first mission, while I gathered more dirt on him.

I did what most smart people do when faced with a challenging situation. Relit the reefer and took a long drag.

31

The early evening light was deep lavender, with a vast orange button, the sun, gently bouncing towards the horizon. The colors reminded me of Dede's Dedeaux's outfit, the last one I'd seen her in. Horns from frustrated drivers mingled with the cries of news sellers. The traffic was snarled up so I was glad to walk, the hard edges of life rubbed off by overindulgence.

I had a night to kill before Lauder would be back, angry at my failure. It seemed like an eternity. I didn't want to hurry back to my mustard bedroom.

Dusk fell fast. The streetlights glowed, shopkeepers pulled down shutters and in the bars, bartenders switched on low table lamps. I still didn't know the city but I liked it. I liked it a lot. You could be insignificant and invisible here.

And maybe just one day, I could settle down here, in my own place. Or was that just a pipe dream?

I went to light a cigarette, only to realize I had left my matches at Shimmer's place.

In the distance, a short and stocky man was slowly ambling with a small fluffy dog on a lead. I caught up with them as the dog sniffed around a garbage bin. The man was looking into the night sky, lost in his dreams. I coughed. 'Got a light, sir?'

He turned. He was mid-fifties, with thick, bottle-bottom spectacles that gave him an unfair advantage. He could see out but no one could see in. He held the dog lead in one hand, a flask of something in the other. Booze had permanently bloated his features, ageing him prematurely. An expensive-looking fountain pen stuck out of his jacket pocket.

'Why, certainly, madam,' he said, rummaging for a lighter in his pocket. He found one. I lit up as he cupped the flame. I leant in, inhaling. 'Thanks.' He reeked of strong spirit. I could imagine us both igniting if the flame got too close.

'Fine evening,' he said.

'Yes, it is.' The mutt jerkily sniffed around the trash. 'What's his name?'

'Her. Veronica. My wife named her.'

'Good name for a dog.'

'Darned beast doesn't even respond to it. Not when I say it, anyways. Have to keep the damn thing on a leash. My life wouldn't be worth living if I lost it. Now if *I* got lost, my wife would throw a party.'

I grinned. It was a relief to be having an inane conversation with a stranger. He seemed harmless enough and quite eccentric.

He was tutting. 'Forgive my crass blathering. Don't get out enough, so when I do see people, the verbal runs ensue.' He smiled. 'Troy. How do you do?' He tucked the flask under the arm with the lead and held out his hand. I took it. It was warm, a little sweaty.

'Elvira.'

'You have an accent? A twang of Brit, if I'm not mistaken.'

He had a good ear. I gave the old story. 'I lived in England, in London, before the war.'

Troy went on. 'A wonderful city. I was posted there as a reporter. Back in the day, before the world decided to go loony.'

I grunted, not relishing the prospect of a late-night trip down memory lane, his or mine. Troy had an English look, thinking about it – wearing expensive tweeds, baggy and disheveled. I'd met his type before, on Fleet Street. Chatty and charming hacks, masters at getting the dirt out of you, and fast.

'To London!' He raised the flask, swigging hard. He wiped his lips with a spotty handkerchief.

We began to slowly stroll, matching the pace of the meandering Veronica. I said, 'You still write for the press?'

'Not anymore. Nowadays, just the lower but remarkably more lucrative form of screenplays. I've got a big old coot of a block, not helped by churning out garbage under contract. Hence the evening stroll. I was hoping the ambience would shift something, shake a few cobwebs. No such luck.' He raised the flask.

'Lucrative – that's got to help.'

'You'd think. The more it pays, the bigger the pressure. Just can't say no to those dirty dollars.' He told me he'd had a couple of movies made, after one of his novels was a hit. Now he was in demand. 'Make hay while the sun shines, etcetera, etcetera.' The studio was so enamored of him, they'd equipped him with a swanky office and secretary. He'd had it furnished with floor cushions, Persian rugs and a reproduction statue of Venus but spent most of his time avoiding it and taking cabs to downbeat neighborhoods like this one. He lived with his wife in Mandeville Canyon but came into the city for inspiration.

I asked about his movies. He groaned. 'Well, *A Close Call* came out last year.' I said I hadn't seen it.

'Where have you been? Jail?!' He joked. I laughed. We caught eyes for a second and I looked away.

'So, what brings you to the city of angels?'

'Change of scene.'

'Ah, a woman of mystery.'

159

'Just a little man trouble,' I glanced. If he wanted mystery, he'd get it.

He chuckled. 'A fine girl like you shouldn't be jerked around by the inferior sex.'

I liked the game so decided to take it up a notch. 'The louse won't jerk nobody around anymore. He's dead.'

'Ah. So you killed him?'

I gave a twisted smile.

'Ah, a femme fatale.' Troy chuckled.

I wondered if we were flirting. He had a certain sex appeal with his brainy cynic look. If we were, he'd be the oldest guy I'd ever flirted with. Maybe one night with an older man would be a good thing. He'd be happy never to see me again. He asked what work I was in. I told him I was between jobs but he wasn't really listening. He didn't want my reality, now that I'd inspired some kind of fantasy.

Out of the blue, he said, 'You know, you may have cured my block. May I treat you to a night on the tiles? There's a new nightclub opening on Sunset. Swanky. First I have to deliver the mutt home to my better half.'

Going to a nightclub, under Lauder's watch? Actually dressing up and dancing and doing what I had meant to be doing in L.A.? I was more than tempted. Still, I'd feel like Cinderella, needing to be home before the clock struck Lauder. Surely he wouldn't show up tonight? He'd made it plain he would wait to see if the girls got back the next day as instructed. Anything would be better than counting the roaches at the Astral. I'd just have to slip out without catching Malvin's attention.

I tried to sound relaxed about the whole thing. 'Sure, why not? Just don't write me into your next picture, okay?'

'Your secrets are safe with me.'

Troy hailed a taxi. It screeched to a halt. He offered it to me, but I said I had time to kill. He then picked up the dog and crawled in. Both their faces appeared at the window. 'Seven Palms, on Sunset. I'll be there from ten.'

The light in the front office of the Astral was on when I got back. The lonely silhouette of Malvin reclining with his feet on the desk was visible through the blinds. He didn't hear me come in, engrossed in a boxing match on the wireless.

I pinged the bell on the desk. He spun around. 'Miss Slate. Are you okay?' He went to turn the radio down.

'Malvin, about the roach situation. It's out of hand.'

'Gee. Sorry, Miss Slate. We had the pest guys in a while back.'

'I can't sleep with the lights on all night, which is the only thing that makes them hide away.'

Malvin looked apologetic. 'I could go to the store tomorrow, see if they have anything.'

I got to the point. 'Who owns the joint, anyway?'

'Mrs. Thurlow.'

'When does Mrs. Thurlow show her face?'

'If I have a problem, I call her secretary, April. She's nice.'

I made a mental note of the names Mrs. Thurlow and April. The fact that I had no rent to pay on the room either meant Lauder or Clarence was in cahoots with Mrs. T. for their own reasons, or she was doing one of them a favor.

Mrs. Thurlow. Mrs. T. How about that? Could it be Mrs. Reba T.? That would fit. For keeping quiet, Lauder could get a free room at the motel if he needed it. And she could launder her ill-gotten gains through an outfit like this. I wanted to ask

161

Malvin if Mrs. Thurlow had other businesses, but didn't. As easygoing as he was, I couldn't trust him.

Mrs. Thurlow's identity was another lost piece of the jigsaw. If I found it, a lot else could fall into place.

I shifted my features into something that could pass as a motherly smile. 'Please tell April the fumigators should come back.'

He wiped his brow. It was hot in the office, and Mrs. T. hadn't thought to give him a fan.

'Sure. I'll make sure the maid cleans your room extra good.' Malvin offered me a candy and I took one. It was banana flavored, and delicious. 'Gee, I can see why you like this stuff!'

He grinned. 'Yeah. They're real good.'

I hesitated. I had a few hours to kill. I pulled up a stool. 'Can I join you?'

Malvin thought about it then nodded. We listened to the rest of the boxing match, sucking on candy in silence.

32

In the gloomy reflection of the bathroom mirror, I troweled on foundation and red lipstick. With little time and no patience to redo my chipped nail polish, I touched it up with a darker shade. I sprayed hair lacquer on my pin curls, then slid out the grips to liberate the curls.

I wore the long black gown, the Manhattan indulgence. The fabric was silk with a full long skirt cut on the bias so it hung down in soft gathers, reminding me of an elongated black tulip turned upside down. The sleeves were puffed; their fine tulle net, also black, extended over the top of my chest. Edging the cuffs, the neckline and the darts to the waist were rows of tiny brilliants, with the occasional loop shape breaking the straight flow.

I jazzed it up with faux diamond earrings and matching bracelet.

Was it too much? No. Make hay while the sun shines. When would I get another chance to feel like a society girl?

I threw the white stole over my shoulders and donned a tilt hat in white satin with black feathers.

I slipped my feet into black satin peep-toe sandals with diamante buckles and bent down to cover the tips of the toenails in red. A lazy do-over, but the overall effect worked. I was excited. I would enjoy my own company, looking like this, tonight. Screw Lauder.

My new life was like an open prison with large sunny grounds. I just shouldn't go too near the fence.

I stood back and examined as much of myself as I could in the mirror.

Not bad, Elvira Slate. Whoever you goddamned are.

I blew myself a kiss for good luck.

The Seven Palms was a stylish and sophisticated palace, with a vast cream and gold canopy gracing the sidewalk. A string of flashy soft-top cars rolled up outside, depositing a never-ending flow of the rich, the powerful, the beautiful and the pampered onto the gold and pink carpet.

The wail of the big band pulled me in like a siren. Beyond, a vast arena, where tables topped with low red lamps edged a ballroom. On stage, a dazzling female crooner sang about mischief, wearing a cream and gold frilly off-the-shoulder dress. A chunky gold necklace set off her skin. Her full skirt cascaded to the ground in huge tiers like a wedding cake. The central panel of the skirt was cut open, revealing her swaying legs, covered in some kind of gold sparkly net stockings. Her high sandals were also gold, delicately stepping in rhythm. The male members of the big band wore gold blazers and gold bow ties.

Suspended above the dance floor, huge pink chandeliers illuminated the couples. Beyond tall arched doors at the end of the dance floor, a roof terrace overlooked the twinkling lights of the city. A fountain spewed frothy pink bubbles into a shallow pool lined with seven palms illuminated by pink lights. This joint reeked of exclusivity. Even the overfed pink flamingos waddling around the terrace probably kept a social diary.

Going home to the Astral after this would be a serious downer.

Cinderella could wait.

'Attagirl! Expected a no-show.' I turned to see Troy bouncing up with a fat grin on his face. 'Well, doesn't the lady of mystery look the part?' His breath stank, his white tuxedo was stained, and his eyes were bloodshot.

Romance was off the table. He was a soak, if an amiable one. But drunks could be unpredictable and hard work. I had enough on my plate.

Unsteady on his feet, Troy led me over to a corner of the club where a group of men lolled around. Troy explained they were all screenwriters, rolling off names like Gill, Hermann, Dare, Milton, Eugene and Drew, 'hack writers at the Mercer Studio and the other graveyards'. Some of them waved, some looked me over, surprised. Some of their expressions implied *'Troy's latest?'* It was clear he was top dog, as they all treated him with some kind of reverence. Troy joined in their banter, but I clammed up. I couldn't talk movies, clubs, stars or other gossip. The guys took no notice, liking their own jokes and banter better anyway. I turned away from them, focusing instead on the band.

Troy ordered me a drink and escorted me to a corner booth. One drink and I'd push off. I didn't belong here after all.

'You're leader of the pack,' I pulled a cigarette from a box on the table. It looked pink, but maybe it was the light.

Troy waved his hand dismissively. He fumbled for his lighter and lit my cigarette. 'Movie business. Everybody loves everybody till we're stealing each other's ideas. I jest, of course. They're my brothers-in-arms, us against the bloodsucking machine.'

The waitress soon returned with the Seven Palms bright pink cocktail. I took a sip. Heaven in a glass and dangerously divine.

165

'Hello, old boy. Why aren't you at home finishing my screenplay?'

We looked up. A pair of warm brown eyes was laughing at us. The kind of eyes that laughed through life, set in a handsome face. The dreamboat was around thirty-five, his dark brown hair flopping over his brow.

Troy gave a sarcastic smile. 'Checking in with my muse, can't you see? Now run along.'

The dish didn't move. His skin was peachy; the vital, outdoor type. In comparison, Lauder was a sickly creature of the night. I caught myself. Why was I even comparing them?

Then he turned to me, undeterred. 'Muse, huh? I sure need one of those. Lyle Vadnay.' He thrust out his hand to me, so I shook it. His grasp was warm, inviting and went on rather too long. The name rang a vague bell. Had I read about him in one of June's gossip magazines?

'Elvira Slate,' I said.

Lyle Vadnay turned to Troy, with another fake apologetic smile. 'Mercer's looking for you. Can't bite another hand that feeds you, old boy. I'll take care of Miss Slate.'

Troy was clearly snookered. He looked a little preoccupied. 'My dear, I'll leave you in the hands of this bounder for five minutes, tops. Don't fall for any of his guff.'

I smiled. 'I'm immune to guff.'

Troy shuffled off. Lyle slid into the booth, like a shark sliding into a lagoon. But I was no unsuspecting bather. I gave him a sweet smile, circling back.

'So Miss Slate, what brings you to L.A.?'

'Sunshine, cars, good times, Mr. Vadnay.'

Escaping the law.

166

'And what's your big dream, sweetheart?'

I cringed, inwardly. The tone was patronizing. Did he take me for some kind of dumb blonde?

'My dream? Right now, another house cocktail.'

He snorted with a hearty laugh. 'All right.'

His eyes landed on an observant waitress in a pink feathery outfit that seemed to be inspired by the flamingos. 'The lady would like another of these. And a Rusty Nail.' She nodded and flounced off, her tray held high above her curls in which was stuffed a swaying pink ostrich feather.

'I'm a film producer,' he announced, proudly.

'Swell,' I said. I still got a buzz out of saying swell. It was about as un-English as you could get.

Lyle told me he'd commissioned Troy to write a thriller, something slick and dangerous. Troy was proving troublesome. Drunk too often, and late in delivering. I felt bad for Troy that Lyle was so blatantly trashing his reputation. Lyle leant forward. I could smell his eau de cologne, expensive and probably French. 'It's about a *femme fatale*.' He delivered this with some gravity.

'Hate to disappoint you, but they don't exist,' I said.

Lyle laughed as if I was clueless. 'Sure they do.'

'You mean girls making hay while the sun shines? You never hear about old femmes fatales. Do they just vaporize?'

'Oh, you're one of *those*.' He looked disappointed, as if he'd been sold a dud.

I was warming up to my theme. 'Yeah, the *really* dangerous type. A woman who speaks her mind. You better watch out, sitting so close.'

Whatever was in the pink drink, I was suddenly enjoying not giving a damn.

167

Lyle crossed his legs, put his arm over his stomach, and sipped. He looked around the room. Now he was trapped with a snarky female.

'You don't have to wait until Troy gets back. Feel free to go,' I blurted.

Lyle thought about this. 'You're too pretty to be so cynical.'

'Oh, pretty girls shouldn't have opinions? That makes them *cynical*?'

'Jeez! What is your problem?'

'I don't have a problem. Maybe you do? With any female with a brain,' I sneered.

Well, this was going well.

Our drinks arrived. Lyle gave the waitress an intense smile as he tipped her. She beamed at him. Lyle puffed up a little more, his faith in cute women restored.

'Poor girl,' I said.

Lyle shot me an irritated *'what now'* look.

'She doesn't stand a chance with a guy like you. You'd label her a wannabe.'

'That's called harmless flirting. You should try it. It's fun.'

I jerked my finger at a few glamorous gazelles, hanging around, shooting Lyle admiring glances. 'And those raving beauties don't stand a chance, either.'

Lyle laughed. 'Oh, don't worry about them. They know how to play it. You all do. Like you're playing with me now. I bet your sourpuss act is just that. One big smokescreen. Hey, don't tell me. You are an actress, just playing hard to get!' Lyle took a slug of his Rusty Nail. 'Secret's safe with me, sugar. You'd make a great femme fatale. Anyone ever told you that?'

Lyle Vadnay's opinions of women were set in stone and one

sloshed girl wasn't going to change anything. Enough women probably threw themselves at him and hung on his every word. He never had to question himself. Still, I didn't need a foot in his door. It was just annoying that he was so physically desirable.

I yawned. 'Troy said something like that. He suffers from the same delusion as you.'

I looked around. No sign of Troy. A heavy fog of smoke hung low over the tables, illuminated by the pink lamps. It veiled the secret deals, trysts, intrigues and strategies. Bored, I pulled another pink cigarette out of the pink marble tray on the table. Lyle lit it for me, and our fingers touched, our faces closer.

The band took the music up a notch, the saxes and trombones wailing like tuneful alley cats. A glow descended on the place. Everywhere, the beautiful people smiled, danced and talked. On stage, the singer now purred a romantic number in harmony with a quartet of male singers, a queen bee with two crooning drones on each side. The harmonies were seductive. Her gold skirt swayed in the dark to the rhythm.

It had to be the booze, but a pink and cozy bubble where nothing had any consequence was enclosing me.

'Want a dance?' Lyle whispered.

I hadn't danced in five years. Would I remember how? Would gossip columnists observe me, this stranger with the up-and-coming producer? Surely breaking the long, dark curse of my life with Lyle Vadnay was worth the risk.

Live in the present.

Seconds later, Lyle Vadnay, Hollywood hotshot, led his femme fatale out onto the dance floor. He was confident and held me close. I relaxed. They could all stare and gossip. I wouldn't be back. I didn't care. I leant my head on his shoulder, my eyes half closing.

Something, at the far end of the club.

Ivory blonde hair.

Starlet's hair.

Lena?

An elegant female figure, in white furs and a silvery dress, breezed towards the entrance. Her arm was interlocked in a man's. Right height. Same moves.

Impossible.

Lena was rotting in a common grave in cold England, or a numbered coffin in the bowels of a ship bound for Australia.

Then she was gone.

I shook off the apparition. In a city that specialized in myriad shades of fake blonde, this head had to be just another.

'What's wrong?' Lyle asked, his dark eyes peering into mine.

I couldn't answer him.

The pink bubble burst then and there. Five years of dank and decomposing memories splattered from the ripped membrane, surging all over the club.

My prison dress. The stained mattress. The itchy blanket. Endless days. Piss turning green in the pot. The skin of potato chits planted with frozen fingers. Dirty baths that never got you clean. The vast crater that was the remains of Suffield Road.

Who the hell was I kidding, swanning around in this place, dressed to the nines and flirting with handsome film producers? It was just one big pink booze-induced sham. I was a total fraud.

And frauds get found out, don't they? They should lie low.

What the hell are you doing? There could be eyes on you. Get out, get out now!

Lyle was still in the moment, oblivious to my turmoil. He pulled me closer him. I felt trapped and suffocated. I raised my head, meeting his eyes. 'I've got to...'

Get out! Fast!

And then Lyle Vadnay did the unthinkable.

He kissed me.

33

The convertible zoomed along the Roosevelt Highway. The ocean was a vast expanse of indigo velvet, under a luminous pearl moon.

Tall silhouettes of abandoned look-out towers were the only sign that the city had just been in the grip of war.

Chatting was pointless; the wind forced us to gulp back our words. Occasionally, Lyle would grin at me. I'd grin back, hair in my face, insanely happy that if Lauder shot my brains out tomorrow at least I'd have come to L.A. and, for a brief moment, been one of those girls next to a hunk in a luxury soft-top.

The car slowed down to cruise through a couple of white pillars with a sign that said Malibu Colony.

We pulled up outside the double garage of a white gabled house, occupying a double lot. A hedge hid the enclave from the road. Explaining he'd bought his beach house for peanuts in '41 from a celebrity who feared a Jap invasion, Lyle led the way through a tall wooden gate into a garden. He'd bought a little piece of paradise in the same year I entered hell.

It was nothing short of paradise. Lush banana and palm trees, illuminated by lamps buried deep in the foliage. White wooden recliners, were dotted under trees, in bowers. If I lived here, I would never leave.

I followed Lyle around the side of the house but paused to look back, to where the garden met the beach. Curving its way around the rear of the garden, a swimming pool shone like dark emerald under the moonlight. Dark glossy boulders informally edged the pool, interspersed with some kind of tall grasses, waving in the breeze. As Lyle fiddled with his keys in the lock, I slipped away, drawn to the dark water. On my way, a fountain suddenly sprang to life. As I got closer to the pool, its light flashed on. I turned to see Lyle at the back of the house, waving.

'Champagne?' he called out.

'Sure!' I yelled back.

He was putting on quite the show.

I slipped my sandals and stockings off, sliding down to dip my toes in the water. Circles of ripples invited me. A midnight swim in Malibu. I might never get another chance. I flung off my dress and slid in.

Floating, I lay on my back, arms out, looking up into the universe above me. This was freedom.

Lyle's face appeared above me. 'So you're not such a tough cookie.'

I straightened up, splashing him. 'And you're a real slimeball.' He jumped back to safety, managing to keep the silver tray upright. He popped the bottle and filled the glasses.

Forget Cinderella, I'd been Alice in Wonderland, and he'd witnessed it. It was exposure I hadn't intended.

I got out of the water and let Lyle wrap me in a fluffy white bathing robe. My body wasn't used to being coddled and it shuddered, shocked by the sensation. It fit me perfectly. A woman's. At least it wasn't emblazoned with her initials.

We sipped, reclining on the sunbeds. Lyle felt the need to explain himself. His father was in property – oil and shipping – and thanks to the creamed-off interest of an endowment fund, Lyle had set up his production company. But he wanted to pay every penny back from the profits of his movie masterpieces and establish a foundation with the rest. 'Dollars lined my diapers. I don't want laziness or complacency, not in me, or in any project I work on. I want to work with real talent, even the ones who haven't had a shot, who aren't spoilt by a contract they've long outgrown.'

'Like Troy?'

'Exactly. He's my first real lesson of what not to do. I went for the name, and where did that get me? Twiddling my thumbs waiting for a draft that won't show up any time soon, while he's pickling his liver and resting on his laurels. Hunger creates art.'

I sniggered. 'Odds are you'll have to settle for the hunger to feel hunger.'

His face fell, deflated. 'You think I'm a hypocrite?'

'No. It's good to be hungry. Keep on the edge,' I lied. My cynicism would wreck the night ahead. He didn't need me giving him a hard time.

But somebody had to, right?

Later, I had a long hot bath in a white marble bathroom swirling with white bubbles. I curled up in immaculate crisp linen sheets in a big soft bed in a vast bedroom with doors opening out onto a balcony, the roar of the ocean providing the music.

As far as Lauder knew, I was still tossing and turning in the seedy Astral. Why did the jerk always manage to waft in to my thoughts, like a bad smell?

Lyle came in, with another bottle of champagne and two crystal flutes.

And a little later, I let the guy who always got what he wanted get what he wanted. I wanted it, too. Badly. There was something irresistible about this once-in-a-lifetime fairytale night.

Cinderella's compromise position.

For someone so self-interested, Lyle was a very tender and attentive lover. Billy and I used sex to communicate. We knew how the other climaxed, and in later years we'd become too efficient. I wasn't used to generosity in bed. 'Relax,' Lyle murmured. He has a lot to give, and he wants to, I told myself. So let him.

Afterwards, we lay back, exhausted. I smoked, blowing smoke rings that floated up to the gables. Lyle turned onto his side, looking at me. His eyes were massive and liquid in the dark. He wound his finger around a lock of my hair.

'I'm married.'

This genuinely surprised me. I glanced at him. 'I won't hold it against you.'

I'm a felon.

It was funny. He'd made the confession after sex. Any other girl might feel tricked and stomp off right now. Lucky for him, he'd picked one fat liar himself. Wait a minute! Had I missed the point of his post-coital confession? I sat up. 'Is she about to show up?'

'No. Barbara doesn't like Los Angeles. Thinks it's full of shallow, greedy fools. Prefers to hang out with her lofty intellectuals in Manhattan.' He said the last sentence with bitter derision.

'She doesn't approve of what you're doing?' I was suddenly thirsty and leant over to grab the bottle of water on my side of the bed. I knocked it back and wiped my mouth with the back of my hand. We'd screwed. Intimacy always lowers the bar on manners.

'She despises mass entertainment.'

'Oh.' There wasn't much else to say. 'What does she do?' I asked, without caring. Barbara was already boring me.

'She's on the board of her family's bank. We were childhood sweethearts. Married young. It went sour pretty quickly. We practically live separate lives.'

'Kids?' I lay back down.

'No. Thank God. I want some, though. One day. A whole bunch.'

I giggled, turning to him. 'So much for femmes fatales! You're a cheating cad, a real heartbreaker.' My joke went down like flat champagne as Lyle pulled an affronted look. 'We're both cheaters. She's got Harold, her *playwright*. She even had the nerve to ask me to read one of his damn plays. Tedious, self-indulgent bullcrap.'

I rolled away from him, on my side, my hand reaching for a packet of cigarettes. Hearing about his domestic woes was frankly boring. At least the announcement that he was married provided a handy excuse. I said, 'So, this is a one-time thing.'

'Doesn't have to be.'

'You're spoken for.'

'We don't even sleep together anymore.'

Sneaking off to Lyle's place for sex would be like having a gleaming yacht in a secret bay on tap. Somewhere to escape to, float around in for a little while and be coddled and pampered. Jemima Day wouldn't bat an eyelid. That had been the deal with Billy, after all. Elvira Slate knew it was doomed. I would just bring us both down. Lyle had it all, his star was rising and soon enough the fawners and hangers-on would be replaced by press and gossip columnists. I had to steer well clear.

Lauder would see my face in the paper and kill me. The Mob would be next in line. And bringing up the rear? The Old Bill.

The Lyle Vadnays of this world weren't designed for jailbirds like me or intellectual uppity types like his wife. Lyle needed a nice girl, somebody straightforward and wholesome. He'd probably be faithful and the brats would be plentiful.

I rolled back to face him, and ran my finger up through the hairs on his chest. 'You know what? Let's forget all about your wife.'

I ran my finger down again. All the way.

The second bout of sex was less polite now his confession was out of the way. We both let ourselves go.

Later, Lyle clutched me to him as he drifted off. I felt hot and stifled by his embrace and wriggled out of it, whispering something about needing the bathroom. His arm was heavy and floppy as I slid out of bed, his face calm and angelic. I kissed his forehead, like a mother would kiss a child.

An abandoning mother.

The next room along the passage appeared to be his office. Tidy, dominated by a huge desk overlooking the sea. There was a neat stack of correspondence on the desk. I flicked through it. Boring things like bills and contracts. One between Troy and Vadnay Pictures, dated from July.

There was a small framed photograph in faded sepia. I held it up to the moonlight. It showed an old castle with turrets, romantic and mysterious. Looked like central Europe, maybe Hungary. The ancient Vadnay homestead?

If so, he really was Prince Charming.

Prince Charming – with a touch of the slimeball.

I left around four in the morning and walked along the beach, sandals in my hand. Here and there, glowing embers. Soldiers lay around the fires, sometimes with a girl in their arms, sometimes alone. Demobilization washed up more guys every day, the beaches providing a strange haven to the uniformed driftwood. How many didn't have homes to go back to? How many had wives who had moved on? Maybe the GIs dreaded their old civilian life, or were just too shell-shocked to put one foot in front of another.

Maybe the lapping tide was the only comfort that made sense.

34

It was one o'clock, and no Lauder.

I sat at the table, puffing away. I varnished my nails with a lacquer, *Crimson Delight*. What the hell was a crimson delight anyway? A beautiful sunset? An oozing jelly dessert? I mentally came up with some more fitting names, to pass the time.

Blood Wedding.

Fevered Lust.

I still had sex on the brain.

Three o'clock came and went.

So did five cigarettes. Four o'clock passed, still no sight of him.

I lay back down on the bed, stiffly, careful not to crumple my dress, made of a simple gray lawn, with a white collar and cuffs. My curls were fresh and bouncy, too.

The better I looked, the easier I could play Lauder. At least, that was the hope. So far he had proved pretty immune to any attempt to charm him.

Four-thirty.

Maybe the whole thing had been a test, something he dreamt up just to keep me busy. Shimmer was just an informer, who could report back.

No. She had been straight with me. I'd bet on it.

I peered through the window.

Two cars in the lot, Malvin's and one other. Heat waves danced off the hot tarmac.

I was starving. Malvin could just tell Lauder I was at Tina's having a coffee and a sandwich. I pinned on my hat, stuffed a few coins in my pocket and walked out.

As I locked the door, I heard an engine. Typical.

Lauder's car cruising into the dusty lot, like a snake in the desert coming out to hunt. No point retreating inside as he most likely had seen me.

Lauder turned off the engine and slid out of the car. He looked hot, wiping his forehead with a cream handkerchief.

'Hi.' I kept my voice steady.

Lauder came up close, his eyes shadowed by his hat rim. He scowled, 'Where the hell do you think you're going?'

'Grabbing a bite. I'm starving. Thought you'd be here much earlier.'

He barked. 'Great fucking job. I should've known better than to send you.' Pure hatred laced his eyes.

'Don't be sore! They're coming back. Shimmer said she knows it was a mistake. But she wanted me to tell you something. Let's go to the café, I can fill you in.'

Lauder's expression was irritable, confused and incredulous. 'What?'

I fed him the line we'd concocted. 'She says they're out of town, for a family matter. A funeral or something? They'll be back at the weekend.'

His face darkened. 'You're coming with me.' He grabbed my arm, propelling me towards the car.

'Give them a break! It's a funeral.'

Lauder guffawed, all sarcasm. 'Funeral? Knock it off. Shimmer's going to a funeral all right. Her own.'

'I did what you wanted.' I muttered. Lauder heard this but ignored me.

We reached the car. He flung the passenger door open and shoved me inside. Alberta's hat was on the passenger seat. I guess he was giving it back.

'Can we go eat? I did it. Shimmer agreed.'

He turned, facing me down. 'Shimmer agreed fuck all. She's dead.'

35

The Flamayon Hotel was a grand hotel built towards the end of the last century, long past its former glory and now something of a dump. The striped awnings on the ground floor windows were stained and tatty, battered by the Santa Ana winds year on year. The original clientele of prospectors now had to be tucked up in retirement homes or the cemetery.

A mob of ravenous reporters surged behind a yellow police cordon. Behind them, the real vultures, the clamoring public, drawn to the morbid events within. Irate cops pushed back. Police cars and a forensics van lined up along the street like zipper teeth.

This had to be the scene of Shimmer's last moments. Lauder hadn't spoken to me the whole journey and had refused to answer any of my questions. 'Shut the fuck up,' he'd just barked, when I'd pressed. Now we seemed to have arrived it was worth a shot.

'Is this where she died?' My voice came out flat. 'What happened to her?'

He finally turned to me, a look of disgust on his face. 'She mention this place?'

'No. She didn't tell me anything.'

'Liar. Told you about the funeral, right?'

I nodded. 'When did she die? How?'

'Crime scene coroner reckoned she's dead almost twenty hours.'

'*Crime scene*? What happened?'

He didn't answer.

Had Reba T. found her?

Beyond Lauder's profile, I noticed a couple of detectives left the building only to be mobbed by reporters. Cops came to their assistance and got the better of the mob. Beyond the commotion, scattered bungalows were just visible in the grounds of the Flamayon. Past their prime, tatty little cubicles only fit for the desperate and the broke.

The car suddenly lurched forwards, jolting me. Lauder had noticed the detectives and put his foot on the gas, picking up speed. He didn't want to risk being seen with me. At the end of the street he turned left onto a main drag. After a while he said, 'It was an overdose.'

'What?' I couldn't square this with the woman I'd met. Shimmer was a tough bird with her head screwed on, off to her meeting to make some money. Crazy. Even now I could see Shimmer's eyes sparkling at the thought of getting out of L.A. So much for her fresh start with the love of her life. 'Alone?'

'Why?'

'I mean, was she with Rhonda?'

He was slowing for a red light. 'No. Rhonda's taken off.' He spoke flatly, without emotion.

'What?'

'You heard. See her when you went there?'

'Yes. Briefly.'

'She say anything?'

Trick question. He might be looking for her, for Reba T. I gulped, looking down. 'No. I just talked to Shimmer.'

Think fast. Keep all the dirt you've got on him. It's your little secret.

Lauder grimaced but he said nothing. It was better for me to go along with things and act as if I'd been duped. 'Shimmer didn't look the type to use.'

'Yeah? You an expert on addicts or something?' He glanced at me. 'Guess you could be one yourself.'

'I'm not.'

Lauder ignored this. He pulled onto Sunset Boulevard and joined the flow of traffic heading east towards Downtown.

What did I know? Shimmer couldn't refuse an old bad habit? She was selling heroin at her mystery meeting? Did she taste too much of her own wares?

A suspicious mind wouldn't help now. It certainly wouldn't lead to Rhonda. She was now out in the big wide world. I hoped she was with company who could take care of her.

Good luck, girl.

'I need a drink,' I blurted out, without thinking. Lauder looked at me. Then he said something I didn't see coming. 'All right.'

The tavern was quiet, virtually empty, a Downtown watering hole. A long bar with around twelve chrome stools with tatty leather seats lined one half of the room. Years of grime had solidified in pockets on the cracked floor tiles.

I sat in a booth at the back while Lauder ordered drinks. The fact he'd acted on my wish and brought me here was slightly unnerving. I had ordered a scotch with ice. He didn't flinch or give me a lecture. Maybe he'd bring back a double.

I needed it. Shimmer was dead. Had I somehow played a part?

A painfully thin woman, somewhere in her mid-forties, sat alone at the bar. Her dress had seen better days. It was faded dusty pink, with yellow stains, and too big for her. A round faded lace collar told me the dress had to be a decade or more old. She was checking out Lauder as he paid for the drinks. As he walked past her, she mumbled to herself, waving a long cigarette holder as if to make a point. Lauder gave her a nod. Thoughtful of him, but she missed it, knocking back her drink.

A trio of young GIs fooled around at the end of the bar, sniggering at the tragic wreck. Easy prey. I felt sorry for her. I had a soft spot for female drunks. One theory I had about Violet was that, once rid of me, she'd hopped on a boat back to the US. Now she could search for her Monty unfettered by me, a kid. But the trail ran cold and the bottle gave the warm comfort she needed.

So I always did a double take at female bums and soaks in case of any family resemblance.

What I really liked was that female drunks really didn't give a damn. With each hiccup, they stuck two fingers up at all society's notions of being ladylike.

A harmony group crooned out of the jukebox, the volume low. They sang about love like candy that they couldn't get enough of.

A couple smooched in the first corner booth. The guy was about fifty, well preserved, sliding his hands up and under his younger lover's jacket. All the hallmarks of an office romance. Maybe Lauder and I looked like one, too. One that had long gone sour, with nothing left to say, fueled by habit rather than affection.

Lauder sat down opposite, sliding over my drink and a packet of nuts. 'Thanks,' I said, avoiding his eye. He grunted some kind of acknowledgement.

As awkward for him as it was for me.

He'd got himself a glass of beer. Without saying anything, he offered me a smoke. I took it. This was a first.

I leant into the flame of his lighter, inhaling. I didn't like admiring his thick lashes so I pulled away abruptly, inhaling too fast. My coughing fit, which left me puffing out spurts of smoke like a novice dragon, was timely. Lauder seemed too preoccupied to notice or smirk.

He spoke quietly. 'Tell me exactly what happened. From the moment you got there.'

'I've got nothing to do with it!'

'Talk.'

I took a deep breath. 'Shimmer answered the door. She wouldn't let me in. I gave her the message as well as I could through a one-inch gap. She said she understood. As I was leaving, she called me back. She had a message, she said. So I went back, with no intention of staying long.'

'Your first fuck-up.' Lauder exhaled over the table, virtually into my face. I wafted the smoke away.

'I figured I should hear her out. But she tricked me, played me. Talked about me being sent by "Kaye", and I fell for it. Hook line and sinker. I wasn't exactly prepared for chat, remember? Then she pulled a gun on me!'

'What?'

'A pistol. Looked like I wasn't getting out alive unless I talked. So I did.' I took a ladylike sip.

'What did *you* say?' He controlled his voice. The same muscle woke up in his cheek. If not for the fact that there were witnesses, I would be on course for another clip round the ear.

'I said that a cop sent me because I was running errands for him. I invented a name. Lee. She bought it.' Was *he* buying it? I met his eyes. They were opaque, giving nothing away. We were both hardened poker players but I fancied my chances today.

'Go on.'

'She said they just had this funeral to go to.'

'Whose? Where?'

I shrugged. 'Maybe family? I don't really remember. I was focusing on getting out in one piece.'

'What else did she say?'

'Nothing at all,' I lied. 'She sure didn't trust me. Just gave me the message.'

Relax. Your sordid affair is safe with me. For now.

'She say anything about anyone else?'

'No.'

'Then what?'

I shook my head. 'She let me go. Whole thing lasted a couple of minutes, tops, give or take thirty seconds of her beating on me.'

'Where is this funeral supposed to take place?'

'No idea. Maybe that's where Rhonda's gone? You know if she had family?' I asked, to pad it out a little.

'See anything else that strikes you now? In hindsight?'

Yes, there is, as a matter of fact. Rhonda is sick as hell and you don't care.

Sticking to the lies I concocted with Shimmer felt good. Honor among fallen women.

Lauder leant back, taking another glug of beer, staring into space. His face was back to normal; no emotions visible under that finely chiseled veneer. Was he cut up? Something was up

187

but I had no idea. But I'd spent my whole life concealing my feelings and I knew when somebody else was doing the same.

A GI was feeding the jukebox. On his way back to his pals at the bar, the soak used her arm as a barricade. 'Soldier boy,' she bawled. 'Buy a lady a drink.'

He halted, saluting her, the uniform lending him more gallantry than he deserved and she beamed with pleasure. Maybe he'd wear it when he fucked her a few hours later. I tried to switch off my dark thoughts but the other GIs cracked up laughing as their buddy opened his wallet. Maybe they'd all take their turn with her.

Lauder gazed at me, watching the drunk. 'The trouble is we both know you're a very good liar.'

'What? I'm not lying! What have I got to lie about?'

'Maybe Shimmer paid you to bullshit me.'

'That's crazy! She nearly killed me. I know my place with you. You think I'm going to blow it, with all the stuff you've got on me? I'm doing exactly what you want. And even if she had, it didn't get her very far, did it?'

He stared at me. Unreadable as ever.

The possibility that Lauder could have set the whole thing up with Shimmer, a test of my obedience before he really put me to work, still had some currency in my calculations. If she was in cahoots with Lauder, she could have warned him in advance that she'd given me fake leverage. Maybe *she* was his little piece on the side. No. I couldn't see Shimmer being his type, but nothing would surprise me anymore.

With her death, this theory was fading fast. Even if the visit had been an elaborate test of my obedience, Shimmer had died before she reported back to him.

An ugly thought crossed my mind. Shimmer's death meant she could never let slip – even accidentally – that she'd given me dirt on him.

I knew about Lauder's mistress. I just had to find out her name.

'Anything else I should know? She say anything about going any place after?'

'That's it.' I glanced at him, trying to read his mask of a face. 'Why, it is suspicious?'

'Nope, straightforward OD. Along with the other two. Frank Acker and Darlene Heymann. Movie types. OD-ed as well.'

I stared at him. 'She was with a *couple*?'

'A man and a woman.'

What? So, possibly not a couple? He wasn't going to reveal much to me.

Shimmer had said a business meeting. Rhonda had mentioned a guy. The grass had hit me by that point and my memory was hazy. I could have got it wrong. She was dead and Rhonda was gone. What could I do about anything now?

It was pointless asking but I did anyway. 'Who are they?'

Lauder looked at me and thought about it, weighing up how much I should know. 'Darlene Heymann is Otto Heymann's daughter.' Clearly I should know who he was. My face must have blanked.

'Heymann Brothers?' Lauder said. 'The Heymann Brothers Studio? Darlene is – was – the middle one of three. In her forties. Used to be a wild child. Typical rich kid problems. Maybe she had a mid-life relapse and went back to her fun-loving ways. Frankie Acker is an actor, twenties, signed to the studio.'

'They were dating?'

'Unlikely.'

'But they knew Shimmer?'

'You tell me. Not exactly from the same side of the street. Somehow they hooked up. Shot themselves up, that's it.'

'Was it...sexual?'

'No.'

He talked as if he trusted me. It was unnerving. I knew he could turn nasty as quickly as a toupee spins in a hurricane.

I focused back on the soak, proving herself to be the main attraction. She had perked up a bit, swaying on her stool, clutching her newly acquired man's muscular arm for dear life.

If there had been a sexual element to the deaths, he wasn't telling me. Maybe the Hollywood machine would kill that story. But I saw Shimmer entwined with a couple, vomit drying across their faces, eyes lifeless like worn-out marbles. But she was as dyke as they come. And in love. Really in love.

The whole time I'd been with Lyle, she lay dead.

Was it my fault, somehow? Failing the first Lauder mission?

In my keenness to get leverage, had I failed her somehow? No. She had laughed in my face at Lauder's threat. Anyhow, he had given her two days to get back, and she was dead within that time. She was intent on her meeting, a little smashed. She had been sober when I arrived, though. She partook with me and I'd encouraged it. Rhonda had wanted her clearheaded, hadn't she?

I suddenly felt sick, my mouth dry.

No. Don't blame yourself.

Lauder loosened his tie.

I stubbed my cigarette out in a tin ashtray advertising root beer. 'Poor Shimmer,' I said, without thinking.

Lauder looked at me. 'What?'

'Just sad, isn't it?'

Lauder shot me another hard look. 'Shimmer messed up. She should have paid up when asked. You did what you were told to do, *if* you are telling the truth.' He looked at his watch and reached into his pocket. He pulled out a small purple card, tossing it on the table in front of me.

I picked it up and read it in the gloomy light. *Nightshade Club* was written in a curling, embossed silver font. 'Malvin's got a load of *Chronicles* for you to check out. See if you can find a link between anything in the personal columns and that card.'

I didn't quite get it. 'What's the *Nightshade Club*?'

'I don't want to see your ugly mug for a while, so this is homework. Don't get any funny ideas about going walkabout.'

Then he got up and headed for the door. So much for goodbye.

I slumped down in my seat. I remembered I had no idea where I was. 'Wait, you're just leaving me here?'

Lauder turned, at the door. 'Work it out,' he snapped, in earshot of the whole bar.

My face must have fallen. A romance gone very sour.

The soak giggled loudly. 'Some gentleman you got yourself. Not like my guy.'

36

I was in the garden at Holloway. Digging for something I dreaded to unearth. The screws hovered around me, forcing me on. The spade struck something hard. A skull, encrusted with mud and stones. Billy was there, pleading with me to leave, but I screamed at him that I couldn't. They wouldn't let me go! I had to dig. Billy suddenly became Lena, immaculately dressed, her hair in a turban with a large ruby brooch. Mud from the spade splattered her shoes. She held up a couture gown for me; a silvery satin number, with sequins over the shoulders and waist. She taunted me – time was running out to change into it for the dance. Impossibility paralyzed me, but I had to finish my work first. Why wouldn't she understand that? Lena was knocking back the champagne now, warning me a storm was brewing. Suffocating, dark clouds filled the sky. And then she was gone. I was quite alone in the grounds of the prison. Fear gripped me and I wandered aimlessly around, calling out. And then the wave came; huge, solid, curving, bigger than St Paul's Cathedral, rising up like a gigantic wall, coiled like a cobra before its fatal strike. I couldn't run. It was crashing down on me and I was stuck on the spot, unable to move.

I lurched up, covered in cold sweat. A recurring dream, every bit as dreadful as the time before.

I jumped up and showered. Lauder's homework could wait. I wanted to know what the papers reported about Shimmer and the couple.

Shimmer, dead. It still didn't seem real.

Out in the street, the headlines screamed '*Hollywood Socialite and Young Actor's Tragic Death*' and '*Heymann's Daughter's final troubles*'. I bought the *Los Angeles Chronicle* and a couple of Hollywood gossip magazines from the newsstand and headed to Tina's for my morning coffee.

I settled down in my usual chair on the sidewalk, to read up on the life and times of Darlene Heymann and Frankie Acker.

There was a photographic portrait of Darlene's family, from the 1920s. Otto Heymann and other suited men flanked the lavishly jeweled Heymann women in some enormous drawing room. Young kids trussed up in formal clothes stood at the front. The men were large, balding and with moustaches. Darlene was about twenty, her eyes focused somewhere just beyond the lens, giving her a dreamy look behind a thin smile. She was just going through the motions. Next to Darlene, her skinny mother Nancy Heymann was an elegant creature, who knew exactly how to pose in her straight flapper dress. Standing next to her elegant and petite mother, Darlene was a giantess in the making.

That must be tough. Hollywood didn't exactly love Amazons.

I flicked through the papers. There were no photographs of her beyond twenty years old. Strange, as she was now considerably older, just the odd reference to her living in *an artistic community*. A few gossip columnists assumed Darlene and Frank were even dating, using the words 'her young male confidant,' the article loaded with innuendo. Frank had had minor roles in a few Westerns before the war, signed to the Heymann Studio. He came from Wyoming where his parents had a ranch. He was one of three brothers. One had died in the war, a hero. Frank had served but was discharged due to losing the hearing in one ear in an explosion.

The message was the same in all the papers. Darlene and Frank, odd buddies, were just victims of a low-lifer who supplied the evil narcotics. The families requested privacy and gave no comment. It had been a bad year for the Heymann Studio. A series of flops and now this, a nightmare.

Shimmer was pronounced as being an Ellen Cranston. Just a nobody from Compton, a desperado who preyed on a rich couple. The drugs were found in her bag.

No family crisis for the likes of the Cranstons, no posh portraits.

No mention of the true family she'd made, with Rhonda.

I folded the papers and pushed them away. I sipped my coffee.

Maybe she had been a pusher. I had no idea.

One thing I did know – girls like me and Shimmer dragged our pasts around as if they were trickster cartoon shadows mocking us behind our backs. The city she had been so intent on leaving now ensnared her forever, because she'd been born on the bottom rung and needed to fund an operation.

I lit a cigarette and pondered. Would Rhonda claim Shimmer's body? Or would Shimmer just end up cremated, her ashes flushed down the toilet of some facility? Lauder would know, but I wouldn't ask. I shivered; he could end up doing the same for my unclaimed remains one day.

I couldn't get Rhonda out of my mind. Who would take care of her with her fragile health? Unease niggled at me but I was powerless. I had to forget it.

Maybe Lauder's stupid homework would be the distraction I needed. I took out the card again and examined it. *The Nightshade Club*. Probably some den of nastiness he had stuck his claws into. Lauder would get a kick out of me sitting on the bug-infested carpet of the Astral, wading through columns pointlessly for hours on end.

Boring.

Damn him.

I'd do it my way.

I went to the phone booth and asked the operator to put me through to the *Los Angeles Chronicle*. When I was connected, I asked for the office where I could place a wedding announcement. A young man's voice came on the line. A pleasant, slightly bored voice. 'Barney Einhorn speaking. How may I be of assistance?'

I asked, 'Dumb question, but how do I place an announcement? Do I have to come in person?'

'You can dictate it to me now or you can come in. Payment upfront. Dictate it, it won't go in the paper till you've paid up. Post your check, or come in and settle in cash. We're very accommodating in how we take your money.' His ironic tone was amusing. I felt a smile on my lips for the first time in weeks.

'Want to go ahead? Let me guess. You're getting married?'

'Nope. Not the marrying type.' I quipped. 'Nor the maternal, for that matter.'

He stifled a snigger. 'So no weddings, no babies. That leaves sad news?' His voice took on a mock-tragic tone.

'Where do I start? But no, nobody's dead.' I bit my lip, thinking about Shimmer. 'It's a rather delicate matter.'

'But you want to place an announcement and tell the world? Now I'm confused.'

I laughed. 'It's mysterious. Maybe I should just come down and explain?'

'Do! You'll brighten the most boring day imaginable.'

He told me to come to the Chronicle's offices on Broadway, and ask for him. Barney Einhorn in Classifieds on the ground floor.

'Thank you, Barney Einhorn in Classifieds.'

'I look forward to seeing you, Miss…?'

'Slate. Elvira Slate.'

37

'I'm not sure I understand.' Barney Einhorn looked baffled. He had a bookish look and an incongruously lively face. His suit was old, darned on the lapel. I instinctively trusted him. His dark eyes reminded me of the homeless Jewish boys in London I ran around with aged eight after I'd fled the orphanage. They'd fed me warm bagels they'd stolen. Barney looked like how I imagined they'd be, grown up.

It was a quiet day for the Classifieds department. Behind the wide counter, Barney was one of the few servers. Behind him, staff gossiped lazily at their desks. It looked friendly. Maybe I could get a job here one day.

I said, 'Truth is, neither do I. It's a favor for someone. I need to find a link between something in some back issues, and something else.' I slid a five dollar note across the counter. 'And I'd appreciate your discretion.'

He eyed the note. 'What's that?'

'What does it look like?'

'It's a rhetorical question. You don't have to pay me. You're not placing an ad. This is fun.'

I'd stung his pride. I slipped the note back in my purse. 'All right,' I smiled. 'Here's fun.' I bent down and picked up Lauder's papers, dumping them on the counter.

'That's a century's worth in the world of personal columns,' Barney said. 'That won't be quick. I can only do it when things are dead around here. Lucky for you, it's pretty slow this time of year. Thanksgiving is around the corner, hardly any betrothals or weddings. The California winter doesn't kill off so many old people in L.A., so we're slow on funerals, too. It's mainly births, which goes to show that there's something to Valentines after all.'

I took the purple card out of my pocket and slid it over the counter. 'This is the connection. I have to find something, anything relating to this. I have no idea what to look for.' I knew full well this could all be one big Lauder joke on me.

Barney picked it up and examined the card. His brown eyes looked into mine. 'Are you some kind of *sleuth*?'

'What? No!'

He smirked, his hand flying up, as if he wouldn't press any further but knew he'd got it right. 'All right. Nightshade Club. One of them!'

My heart skipped a beat. 'You *know* it?'

'No. Not this one in particular. Wouldn't be the first time the classifieds spread the word about a secret meeting place. Crackpots, spies – heck, I can't tell the difference.'

'So you'll do it?'

'I love this stuff. This kind of thing went on a lot in the war. The occasional christening at a church that didn't exist. Then I'd figure out the date would be the same birthday as some fanatic. Like Hitler or Mussolini.'

'Queer.'

'Very.'

I widened my eyes. 'Did you ever figure out what was going on?'

'A couple of times I had a hunch. I even called the cops once.'

'Some job you've got. But don't call the cops, please. This isn't sinister, I'm sure of it.' I averted my gaze from those big brown eyes.

198

'Your wish is my command.' Barney concealed a highly ironic look. 'But it's a job. Not a great job.'

'Why do it, then?'

'Pays the bills. I don't have a lot of options and it beats selling insurance.'

I noticed a walking stick, propped against the edge of the counter. 'Oh, sorry.'

'Souvenir from France, courtesy of Uncle Sam. At least I got to come home. And now, I get to meet people like you. Female P.I.s!' He winked.

'I'm not a P.I.,' I mumbled.

He slammed the palms of his hands on the counter. 'If you say so. Leave it with me.'

As I went down in the elevator, I had a fat smile on my face. Barney Einhorn had lifted my mood.

I walked away from the office and a few blocks along, found a movie theater, practically empty during the daytime. A slushy romance was playing. I bought a ticket and sat in the empty auditorium. As the miraculous couple exchanged passionate glances on screen, I remembered Rhonda's face, lighting up when Shimmer kissed her. As short and fragile as my allegiance had been to Shimmer and Rhonda, I still felt uneasy.

Bright girls, bad starts.

I left the movie before it ended, too restless to concentrate on the flimsy plot.

I considered calling Troy for a drunken diversion but he might be offended I'd gone off with Lyle and I didn't want to be grilled or to have to endure any witty innuendo. Besides, a night out with the cynical screenwriters wouldn't help. If anything, their shallow minds would annoy me. They knew nothing, just peddled fantasies and lies about non-existent women. In real life, nobody looked out for girls like us and nobody would.

We had to do it for ourselves.

With Shimmer dead, did Reba T. find Rhonda? Had Lauder told her where to find her? Lauder was just as good a liar as me. And he was a coldhearted bastard.

Damn it, Rhonda!

Back in my room at the Astral, I sat cross-legged on the mustard floor, cupping the dice.

Odds, I'd forget all about Rhonda, just wish her well and get back to my empty life of following Lauder's orders.

Evens, I would do something. I had no idea what. Maybe I could get a taxi back to the house in Fauness Avenue and check if she'd come back. Maybe I'd find something so I could quit worrying about her. Maybe something else would be there, a sign. Like a fresh pint of milk, or Rhonda in bed with another woman. Then I could just walk away.

I rolled the dice.

Double six.

Evens.

Something like relief washed over me.

It was what I wanted to do.

38

The wind was picking up. Oranges rolled over the sidewalk as if lined up by a drunken pool player, and the air was full of their sweet aroma, as if the Santa Ana was a giant perfume atomizer scenting the pool room.

I stood outside the house, now plunged into darkness.

No lights. Nobody home. I should just leave.

No. Get in, poke around, get out. Peace of mind, remember?

I crept quietly up the front steps of the house. I was wearing dark gray flannel pants with side pockets, and a black sweater, topped off with a gray and maroon patterned silk necktie. I flung a gray jacket over my shoulders and had tilted my gray felt hat over my face, my hair in a hair net. The aim was to blend into the shadows while I worked.

Earlier in life, I'd done my fair share of smash-and-grab jobs but I hadn't picked a lock for years. A quick brick through the window would attract the attention of ol' Nosey Parker next door.

I pulled out a hatpin, kneeled down and got to work. I kept my gloves on the whole time, which slowed me down. If I got in, and then had to make a quick getaway, I wouldn't have time to wipe anything down.

Footsteps! I froze. Out in the street, somewhere behind the shrubbery, someone was whistling a romantic tune. I listened for a while. A woman's voice, calling to her dogs.

Just a nocturnal stroller.

I got back to the task, and in a few seconds, the lock clicked open.

201

I pushed the door open, flicking the light of my small torch around the front room. I ventured in, softly closing the door behind me.

The smell of beeswax hit my nose. Someone had been cleaning.

Through the front door's glass panel, the streetlights provided enough light so I put the torch back in my pocket. There was no mail on the doormat. Instead, it had been stacked up on a side table. Interesting. I checked the date on one item. This morning.

Wait – the three suitcases. Now there were only two. A good sign, surely? So when had Rhonda left?

I moved out of the front parlor along the corridor, making my way into the dining room where we'd smoked the weed. I got the torch back out.

Spick-and-span in here too. No sign of smoking, drinking coffee and cookies. Rhonda could have cleared up after Shimmer left.

No chess game.

The general tidiness and the missing suitcase pointed to Rhonda leaving of her own accord, as Lauder claimed. He didn't tell me how he knew she'd gone, I suddenly realized.

There were three other doors. I'd try each room, just to be sure. Sure of what? There had to be a bathroom as well as the bedrooms. I peered inside the first room along the corridor. It was another parlor. Sofa and armchairs covered in sheets, ghostly in the low light. The curtains were drawn.

On the wall, the torchlight hit a chalk bust of a Madonna and child on the mantelpiece. Her face made me jump. I cursed, and retreated.

The next room was smaller. Heavy lace curtains covered the small back window. There was a single bed with a tall metal bedstead, hospital style, which was also covered in sheets. An invalid's bed. Rhonda's granny's last bed, before she snuffed it?

I stepped on something soft. A rag doll lay on the floor, her face to the ground. Shimmer had been right. The place was creepy. I bent down to pick the doll up.

'Stop right there.'

I froze, halfway up.

The voice of an old woman. Frail and nervous. 'Turn around, hands up. Show me your thieving face.'

I did as she asked. Nice and slow.

A little bird of a woman stood in the doorway. She wore a floral housecoat, and had her rollers in under a scarf tied at the top of her head. Her hair was white. She was skinny as a rake, and her hands shook under the supreme effort of training a rifle on me.

I recognized the face.

Nosey Parker, from next door.

'It's not what it looks like, ma'am. I'm Rhonda's friend, Gina. Just checkin' in on her, or hoping to.'

'What kind of pal breaks in? I saw you pickin' that lock.' She eyed me suspiciously, steadying the gun. 'I'm gonna call the cops!'

'Wait a minute! I just thought Rhonda might be sick or something. Didn't want to get her up. Opening the door like that was just an old trick my daddy taught me in case I locked myself out. Hatpin, see?' I showed the bent pin to her, grinning moronically.

She grunted. 'Saw you here other day. On the doorstep.

Didn't look like pals then. How come you're back? You robbin' the place?'

'No! Me and Shimmer don't always see eye to eye. I mean... *didn't*. May she rest in peace.' I made the sign of the cross on my chest.

The old woman shook her head. 'Didn't surprise me one bit when that cop said she came to a bad end. Knew she was trouble, the minute she rolled up with Rhondie.'

That cop. It had to be Lauder. And the way she said 'Rhondie' was full of affection.

'A cop came?' I said.

'Two of 'em. One after the other. What's it to you?'

So Lauder and a partner had come here before seeing me. That's how he knew Rhonda had gone.

'When did the cops come? The next day?'

Thelma nodded. 'Yeah. In the morning. That's when I got the news.'

'Can I lower my hands now, nice and slow?' I pleaded.

The old bird thought about it, then nodded. The rifle stayed high, wobbling rather alarmingly. I grinned, nervously. 'How about you meet me halfway and put the gun down? Sure looks heavy. I promise you I'm no thief, just a pal. A concerned pal. Do you know where Rhonda is? If she's okay?'

We stood there in the gloom as she weighed it up. Loneliness seemed to win over distrust as she finally lowered her weapon. 'No, I don't. Truth of the matter is I was hoping you was her.'

'Did you see her leave?'

'Sure I did. It was darned late, too. Went off in somebody's car. Don't know who, never saw their face. Same night you came over.' The old lady looked around, a little bewildered. 'Rhondie's granny Gladys was my best pal. This is her house. Left it to Rhondie when she died. Promised Gladys I'd take care of things, keep the house for Rhondie.'

'Ain't that a nice thing to do?' I tried to sound soothing.

'Well, we'd been neighbors for forty years and counting. Took her into hospital myself last winter. I knew she wouldn't be coming home again. Gladys had a son, Rhonda's pop. Hailed from Wales, original. Mining family. Took it upon himself to go down to Tijuana, married a Mexican. She came back here with him.'

I wondered if the whole stick-up was just a ploy to get some company. You didn't see many old women on the streets of L.A. Walking sticks, wheelchairs, wrinkles and gray hair wouldn't get you far in this town.

'What's your name?' I asked.

'Thelma. You?' She'd forgotten.

'Gina.'

Thelma sat down, nodding, using the butt of the gun as an armrest. I hoped the safety catch was on. She went on. 'House stood empty for a couple of years, then that Shimmer shows up, acting like she owns the place. "Who the hell are you?" I ask her. Tells me Rhondie's sick and the place is gonna be sold. To that real estate mob, the ones sucking the life out of this neighborhood. Broke my heart when I saw the poor child, suffering like that.' She crossed her chest.

I cut her off. 'But Rhondie left, taking a case, getting in a car. That sounds like she knew what she was doing.'

'How do I know? She left. I'd been bakin' that day. Another batch of peanut cookies. Don't eat 'em myself but kids round here like 'em, sure enough. I pay 'em in cookies to pick up my oranges. Where was I?' She had already forgotten her train of thought. 'Oh, yes. Thought I'd give Rhondie a few cookies. Her favorites.'

'About what time did you go around?'

'No 'about' about it. Nine o clock, on the dot. Rhondie took 'em but she wasn't hungry. I stayed for a while. We chatted about this and that. She never even said goodbye. I just been praying she'll walk back in.'

I wanted to leave. I could feel reassured. Thelma was just feeling rejected Rhonda hadn't looked in.

Time for bed, Elvira. Get the hell out and forget all about it.

Thelma suddenly burst into tears. 'Oh, Gladys,' she sobbed. 'I let you down.' She suddenly dropped the gun, and it clattered on the floorboards. She crumpled on the bed.

I hovered, uselessly. 'Hey, hey. You did your best. Sounds like Rhonda knew what she was doing, that she went of her own accord. She'll be fine.'

But surely, Rhonda had left before she knew Shimmer was dead. Shimmer hadn't returned, so Rhonda could have got worried and stuck to the plan to leave, or called a friend who'd picked her up. Lauder had indicated the bodies had been found in the morning. Rhonda would have found out like everyone else, in the news. She would have been devastated. I had no doubt about their love for one another.

The old dear looked up, her eyes watering. 'Suppose so.'

'You did your best for her.'

Sniffing, she said, 'Can I fix you something to eat?'

I reluctantly said a coffee would be good. Thelma picked up the gun and went to the kitchen. She filled the kettle and shuffled around, talking to herself.

I tucked the rag doll into bed. 'Sleep tight,' I said, for no reason at all.

As I left the room, I inwardly repeated the obvious facts. Rhonda must have gone willingly. Shimmer didn't come back on time. So Rhonda called a friend, she wasn't going to be a sitting duck.

But. There's always a but. And one was niggling now.

Reba T. could have collected Rhonda at Lauder's behest.

Maybe someone else had helped her run.

Maybe not your problem.

I half-heartedly opened the chest of drawers, gloves still on. Perfume, cheap cosmetics, a few dimes, costume jewelry. It looked like the kind of stuff Shimmer would wear. So they hadn't packed up any of this stuff for their departure. I wouldn't bother examining the suitcases. They were probably full of things for their new life.

I returned to the kitchen. Thelma poured the coffee into two china cups. I removed my gloves, and lit a cigarette. We chatted about the neighborhood, how the city had changed since she grew up here, that it never stopped changing. 'They' wanted to knock down this road for apartment blocks, and were buying everyone out. 'They' had bought out Rhonda – on the cheap, as far as Thelma was concerned. Then she told me to sit down as she served me coffee and cookies.

I took a sip and burnt the roof of my mouth. 'What about you? Selling up?'

Thelma shook her head. 'Nobody's booting me out of my home before my time. They try it, they'll be sorry.' She suddenly fixed her bright eyes on me. 'Say, you can help me find Rhondie!' It wasn't a question.

'Rhondie's just fine. Gone off with a pal.' I snapped. I put the cup down, feeling the roof of my mouth swell up. 'Did you tell the cops about her?'

'One of them said to call in a day or two if there was no sign of her.'

I needed to give her something to hang on to. 'Well, there you go. Call the cops, like he said.'

'They won't lift a finger. Especially when they hear she got Mexican blood. She can pass as white, mind you. Her mom was Mexican, pretty thing. Gladys' son, Thomas, his family line was Welsh. Miners. A lot of them came over here for a better life. Did I say that already?' She was rambling again. I curbed my irritation.

'How about getting a private investigator to look into it?' A private detective could take Thelma and her problems on.

She gawped at me. 'I don't have a bean.'

'Call one up, see what they charge.' I stood up. 'Now we ladies should be getting our beauty sleep. I bet you Rhonda is safe and sound.'

Thelma's watery eyes followed me but she seemed miles away. 'Could sell my wedding ring?'

'Do that.' I edged back towards the door. 'So long. Nice meeting you.'

She looked up, her eyes red. 'You say you're her pal. So help me. I don't get out of the house. I don't know the first thing about investigators. You call one for me!'

I'd done my bit by coming here, assuaged my conscience. Now it was Thelma's turn to feel she hadn't done enough. 'All right. I'll speak to one for you. Give me your number and I'll let you know what they say.'

208

Thelma smiled. 'You're a good girl. I always can tell from the look of someone.'

Well, that was a first.

39

The office of Falaise Investigations was shielded with heavy double glass doors, the kind that forced you to slow down and compose yourself. Beyond, a Hedy Lamarr look-alike sat behind a stenograph in the office. She wore a pair of tortoiseshell spectacles. Her glossy walnut curls arranged themselves on her shoulders like dollops of forest honey. Her dress was like pewter, a heavy chenille trim little number, with dark blue piping on the cuffs, the pockets, and the bodice. A serious look, but sexy with it. She would certainly cheer up any jealous husbands.

The glamour-puss secretary looked up, pulling her glasses down to survey me.

I'd put on a black wool skirt topped with one of my more decorative Manhattan purchases, a black silk blouse printed with white cobwebs and pink roses all over. It had a pussy bow necktie and puffy long sleeves with neat pleats at the wrist. Its flamboyance reminded me of my Hollywood dreams before they were crushed. I'd even stopped at a florist and bought a fresh pink rose corsage, now pinned to my pink jacket. I'd bought a cheap string of pearls and matching earrings at the same time. Totally inappropriate for Lauder's errands but today, I had a use for it. The outfit said '*stylish do-gooding lady about town*'.

It felt good to dress up. Screw Lauder.

'May I help you?' Her accent was French.

I walked up to the desk, confident. 'I'd like an appointment with Mr. Falaise.'

'Mrs. Falaise?'

'Okay. Mrs. Falaise then.'

'For why, please?'

'It's a missing person situation.'

She frowned. 'Oh, for the vacancy?'

'What? No. I've come about finding a missing person.'

'Oh. Mrs. Falaise only does the divorce.'

Suddenly the intercom system buzzed. A gruff female voice said 'Send her in, Therese.'

The girl got up, a little miffed to be overruled. She towered over me, a giant in her heels. She pointed at a closed door at the end of the office.

I walked past a large framed photograph above a mantelpiece showing a motley assortment of suited women. *Association of Women Private Investigators of Southern California* was embossed in bold gold capitals at the base of the photograph. Smaller brass frames housed various certificates, duly stamped and sealed, testifying to various achievements in the snooping business. A large mirror, with open curtains, sat on a dividing wall. This had to be the double mirror.

Beatty Falaise was like a tropical parrot. She wore a jade suit and a chartreuse silk skirt with lots of ruffles forming huge downy plumage over her substantial bosom. Neither color did much for her putty skin and fuchsia lipstick. Her hair was blue-gray, scraped back into a severe bun. Her gold-rimmed glasses glinted, the thick lenses magnifying her green eyes. Her hands were weighed down with an assortment of gold rings with turquoise and yellow stones that matched her earrings and bracelet. She had a style all of her own – if not giving a damn what anyone thinks is a style.

Her office was simply done but with quality fittings. In the corner, an exotic plant grew in a large Chinese-style pot, standing on a brass and marble stand. The venetian blinds were of a rich reddish wood. The whole effect was sophisticated and civilized. A box of tissues discreetly lurked in a brass holder on a low table between the chairs.

A fog of smoke swirled up from a short, fat pipe. The smoke subsided. She thrust out her other hand over the desk. 'Beatty Falaise. How do you do?' Her handshake was firm and hearty.

'Elvira Slate.'

'Pull up a pew, Miss Slate, and tell me all about your missing person.' She nodded at the two high-backed leather chairs, positioned in front of her desk.

I jerked my head at the internal window, edged with short velvet drapes on a brass pole, where Therese and the office were in full view. I asked, 'You can hear through that as well?'

'I'm not a bad lip-reader. Be a doll and close those drapes.' I did as she asked and sat down.

'Well, what's your trouble?'

I began. 'A certain party is missing, and another certain party is worried about her. I'm helping the concerned party. I offered to help secure the services of an investigator. The concerned party hasn't much money, and is elderly. Not to mention that the missing party might be just fine, and all the concerned party needs is reassurance. A recommendation of someone good but affordable is all I need.'

'Good and affordable don't gel like Fred and Ginger in this town.' Falaise grunted, tapping her pen on the blotter. 'How long has the missing person been gone?'

'It'll be thirty-six hours by tonight.'

Falaise whistled. 'All right.'

'Can you help?'

She raised a hand to silence me. It looked quite an effort with all those rings on. 'You said 'her'. How old is the missing person?'

'She's around eighteen, twenty? I met her one time.'

Falaise leant back. I could spot a hair on a small mole. She surveyed me like she was vetting me. 'Have the police been notified?'

'Kind of. A cop said to give it time. Besides, the girl was seen leaving with a suitcase and with somebody else. Without a struggle.'

Falaise eyeballed me over her spectacles. 'Could the missing girl be in some kind of trouble?'

Straight to the jugular. I shifted in my seat. 'I wouldn't know.' I couldn't mention Shimmer's death yet, or the fact the pair had pinched dough from a shady nightclub boss. That was one big can of worms I didn't want to open, let alone discuss with a P.I. I began to regret coming here. 'Look, she's probably fine.'

Falaise considered this, tipping out the ash of her pipe into a green marble dish before refilling it. She said, 'True. Could be a false alarm. But here you are anyway, helping out the broke but elderly concerned party who's fretting. Unfortunately, my associate, Gloria, who handled this type of case, has run off to the circus. Not literally, but she got it in her head to set up an alpaca farm, God help her. Kind of thing that happens when you hit the big five-zero. But you don't have to worry about that. How old are you?'

'Twenty-six.'

Falaise drummed her nails on the blotter. 'A few folks could take it on. Lanie Shaw, but she could still be in Chicago. Then there's Celeste Rogers... But she let rip at a client a few weeks ago. Unprofessional behavior. Ruffled clients toss their complaints up the food chain to the president, yours truly. Tedious for me to handle, but I can't have any of our members losing their license. Too few of us girls in this business already.' She shot me a wicked smile; it rejuvenated her careworn face. 'Exactly how much – or should I say how little – can the client afford?'

'She's broke. She might need to sell a ring.'

Beatty cracked up. 'Jeez, haven't heard that in a while. Can't you lend her any money?' She looked me up and down. I probably looked well-heeled.

'No. I'm new to town and looking for a job myself.'

She said, 'I can put in some calls. The going rate's twenty-five a day minimum, and a retainer of fifty.'

I whistled. 'That settles it. We'll have to leave it to the cops.' I stood up.

Falaise waved her hand for me to sit back down. I obliged but this was a waste of time. She swiveled around in her chair to look at the view through the blinds. 'You ever heard of a blue-footed booby?'

I said I hadn't.

'A seabird. Shows its face every few hundred years and then disappears again. I saw one the other day, at the Marina where Mr. Falaise and I moor our little boat. Couldn't believe my eyes. But twice in one week is something again.'

I raised my head to peer out. 'Where?'

She spun back. 'Right here. You are a blue-footed booby.' Falaise eyeballed me. 'Forty years' experience tells me you aren't just a worried go-between, no more than I'm Deanna Durbin on a bad day.'

214

I stiffened. 'Whatever are you insinuating?'

Beatty pulled off her spectacles and wiped the lenses with a tissue. 'Sweetheart, you're awful good but you're dealing with Beatty Falaise. I didn't get where I am today by being dumb. You feel obligated.'

'Very entertaining, but I'm kind of busy.' I stood up.

'Oh, get off your high horse. I might have a proposition.'

I sighed, impatient. 'What?'

'You do it.' Beatty Falaise looked straight in my eye, rather pleased with herself. 'You want a job, right? I have a vacancy. I could train you up. You're no dumb blonde, you're quite a gal. But mousy would be better. Take off that getup, wash your face and you could have the bland P.I. look in no time.'

That was rich, considering her rainbow outfit.

'Take off those pretty gloves. Let me see your hands.' She shoved her specs back on her nose.

'My hands?'

'Mitts speak volumes. Time in the slammer. Liver spots. Narcotics. You got something to hide, Booby?'

Beatty Falaise had made me, in minutes. Probably seconds, with the two-way mirror. I was impressed and horrified. 'Some imagination you got,' I said.

'Helps in this game. But hear me out. Drink?'

A drink. Why the hell not? Playing along wouldn't hurt and I was intrigued. She had my fake name, but that was all. And I bet her liquor was good. 'Sure. I could use a drink.'

Beatty buzzed the intercom. 'Two bourbons on the rocks, Therese. Oh, and bring the bottle.'

She relit the pipe. 'I got my fair share of honey trap girls but I'm choosy as hell about who I work with. Gloria had what it

215

takes but I'm done with pleading with her to come back. Missing person work pours in for her, but I can't do it. Too old, too fat, too rich. You hear the number of times that darned telephone rings?'

On cue, in the next office, the telephone began again.

Beatty went on. 'I like divorce. Town's riddled with it and I'm top of the game, making sure neither party is too injured. Always takes two to tango. In my younger days, I'd jump at the chance of a missing person, hooch wars, embezzlement.' She had a misty-eyed look as she reflected. 'Those jobs sure get old when you get old.'

Therese flounced in with a silver tray bearing a couple of glasses, a bottle of bourbon, an ice pitcher and some olives in a dish. She carefully placed the olives on the side, and passed us each a substantial cut glass tumbler.

'Merci beaucoup, sweetheart.' Beatty grinned. She waited for Therese to leave the room. Then she raised her glass. I did the same. We chinked over the dark green leather.

'I trust my instinct. Never lets me down. I depend on that more than I do on my darling husband, an angel incarnate. My instinct tells me you've got a lot going for you.'

I avoided her gaze. 'Appreciate it.'

'And this town needs more lady P.Is. A P.I. is like an invisible public service. Underappreciated, for sure. But the real job satisfaction comes from in here.' She tapped her heart. Then she put her pipe down and looked me straight in the eye. 'So how about it, Booby?'

Private investigator? The suggestion was mad. I had to stop myself laughing. A secret life that Lauder wouldn't ever know about? As if. But when he was done with me, if he ever was, I'd either be dead or need some kind of living. Investigating could pay; it would certainly beat learning the stenograph and serving coffee to a creep with wandering hands. And it might lead me quicker to Rhonda.

'I don't know. A lot to get my head around.' I said, finishing the delicious bourbon. I couldn't work out her game. She didn't know me. I had done time in the slammer. I didn't have liver spots as far as I knew but at this rate, they were only a matter of time. Besides, I'd never met anyone like her. It felt like spending too long in a fortuneteller's cave and getting sucked into a magical world of drama and exciting potential. How long before the effects wore off?

When I walked out of here, that's when. That's when reality would bite.

Trust me to find the most eccentric P.I. in town.

Beatty motioned me to slide my glass over to her. She generously refilled it. 'Maybe I sprang this on you a little too quick. I'm not one to beat about the bush.'

'Say I'm interested. How exactly could it work?'

'I could train you, show you how to handle a missing person case. Step by step. You'd be my protégé! You can operate under my agency's license. Your concerned party won't have to pay a penny. Or your interested party sells her ring and pays you. If she does, you throw me a small percentage. If you like the work, stay on and work for me, or set up your own establishment. P.I. licenses are issued by City Hall. They'll check you are a *bona fide* individual, no record, no debts, the whole enchilada. A reference from yours truly and you'll be in business.'

In-house operative, licenses, credentials, associations.

The legitimate world I'd never inhabited. This is exactly what the lost blue-footed booby felt like in an alien human world.

'Is there a problem?' Beatty peered over her specs.

I acted blasé. 'Not at all.'

Beatty lit her pipe and took long languid puffs. 'See how you like the gig. In the meantime, you better make a decision fast. If something bad is gonna happen to your missing girl, it already has, or it will soon.'

I met her eyes. The clock was ticking.

40

It was almost lunchtime when I walked out of the office block. The city was gently humming, business being done, relative calm. It reminded me of how London could make me feel in the days before the war, the way only a big city can make you feel – at the heart of life, that you counted, that your life mattered.

And Beatty Falaise was offering me a chance to be part of it.

Traffic roared past me. I wasn't interested in catching a taxi.

The fact was Beatty's offer had stunned me. It was the second time somebody had done that, shown me a fork in the road.

It hadn't been Billy, as much as he'd like to have thought so. No, he'd just caved to my pressure to let me join him in his world. I was his woman, just the piece on his arm and I'd been happy with that.

It had been my foster mother Gwendoline, a high-brow romantic from a posh family, who had seen something in me. I'd been fifteen when Gwendoline plucked me out of reform school to fulfill her maternal instinct. She gave me an education. She thought I could achieve.

But what the hell was Beatty's motive?

Was she just bored shitless of disintegrating Hollywood marriages and up for a gamble? Maybe I was some kind of surrogate daughter. In her colorful getup and flashy jewels, she looked like the biggest hustler in town, probably sailing each weekend to Catalina Island. Surely, with me, she was just betting on a hunch. Right from the moment I'd walked into her office, she'd read me like a large-print book. When she made her outlandish suggestion, any normal person would have told her to get lost. But I hadn't. I'd pricked up my ears and she knew then and there I was her match, the latest player to the table. She knew damn well I could be anyone. But she was running the game and it was her job to vet the players.

The real test would be telling Beatty Falaise the truth about Lauder's grip on me, and my murky past, but that wasn't going to happen. Say too much now, the offer would go up in a puff of pipe smoke. She didn't want to know the truth, she wanted the gamble, the danger. You only declare a hand when you're either bust or winning and so far, I could play on. She would want me to stick to the rules of the game.

But she wouldn't have offered it to anyone. She'd seen potential in me to be a private investigator.

I had to pinch myself.

Me.

I stopped to cross over at a traffic light. In seconds, I was surrounded by a bunch of uniformed school kids being led like ducklings across the street by their jolly teacher. The kids were babbling and laughing, with bright, gap-toothed smiles. Cute. Maybe I wouldn't cross here.

Lurking underneath everything was an uneasy sensation, down in the deep jelly of my bones, maybe something only a shrink could diagnose. Forget Beatty's foibles, *I* was my problem. Even I wouldn't put my faith in me.

The painful truth is that I had never got to know what it felt like to pull it off. To achieve, to prove myself to anyone. Gwendoline died too soon, Billy treated me like a spoilt kid.

Wait a minute. Beatty's training could equip me with skills

to investigate Lauder as well, not that she would be any the wiser. I'd obtain more dirt on him for the day when he dragged me back to the desert. Investigating Reba T. would surely have to be the first step. What if Rhonda was in Reba T.'s clutches? What the hell could I do? Steal her away? Going back to her granny's house wasn't an option. Lauder knew where to find her there. He'd just take her right back, if he and Reba T. were working together.

Maybe Beatty could help with this, too. She'd be clued up on watertight methods to help Rhonda disappear, if I found her; I bet she'd have all the right contacts for fake documentation.

I'd love to pull that one off under Lauder's nose!

I turned right down a side road. I was lost. The neighborhood was classy, big apartment blocks with lush front gardens. I peered in at the lovely homes. If it all went well, maybe I could live in one of these, one day. My own sprawling apartment, stuffed with modern art and a wide balcony overlooking the city. I could swan around in an ivory housecoat and painted nails.

As if. I burst out laughing.

Me.

Lie low. Do Lauder's bidding. Get on his right side. Make him see you deserve a new chance. Forget this craziness. Rhonda is fine. Shut the door and bolt it. Tomorrow is as far as you can think and that's pushing it.

No. I *could* do this. What did I have to lose?

The mid-afternoon sun was belting down. I found a drugstore and bought an ice-cold cherry soda. I headed for a pay phone.

I had two calls to make.

First, Thelma. I told her a lady P.I. would do initial enquiries for nothing, and she didn't need money upfront, so to hold off selling her ring. Thelma's voice cracked with relief. I told her not to talk to any more cops. She hesitated, but agreed.

Secondly, I dialed Falaise Investigations. Therese was friendlier. She purred that Beatty was ensconced with a client, 'a very complicated case'. Beatty had left a message for me to meet her later at eight at an Italian restaurant – *Luigi's*.

Beatty had known I was in before I had.

A wind of change, and this one didn't have a chill. The Santa Ana was soothing me, coaxing me along gently.

I was carving a life out for myself, away from Lauder's noose. The sobering thought followed that it was all on the back of Shimmer's tragedy. I had her to thank for it.

RIP Shimmer.

41

The restaurant was off Melrose, a small buzzy place. Most of the diners were rowdy Italian-Americans, babbling over red and white gingham and spilt Chianti. Wall murals of fishing villages and olive groves drove the message home that this was a defiant outpost of the homeland.

Beatty was already there, filling a corner booth. She had changed for dinner, now sporting a dark purple suit and floral silk shirt with black and beige flowers. Around her neck was a triple rope of black seed pearls, which matched her earrings. She wore a large brooch with a massive amethyst surrounded by onyx. On her wrist, a chunky bracelet with emerald-cut amethysts gleamed away. A little purple tilt hat with gold trim and black lace perched on her head. She clearly relished fashion.

As I approached, Beatty looked her new associate up and down. Something like approval gleamed in her eyes. I'd changed into my navy suit with the simple polka dot blouse. I'd blotted off most of my lipstick. I was now somber, professional-looking.

She was already celebrating, a fluted glass in her hand, a bottle of something fizzy in an ice bucket. There was another flute on the opposite side of the table. I guessed it was for me.

Celebrating the rehabilitation of an offender and she didn't even know it.

We shook hands. Regular business partners having a meeting over dinner.

So this is what being a career woman felt like.

We sat down. Beatty told me her beloved dachshund Florabel

was at home giving birth. She'd left the whole matter with Mr. Falaise to deal with, as he wasn't squeamish. 'Another reason I just do divorce. No nasty surprises, no dead bodies to trip over.' The way she said it implied she'd seen her fair share. By the time our meeting was over, she'd return to a basket of squirming pups in her house, and did I want one? I said no, no dogs, no cats.

No entanglements, period.

Beatty grabbed the empty flute and filled it up, handing it to me. 'Anyway, to finding your missing person.'

The proprietor, Luigi, approached the booth. His dried-out walnut of a face cracked into a stained smile at the sight of Beatty. 'Hey, Signora Fa-lay-zee, why you no come such a long time? Where is Florabel? Ah, she have the bambini, yes? Very good. Very good. Who is la bella signorina? Bellissima, caro. A friend of Signora Fa-lay-zee, a friend of mine.'

I was tempted to answer in pidgin Italian but shut up. There was no point in drawing unnecessary attention to my past, however relaxed I felt. As they chatted, I got the distinct impression that Signora Falaise had helped Luigi out of a tight corner or two.

Eventually, Luigi sauntered off. Beatty smiled fondly after him. 'This place was shut down when the family were interred in '41. Never mind the fact his sons were born here, and fighting for Uncle Sam. I gave a helping hand after, to get them up and running again. They paid me back in free lunches in less than a year. Still won't take a penny.'

Billy and his friends had of course suffered the same, but I nodded as if I was learning it for the first time.

Beatty spread out her napkin over her lap, as if it was a map. 'Sicily. Now that is one place in Europe I'd like to go.'

I'd had similar plans once. The way Billy described it, it sounded like going back in time. Olive groves, temple ruins, the azure sea, the slow pace of life. There was a darker side he didn't dwell on. Complex, everlasting feuds, one of which eventually caused the death of his father. He never told me how, exactly. Billy had been just a kid, but I knew he'd witnessed something bad. 'Bunch of nutters,' he'd say, dismissively. So we never went. He built his small empire in the Elephant and Castle, and made his own way in life. He'd been proud of that. 'Never took a penny from any of them.' He never wrote to his remaining family, never mentioned them. Whoever they were, they didn't belong in our life.

'Hey, daydreamer! Back to business. Give me the lowdown on the missing girl.' Beatty relit her pipe, leaning back, attentive.

Elvira Slate needed to eat in a local Italian without trips down memory lane. The memory of Billy belonged in the life of someone I had ceased to be.

I folded the corners of my napkin. 'She's called Rhonda. About eighteen, like I said. She's half Welsh, half Mexican. Something like that. She's sick, got a brain tumor and needs an operation. She lives in her dead granny's house, next door to the old lady, Thelma, who's worried about her.'

Beatty absorbed the information without batting an eyelid.

'How do you know them?' Beatty enquired. I rattled out my prepared answer. 'I rented a room from Thelma. She was pals with Rhonda's granny. Rhonda inherited the place. She lived there with her girlfriend.'

'Lovers?'

I nodded, taking a big gulp.

'I saw Shimmer – the girlfriend – before Rhonda left that day. I was over there checking on Thelma. Shimmer was brimming

225

with plans to get out of town, they were selling up for the operation. I know they'd had trouble with a boss. Shimmer creamed off some money.'

'Stole it?'

'She figured she was owed it. But there was bad feeling about it.'

Understatement of the century.

I remembered Lauder's threats. Reba T.'s nasty reputation. And Shimmer's words. *Hush money.*

I went on. 'Last time I saw her, she was off to some meeting, said it was a nice little earner. Next thing I hear she's dead.'

'How did she die?'

Time to reveal the big-ticket item. 'The girlfriend, Shimmer, was Ellen Cranston.'

Beatty puffed, looking blank. 'Who is…?'

'Ellen Cranston was found dead with Darlene Heymann and Frank Acker.'

Beatty spluttered into her bubbles, almost dropping her pipe. 'Darlene Heymann? Frank Acker? Jeez!'

'Rhonda left the same night the three died. Later, I think.'

Beatty shifted uncomfortably. 'Go on.'

'I got a call from Thelma, who'd heard the news, and was upset Rhonda had left without saying goodbye. Somebody picked her up.'

Beatty contemplated this. 'Overdose. Young folks today. When they gonna wise up? Tragic.' She took a slug of wine. 'Sounds like a narcotics hook-up to me. Word is Ellen Cranston was the supplier, who liked to partake of her own wares.'

I pulled a blank expression. I wouldn't throw Shimmer under the bus on principle. 'She didn't look the type.'

'So where are you living now?' Beatty asked. It was an odd question. I squirmed, avoiding her gaze. 'Just some boarding house. In the Palms.'

Beatty gave me the fisheye but didn't press. 'Know who the boss is? The one they had trouble with?'

'Name of Reba T.'

Beatty puffed. 'Reba T. Don't know her.'

'And her ex-husband now passes as a woman. He has his own nightclub. *Joyce's*. Shimmer liked him...I mean *her*.'

Beatty put down her pipe and took a slug. 'Real underworld stuff. Your girl ain't no missing person, honey. She's running from the law and the old boss. Probably a good thing, too.'

It was the confirmation I needed. I tried to hide my relief. The cold facts pointed to the fact Rhonda decided to leave and she had her own reasons. Maybe she and Shimmer had a plan that if things went bad, Rhonda should run with the money in any event. It was hurtful to the overprotective Thelma but she was losing her marbles and maybe they'd decided to keep her in the dark.

Beatty looked intently at me. 'About the Darlene Heymann and Frank Acker deaths. Cranston, I mean this Shimmer girl, could have supplied the drugs, she's from that world. Rhonda could have cleared out fast because she didn't want to get implicated.'

Beatty might be relieved, too. Narcotics and death were far more sordid than her customary uptown divorce cases.

'So I guess that's it?' I said.

Beatty took a puff on her pipe.

'Sure. Until her body shows up and you feel rotten as hell you did nothing about it.'

42

Beatty leant forward and lowered her voice. 'Lesson number one. No matter how pretty the path, leave no stone unturned.'

I prodded an olive, uncomfortable. Beatty had reactivated my anxiety. 'You think she could be in danger?'

'Lesson number two. Assumption? Until you see her with your own eyes, you don't know. I don't know. Nobody knows. I can assume from the facts, so can you. But an assumption ain't gasoline. Won't get you anyplace, anytime soon. But sometimes, it's all we got. That's where lesson number three comes in. Follow your instincts.'

I tried to keep up. Check everything, assume nothing, listen to my gut. 'So where do I start?'

'Known associates. Maybe the transvestite ex knows something. Start there.' She fished a car key out of her bag and slid it over to me. 'I see you're taking taxis. Wheels are on the house, till you get your own. There's a car for you in the street opposite. Maroon. There's life left in the old boneshaker. I'm fond of the old girl so try not to get into any scrapes. Let Therese know when she needs filling up. She's got the coupons.'

'Gee. Thanks.' I wouldn't be able to park it at the Astral. Malvin could report back to Lauder I had a set of wheels.

'Temporary driver's license in the glove box. I guessed your date of birth. If you've already got a license, you can toss this one.'

She knew damn well I didn't have one. That she'd forged a license was interesting.

Beatty rummaged again in her purse, this time pulling out a small box. She slid it over to me. I took off the lid. Business cards. I pulled one out, a firm piece of white card. Embossed in black were the words *Falaise Investigations*.

I'd never had a card. I visualized my name on top in swirling gilt letters.

Elvira Slate. Private Investigator.

That would take some getting used to. But it would never happen. Somebody else's business card was as good as it would get. But it was better than nothing.

'If any boys from the LAPD rub you up the wrong way, slip 'em one of these. Should smooth things over. If not, put 'em onto me. Try not to antagonize the cops unduly. Some don't take female detectives too seriously, which has its upside. In my younger days, I got many a guy to say more than he should just by looking cute. Men just love explaining things to us gals, don't they?' She chuckled into her drink. 'Not so much Mr. Falaise, thank the Lord. He knows better!'

Beatty continued with the practicalities. Like what to wear. 'Nothing like that cobweb blouse you had on earlier. Don't get me wrong, it's pretty. But I sure as hell won't be forgetting it anytime soon. Stick to what you've got on now. Bland is best. Pantsuits and low shoes that you can sneak around and get out fast in.' She also suggested a pair of clear glass spectacles. 'Men don't make passes at girls who wear glasses. Don't remember them, either. And gumshoes,' she said. 'By name, by nature. Keep a pair in the trunk. There could be some there already, come to think of it. Gloria's. See if they fit. And something girlie in case you need to use your charms. You packing?'

'What?' Then I got it. 'No. No gun. Should I get one?'

She thought about it, rubbing her chin. 'Don't like firearms, personally. Tempting fate. We'll see how it goes.'

Beatty plonked a set of keys on the table. 'Keys to the office. I like to spend my weekends with Mr. Falaise, on the water, not as the hop to my new associate.'

I swallowed. If she really knew the truth, would she go so far? Open up her life, her possessions, her confidential clients' information, to a former jailbird? My instinct told me she knew I was damaged goods, but not half as broken as I really was.

Beatty surveyed me. 'Just don't lose them. I can't abide disorganized people.'

I picked the keys up and slipped them into my purse. 'Thanks.'

Her gaze roamed over the tables. 'One day, this town will finish me off. But not yet.'

Then she waved to Luigi, pointing at our empty bottle. 'Darn it! We're celebrating.'

Then she turned to me and said something I'd rather she hadn't. 'Don't let me down.'

43

Beatty and I had got through two bottles of fizz, huge helpings of spinach cannelloni and two espresso coffees. I was almost sober by the time I found the car. I took one look at the plush maroon vehicle and it was like meeting an old friend from a former life.

If this was a beaten-up car by Beatty's standards, I wondered what model she was driving. I hopped in and breathed in the old leathery smell. The steering wheel looked like polished walnut. I checked the glove box. Sure enough, there was the temporary license with my details, issued at Hollywood. It had all the required information and an expiry date. It even had a stamp and a number.

Beatty knew a thing or two.

Driving again was a piece of cake. There was little traffic and I glided along, unable to wipe the grin off my face. It was like floating on air.

In some respects, the case felt like I was helping June again. Except this time, I would tread very carefully, guided by a professional, instead of blundering around, burning places down. Best-case scenario? Rhonda would turn up safe and sound. Worst-case? Reba the boss bitch was handing out punishment.

With these thoughts running around my head, I parked on the same street as Joyce's nightclub.

I was even looking forward to being somewhere with music. Somewhere that wasn't likely to be full of gossip columnists with their beady eyes on who was dancing with who. Low-key was the name of every game from now on.

Joyce's was written in pink neon above the door of a low building. Luigi had put in a few calls and quickly found the address for the club.

A stocky woman in a man's dinner jacket, a fedora and flats walked arm-in-arm with a glamour-puss with seamed stockings, high heels and fox furs, towards a narrow door in an inconspicuous building. I followed the butch and femme, but stayed on the other side of the road. They rang a bell, waited a while. Eventually, the butch spoke through a hatch. Someone on the other side let them in. The butch stood back, letting her lady enter first.

I approached the door. After ringing the bell, the small hatch slid open. A woman's eyes, devoid of mascara, flashed up and down me. 'Members only.'

'My lady friend's a member.'

'Yeah? What's her name?'

'Tell you later when I've got lucky.' I winked.

The hatch slid shut. Had my looking-for-action act worked? It seemed to, because seconds later, the heavy door opened.

The hunky doorwoman impatiently summoned me in. Her muscular chest was crammed into black tails and a dickie bow, her short hair greased back. She looked me up and down. 'You already got lucky, Trixie. You know where to find me for that dance later.'

I told her I'd remember that.

The club was dark, smoky, and at ten o'clock, already heaving. The heaving dance floor writhed like a pond of breeding carps. Women outnumbered the few men. I could blend into the dive of misfits. I could relax here.

Now I was under Lauder's control, the company of women *en masse* was a pleasant change.

Perspective is an amazing thing.

On the small semicircular stage edged with blue lights, a female swing outfit pelted out a good beat. The big battered drum revealed the name in flaked writing. *The Charmettes.*

The singer was a tiny blonde, in a cheap-looking satin aqua floor-length gown covered in sequins and tulle. Even from the back of the club, I could see her hem was coming loose. She had a vivacious face, but dark rings under her eyes. Still, with a voice like honey, she might have been good enough for an uptown joint in a better quality dress.

I glanced over the band. They were pretty good, made up of about twelve women of different ages and races, in jade jackets edged with an aqua trim. The saxophonist was giving it some and more. I did a double take. *Wait a minute!* She looked familiar, really familiar. It took a moment to place her because I'd only seen her in a certain situation.

Alberta, Dede's maid. Hotel maid by day, tenor sax by night, dishing up the solos in a lesbian club instead of doing the dishes. Now her hair was elaborately piled up on her head, with a green flower pinned to the side. She was engrossed, and I could have watched for hours. Was she a lesbian too? Were all the Charmettes? Alberta and Dede were cozy. Could *they* be an item? The whole maid and mistress relationship one big act to enable them to live with each other? Clever, if so. That could explain Dede's assault on me. Was she here, too?

I inwardly cursed as I looked around. It was hard to focus. Alberta was safely installed on stage, and I was pretty sure she hadn't seen me. If I bumped into either of them, I would just have to bluff it. Better to just get my business done here fast. Lauder's orders were fresh in my mind. My recent past as

Connie Sharpe and my very new present as Elvira Slate had to stay strictly divided. Then it struck me – if Alberta played here a lot, she might even know Shimmer. But I couldn't ask her. Joyce was my lead, and that was who I came to find.

I moved deep into the crowd, scanning it for any sign of a transvestite.

In another corner of the club, a slim, exotic-looking creature sat at a small table protecting a box. The resident drug dealer. Her angular bare arms moved fast, dishing out Red Devils, Yellow Jackets, Blue Velvets to her customers. She was a busy spider, weaving her toxic web; there was nothing discreet about it. My eyes moved on and then I saw her. Joyce. The tallest woman here, swanning about in a dark red velvet gown like she owned the place, making sure everyone was having a good time. An elaborate red and silver corsage was pinned to her breast. She wore a lot of faux ice, matching her twinkling but wizened eyes. Under the layers of white foundation was a hawkish bone structure that no amount of mascara and lipstick would soften. She would have been quite handsome as a fellow. As a woman, she was striking and elegant, lady of the manor, fussing over her regulars, laughing gracefully with a tinkling voice. She had more feminine panache than the rest of us women put together.

Propping myself up at the bar seemed the best move, and I pushed my way through the throng. The bar itself was U-shaped, attended by three girls in silver short pants, and turquoise bikini tops. An assortment of silk green and blue tropical flowers topped their pin curls like decoration on a pie, bobbing about as they mixed cocktails at a frenetic pace.

I perched on a stool and it wasn't long before I felt Joyce's gaze land on me. It hadn't taken her long to clock a stranger. Within seconds, she cruised up to me, wafting perfume.

'First-timer?' Joyce stood opposite me, mirroring my posture, elbow on bar. Behind us, two women in identical dinner suits and top hats were sucking the lipstick off each other's lips. It was distracting.

'Yeah. New to town.' My eyes moved to one of the bar girls. 'How about yourself? A regular?'

'You could say that. I'm Joyce. This is my place.' She said this rather pompously. 'How did you find about us?'

'Strolling past. Liked the sound of the band.' I caught her eye. I'd soon be contradicting myself but I wanted her to lower her guard.

She clicked her fingers at one of the bouncy bar girls and within minutes a tall orange neon cocktail was delivered to me. 'Zombie – on the house, my compliments.'

'Thanks.' I took the glass and sipped it. 'Nice.'

'We add something to give it a little kick. Don't worry,' she said, catching me freezing. 'Nothing too naughty!'

There was no point in beating about the bush. 'Turns out we've got mutual friends.'

'Oh?'

'Rhonda and Shimmer.'

It's funny how a smile changes from genuine to false without a muscle moving. It's all in the eyes. And Reba's suddenly became opaque. She pursed her lips, shutting down already.

'Really?'

'Uh-huh. And I'm a little worried about Rhonda. Thought you might know where she is.'

'Me? No, not at all. Is something wrong?' Joyce's voice

softened with fake concern. Those perfectly arched painted brows disappeared into the horizontal folds of her forehead.

'Other than her lover dying?'

'I heard about that. Very sad. But is there anything the matter with Rhonda?'

'Mind if we sit down?'

The mask didn't crack. 'Certainly.' Joyce gracefully pointed to the far side of the club, where booths lined the wall. In the middle, one stood empty. It had the best view of the band. Joyce's throne.

Joyce waited for me to sit down, then elegantly lowered herself onto the opposite side, crossing her legs. She maintained a bemused look on her face. 'So. Rhonda?'

'I just need to know if she's okay, considering recent events. Thought you could put my mind at rest.'

Joyce flinched slightly. 'Who are you, exactly?'

'A friend. Shimmer told me she got along with you, so here I am.' Should I be Gina or Elvira? Until she dished, I was under no pressure to share, either. 'If you don't know, maybe for old times' sake you could find out through the grapevine if Rhonda's with your ex.'

Joyce leant forward on her elbows, holding her lighter back. 'I'm of the opinion that divorced couples should proceed as if they had never known one another. I don't speak to Reba.'

'So you won't help?'

'*Can't.* You've wasted your time. At least you are drinking the best Zombie in town.'

'Last thing anyone saw of her, she was going off in a car. Did you pick her up?'

Joyce gave me a cold look but her voice stayed calm.

'Whatever tree you're barking up, it's rotten and about to crash down on you, sweetmeat.'

'Relax. Rhonda's not exactly in the best shape to look out for herself.'

Joyce stood up. 'Then let's hope she's all right. Enjoy your Zombie. I trust we won't have the pleasure of seeing you again.'

I was blundering, and hadn't achieved anything except antagonize her. But my instincts told me she knew something. I stood up, not caring how loud I sounded. 'Scared shitless of your ex-wife, or something?'

Joyce hissed. 'Keep your voice down. Now would you leave, or do things have to get unpleasant?'

I leant back, defiant, smugly slugging the cocktail. 'You're right. It's darned good.'

Joyce bent over the table. She snarled, 'Hop it.' Her voice growled, menacingly. It matched her knuckles, large and white. A standoff with a transvestite would be a first. So would a fistfight with the doorwoman.

I'd come off worse in both cases.

I had a last shot, looking up at her. 'You're now a woman, right?'

'No. I was always a woman, inside.'

'Whatever. But what type of woman? A fucking bitch, just like your ex? Or a compassionate woman who does right by a sister in need?'

'You think I'd run a place like this if I didn't care, dumbass?'

'I don't know. Maybe you spotted a gap in the market.'

Her nostrils flared. 'You got a nerve.' She raised her arm. In seconds, two beefcakes muscled their way through the crowd. 'Problem, Boss?'

'Escort the young lady from the premises.'

I stood up. 'Keep your dogs on the leash. I'm leaving. Just wanting to make sure Rhonda's all right. Some folks are worried about her.' For added flair, I slipped her one of Beatty's cards. 'Call this number if you remember something.'

The doorwomen grabbed my arms. Joyce scanned the card. 'Of course. A professional Nosey Parker.' Joyce raised her finger, and wagged it. The women released me.

'Alright. Let's talk.' With another wave, she dismissed her guards. She turned to me. 'Maybe we got off on the wrong foot. Sit down.'

The change of tune was interesting.

I sat as Joyce signaled a passing waitress. 'Another Zombie?' she enquired. I nodded, keen to help the truce along.

The girl glided away, a tray of empties held high above her head, her cute ass wiggling. I snuck a look at Joyce to see if she was also appreciating the sight. Joyce's eyes, if they had been roving, were already swiveling back to mine.

Joyce leaned forward slightly. 'Who's footing the bill for your services?'

'A client.'

'And you expect me to dish.' Sarcasm pushed the brows up again. Then she sighed. 'All right. I'd like to help. I read about the tragedy just like the rest of the world, but I have no idea where Rhonda is. If you must know, I've already asked around. Even asked people in with my ex. Nobody knows a thing.'

'How did you find out Rhonda was missing?'

She turned back to me, struggling to get over her dislike. 'I have an apartment block in San Diego, my hometown. They were going to rent one of the apartments for a while. Shimmer

238

was due to come in here to collect a key. The plan was for Rhonda to have the operation down there. Shimmer didn't show. Then I hear the news. I assumed Rhonda would come and collect the key – her house is sold, after all. But no. So I rang. No answer. No word, *nada*. But they knew people, people liked them. So maybe she's with friends.'

They were even more pally than Shimmer had let on. Joyce was part of the whole escape plan. 'You knew they skimmed from Reba T.?'

'Yes. It was foolhardy – I made that clear. Reba lives by the law of the jungle, particularly when it comes to money. Anything goes for her. Anyone else tries it, big trouble. Queen of double standards.'

I nodded. 'On the last day she was alive, Shimmer said she had a sweet deal, some gig that would pay good. Some meeting?'

'She told you that?'

'Yes. Could she have been selling drugs?'

Joyce shrugged. 'I don't know and I'm hardly one to judge. They needed money fast. She never told me if she was dealing and nobody I knew supplied her.'

'Could Reba T. have set it all up, as a punishment for Shimmer? The overdose?'

This surprised Joyce. 'You mean, murder? That she somehow got them all there and drugged them?'

'Why not?'

Joyce laughed, throwing her head back. 'Reba is many unpleasant things, but a murderer? No. Shimmer and Rhonda were small fry. She would play the long game to get her money back.'

'You said anything goes with her.'

'Anything but killing.' She met my eyes. Had years of marriage set some kind of deep-rooted loyalty, like the foundations of an old house? You pull one down and build a new one on top, but the whole time the original bricks are still stuck in the ground, immoveable markers of a previous existence.

We fell silent as the waitress sashayed over with my second Zombie and a small shot glass of something clear for Joyce. I tipped her. She gave me a flirtatious grin before bouncing off. Joyce observed the interaction with a coy smile. 'When you're done, feel free to stick around. Enjoy yourself.'

'Thanks, but I'm working. Guess your ex didn't appreciate you becoming a wife?'

Joyce took a cigarette out and placed it in a long ivory holder. 'Reba is one-way traffic. She cannot think beyond herself. She always wants more, the best of everything. Being around that is like living in the eye of a hurricane, exhausting. You don't exist. It's very tiresome, after a while – pretending you don't exist.'

She seemed to be waiting for me to light her cigarette, so I obliged.

'My major crime, becoming my true self... Well, you can imagine.'

She shook her raven curls slightly.

'What are her clubs like?'

'Cater for a wide variety of tastes. Some classier than others, that's all I can say. We don't talk anymore, and even if we did, this place doesn't let me have a social life outside. I'm no entrepreneur, like Reba.'

I looked around. 'Business looks good to me.'

'I'm doing all right.'

I tried a new track. 'Shimmer was crazy about Rhonda. Seems odd she was found with a straight couple.'

Joyce studied me for some time. 'Darlene Heymann wasn't in a relationship with Frank Acker. They were just friends. Darlene's girlfriend is the artist Olive Harjo. Been together for decades. Regulars here.'

Olive Harjo. Another name the papers left out of Darlene's sob story of a life. Now it added up. '*The artistic community.*'

Subtext – abnormal, by society's double standards. Shimmer and Darlene. Two women, both in relationships with other women, found dead together.

'Think there's anything fishy?' I tried to keep the intensity out of my voice.

'I'm not thinking anything. You're the P.I. I just run a nightclub and two of my regulars met with tragedy. I expect you're hitting a dead end because there's nowhere else to go. Maybe Darlene just went too far. Maybe Shimmer was selling. Maybe that's all there is to it.' Joyce arched a brow, exhaling.

'Did Darlene and Shimmer know each other from here?'

'I asked myself that question. We're packed out all night, every night. I don't keep tabs on who know who knows who. Anyhow, Darlene and Olive are the kind of couple that prefers their own company. Most nights, they sat alone, sometimes they'd join me.'

Shimmer and Darlene's fatal encounter felt like an itchy scab. I knew I should leave it alone. But here it was again, a fat and inflamed hive, demanding I have a damn good scratch.

'How often did Darlene and Olive come here?'

'Oh, once or twice a month. Olive hasn't been back. Guess she's pretty cut up.'

'Know how can I find her?'

What are you doing?

'My, oh, my! You are a persistent little thing. All right. I'll give you Olive's address, and I'll double-check Reba hasn't done anything stupid. If you don't hear from me, I've got nothing.'

She got a pen out of her purse, scrawled an address on a napkin. 'Olive lives up in the Hollywood Hills. Don't say I gave it to you. I don't want my regulars to think I'm indiscreet. You could say you like art, you want to see her work. She might be cut up but she'll show you. They were flat broke. Heymann had completely cut Darlene off, you know. All that money and she never got a penny.'

'What? Why?'

'Guess he thought she didn't deserve it. Powerful men like to control people. She liked to live her way.' Joyce waved my card. 'Now, I've played ball. Tell me who's paying you to do all this?'

She may have opened up but I wasn't going to break client confidentiality on my first outing.

'A compassionate woman.' I downed the dregs of my drink, avoiding her eyes. 'If you do hear anything, call the number and leave a message. For Elvira Slate.'

'That's you?'

I nodded. It was beginning to feel like me.

44

I drove back to the Astral, enjoying cruising along the wide empty streets. The moon was high, the air sticky. I had the window down, letting in the warm breeze. I wouldn't go back immediately. I wanted to drive for longer and didn't feel ready for bed. I felt strangely alert. I signaled left and headed towards Sunset.

Soon the bright neon lights and signs gleamed like jars in a candy store seen through a kaleidoscope.

The old car glided through the main drag of the Strip. The nightclubs were at full throttle, swing bands blasting out from various venues. Creatures of the night glided in and out of clubs and restaurants, into taxis, into big fancy cars with exhausted chauffeurs holding open the door.

I turned again, down Genesee. I passed houses and apartment blocks. Soon, a velvety darkness descended where the odd bum and a black-and-white prowl car were the only signs of life. Then through a barren wasteland of roads where hoardings hid demolition sites, new structures towering into the darkness. Far beyond these stood deserted oil derricks like giant scarecrows in barren fields. Yesterday's dream.

I checked the gauge. My gas wouldn't last forever so I changed direction and returned to civilization.

Now I was back in the land of blocks with silent malls, shuttered newspaper stands, closed tobacconists. A dead city in the dead of night. But was it all so dead? Surely the fashion shops' ghostly mannequins would whisper gossip once I'd gone by. And in the shoe shops, the high heels and gumshoes would be clicking their heels and dancing. In the millinery shops, hats would spin off their poles and fly through the air. And the giant cup of coffee on the roof of the oddly illuminated café, surely some being from the night sky would descend and drink it; a hand would take the giant plastic cone from the top of the ice cream parlor and lift it to the heavens.

What exactly was in that Zombie? I laughed, remembering Joyce had said it had a kick. I drove on, anonymous and safe, just another tiny car crawling through the big city.

Olive Harjo. An artist living out in the hills, mourning a dead lover.

A new lead? Or a dead end? Should I go there? Me, Elvira Slate. P.I. A charlatan by most people's standards. But Beatty had encouraged me to turn stones over, and that was what I was doing. Being a professional, for the first time in my life.

This new responsibility filled me with a renewed sense of dread, simmering beneath the surface, ready to burst out. It would drag me down to a new kind of hell, where only I would perish.

I parked a few blocks from the Astral and walked the rest of the way. Just as I approached the motel, I felt an incredible sensation. An unusually warm current of the Santa Ana suddenly engulfed me. I stood still, pulling up my sleeves, and unbuttoned the top buttons of my blouse, letting the air onto my neck. I removed my hat and shook my hair. How could a wind feel this magical? I lifted my head to the night sky, standing there, breathing it in, letting it caress me. The wind was soothing me, encouraging me, empowering me.

I was being cleansed, refreshed, renewed.

You can do this, you can be this. You are Elvira Slate. You can be this.

And then I knew. The wind was blessing me.

As I turned into the parking lot, my stomach lurched.

Lauder's car. The silhouette of his fedora in the driver's window.

Had he seen my private Santa Ana benediction?

No, that was my moment. Not his, not anybody's. He wouldn't steal the effects.

What did he want at this hour?

My hat under my arm, I marched up to the open car window. His head was lolling awkwardly, in the manner of someone desperate not to be caught napping. So he hadn't seen me.

'Pretty late hours you cops work.'

He stirred, blinked and looked up at me. He coughed as if to assert he had been awake the whole time but his husky voice gave him away. 'Where the hell have you been?'

'Picture house. Then took an evening stroll, followed by a couple of cocktails.'

Lauder decided not to pursue it and got out of the car. He looked me up and down. 'Kind of dressed up for a date on your lonesome. How's the homework?'

'Slow progress.' If he actually came into my room, he'd soon realize I had got rid of all the papers. And if he got mad and poked around, he might discover Beatty's cards and the car key in the cheap purse I'd bought to replace Violet's.

Stay in control.

'Want me to run an errand tomorrow?'

245

Please not tonight, anything but that.

'Yeah. Minnie Groader has places to go, people to see. First thing. Figure that's around eleven, for you.'

'What?'

Minnie Groader!

Lauder leant against his bonnet, crossing his legs. He looked me in the eye. 'Don't dress so fancy. Minnie's desperate, as I recall?' The sarcasm was obvious.

'You found Caziel?'

He peered into my face. 'Who's asking?'

'Oh, I get it. The big lure.' Hairs stood up on the back of my neck.

He noticed my surliness. 'We have a deal. You do what I say, when I say. No questions. Not like you've got anything better to do.'

My own investigation, for starters.

I would have the last word. The new me would. 'Some deal.'

It was dark, but was that a small smile on Lauder's normally straight mouth? He looked aside for a second. 'Make sure you're ready.'

45

The mid-morning sun was already like an oven. I'd overdone the make-up and cheap scent, and my skin was starting to sweat. Going as Minnie Groader meant wearing my old blue dress. I plonked on Alberta's hat. It stank of smoke from the fire.

I hadn't dared creep out to Tina's to call Beatty and fill her in on my conversation with Joyce. That would have to wait.

There was a rap on the door. Eleven on the dot.

Well, Lauder was a stickler for timekeeping.

An unlit cigarette dangled from his mouth as he stood in the doorway. Cool as a cucumber. He looked me up and down and gave an affirmative grunt. 'You look the part. Good.'

I nodded, suddenly nervous.

'All right. You ready?'

'You tell me. Last time I was Minnie Groader, I didn't know what I was walking into but at least I had a weapon.'

'Let's go.' Lauder turned away.

Lauder kept his eyes on the road. We drove in silence, the odd couple on a bizarre mission together. I asked, 'Aren't all detectives supposed to have a partner anyway?'

'Sick leave.' He gave a mind-your-own-business grunt.

That, and the knot in my stomach, put an end to the small talk.

The journey seemed to go on forever. Finally, a drab suburban stretch turned into an industrial zone. There was no traffic, no pedestrians. I peered out as we passed lumberyards and depots selling sanitary ware, sand, cement and building supplies. The places that pop up to serve a hungry, ever-expanding city but that can be ripped down fast. Factories and warehouses that the war had laid waste to still lay empty, with broken windows and boarded-up gates. We passed a car pound where turn-of-the-century motorcars were stacked high like dead bats in a belfry, the soft tops hanging down like decaying wings on rusting metal skeletons.

Finally the car slowed down. Just before a dead end, a strip of painted beige warehouses edged the road.

Lauder pulled up in front of a large truck parked at the side of the road. It was covered with thick dust as if it hadn't been driven for years. He looked at me. 'Get out, turn around and go left. You'll see three warehouses. Head for the one in the middle. *Jackson's Linoleum*. Go in, and announce yourself. Say you're here for work.'

'What?'

'You heard. And use your eyes and ears. Note anything that strikes you.'

'What kind of work?'

'Use your imagination.'

'Sounds like fun. So long.' I began to open the passenger door, my mouth dry. Great. Minnie would be stripping for creeps.

'Wait.' Lauder bent down and handed me something. It had been so long, I almost didn't recognize it.

Violet's handbag! Intact, musty and battered as ever.

'Open it.'

I opened the clasp. Inside, scrunched up in a ball, was Prison Governess Seldon's handkerchief with the violets on.

And another unexpected item.

Dede's pistol.

I met his dark eyes. 'You think I'm going to need this?'

He shrugged. 'If you don't want it, fine.'

I glowered at him and clutched the bag closer.

Lauder checked his watch. 'All right. Bang on time.' With that, he leant back, and stretched out on the front seat, adjusting his hat to lessen the glare from the sun.

A fine time for sunbathing.

I didn't want to go inside, but there was no choice. I hesitated.

'Beat it.' Lauder said, from under the hat.

I had no choice. I got out of the car for my rendezvous with a perv.

Around the corner, the three warehouses occupied a gravel yard divided by chicken wire. The yards of the end two were piled high with junk but the middle one had been cleared out at some point. Weeds inhabited the cracks in the tarmac, the only sign of life.

I entered the yard, wondering if eyes were already on me. It felt deserted, but there was no telling.

The main door was half open. I pushed it and stepped inside. A layer of dust already soiled my fine white gloves. 'Hello?' I called out, in Minnie's drawl. 'Anybody home?'

I stood on a bundle of unopened mail and peered into a gloomy corridor. Fishy. 'Hello?'

Silence. Keeping my hand on the pistol concealed deep within the purse, I edged down the dark corridor, doing my best to tread lightly on the concrete floor. There were a couple of doors on each side; both were padlocked. At the end, a sign announced *Main Office*. I approached. I went to knock. The door swung open at the touch of my hand.

Large metal-framed windows, divided into smaller square sections, lent the room sunlight. It was bright but cold, as the broken panes let in a permanent draft. The only other features were a high stack of rolls of colored and patterned linoleum, and a long wooden bench with nothing on it except a broken pencil. A stool with a broken leg lay on its side.

Pushed or kicked?

I paused, alert. Surely Lauder's information was old. No telephone anywhere. No sign of life. Certain no porno studio. Wait! The stack of linoleum rolls was propped up against two sides of some kind of inner office sectioned off in the corner of the room. The door must have been on the other side, not obvious. I approached cautiously. Something was in there! Music? It was a tinny buzzing sound, like a radio stuck out of range, in desperate need of tuning.

I crept up to the door, hidden by the end of the stack of rolls. Through the deeply marbled glass panel, I could just about make out a figure. A man's figure, dark-suited. He seemed to be dozing, head on desk. I called out, 'Hi, there. I got an appointment.'

I gritted my teeth, coughed loudly and approached the door. 'Hello?'

No answer. The buzzing noise was very strange.

I knocked again with my free hand. Nothing doing. I turned the metal handle and pushed the door.

A swarm of bluebottles buzzed angrily at me.

An appalling stench hit my nose. A putrid miasma of

rottenness. I gagged. Somehow I lifted the gun and pointed it. Nobody was moving. Certainly not the corpse slumped over the desk.

The back of his skull had been blown to bits, leaving a wide crater edged with dark, dried blood. His arms weren't visible, hanging down limply. What must have been the rest of the man's brains formed a violently splattered brown and black spongy mudpack on the back wall, with dried brown rivers flowing down, like open veins. A lank and mousy toupee lay on the desk, floating in a pool of dark blood. The same toupee I'd seen before.

Elmore Caziel.

Dead at his desk.

The impulse to heave threw me back.

Had Lauder sent me in here, knowing this all along? *Damn him!* Lauder was lazing in the sun outside. I wanted to run out to him, to yell at him for risking my life. But wait! Was this all a set-up? His way of pinning a murder on me?

I had a gun on me. Maybe Lauder had already used it on Caziel. That's why he wasn't here. Were the cops about to storm in?

Just run!

I backed out of the office. I had to flee. This would be my only chance to loosen their grip on me. Somehow, I had to escape the notice of Lauder.

No. Wait. Be reasonable.

Lauder had given me a gun to protect me. Maybe he just wanted to check if Caziel was really here. Maybe I was meant to just injure Caziel if he got nasty, so he could arrest him.

But I couldn't be a witness. Lauder knew that. So was he

killing two birds with one stone? Lauder could be finally done with me.

I was paralyzed, rooted to the spot. To bolt or not to bolt. To trust or be proved a fool.

Seconds going.

Going, going, gone.

If I was going to run, it had to be right now.

I swallowed hard. I'd choose trust, today. And maybe live to regret it tomorrow.

Eyes and ears. Find something. Brownie points.

Covering my nose with Seldon's hanky, and with the gun in the other hand, I went back in.

Caziel's feet were neatly pressed together under the desk, although his knees had fallen open at a strange angle. His dapper shoes were sprayed with fine blood spatter.

Bluebottles bounced up, their feasting disturbed. The more blasé among them didn't rise from the wound.

This was not a fresh killing. I'd seen one of those firsthand in London and would never forget it. Billy's eyes. Scarlet, glistening, new blood.

Suicide? Surely his head would be flung back?

I looked around for any sign of the weapon, on the desk or the floor.

Nothing.

Caziel and his ilk would always have plenty of enemies. Someone could have forced him to shoot himself and then shoved his face onto the desk.

No briefcase, no possessions. I approached the side of the desk. Flies circled around my face. I waved them off. I would have to drop either the hanky or the gun to feel inside Caziel's pockets. I slid the gun back in the purse. Through the hanky, I took a deep breath then bent down and slid my hand into each of his inside pockets. His hands hung low between his legs, near his dick. Revolting. It was odd, confirming my thought he'd been positioned. Directly beneath his hands, a pool of blood had formed. It could only mean one thing.

He had been shot in the genitals.

I tried to stop my thoughts bouncing around. I forced myself back to the task, shut my eyes and plunged my hand into all visible pockets.

A few dimes, a lighter. Nothing of significance.

Time to go. I moved towards the door.

Wait! There was a tiny shred of something cream and fluffy, stuck between an edge of linoleum and the plinth. It was too clean, out of place amidst the grime.

I kneeled down and plucked it out of the crack.

A feather, silky and fragile. I slipped it into my purse.

I finally left the office, and as soon as I stepped into the larger work areas, the nausea got the better of me. I heaved, vomit splashing the base of a linoleum roll.

I felt a hand on my shoulder. I glimpsed a white hand.

Lauder.

I glanced around, through retches.

He held a gun in his hand. Had he been covering me the whole time?

46

'You knew he was there, didn't you? You sent me in there,' I mumbled, my legs jelly, wobbling towards the rear passenger door. My only desire was to curl up like a baby. I slid in and pulled the door shut, collapsing on the seat.

Lauder got in and slammed the door.

He turned on the engine. 'Didn't know the asshole was shot to pieces!'

I said, 'He could have killed me...somebody could have...I wouldn't have stood a chance in there.'

Lauder spun around. 'Shut up!' Suddenly he began to slap the steering wheel hard. 'Fuck, fuck, fuck!'

I slowly sat back up, confused. I'd never seen him lose it. Now he was punching the living daylights out of the front passenger seat. His rage abated. He cursed, and swerved the car around the truck, the wheels crunching on gravel. He checked on me once in the rear mirror. His eyes were like steel.

He and his temper tantrum could stuff it. It was hardly my fault Caziel was dead. I wouldn't tell him about the feather. Lauder didn't deserve clues. Caziel's death meant one person off a long list of people who were after me. Who gave a shit if the killer got justice or not? Not me. I should be sending the killer a gift basket and a big bouquet.

Good riddance to bad rubbish.

I yanked off the gloves, my hat, anything that the stale stench of death might have permeated. Had I left any trace of myself there? No, I had worn the gloves. That had been

Lauder's instruction. So he hadn't wanted evidence of me there, either.

Then I sank back into the seat, my breathing slowly becoming controllable.

'Want some?'

A silver flask appeared, offered by Lauder's hand stretching backwards. I sat up and took it. 'Thanks.' I unscrewed the lid, sniffing before I drank.

Brandy.

I gulped it down, spilling some down my chin.

So what.

I glugged more. I lay back, shutting my eyes again, willing away the image of a rotten skull. 'That's why you let me have a weapon. An untraceable weapon. I could have been killed!'

'But you weren't.' Lauder snapped. 'What did you see?'

'You saw it yourself, didn't you? A carcass and bluebottles.'

He shot me a look via the mirror to shut up. 'I mean, any clues? You were in there longer than me.'

'A bench, a chair on the floor. Could have been a fight. Nothing in the office.'

Lauder drove on in silence.

After a couple of miles, we passed a small painted chapel. An old lady was tending the strips of flowerbeds edging the grassy yard. The dahlias, hydrangeas and late summer roses were soothing after the horrors in the warehouse.

I said, 'Aren't you supposed to report murders?'

'He can rot in there.' But his eyes glanced at the chapel and then he added, 'Somebody will find him soon enough. And you won't mention it to anyone, either.'

'You think I'm nuts?' I glared at him.

But how I'd love to tell June and Dede. I hoped in time they'd read about it. I hoped it would make June feel safer, it could aid her healing a little. The thought calmed me down somewhat. 'At least he can't do any more harm to girls like my friend, or produce any more sleazy publications.'

Some kind of errand girl I was turning out to be. I felt bleak, a million miles away from Elvira Slate.

Lauder cleared his throat. 'Types like Caziel don't stay out of trouble for long.' His voice had a more gentle tone.

'You got any idea who did it?' I asked. He thought for a moment, then shook his head.

Had Lauder wanted *me* to murder Caziel? Had he set me up? Was that what Dede's pistol was really for? Or had Lauder killed Caziel before I got there? The corpse had been there for a while.

None of these theories felt right. Why the tantrum? Why force me to wear gloves?

Lauder lifted his hat for a brief moment to wipe sweat from his brow. I blinked the vile images away, taking another swig from the flask I hadn't handed back.

The image of Caziel's red eyes bored into my eyeballs. I saw the rotting and gnarled crater in his skull. I wouldn't forget that anytime soon.

47

Back at the Astral, in my gloomy room, I slumped on the divan. I still held Violet's purse, and the purse still contained Dede's pistol. Lauder hadn't asked for it back. An error? Or a test?

I opened the bag, examining the pistol. Fine lines but chunky. It lay in my hand, a pearly, ladylike killing machine.

It was mine until Lauder demanded it back, as he surely would. Until then, it was a form of protection, a form of power. Something to run with, something to shoot my brains out with, if it came to it.

Never the noose.

Absentmindedly, I opened the chamber.

A single bullet. Just *one*.

Lauder had sent me in to Caziel's with a highly limited means of protecting myself. Another little joke? But now at least I had a gun and that counted for a lot.

I'd never bought ammunition in my life but until he collected it again, maybe I would start stocking up.

I had a long hot shower, standing in the primrose washtub, letting the water pound on my face. The smell of the citronella soap eased the memory of the stench that still made my tummy feel queasy.

Doing Lauder's bidding had rid me of one of my enemies but I had wasted time trying to find Rhonda. I hadn't let Beatty know what was going on. That job had to be the first in the line.

The bathroom was totally steamed up by the time I stepped out of the tub. I smeared a clear patch in the mirror.

Dark rings, white skin. I was the cadaver.

'About time. I was beginning to think you'd had a change of heart.' Beatty's voice sounded relieved. I stood by the pay phone in Tina's. I quickly explained two Zombies with a secret ingredient had kept me up late, and I'd been sleeping off the effects for most of the day. 'I found out Darlene had a long-term lover. Olive Harjo. They'd hang out at Joyce's club. So did Shimmer and Rhonda. So they could have known each other, but Joyce didn't know if they did.' I told her Joyce was even part of the plan for the girls' new start and was as surprised as anyone about the overdose. I didn't need to mention I recognized a certain saxophonist, so didn't.

Beatty hadn't heard of Olive Harjo but she agreed visiting her was a good idea and I should go right away. 'Find out what was behind Darlene's trip to The Flamayon Hotel. Find out if she was using heroin again. Grief could make her wanna spout forth.'

I told her I'd do my best. I hung up, only to see a tall man standing behind me. I assumed he wanted to use the telephone. 'All yours.' I said, stepping aside.

'I don't want to make a call, Goldilocks. I just want to talk to you.' His velvety face split into a grin revealing square, ivory teeth. 'Why don't you and me sit down and get to know one another.'

I'd never seen him before in my life. He was dapper in a crisp, pale gray suit and pale green shirt, flattering his rich warm skin. His tie was dark red with a fine woven diamond pattern in gray and green. His brown hat was edged with thick gray ribbon. Overall, he was well turned out, but in a less exuberant way than some of the neighborhood guys in their baggy zoot suits and gold chains. He was definitely easy on the eye.

'You've got the wrong blonde, mister.' I smiled sweetly. I knew I was a novelty attraction in these parts, but most guys either snuck a quick glance or ignored me. This one was the first guy to actually hit on me and rippled with confidence. As nice as he looked, what good would that do me?

We were alone in the coffee shop. Even Sandy, who normally buzzed around the place, seemed to have gone. If he wanted to buy me a drink, maybe I should let him. Spending a little time looking into these big eyes on the wide, high cheekbones couldn't hurt. I hadn't actually been inside a local bar yet, for fear of talk getting back to Lauder. But there was something about this man that could encourage me to risk it.

'I'm Elvira Slate. You are?'

'Clarence Johnson.' He smiled at me. He wasn't malicious or friendly. He was genuinely amused. Amused – but with an edge.

Clarence. The *Mr. Clarence*? It suddenly dawned on me. Now I knew exactly who he was – the other guy up the telegraph pole near Caziel's dive. Now he was out of his telephone man overalls, he looked very different. I suppose I did, too. The last time he saw me I was in a stained negligee and handcuffs.

It explained the confidence too. He knew perfectly well I could call no shots.

I didn't have to ask, but did all the same. 'Lauder's buddy?'

His pearly whites flashed again, now with the gleam of sarcasm. 'Me and you have got some catching up to do.'

I put my hands on my hips, acting tough. 'Is it all right with him I talk to you?'

He leant forward. 'It's all right with me. Look at you. All skin and bone. Why don't I treat you to a banana sundae? They're real good here. Or are you feeling kind of sick? Something turned your stomach? Seen too many dead bodies lately?'

So Lauder had filled him in already.

I glared back at him. 'You know the latest gossip. Say, as you're asking, I wouldn't mind a drink. A real one. I had a real rough day.' Seeing as Lauder was behind this latest rendezvous, I would definitely take advantage of Clarence's company to enjoy a local bar.

'Here's just fine. And I can smell liquor on your breath.'

'Are you a cop?'

Good cop, bad cop. All the same to me.

'Sit down, Goldilocks.' He jerked his head at a corner table. It was the end of a row of narrow tables that lined the far wall, away from the window. Each table was covered with gingham wax cloth, edged with two banquettes covered in cracked dark red leather. I chose one facing the window.

Clarence took the opposite banquette. There was still no sign of Sandy. I wondered then if he'd asked her to leave.

'Coffee would be nice.'

'That can wait.'

'So no coffee. No liquor. What's this about?'

After a while, Clarence cleared his throat. 'You know, Lauder picked up Caziel's henchman, Jose. That's how he knew where to find him.'

'So?' Indifference could mask an unsettled feeling. The sense I was about to be played. Was Clarence the good cop? Lauder who stayed *schtum*, and gave the orders, but Clarence softened the edges?

'Caziel was obsessed with finding Minnie, or so Jose said. So we figured you could pay him a little visit, surprise him.'

'Why didn't Lauder just go there and arrest him? I'm useless, can't take the stand.' *I genuinely did want to know the answer.*

Clarence read my mind. 'But you are handy for getting him to talk, thinking we have a witness, even if we don't. Caziel had no reason to believe you aren't Minnie. He didn't know about your fake identity.'

'Talk? You mean confess to the porn books? His word against yours, surely, without evidence. I didn't see anything inside, just a load of linoleum rolls. Lauder knows all this anyway. Waste of time. Yours too, by the way.'

His eyes met mine. I raised my brows, as if impatient. He definitely was weighing something up. Finally, he leant back and folded his arms. 'Randall – I mean Lauder – doesn't want you to know any of what I'm about to say. He wants to keep you in the dark. Well, I don't, so pay attention. But this conversation stays between me and you.'

My eyes met his. Here was a stranger to me, going behind Lauder's back? Three words came to mind. Gift horse and mouth. I sat up, totally alert. 'Sure.'

'So your arson attempt worked. Destroyed everything. Lauder and his partner Stan Perrin were down on the porn stuff. Caziel's smutty books travel far and wide, and they were planning to bust him. Then something else happened.'

I stared at him. 'Stan Perrin's the one on sick leave?'

Clarence frowned. 'No. He's dead. Jeez. Is that what Lauder told you?'

I nodded but my mind was absorbing every new fact like a dry sponge flung into the LA river. *Dead.*

'Like I said, he sure doesn't want you to know anything. The whole point of the surveillance job was to catch Caziel and a certain bent Vice cop together. The fire ruined that chance, too, because Caziel went into hiding. Just luck that Lauder picked up Jose.'

'What do you mean, a bent cop?' Wasn't Lauder himself a bent cop? Even sheltering me was morally dubious, let alone everything Shimmer had shared with me.

'Another cop in Vice has been paid off by Caziel. Lauder's partner, Detective Stan Perrin, was found dead at the wheel of his car, shortly after he called Lauder saying he'd got a new lead on Caziel, and it didn't look good for the LAPD. Next thing, Stan's dead.'

I froze, processing this.

'Next, a friend of mine gets picked up, with a gun in his trunk. Matches the weapon used on Perrin. Now Caziel's dead, my guy is facing the death penalty.'

I tried to fit things together. 'So the bent cop framed your friend?'

'Correct. When this cop arrests my friend, that's when Randall...when Lauder smells a rat. He keeps eyes on him, gets on his side even though they aren't exactly work buddies, convinces him he believes his story. It's only a matter of time before he visits Caziel. That's why we were lying in wait when Minnie flounces in. I want to prove my friend's innocence, and Randall wants true justice for Perrin. The Murder Squad buys the cop's story, so nobody's looking for Perrin's real killer. A black man is an easy target. My friend had a few brushes with the law when he was young, but what black kid hasn't in this town? In this nation? He's married, three kids. The last thing the LAPD want is to point a finger at their own.'

True justice. Clarence's version of Lauder had some honor and guts. I had got in the way of their attempt to corner the cop with Caziel, their only chance of helping the framed guy. I fiddled with Violet's purse, realizing Clarence hadn't demanded it back yet.

'Even if your friend was framed, how do you know it was Caziel who killed Perrin in the first place? Even if you'd caught him alive, with pornography, how could you pin the murder on him? He would never have confessed to murder. And the bent cop could just deny it all.'

'Lauder's idea. Along the lines of rats leaving a sinking ship. As I said, that's where you came in today.'

Lauder would turn the screw on Caziel using my identification of him as a threat. The bent cop would have to confess and Lauder would expose the cop to free Clarence's friend.

But with Caziel dead, none of this could happen.

Clarence looked down, deep in thought. Even lowered, his lids had a slight crease in them.

I absent-mindedly picked at Minnie's remnants of pink nail polish. Cheap stuff and one coat. Flakes flew off like miniscule confetti. Realizing what I was doing, I quickly swept it off the table onto my lap before Clarence noticed.

'So you think the bent cop got to Caziel first? Tying up loose ends?'

'No. Somebody else must have got to Caziel. Like I said, Lauder has been keeping tabs on the cop the whole time since Perrin was shot.'

Tabs? Lauder kept tabs on me, this cop, and probably a whole heap of people. He couldn't watch us all, all the time.

'Who, then?'

'You tell me.'

I squirmed in my seat to wipe away the sweat now running down my back. 'Surely that Jose guy could talk? He just has to say his boss killed Stan Perrin and that his boss was working with the bent cop.'

'What planet are you from? A spic gunman versus a white cop? Turns out Jose was kept in the dark. Didn't squeal under pressure, and had no reason not to.'

I could see it. Jose getting a good pummeling from Lauder.

With one hand, Clarence pulled a box of chewing gum from his pocket, and popped one in his mouth. As an afterthought, he said, 'Want one?'

I shook my head. 'How do you know your friend was framed? Is there any way he could be involved?'

Clarence didn't answer for a while. 'He's innocent. I know it like I know the sun shines today. Like I know it's your fault he will die an innocent man.'

He stood up.

Conversation over.

The fire had helped June but triggered a horrendous sequence of events for Clarence's friend. I wanted to help June and find Rhonda, not get pushed into a boiling vat of guilt. I stood up too, protesting. 'Look, I went to Caziel's to help someone, not ruin some guy's life. How could I know it would end up like this?'

He was looking out onto the street. He scoffed. 'Well, now you do.'

No answer to that. Even doing good, I managed to wreck things.

I watched Clarence's jaw relentlessly chewing, a sure sign of anger. It reminded me of Lauder's muscle twitch. From everything I had heard, there had to be a close bond between them.

Clarence resented me now, probably even more than Lauder did. To Lauder, I was a means to an end. A useful tool in getting true justice, whatever that was in his book, for a colleague who was already dead. Maybe some other tasks, before he was through with me. But to Clarence, I was the reason his friend languished inside and would face the chair. I was useless now but at least he could make me feel guilt. And he wanted me to take a form of responsibility. That made me realize he still saw some degree of humanity in me. Lauder just thought I was beyond redemption.

'What's your friend's name?'

I saw the cold glare of his eyes, weighing up if I was worth telling.

'Arnie...Arnold Moss.'

Wait! I knew the name. I dredged my memories. The face in the paper, in Mikey's bar?

'What about the cop? Do you know his name?'

'Jim Fraser. Vice Squad, like Lauder.'

Jim Fraser. The Jim in the pub that Lauder held back from hassling me? I asked, 'Is he a big guy, a drunk?'

'Never saw the guy. But yes, likes the booze. Why?'

Jim's abusive rant. It all made sense. That was why Lauder

was there. He was watching him, the cop who worked with his partner's killers. Keeping tabs.

'I think I know him.'

Clarence turned to face me. 'You know Jim Fraser?'

I explained to Clarence that a drunk called Jim had pounced on me in Mikey's, thinking I was a newspaper girl. That he was shouting about a cop killer facing justice. That Lauder had held him off me.

Clarence listened intently. 'You saying you met Lauder before we caught you at Caziel's?'

I nodded. 'Yes, the day before. Destiny laying it on thick. Did Lauder tell you all about my past?'

Our eyes met again. Clarence's seemed less hostile. 'I got the lowdown. Said you're a killer.'

'For the record, I shot two men to protect somebody and save myself.'

Clarence shrugged. 'I don't know anything about you. You should feel bad about a man going down, but maybe you don't.'

I didn't answer.

He added, 'Don't say a word of this to Lauder. Not if you know what's good for you.'

'If it makes you feel any better, he owns my life. I don't have any say. It's not death row, but I've been close.'

Then he did something that shocked me. He held out his hand. To shake mine? Why? I had ruined everything, in his eyes. I wasn't used to being treated like an equal by anyone. Even so, I slipped mine in his. It was a warm and solid grasp.

'How do you know Lauder?' I asked, seizing the opportunity for information now we were on handshaking terms.

'We go back.'

'Funny, only last night I saw a picture in a magazine of Lauder, with his fiancée. I forget her name. Lara, or something? She's pretty. You know her? Oh, what's her name?'

Clarence let go of my hand as fast. He laughed. 'I don't blame you, asking about Lauder. I'll tell you one thing. He's all right.'

I scoffed. 'Sure. He nearly fed me to the lions.'

Clarence shot me a patronizing look. 'Lions? Is this the savannah, Goldilocks? Are we in Africa? No. You're alive and well, thanks to Lauder.'

He seemed to hesitate, before fumbling in his pocket. He pulled out a card and held it out to me. I scanned it. *Clarence Johnson. Principal and Educator. Johnson's Academy for Gifted Children.*

I looked back up at him. 'So you aren't a cop? You run a school?'

'Uh-huh. I teach Arnold Moss' kids.'

48

I sat in the front seat of the car, the engine still off.

The quicksand feeling. Framed, to rot away for something you didn't do. I had feared execution, too. Paranoia had eaten away at me, with the fear that halfway through my sentence a very different decision would be made about my treasonous behavior. Or my enemies outside, the ones who had pinned gunrunning on me, would somehow implicate me in other crimes. Wasted years as a sitting duck, knowing the hunters were out there.

The whole time, dreading the noose.

I tried to banish the thought. Too late. My breathing became shallow, and I couldn't swallow.

You're fine. You're safe.

Arnold Moss's face came to me. The hunters had already seized him. He was as good as dead, banged up on death row.

He'd get the electric chair, a bunch of strangers watching. He'd go to his death knowing he was being murdered by the state. What kind of death is that? What kind of god can you pray to or curse when that happens? What kind of forgiveness is possible?

Clarence had come to me wanting to tell me something, that in his book, I should feel guilty about. He'd wanted to see if the bungling killer under Lauder's control had some remnant of a conscience. He put me in the picture, behind Lauder's back, laying my culpability on thick.

Did he come with the intention of guilt-tripping me into doing something about it? I doubted it. He didn't know I had a gun. He didn't know, until halfway through our conversation, that I could recognize Jim Fraser. He left as he arrived, content he'd made me acknowledge my responsibility.

But I knew exactly who Fraser was, and I had a gun. Killing Fraser wouldn't help anybody, least of all me. But could I get to him and threaten him?

If Lauder was glued to Fraser, as Clarence claimed, it made any intervention even more difficult.

If I was going to do something, I'd have to do it soon – before Lauder came to collect the gun. Next time he came by with some new errand, I could pretend to be sick. Send him off to get a doctor, then slip out... And do what, exactly?

Impossible.

49

A narrow track meandered up through the hills. Crickets sang in the tall grasses that gently rippled in the late afternoon breeze. The vegetation was tatty and wild up here. No lush gardens, no teams of Mexicans manicuring lawns, as at the white wedding cake style Spanish villas dotted around the lower slopes. This was the wild terrain for a tougher type of inhabitant. The tan skeleton of a dead banana tree, self-seeded from one of the nicer patches, stood upright, its shaggy leaves pointing like a signpost.

This way, civilization. That way, artists.

I marched on, thirsty. It was remote and I only had twittering birds for company, and maybe unseen snakes in the long grasses. There could be a certain appeal in living up here. Soon the sweat dripped down my back, and the suit felt itchy. As I tripped over hard clumps and my calves got scratched by dried-out undergrowth, the appeal soon faded.

Visiting Olive Harjo, the artist lover of Darlene Heymann, now felt as awkward as hell. Should I follow Joyce's suggestion to bluff it as an art collector? If Olive was distraught, she might not even let me in.

I decided to play it by ear.

I was about to give up when a wood cabin came into view. It was a ramshackle affair, a rug thrown over the wooden beams of the wide porch. Large cacti and succulents grew around the base, their strange blue foliage and prickly globes curling like waves around a wooden ship. Some linen was drying on a makeshift line tied onto two yucca tree trunks. A smaller hut, with an open skylight, was just about visible beyond olive trees. Whoever lived here surely had to walk the track I'd taken from the road. Perhaps at the time the cabin was built, the track was wider. But the fact it could have been let to grow over was interesting in itself. Olive and Darlene liked to live literally off the beaten track.

Further back on the porch, a striped hammock was tied between two posts, swinging gently. Someone was home. A breath of smoke danced over the fabric. I called out loudly. 'Miss Harjo? Hello?'

The hammock continued to sway as a long, slim, brown arm appeared, holding a reefer. The nails on the dark tapered fingers were unpainted. They gestured me in.

I made my way up the steps onto the porch. The occupant of the hammock was a Native American woman, about fifty, lying in a long woven shirt. Her thick hair was held back by a woven green scarf. Her expression, as she surveyed me, was one of infinite sadness. 'What do you want?'

'My name's Elvira Slate. I'm an investigator.' No point beating about the bush. 'My condolences for your loss. Joyce told me.' If Olive thought I was part of the dyke demimonde, we might get somewhere faster.

She swung herself heavily out of the hammock. 'A pretty name. Sounds like a bird. What does it mean?'

'I don't have a clue.'

'You do not know the meaning of your own name?'

I do, actually. To me, it means being myself.

'No, as a matter of fact.'

She confronted me. 'What do you want?'

'I'm trying to find somebody. Thought you could help.'

'Me? No. I can't help. I want to be left alone.'

'Hold on, you don't know who it is yet.'

'Rhonda. She was the lover of Ellen Cranston.'

I gasped. 'You know her? Do you know where she is?'

Harjo's eyes narrowed to virtual slits. 'No. I do not know her very well. But I know they killed her, too.'

I froze. 'What do you mean?'

'Darlene was murdered.' She turned away.

I called out after her. 'Wait! Why do you think it was murder? Who do you think killed Darlene?'

Olive Harjo stopped at the door. She surveyed me from under heavy eyelids, weighing up if I was worth the bother. 'He killed them all. Otto Heymann.'

50

I stood awkwardly in the middle of the room while Olive made a jug of lemon juice in the kitchen area. 'Why would Otto Heymann want to kill Darlene, his own kid?' My voice faltered.

The cozy feel of the place eased any apprehension. Vibrant rugs covered the wooden floor. Smaller cacti flourished along shelves and surfaces in colorful Mexican pottery. It felt neat and clean. Cut wildflowers sat in jam pots. The kitchen area was at the far end – a rustic wooden table and an old stove with a pile of logs next to it. Unlit candles stood on ledges and surfaces. Maybe the electricity wasn't rigged up.

I felt something staring at me and looked around. Nothing. Something made me look up. A large green parrot sidled along a central beam, almost directly overhead, its beady eye on me. I moved to one side but the bird hopped along the beam, following me.

Olive answered as if she was musing to herself. 'Strange, for a father to hate a child, no? But it is the purest, coldest hate. He cut her off. Him, the richest man in town. Why? Because she was an embarrassment to him. Yes, she had problems, when she was young. She never fit in her family. So she rebelled. But then she grew up, found her passion. Photography, her films.'

This didn't seem like a motive for murder. 'How did you learn Darlene was dead?'

'When she did not come home to celebrate, I know.' Olive motioned for me to sit down and wandered over to the far side of the room. She filled a jug from the faucet.

'Celebrate?'

'Her big chance. Directing her first movie. She had gone that day to sign an agreement. She had a meeting but she never came back. I read the paper but I already know.'

Movie? Directing? Another thing left out of the obituaries.

Olive brought the jug of lemon juice on a tray. She poured out a glass and handed it to me before sitting cross-legged in a wide leather chair.

'He had her killed to stop a movie going ahead?'

Olive tutted. 'Of course. He was scared of her success. She was going to the lawyer's office, but she never gets there. She dies in that place. It is proof they caught her on the way.'

'She wasn't alone.'

'I know. Frankie, he was driving her. He stays with us sometimes. Poor Frankie. So young.' So Frank was acting as driver to an appointment with a lawyer.

'You know who the lawyer is?' I asked.

'Frederick Lyntner. She was meeting him at his office. Maybe the screenwriter, Martell, too. I do not remember her second name.'

I made a mental note. *Martell.*

'Did Darlene know Martell?'

'Not well.'

Troy might have the lowdown on Martell. He certainly knew enough male screenwriters. I turned back to Olive. 'But if she left here to go Downtown, Heymann – or his men – would have literally had to have stopped her in her tracks? How would he physically get her to The Flamayon?'

'Why you ask these stupid questions? You never hear of gun to the head? Drugging somebody? The woman, this Ellen

Cranston, could be already drugged! I tell you, these men, they can do what they want!'

It felt like a crazy conspiracy theory. Still, it was the only lead I had.

'What was the movie about?'

'The true story of Tatiana Spark's life.'

I looked blank.

Olive was patient. 'She is an actress, from the silent period, signed to the Heymann Studio. A long time ago. She always liked Darlene, from childhood. She wanted to make a film about her life, to tell the real truth. And she wanted Darlene to direct it. A wonderful chance! Darlene even swallowed her pride and asked her father for money, to even give them a producer to help. No, he said. You are wasting your time. I forbid you to do this. Another failure, you shame the family again? She had no place to do this, no way to embarrass him. His words. She came home so upset. He cut her off, and he still thinks he can tell her what to do?'

I sat back, trying to absorb as many of Olive's words as possible.

Olive sipped her juice. 'Men like Otto Heymann, they own everything and everybody in this city. So he gets his people to kill her. Now, Darlene is free from them all. She escaped him. And she is still with me. I am Muscogee. I live by my own rules.'

'So this Tatiana Spark was close to Darlene?'

Olive nodded, holding her drink to her mouth, her eyes wide.

'How well do you know Tatiana Spark?'

'I never meet her. She is Darlene's friend, that's all. But I admire her. After she stopped acting, she travelled the world, before the war. Egypt, Greece, all the ancient worlds. Now, the gossips did not know this. They say she is a recluse, a lonely woman. They make up lies, all lies.'

So this was the drive behind the film. A last chance for Spark to tell the *real truth*.

'Do you know what the true story is?'

'No. It was a big secret. Darlene is not allowed to know, not before she sign the agreement.'

I nodded. 'Did Heymann know about you and Darlene?'

'Maybe. I don't care.'

According to Olive's own theory, she could be in danger, particularly if she made a habit of accusing Heymann to anyone who would listen.

'Was Darlene still in touch with her mother?'

Olive looked away. 'Yes. But it was forbidden. Nancy Heymann is a weak woman. She does not fight for her daughter. You know, the son is stupid but he will take over the business. Darlene would be so much better than him.'

A large canvas of a naked woman hung on an easel. The likeness was incredible; obviously Darlene, with her wayward eyes. Her naked body was very voluptuous. Now she was reclining, in a classical toga pinned by an ornate gold brooch. One pearly breast lolled out. The backdrop was some kind of ancient setting. A porcupine was strolling past a pile of marble columns in the background. The oils smelt fresh. The colors were rather garish and lurid, but there was skill in the work. Art appreciation was not my strong point.

Olive said, 'You like it?'

'Very nice. Why the porcupine?'

'Darlene's guide. I paint this the night she died. I will never sell it.' Olive got up and wandered over to the painting. She traced her finger along Darlene's cheek.

'How did you two meet?' I asked.

'Through another artist, Blandine Hundley. You know her? Beautiful work.'

I said I didn't. 'Had Darlene made many films?'

Her eyes flashed with irritation. 'She could do it as well as any man. Hollywood is full of boys who get all the chances. Darlene had real talent. Photography, art, beautiful work. And she knew Ida Lupino. She was going to ask her to guide her.'

Ida Lupino? *The* Ida Lupino? My ivory blonde fairy godmother who also grew up in Camberwell before she moved to Hollywood?

'She knows Tatiana Spark, too?' Ida, Martell, Darlene. There seemed quite a gang of women ready to get on board with this film.

Olive studied me. 'Nobody can help you get justice. Forget Rhonda.'

She had it very neatly worked out. She'd been gabby with me, a stranger, about the supposed secret. Was she hiding something herself?

I had to look at all angles, turn over all stones. Maybe Olive herself could have carried out the murder, jealous about Darlene's new direction. She could have arranged a lesbian orgy and played on her lover's weaknesses. Maybe she'd taken Rhonda and buried her up here in the canyon. Or perhaps it had all been accidental. Maybe Darlene and Olive like wild parties now and then and it had all gone wrong. Pointing the finger at bad Daddy was a cover-up.

A hell of a lot of maybes. I would play along for now. 'The

way I see it, three people are already dead, and one more could be in danger. If what you're saying is true, it's all to stop a film being made. Heymann should pay.'

Olive smiled, with something like pity in her eyes. 'Darlene would like you. So, for her sake as well as yours, stop. Stop this craziness.'

51

Sunset Boulevard welcomed me back like a noisy family. It was good to be far from the isolation in the canyon and Olive's angry sadness. I felt my shoulders relax.

Olive had messed with my instincts, which were now hopelessly muddled. But on balance, surely she was no killer. Just full of sorrow, her tongue loose, as Beatty had predicted.

But if Olive's murderous daddy theories were true, I'd hit the ultimate dead end. Otto Heymann was a big shot, with power over the law. Snooping around drawing attention to myself was out. I would be up to my neck in more hot water in no time. If Otto Heymann had killed Darlene and Shimmer to get her out of his life once and for all, there was a good chance Rhonda was dead, and had been for a while.

But one thing rang true. Heymann's sabotage of Darlene's ambitions. Not through murder, but by cutting her off, refusing to help, shitting on her ambitions. Typical. A woman tries to break a barrier and the big boys' club closes her down.

An even tougher break if your own father runs the club.

Something about the family portrait spooked me. Darlene's total disengagement. She was a misfit, pure and simple. Born into the wrong family, one in which wives looked pretty and dumb and produced brats, and artistic and lesbian daughters were labeled oddballs, while incompetent sons were fed with the silver spoon. No wonder she rebelled, first with drugs, and then by doing her own thing. She'd have been better off having parents with less money and power. It sounded as if Tatiana

Spark had tried to help her, give her a leg up. It took another woman to do that.

Still, the simple fact that somebody else other than me thought the trio had been bumped off was a strange reinforcement of my own deeper convictions.

But I was no closer to finding Rhonda. My only lead had been supplied by a woman deranged by grief.

Give up!

I stopped at the Farmers Market and wandered around. A chubby man and his wife were shutting up their fruit stall, still loaded with large golden apples and dazzling oranges. Oranges were now my weakness, after years of bleeding gums from barren prison years. I approached the stall and asked the wife for some.

'How many?' The farmer's wife held up an empty paper bag.

'Five.' I paid for the oranges and wandered off to find a vacant table.

I sat down and peeled an orange. Nobody gave a damn; even Olive was closing the door. I was the only person who seemed to care. It would be so easy to walk away now.

Don't give up.

Until I found Rhonda, dead or alive, and until I knew for sure the deaths at The Flamayon were accidental, I couldn't rest.

And maybe, just maybe, in my own private way, I could make somebody pay.

I felt a sudden and unexpected rush of adrenaline.

The peeled orange was now just a baggy ball of soft, firm flesh. I bit into it. The juice was almost perfumed. It ran down my chin, but I didn't care. This was better than any drink. Wiping my face, I looked for somewhere with a phone booth.

A coffee shop occupied a corner plot in the market and was still open. I went inside and found the phone booth and called Beatty. Therese said she had gone for the day as one of the puppies looked sick and she and Mr. Falaise were very worried.

In a way, I was relieved I didn't have to speak to her. Beatty might advise me to stop in my tracks. Making accusations about Hollywood high society figures like Otto Heymann probably wasn't up her street.

Before I left the booth, I flicked through the phone book. The words were typed clearly enough. *Frederick Lyntner, Attorney-at-law*. I took a note of the number; I'd call him first thing. It had been a long day, and now I wanted to curl up in the comfort of my cozy wall bed.

Midnight, and something woke me up. A banging on the door. I hadn't got as far as the bed, I was asleep, fully dressed, on the divan.

Groggy, I moved towards the door and called out. 'Yes?'

'Open up,' Lauder barked. Of course, he was finally here to collect the gun. There was no way he'd forget about that for long.

'Give me a minute.'

'Now.' This time, he growled.

Fucking great.

I kicked Violet's purse under the divan, out of sight. Just in case he hadn't cottoned on yet.

Seconds later, I opened the door, and Lauder brushed past me, leaving a whiff of cedar cologne in his wake. He was unrecognizable in a black tuxedo, and a bow tie. It looked expensive, with satin edging. His hair was greased back, and he was closely shaved. I closed the door behind him.

'Coffee?' I murmured.

'No.'

For the first time, he was standing in my lowly room. His eyes cast around it, taking it all in – the bottle of brandy on the low table and a decaying sandwich next to the overflowing ashtray, and the bag of oranges, half of them on the carpet.

I was frankly embarrassed. 'I didn't have time to clean up.' As quickly, I regretted the words.

He pulled out his wallet and pulled out a wedge of dollars. 'In case you're running low. Enough for a movie twice a day and a takeout dinner.' He placed them on the side table.

The pile of notes looked about fifty dollars in five dollar bills. 'What the hell is this?'

'What does it look like? For groceries, movies. I don't give a damn. I'm going away for a little while. Leaving tonight. Any issues, talk to Malvin. He can get hold of Clarence Johnson. You don't know him. He's the only person you can contact in case of trouble. You do not call the LAPD. You call nobody else. But you aren't going to get in any trouble, are you?'

He didn't know Clarence had already given me his card. But Lauder was going away? A vacation with the deluded uptown fiancée?

'All right. Business or pleasure?'

'What?' He pulled a mind-your-own-business kind of face.

'Well, if you're on vacation, try and have a nice time!' I pulled a smart-alecky smile.

'Just finish that homework.' Lauder walked to the door. No mention of the gun. I willed him to get out without remembering. Then another thought shook me. Was he leaving the gun so I could protect myself in his absence?

He turned back to me. 'Don't stray too far,' was his parting shot.

And he was gone. With Lauder out of town, I had a few days to make my move on Fraser, whatever form that would take.

52

I fancied a large and leisurely breakfast at Tina's to set me up for the day. Fried beans, tomatoes and eggs washed down with coffee. The thought of it propelled me out of bed to shower.

It could be my last meal, after all.

I relished the chance to dress up again. Under Lauder's regime, these opportunities didn't come along that often. I picked out a cream dress with black ferns printed all over it, shiny black buttons in the shape of roses and a patent leather belt. I pinned on a black pillbox hat, and a red crepe jacket which matched my scarlet nails and lips.

Tina's was empty. Sandy, the young waitress, was wiping tables down. She broke into a smiled as I came in.

I wouldn't mention I'd been in yesterday, and she'd vacated the place the whole time I'd been with Clarence. She probably knew anyway.

I ordered my breakfast. 'No bacon or sausages. No meat.'

'Bacon and syrup? Can't tempt you a little bit, Miss?'

I shook my head.

'You're looking real elegant today, Miss. Going someplace nice?'

I did look the part. 'Downtown. Shopping. Maybe catch a movie.' The Downtown part was true – at least I hoped it was. 'That's nice,' she said. I couldn't imagine she gave a damn really.

I made for the phone booth and flicked through the book.

In seconds, I would be doing what Lauder had explicitly banned. Phoning Vice Squad.

I picked up the receiver and asked the operator to put me though.

Lauder was now away, but I wasn't calling to speak to him. I was calling for Jim Fraser.

His eyes were bloodshot and completely blank. Absolutely zero recognition. Jim Fraser growled, 'Said you got something for me?'

He was standing over me.

Fraser wore a lightweight suit with creases from overuse and under-washing, one hand in his pockets. Though he was presumably sober, his face was still blighted by red cheeks, the sign of a permanently angry man.

I was already sitting on a corner table in the coffee shop in Hotel Acacia when he'd wandered in, a fish out of water. I had chosen the hotel because it was another version of the Miracle Mile, full of clean-living career girls. My hope was that he wouldn't easily remember my face if he was surrounded by other women of similar age. On my way, I'd picked up some spectacles from an optical shop. The man had been surprised when I said I'd take the demonstration pair without prescription lenses. The specs were a heavy, horn-rimmed affair. They quite changed my face.

My strategy was flimsy as hell and relied on the big assumption that Fraser still had no idea Caziel was dead. On the telephone, I'd been suitably vague, telling him I'd got information on a crime he would pay good money for and he had to come alone. I hadn't given him a name, just said that I'd be wearing glasses.

I looked up and smiled sweetly. 'Why don't you sit down? You're gonna want to when you hear my news.'

Fraser hesitated, looking me over once again, his eyes roving over my body. I knew the game. He did it to assert power.

'My name's Muriel Seldon.' It was all I could come up with in the drive over here. 'You don't remember me, do you? A jerk of a cop nearly had me slung out of Mikey's but you came to my rescue, and ordered him to go easy on me. So when I got some interesting news you boys would like to know, you came to mind. Thought I could repay your kindness.'

'Yeah?' He was warming to me. I'd flattered his ego and he might have a deal on his hands. He sat down opposite me.

'Turns out we have a mutual friend.'

'Who?' He wasn't expecting this. His piggy eyes narrowed to slits.

'Elmore Caziel.'

It was like he'd been shot. He reeled back in his seat. His ruddy features turned green and his eyes narrowed.

I twisted the knife. 'Just so you know, some people are watching your every move, right now. In the coffee shop, in the lobby. You touch me, do anything sudden, one of them is going to walk out and make a call. Something's going to hit the newspapers that puts you in very hot water.'

The eyes didn't flinch. What had been interest in me had crystallized into pure hate. I went on. 'Elmore Caziel is a houseguest of one of my pals. Now, my friend is not exactly what you'd call a good host but he's very good at making people talk. Mr. Caziel has a lot to say, about you, and Mr. Arnold Moss, who finds himself detained in the county jail awaiting trial for a murder he didn't commit. Mr. Caziel has been...given the impression that if he squeals on you, he's free as a bird. Free to run and hide. His version of events is going to make a very interesting story in tomorrow's papers. We even promised him anonymity. But you'll have to explain to your bosses why somebody's accusing you of peddling smut and framing an innocent man.'

I leant forward. 'Now, seeing as I want to repay your kindness in taking such good care of me the other day, I'm giving you a chance to avoid all this. Nobody wants to embarrass the hard-working LAPD, do they? You're going to tell your superiors Arnold Moss is the wrong guy. You will shift the blame to Elmore Caziel. That's right. You will say that a little bird, maybe one of your C.I.s, told you Caziel dropped the gun in Moss's car. That Caziel's gone to ground but you're looking for him. Hate to break up the friendship with your sleazy pal, but it's your only choice. Your word against his.'

'Nobody will believe Caziel's word in the first fucking place.' He stood up, but he wasn't moving.

'That might be the case. Seems like Caziel believes in insurance. Did you know he had a hidden camera? That's right. He's got a snapshot of you, and it doesn't make a pretty picture. Now sit the fuck back down before my friends get sore.'

'Fucking bitch.' But he restrained himself, wary of non-existent eyes on him. Proof he was buying the charade. It was also proof that he did not know that Caziel was dead. He slumped back in his chair, as if he was relaxed.

'Bitch? Charming. I'm more like your goddamned fairy godmother. You get to free an innocent man and take down that sleazebag Caziel. And not a single one of your colleagues finds out you're a dirty backstabber. There's even a cherry on top. As soon as we hear Arnold Moss is a free man, I'll give you Caziel's whereabouts. When you arrest him, you get the glory.

Nobody will believe him if he tries to drag you down with him. Or you can make other plans for him. Trust me, he won't be going anywhere until we give him to you. Soon as I hear Moss is free, I'll leave a message for you here, at the front desk.'

'Who you working for?' He growled. Perspiration ran down his wide neck, leaving a snail's trail.

'Ain't your business. Caziel's scum of the earth. He's a cop killer.'

But so are you, for framing Moss. Why did you pick on him? He didn't do a damn thing. Hard-working man with a family to support. Doesn't that give you sleepless nights? I couldn't get it out of my mind, but then, I guess everybody's different. Maybe you're in the Klan.

I lit a cigarette.

He reached over for his drink, and downed it in one. Avoiding my eyes.

I exhaled into his face. 'You've got a simple choice to make. Your version of events gets out, or Elmore Caziel's beats you to it.'

53

After the meeting with Jim Fraser, I'd run to the car, whipped off the specs and the hat, and just driven around Downtown aimlessly. I kept on checking the rear mirror in case he was tailing me. For a while, a large black car took the same route as me. I couldn't make out the driver's face as the sun was too bright. A few minutes later, the car turned left and was gone.

My nervous imaginings had to be normal. I'd lost an enemy in Caziel but replaced him with a cop. The good news was Fraser was sober enough this time to absorb my ultimatum.

The bad news was that we sat long enough for him to commit every nook and cranny of my face to memory, even with the specs.

My plan would only hold if Fraser didn't want to chance it, and if nobody discovered Caziel's body in the meantime. I could safely bet Lauder wouldn't be telling anybody. And now Lauder was away. But if Fraser knew Caziel had holed up at the warehouse and went back to check, after meeting me, and discovered the body, then my plan would be blown to pieces.

If he bought my charade, Fraser would need to be very convincing to his superiors about the mystery informant's threat, about the 'fact' that Elmore Caziel killed Stan Perrin and framed Arnold Moss. And on top of all this, the prosecutor would have to buy it too, not just his buddies in Murder Squad, to go as far as releasing Moss. Lauder would be shocked by Fraser's announcement but if he was loyal to Clarence, he wouldn't challenge it. Clarence would pressure him to look the other way. He might suspect I was behind it, but he wouldn't tell Lauder. Anyone could see this was perhaps the first and last opportunity to get Arnold Moss out of jail, even if Fraser got off the hook. Lauder would have no choice but to make out he believed Fraser, even if that meant he lost out on 'true justice', because Fraser was accessory to Perrin's murder. The clock was ticking. If Caziel's body was found, it could all collapse.

I'd done my best, now it was up to the rest of the pieces to fall into place.

I wouldn't call Clarence. I shouldn't want his approval, and he would never give it anyway. Even if he was a more decent man than Lauder ever would be.

I could only tell myself I'd tried to put something right.

It was time to handle the lawyer. I found a small parking lot and left the car, quickly making my way to a coffee shop. I rang Frederick Lyntner's office. An affable male voice answered. I explained I was in need of advice about a project and didn't want to discuss it over the phone. Lyntner offered to meet me as soon as I could get to him.

It was a tall and shabby building on Duquesne Avenue, built last century. An old art nouveau sign hung on rusting metal. *Trenton Towers*. Frederick Lyntner's office was on the fifth floor. On hearing the death rattle of the elevator coming down the shaft from an upper floor, I opted for the stairs. The bannister rail looked like mahogany but was in fact old and unpolished brass, dulled by decades of neglect, and cold to the touch.

Musty air filled my gasping and unfit lungs as I reached the top floor.

A moldy smell dominated in spite of a marbled window opening out onto the street below. I walked down the corridor looking for Lyntner's office, passing a ticket agent's office where somebody had scrawled 'asshole' in the dusty paint; a musical performers' agency with a dent in the door that looked like a kick; a tobacco and cigar importer that had no less than three padlocks. Other than the distant growl of traffic and the click-clack of a typewriter, it was still a dusty tower where fledging businesses failed to get off the ground, and older ones curled up and died.

The door of the last office had a small white plaque which stated *Frederick Lyntner, Attorney-at-Law*, in small, blunt lettering. I rang the bell, coughed, and adjusted my hat.

I would definitely not mention Falaise Investigations, and I wouldn't be sharing Beatty's cards with the lawyer. Until I'd got a clearer picture, things didn't need to lead back to Beatty. I didn't want Beatty to be embarrassed or put in jeopardy. If Heymann was somehow involved in his daughter's death, the lawyer might have been bought off already.

Time to tread carefully.

The door opened partially, but jammed instantly as the security chain was on. A pair of large blue eyes twinkled at me beneath blonde bushy eyebrows and the voice was as friendly as it had been on the telephone. 'Damn, forgot that was on. You the lady who called?'

I gave a polite smile and a nod. So far so good. Affable, and sane.

Lyntner pushed the door shut, unchained it and held it open. I stepped inside a dingy front office. A low lamp gave the only light, as the venetian blinds were fully closed. A couple of leather armchairs sat either side of a coffee table, which was covered by several open legal reference books. Many other tomes lined a metal bookcase, and even more were stacked on top of a row of filing cases. There were several doors, one marked *Private*.

'I leave the chain on because the actors' agencies down the corridor attract a rowdy bunch and occasionally one bursts in. And not for any legal advice, I can say. Crazy kids. Frederick Lyntner. How do you do?' Lyntner offered me a large, freckled hand. In his late forties, he was tall and blonde, with a weather-beaten, rugged look. He didn't look like a lawyer. In this stuffy box, he was a beefcake in a suit. His nose was wide, as if it had taken a beating or two, and one of his ears bulbous. It had to be from boxing or football.

'Elvira Slate. Maybe having a guy at the front desk would help. No sign of life downstairs.'

Lyntner tutted. 'Bill's a hopeless case. He's probably sleeping. I don't tend to meet clients here. I go to them. This is my Downtown bolt-hole.' It was sweet he was embarrassed about his premises. If I took a date back to the Astral, I'd be feeling the same.

Wait! He *normally went to his clients*. Didn't Olive say Darlene was coming here to sign the contracts?

I smiled. 'Thanks for making an exception.'

'I'm intrigued by your call.' Lyntner guided me in. 'Can I get you something to drink? Iced water, coffee?'

I accepted his offer of coffee and sat down on the chair nearest the door.

Lyntner opened the blinds and went into the back office, leaving the door open. I could hear him opening drawers, assembling cups and filling the kettle. I looked around. There

292

were several framed antique prints of racehorses with docked tails on the wall. A photograph of a horse, being led by a jockey, lay on the desk. I called out, 'You like the ponies?'

'Yes. Very much. As a matter of fact, I'm starting to breed them. My other life, one that's waiting in the wings. I'm winding things down here. Moving back to Philly as soon as I can.'

'Gee, quite a change. Quitting the law?'

'The rat race loses its charm when you get to a certain age. And this city isn't home. Most people come here chasing dreams that lead to disillusionment. It's soulless. How about you? Have I just insulted your hometown?'

'Not at all. I'm from New York, new girl in town. So far so good, but I guess I'll go back one day,' I said.

Lyntner came back in with the tray bearing a steaming cup, a sugar bowl and a small jug. He went on. 'I'm fond of L.A., but at my age, it's imperative to do what gives you most pleasure. In my case, that's time with the nags.' He smiled, putting the tray on the desk. The tray wobbled as he lowered it. His hand had a slight tremor.

'You don't look so old,' I smiled. The charm offensive was increasingly feeling like the right approach, not because he seemed particularly vain, but there was something I liked about him.

His look was reproachful. 'Very flattering, but not true.'

I relieved him of the coffee cup he shakily offered me. He said, 'It's instant. I'm mortified but it's all I have.'

I reached over the table to load my cup with sugar from the silver bowl. He raised a brow. 'Some sweet tooth you got there.'

'Turns out I'm not sweet enough,' I joked. He laughed out loud.

'And some sense of humor,' he added. I felt myself starting to relax.

Don't push it. Be the professional, not the flirt!

My sweet tooth was another legacy from Holloway. After years of gray liquid that passed for tea, even instant coffee with a couple of cubes was manna from heaven.

I leant back and sipped what was now brownish syrup. 'Perfect.'

Frederick Lyntner sat back, crossing his long legs. Blonde men had never been my type, but he had an earthy appeal. I could run away to his farm and hide with the horses. Lauder wouldn't have a clue. In my experience, attraction tended to be a mutual thing.

I kicked myself inwardly. Sizing up every guy I met was idiotic. Was I that lonely? I had a job to do, and that was to find Rhonda.

He said, 'Well, I'm all ears.'

'I'm here on behalf of my client. He's a film producer. He heard about the Tatiana Spark project and wants to know its status.'

This little invention had occurred to me as I had parked the car. Olive had said Otto Heymann wasn't willing to help Darlene, so I could just pretend I was working with an independent producer. Lyle had provided enough information about that ambition, unwittingly. If somebody had intercepted Darlene to prevent her from making the film, maybe Lyntner would have information that I could persuade him to share. And that would take getting on his right side. But if Lyntner had been bought, he would quickly shut me down. It would boil down to instinct.

Lyntner laughed a little, as if nothing surprised him anymore. He pulled a packet of thin cigars out of his jacket pocket, offering me one.

I shook my head. 'I'm not at liberty to name my client at this stage, but he's very serious. He also respects the fact that this project is a private matter.'

'And you're his what...attorney?'

'I'm an intermediary.'

'Oh, some kind of fixer? I just don't recognize your name, not that it has any bearing. Oh, of course I don't. You're a new girl, right?'

I nipped his questioning in the bud. 'My client wants to know where things now stand, considering the recent tragedy.'

Lyntner's bronze brow furrowed like chamois leather. 'How did your client find out about the project?'

I met his eyes. 'Darlene Heymann herself.' Blaming the dead had to be a safe enough bet.

The cynical laugh again. 'Darlene shouldn't have done that. Still, that was the whole point of the agreement she was on her way to sign. Nondisclosure.'

'Don't worry. She swore him to secrecy.' Now I felt bad for tarnishing Darlene's reputation by implying she had a big mouth.

Lyntner brandished his unlit cigar, his eyes on me. 'With all due respect, you're asking me to break confidentiality. I don't even know who hired you. You could be a reporter, anybody.'

So he had standards. Admirable. I said, 'I understand. Maybe I should tell you what I know from my client, and that might convince you he is totally genuine.'

'Go ahead.' He lit his cigar. The aroma filled the room. It was comforting in a way.

I was really diving in the deep end now but I had no choice if I was going to get anything useful from the visit. I made a final quick prayer that Olive had been straight on the facts. 'Darlene Heymann called my client on the same day she said she was signing an agreement with Tatiana Spark. Said she was coming Downtown to do the deal. She wanted my client's permission to suggest him as a potential producer for the project, and he agreed. Next thing, he finds out she's dead. He is a huge fan of Miss Spark's work. He's just set up his company and has big ambitions. Working with Spark would mean the world to him and he'd do everything he can to make the film a masterpiece. But confidentiality has to work both ways. He doesn't want anybody to beat him to the rights.'

'Why not come to me himself? It's very nice to meet you, but a go-between's hardly necessary, surely?'

It was a good question. I thought on my feet. I told him my client's company was new but his money was old, and there was a lot of it. 'He wasn't sure of your setup, doesn't know who to trust yet. He doesn't want the news getting out he is looking for projects and has money to burn.'

Lyntner laughed. 'Wise. Fending off vultures can eat up most of your time. How did your client get to know Darlene?'

'No idea. I'm just the girl he calls when he wants a job like this done.' I hoped I sounded appropriately ignorant.

Lyntner sighed. 'Poor Darlene. A blend of class, fragility and impulsiveness. Now it turns out she still had her demons. God bless her soul.'

He stood up, finding an ashtray on a filing cabinet and looking straight at me. 'Still, I've got to say I find this odd. Darlene should not have been shopping around for producers.

296

Miss Spark was handling that side. And she was calling the shots, her life story. First they had to get a script, then find a star. The producer would follow.' Lyntner sat back down. 'It was my idea to have an agreement between Darlene and my client.'

'Why? You had your doubts about Darlene?'

'I wanted it to work, and who doesn't have ghosts from the past? Yes, I suppose there remained a question mark. I thought a nondisclosure agreement wouldn't hurt.'

It was good he was finally opening up, so I flashed a smile of encouragement and reminded him of my client's preference for confidentiality. 'He just wants to know if there's any chance of moving it along.'

Lyntner waved a dismissive hand in the air. 'The project's as dead as a dodo. Tragedies compound. The movie was supposed to be Tatiana's comeback. Obviously she was only going to play herself as an older woman, and find the big name to act her younger self. She can't face it now. I won't pretend the project stalling won't hurt me. God forbid, it might never happen.'

I nodded. 'So Spark won't work with anybody else?'

He shuffled in his seat, a little uncomfortable. 'It's not that. She might, given time. But Darlene's death, the circumstances, it mortified my client. She was extremely fond of Darlene. She kind of lost faith in her own judgment.'

'So on the actual day she died, Darlene was coming here to sign?' Now I could tease out his earlier contradiction about only going to clients' places.

'What a strange question. You aren't a newshawk, are you?'

Damn. I'd pushed it too far. 'Of course not! Just strange everything was going well and she blows it at crunch time.'

297

'I'm no shrink but some people just sabotage themselves when it's finally going good. Maybe Darlene had a relapse? Who knows? It's an overdose and the cops aren't interested, anyway.'

'Very sad.' I shook my head and took another sip.

'The fact of the matter is that Darlene was supposed to collect me, then we would go to Miss Spark's for the signing. I don't drive, I have this condition. She must have had the Acker kid acting as chauffeur. They never showed up.'

This was all very plausible. Lyntner had stood to make a buck or two to fund his retirement hobby. Maybe his illness had put a ticking clock on his own life. He probably had more to lose than Tatiana Spark, who wanted some kind of comeback. The fact that the Heymann Studio weren't interested could be purely economic. A forgotten star's life story? It all reeked of desperation, Darlene's to prove her father wrong and Tatiana's to regain some former glory.

Olive's paranoia was either deflection or craziness. It looked increasingly likely Darlene had wanted narcotics, possibly influenced by Frank Acker.

I tested the water. 'What about this Frank Acker? Was he going to be in the picture?'

'Doubt it. They hadn't even got a script so casting would have been premature, especially bit parts. I never met him. I heard he was the bad boy type.' He puffed on his cigar but it had gone out. 'Shame. There aren't really any female movie directors. You may have noticed, I'm all for equality.'

I hadn't, in fact, but it was good to know. 'Oh, what about the writer? Darlene mentioned a Martell somebody?'

'Martell Grainger. My client knows her, but there was nothing formal with her.'

I put my cup down and stood up. 'I've kept you too long. But I have to ask. Can my client make an approach to Miss Spark? He's genuine. He really would like to make her life story.'

Lyntner let out a big sigh. 'By all means get your client to write a letter of interest. Send it to me, here. Give it a little time. A month or two? The fact Darlene talked to a third party won't go down so well right now, but I'll do my best to smooth any ruffled feathers. Better tell him to factor that in. And be prepared for a no.'

'How long before you close up shop?'

'I'm sorry?'

'To go back to Philly?'

He rolled his eyes, standing up. 'Oh, these things always take longer, don't they? I need to be around for a few other negotiations. Ask me this time next year.'

We laughed and shook hands.

As I reached the door, I turned. 'One more thing. Darlene mentioned something about the story giving the truth at last. Can you give us just a little tidbit?'

Lyntner laughed. 'I'm just the attorney. I wasn't privy to any story conversations. Even if I had been, they would be *strictly* confidential.'

I went back down the blue stairs, frustrated. If there was a rat, I couldn't smell it. At least meeting the lawyer had confirmed the basic facts Olive had supplied, that there was a film project and Darlene had an ambition. Darlene Heymann and Frank Acker, for whatever reason, had gone first to The Flamayon Hotel.

By the time I reached ground level, the front desk was still abandoned. I noticed a pile of envelopes lying on the desk. I looked around before quickly flicking through them. Most were addressed to unfamiliar names, with different offices. The majority was for the actors' agency, no doubt resumes and photographic portraits from the hordes of desperate wannabes.

Amongst them, a small envelope was addressed to *Mr. Frederick Lyntner*.

It seemed like a good idea to slip it into my pocket.

54

I drove away from Downtown, heading west. I pulled up outside of a café and jumped out. It was cool inside, with the shutters down and a fan spinning creating a pleasant breeze. A Greek-looking woman was slicing cheese behind the counter and I suddenly felt ravenous. I ordered a glass of milk and a cheese sandwich as an early lunch and occupied a corner booth. The leather of the padded seat was battered and kidney-colored, a cozy enclave in which I could safely poke my nose into somebody else's mail.

I ripped open the envelope. A cheap rose scent hit my nose, as I pulled out a floral card covered in red roses. Inside, a message was written in large, childlike handwriting.

'My darling Freddie, forgive me. I promise I won't embarrass you again. I'm just so crazy about you, I can't help it. You've turned my world upside down. I'll be more careful next time, my sweet. I just can't wait until I take care of you and nobody else! Here's my address. 7, The Laurels, halfway up Cuesta Avenue. I can't wait until Wednesday night when we're in each other's arms. Passionately yours, Janice.'

An affair? I felt a momentary pang of dejection but quickly shrugged it off. Beefcake like that would be taken. But unless I snuck the letter back into Trenton Towers, there'd be no rendezvous for Janice and Frederick. Bill the lousy doorman could get the blame. Lyntner hadn't indicated he was married but the fact she'd sent the note to his office, and the wording itself, gave the strong impression Janice had put her foot in it somehow.

I wondered about the other ball I had in the air. Jim Fraser could have put the wheels into motion that could lead to Arnold Moss being freed. I still had Clarence's card in my pocket. It would be good to call him, to vindicate myself, to find out what he knew, but I wouldn't.

My next obvious lead was Martell Grainger. I went to the payphone and called Troy's office. It was a long shot but he answered.

'Camberwell Beauty!' He sounded very merry and I was pleased he wasn't holding a grudge about my disappearance. I thanked him for the night at the Seven Palms before I got to the point.

Troy roared with laughter. 'Martell Grainger? Darling girl, she's a monster. What on earth do you want with Dragon Lady?' He hiccupped loudly. 'Pardon me.'

'Oh, something about a job,' I bluffed. 'For a friend of a friend.' A drunk Troy wouldn't remember the whys and wherefores.

'Peddles romantic garbage from her Beverly Hills mausoleum. Me and the guys have a running bet on her age. Your friend can find out.'

This irritated me. Nobody had running bets on men's ages. I bit my tongue. 'Okay. Can you get me her address?'

'Sure, Patsy, my secretary – my favorite secretary, I'll have you know… Dammit! She's gone for the day. Hey, is the job for you, sweetheart? If you're that hard up, you can always work for me. Got to be something you can do.' I realized by the sound of his voice he was already drunk, and it was only midday. I asked again if he could get Martell's details.

'Your wish is my command,' he hiccupped and then went

off the line. There was a crash in the background. I heard him curse. Eventually he came back on the line. 'Got it.'

'You okay?'

'What? Never better. Did I tell you my beloved kicked me out?'

'Your wife did? That's too bad.'

'She'll calm down in a few days. Say, why don't you come over? Now? C'mon! Come see me. I'll take you out.'

I tensed up inside. Troy was rejected, boozed up, and wanting to lick his wounds.

I gave my excuses and hung up. I felt bad for Troy but I hardly knew him. I needed to cut ties now, not tighten them.

I called Beatty but she was busy with a client. I told Therese I'd check in later.

Then I rang the number Troy had given me for Martell Grainger. A bubbly young woman picked up. She said her aunt couldn't talk right now, but I should come immediately.

55

This was as far from Holloway Prison as you could get.

No roaring engines, no horns. No electric lines crackling. No doors slamming, no bums yelling, no sirens wailing, no haunting saxophone, no spilled garbage rattling along the gutter. No desperation. This was the silence of nobody having anything to prove – or to lose.

The hot, lazy sun had burnt off the mist in record time. I parked the car under the shade of a large magnolia tree and walk the distance to Martell's house – *Perpetua*, the bubbly girl had called it.

Walking gave me the chance to admire the view; velvet emerald lawns with edges clipped as straight as a ruler, twinkling with dew diamonds; ornate fountains spewing froth like champagne in front of beautiful houses; hummingbirds and bees, spoilt for choice, buzzing on the exotic blooms and lustrous French roses. Even the air smelt expensive here. I heard the occasional distant whack of a tennis ball. Maybe it was the sound of a slapped buttock on a satin sheet. Maybe the devil had slipped into Beverly Hills and was having some fun.

Nothing like life in prison. Going back was my worst fear. If hunting for Rhonda got me in too deep, then I'd run. Dede's pistol would stay right by my side, in my one family heirloom, Violet's purse. By giving me the gun, Lauder had enabled me to be mistress of my own destiny.

Perpetua appeared behind a tall manicured hedge, a large white villa that wouldn't have looked out of place in the French

Riviera. A majestic blue cedar tree dominated the front garden. White hydrangeas bloomed beneath statues of dancing Greek goddess nymphs. I took my time, enjoying the stroll up the terracotta tiled path to the marble steps nestling between high white fluted columns that led to the covered porch.

An enormous red convertible was parked underneath.

Whatever corny guff Martell Grainger was churning out, it was working for her. That, or she had married – or divorced – well. I rang the bell, wiping my brow. There were sticky patches under my arms. I hoped I didn't smell. *Perpetua* wouldn't do dirty.

Inside, a dog started yapping. Behind the polished wood door, a young woman's voice yelled, 'I'll get it!'

The door was flung open wide, without caution. She was around twenty, and bouncing up and down. 'You the lady who called? Finally! My life depends on you, you have no idea! Come in! I'm Pammie!' She spoke in the over-dramatic tone of someone who has never had to worry about a thing in her life.

Pammie wore crisp aqua linen shorts, a white sleeveless tennis shirt, and blue sunglasses. Her toes were varnished with a pale pearly pink as if dipped in candy floss.

She yanked me inside an inner lobby with a white polished marble floor and palms in burnished copper pots. A bronze sculpture of a wolf and three cubs sat on a white marble plinth.

A housekeeper, around sixty, silently appeared from nowhere. She was tall, her elegance wasted on her white starched apron and blue dress. She looked at me, more than a little surprised. 'May I help you, Miss?'

'Miss Slate called to see Auntie. I said she could,' Pammie butted in again.

'That's a lie, Pammie. You know it, and I know it. She's writing.'

Pammie blushed.

I looked from one to the other. 'If this is a bad time...'

Pammie interjected. 'Even so, Miss Slate is a very important visitor.' She turned to the housekeeper. 'Phyllis, tell Auntie I've gone to the movies, to see *Reign over the Heart*. I'll read her lines later.' She spun back to me. 'Isn't Grayson Carling to die for? I *love* him.' Pammie grabbed her purse and gave me a grin. 'You're a lifesaver.' She ran out of the door, her sandals not fastened properly.

Phyllis suddenly yelled, 'Frou-Frou!' I jumped. What the hell?

Suddenly a massive white ball flew past me, knocking me off balance. It was a giant French poodle. Phyllis grabbed it by the scruff of the neck, and dragged the animal to the car. 'Pammie, you ain't going to the movies, so you're taking the darned dog. Needs its walkies!'

Pammie groaned but Phyllis lowered her voice. She seemed to win. Pammie nodded and the dog jumped into the car.

Pammie zoomed off. Frou-Frou's ears flapped in the wind from the front seat, as if to wave goodbye.

Phyllis returned, laughing at me. 'So she fooled you? Pammie's little tricks, Miss. You better go. I'm sorry. Miss Grainger don't like interruptions. Would you like to leave a card?'

I hesitated. I wouldn't be able to talk her around. 'Fine.'

I must have looked fed up as Phyllis looked at her watch. 'She'll be having a break soon. Let me see what I can do. What's your name again, Miss?'

'Elvira Slate. Thank you for trying, but Mrs. Grainger doesn't know me.'

'*Miss Grainger*,' she corrected me. 'There ain't been no Mr. Grainger for years.'

After a few minutes, Phyllis came back to the room and nodded, gesturing to me to follow. We walked along a wide white corridor with windows that overlooked an idyllic rear garden. I soaked up the garden views. The opulence was alluring; the pool was the jewel. An oasis of pure azure, gently rippling in the breeze, with curved steps descending into the water. There were palms, exotic trees in blossom, and several more fountains. If a unicorn had trotted past, I wouldn't have been surprised.

'Not bad,' I said. 'You live in, Phyllis?'

'Weekdays. I take the car home every Friday night, and I take care of my grandkids. Got five now, all under five. And all together still less work than Pamela Grainger.' She shot me a meaningful look.

She led me into a drawing room. French doors at one end opened out onto the garden, letting in the evening sun. The walls were adorned with framed portraits of movie stars, all personally signed. '*Martell, dearest collaborator, dearest friend, keep the creative rivers flowing, darling. Yours, Laura.*' And '*My partner in crime, John*'. Another declared, '*Missing your imagination, many thanks, Cx*'. And a row of framed photographs – Martell arm-in-arm with stars. No kids, no husbands. In each one, Martell had the same glossy dark auburn hair, the same smile. The only thing that changed was the style of her gowns.

'So Pammie was off to see that hopeless dope. Gee, she frazzles my nerves. So...Miss Slate, was it? I don't think we've met.' I turned to see Martell Grainger floating in in a satin pink housecoat. The collar and cuffs were a darker pink, with matching covered buttons. The skirt was full and swished as she walked, revealing pink satin slippers topped with pink fur, her toe nails painted the same shade of pink at the housecoat. Against the rosiness, Martell's chestnut hair and green eyes were brilliantly set off. I scrutinized her face. No lines, no wrinkles, no furrowed brow.

She looked me up and down as sharply.

I was glad I'd dressed the part.

We shook hands. 'No, we haven't. I called, there was some... confusion.'

'My niece is supposed to be reading my dialogue. It bores her. She says she wants to act, but I think *that's* the big act. Still, now you're here, what's the story?'

Her arm waved me over to an ivory velvet sofa. It looked far too immaculate for human use so I perched on the edge. Martell Grainger sat down opposite on a high-backed armchair covered in gold brocade.

I fed her the story about my client, the well-to-do producer I was working for, wanting to make Tatiana's life story. I hinted that Darlene had mentioned Martell as a possible writer.

Martell Grainger studied me. 'Oh. May I ask who this producer is?' Her brows arched high, in anticipation of juice.

'He wants to stay anonymous, for the time being. He's really interested in picking up the project again.'

'He hasn't talked to my agent, then? Harry Freeland?'

'No.'

'Good. Tell him to keep it that way. But tell your producer to get in touch when he can at least introduce himself.'

Frederick Lyntner was a gabby kid compared to Miss Fortress. 'If he gets involved, he would consider asking you to write it.'

Martell burst out laughing. 'Poor child, you just haven't got the facts right, sweetheart. Don't embarrass yourself by saying any more.'

She was talking herself up; Lyntner had played her importance down. 'Wait a minute. You've signed an agreement already?' If so, Lyntner hadn't said that.

'You don't take a hint, do you?'

Martell looked at me like I was the biggest fool in town. She got up and went back to the bar to retrieve an ivory cigarette holder, stuffed a cream cigarette in the end and lit up. She stood with her back to me, admiring the garden, one arm folded across her waist, the other holding the cigarette up.

'I'll say just one thing. Darlene's demise kicked my and Tatiana's butts. Skate on thin ice, gonna fall in some day.' Then she turned around. 'Have you seen any of my movies?'

I squirmed a little. 'Not really.'

'No, you don't look the romantic type. I bet you're more of a thriller lady, right? Well, I'm not ashamed of all the sentimental stories I've penned. The public wants its happy endings. But I'm craving something a tad less corny to do. This story is it, and the project is mine. Tell your client I look forward to discussing the project in person with him, *then* I'll see about introducing him to Tatiana.'

'What about Frederick Lyntner?'

'What about him? He'll do the paperwork when required.'

'So you know Darlene was on her way to sign an agreement when she died?'

Martell hesitated for a moment before declaring that of course she did. I got the impression she didn't like to reveal ignorance of anything. If she hadn't been asked to sign an agreement, it meant her position on the film could be uncertain. She just didn't want to admit it.

'Well, tell your producer to get his skates on if he wants to hear more. I'll show you out.'

The only one of us who could have gained much from this meeting was Martell Grainger. All I'd found out was that she was very good at protecting her interests, making out she was in with Tatiana Spark. I wondered if my next lead should be Frank Acker, but other than going back to Olive and asking her if she knew anybody who knew him, I had no idea how to go about finding his connections. I certainly didn't want to be poking around the Heymann Studio.

Martell led me back to the lobby. Before she opened the front door, she turned back, almost blocking the way. 'Do you work for your client on an exclusive basis?'

'Not at all. Why?'

Martell leant back, musing. 'I might be interested in having some individuals vetted. Pammie's beaux. There's a number of them. How can I get hold of you?'

I had Beatty's business cards on me but I didn't want to give one to Martell. She just knew too many people. I told her I was moving offices and getting a new number. When I came back in the next day or so, we could talk.

56

The client was around fifty, a fake yellowing blonde bob, with heavily caked white skin and something dead about the eyes. Her style was a hangover from the Twenties, as if she hadn't realized times had moved on. Her hat perched dramatically on the front of her head, a complex affair of thick beige felt, cream velvet and gold-edged ruffles. She was dressed in pale ivory – a silk coat edged with pale mink. The triple string of pearls around her neck gleamed and the pale feathers of her boa rippled softly around her neck like tiny writhing worms.

I'd seen a feather like that very recently.

And it was still in my purse.

The atmosphere in the office was tense as hell, almost as thick as the veiled disgust on her face. Beatty's eyes glanced at me, then back again, barely acknowledging me. She gave my flashy cream and red 'fixer' getup a despairing look.

The client looked me up and down, a long gold cigarette holder in her mouth. The ivory cigarette protruding from the end was unlit. She growled, 'This her?'

Beatty shot me a sharp *play-it-cool* look. 'Elvira, this is Mrs. Reba Turlington. Take a seat.' I couldn't quite read her mood.

Reba T. How the hell had she found me here? Joyce. It was the only link. Had Joyce been careless in finding out about Rhonda? Or was she more in cahoots with her ex than she had admitted to me?

I pulled a chair away from the back wall and positioned it

311

as far away as possible. I lit a cigarette. Playing it cool. I had the gun, I reminded myself, if things got nasty.

Reba T. noticed my hand on Violet's purse, giving it a withering look. She removed the cigarette holder, pointing at the purse. 'That purse is an abomination.' She turned to Beatty. 'Your associate needs to pay attention to her couture.'

I looked at Beatty. 'What's going on?'

Reba T. pulled a strange grimace. It probably was supposed to be a smile. Her teeth weren't in such good shape. 'Let me explain, sugar. I was telling Mrs. Falaise here that I don't appreciate snoops sniffing around my business uninvited. You want to know something, ask me straight to my face.'

So Joyce had talked. 'All right. Where's Rhonda?'

Reba T. let out a tinkle of a laugh, addressing Beatty. 'She's got some balls on her.' Beatty glanced at me. *Cool it.*

Reba T. went on. 'Listen good, sugar. First, I don't know Rhonda's whereabouts. And don't you dare shoot your mouth off around town suggesting I've got anything to do with anything. As for Shimmer being dumb enough to OD, girl could add up but she was a fool at the best of times. And a darned thief. Dumb, too, trying to pull that off under my nose. I'd like to know where Rhonda is because I want my money back. She should've just come back and I'd have let her work off what Shimmer owed me.'

'She's sick, but I suppose you don't care. So why should we believe you?' I tried to sound tough but inside I was quaking. Reba T. just had to tell Lauder to deal with a pesky private eye called Elvira Slate and he'd know all about my new sideline. This was not good.

Reba T. turned to Beatty. 'She ain't very bright either, is she?

Or is she deaf? Did I or did I not just say I don't know Rhonda's whereabouts?'

Beatty gave me a look of reprimand. 'Pay attention, Elvira.'

Why was she being so groveling to the cow?

Reba T. examined her nails. 'So much for gratitude. Shimmer was a useless bookkeeper, only kept her on because I felt sorry for 'em. And Rhonda, seemed like to me I was paying for her not to come to work. What I wanna know is how do you know them?' Reba T. shot me an icy glare.

'We were neighbors. Got friendly. I played chess with Shimmer,' I said.

'Shimmer? That's funny. I thought Rhonda was the chess nut.' Reba T. smirked again, winking at me. 'Chess nut, get it? I'll do you a favor and take your word for it. Just like I'll take your word for it Elvira Slate ain't a phony name. All kinds of folks move out here to make a fresh start. Funny there ain't no record of Elvira Slate in the Hall of Records. So what's your fresh start all about, sugar?'

Fuck.

So she'd been looking into me. She was a damned snake. A slow, slick mover until she spat her sudden dart of venom. That's why Beatty hadn't kicked her out of the office.

Reba T. had been snooping on the snoop. How, and using whom, I had no idea. Lauder? Or did she do her own dirty work?

I glanced at Beatty who avoided my glaze. She hadn't asked for my story, but she would insist on it now.

Beatty lit her pipe, saying nothing. Reba T.'s gaze was fixed on me. Finally, she spoke. 'By the way, I do feel bad for sweet Rhonda. You keep lookin' and get her home. Hell, I'll even

313

cough up for the operation. Just quit badmouthing me around town, or else.'

What the hell?

'All right,' I said, acting calm. Beatty's expression remained inscrutable.

Reba T. finally lit her cigarette. She took a long drag and puffed the smoke out dramatically, in my direction. 'Now we have an understanding, I've got my own missing person case. I want you to find somebody who's been bothering me.'

'Who's rattling your cage?' Beatty asked.

'Goes by the name of Slim Caziel. Elmore Caziel.'

My stomach lurched, aware of two very shrewd women's eyes on me. Reba T. went on. 'Slim used to work for me, some years ago. Back then, I had a small venture, private magazines. They were tasteful. Beautiful girls, classy shots. *Bona fide* erotica. Slim was my photographer. Times moved on and so did I. Running nightclubs now. We all gotta start somewhere, right? I ain't ashamed of my beginnings, and neither are the girls who made a stack of dough with me. It ain't the same for Slim. Kinda went downhill, into the muck.' She sniffed with distaste.

Beatty studied Reba T., pulling her spectacles down her nose a little. 'Why do you want to find him?'

Reba T. sighed dramatically. 'We had a business arrangement. Thing is, he hasn't been around in a while. I just want to make sure he's not in any trouble.'

The feather. Just like the one she was wearing at the place he was rotting. She either had shot him herself and she was playing a game, or she had paid a visit before or after somebody else bumped him off.

Another feather was detaching itself from her boa. I willed it to fall on the floor before she left so I could compare it with the one I had. Maybe stress was making the boa molt.

Beatty said, 'Why not tell the cops? I guess it's too delicate a matter?'

Reba T. bounced back fast. 'Now you're catching on.'

Beatty interjected, 'Where does this Caziel creep operate?'

'He had a flophouse, but got sloppy. Apparently the joint was burned down in a raid. Then I heard he'd flopped in some warehouse near Ventura but he wasn't there when I paid him a visit.'

So she'd gone *before* he was killed?

Beatty asked, 'Any known associates?'

'Slim's a loner. He had a man – Carlos, or was it Jose? Something like that. Cheap muscle. Nobody's seen him around.'

Because he was in custody, I thought. Whatever form of custody Lauder used. He might have Jose in the Astral, for all I knew.

'We don't exactly have much to go on,' said Beatty, looking at me. 'Elvira? You want to ask Mrs. Turlington anything more?'

I turned to Reba T. 'Does Caziel still have anything to do with your nightclubs?'

Reba T. thought about this. 'No! I said that, already.' She stood up, heavily, and completely ignored me as she addressed Beatty. 'You just find Caziel, whatever it takes.'

Then she shot me a meaningful look.

With that she swanned out, paying her retainer in the form of a loose feather.

315

57

Beatty got up stiffly and opened the windows wide, to let the breeze in. 'I don't know about you, but I've got a nasty taste in my mouth.' She buzzed through to Therese.

As she did, I grabbed the feather, which had floated under the desk. The sounds of the traffic did little to shift the atmosphere. 'A couple of brandies, *s'il vous plait.*'

I spoke up. 'I had no idea. Joyce, the ex-husband who runs the dyke nightclub, convinced me he hated her. But he...*she* must have tipped Reba T. off.'

'The same person who lived a lie for most of their life? Hardly the most reliable type.'

I met her eye. 'Elmore Caziel. He's dead. I know it for a fact.'

'What?' I'd never seen Beatty jump but she did now. Her eyes bugged out. 'What do you mean?'

'I saw his corpse two days ago. There's a lot you don't know.'

'You're darned right there is!' I'd never seen her angry before, either.

I gulped. Reba T. could drag Beatty's business through the mud, or even worse.

Time to do some explaining.

Time to jump off the cliff.

'My real name is Jemima Day.'

Therese breezed in, holding the tray high. The tense atmosphere wiped the smile of her face. She set the tray of drinks down and looked at me. 'Somebody call for you, Elvira. Barney Einhorn? He says to call him. He is at the office until six. You know where? He did not leave a number.' Then Therese trotted out as fast as her high heels let her.

I met Beatty's eyes. She took one of the glasses and slid it over to me. 'All right. Give it to me. Fill in all the gaps.'

So we had reached the stage in the game where it was time to put the cards on the table.

A lot sooner than either of us desired.

All the cards.

I wanted Beatty to know everything. If anyone should hear it all, from me, it was Beatty Falaise, whether she liked the truth or not. Lauder had found me out. He used my past as a punishment, a form of control.

Beatty had given me a chance, and she deserved a choice in whether to have anything to do with me. It wasn't fair on her to proceed without her knowing the risk she was taking being connected to me.

She wouldn't report me to the police. If she didn't like what she heard, she would let me walk out of her life and she would forget she ever met me. I could dump the car keys, the keys to the office, the cards back on the desk and walk out of her life. Right then and there, go back to the Astral and just await my fate.

I took a deep breath and looked at her directly. 'I was in prison in England, for something I didn't do. In '41, I was caught with a stash of guns. I was set up. My boyfriend was a gangster, and I think he was involved somehow. He used me. His name was Billy. I was just a stupid idiot in those days, I didn't care about anything except buying dresses and getting drunk. So I spent most of the war in jail. Then in May, on VE Day, I jumped probation. I tracked Billy down, to get some kind of payback. I'd never talked, never dumped him in it. When I got there, he was already in some other trouble. Italian mobsters killed him before he spilled the beans. I shot them dead. It was them or me. Then I found a fake US passport in my name with Billy's stuff. So he kind of came through for me. Guilt, perhaps.'

A neat summary. But as I recounted it, it sounded crazy. Was this really my life? Four and a half years of inertia and despair followed by four and half months of a high-risk rollercoaster. Who the hell was I?

Beatty's face was back in mask mode. 'So you're British?'

'No. Yes. I mean, I was born on a boat, half-way across the Atlantic. I don't know what that makes me. My father was apparently American.' I went on. 'After I fled, I managed to get to L.A. with the counterfeit American passport. I had some delusion I could start over. Things were working out until I did a favor for a new pal who'd got herself in trouble. She was posing for sleazy portraits. Elmore Caziel was the photographer. He had drugged my friend and taken shots of her. Pornographic shots. I thought I could destroy them. I pretended to be desperate for a break and he bought it. While I was there, I set Caziel's joint on fire. He got away, but I wasn't so lucky. A cop caught me, a Vice Squad cop. Turns out he and another guy had the place under surveillance. To cut a long story short, the cop found out everything about me. He discovered I had a criminal record in England, that I'd jumped probation and was wanted for killing the mobsters. He offered me a deal. If I did secret errands for him, he wouldn't send me back to England.'

'What's the cop's name?'

Naming Lauder was terrifying.

All the cards.

I had to do it. I took a deep breath. 'Randall Lauder.'

Beatty seemed unmoved. I rushed on. Told her about Lauder and Clarence Johnson and that neither of them knew about my arrangement with Beatty, or that I was looking into Rhonda's disappearance.

Beatty raised a brow and took a slug of brandy.

'I made friends with Shimmer and Rhonda kind of behind Lauder's back. Then Rhonda disappeared, and her neighbor asked me to help find her. So I came to you.'

I bet she regretted that day. Beatty nodded for me to go on.

'Shimmer told me Lauder is a regular at Reba T.'s club, and he has a mistress all the while he's engaged to a socialite. Maybe true, maybe not. Anyhow, after I'd been to Joyce's, I went to see Olive Harjo.'

'Darlene's girlfriend.'

'Yes. She told me Darlene was supposed to sign a contract the day she died, but she never made it to the lawyer's office. She and Frank Acker drove to The Flamayon Hotel instead, and took an overdose.'

I stopped.

'What kind of contract?'

'Nondisclosure. For a movie. Tatiana Spark... I guess you know...?' I tailed off.

'Oh, yeah. I'm old enough to know who Tatiana Spark is.' She sounded wry but no smile came with it.

'Tatiana wanted Darlene to tell Tatiana's true life story, the facts that nobody knows. And Olive Harjo was convinced Otto Heymann had his daughter killed, to kill the movie, she said. So I paid the lawyer a visit, just to see what he knew. Olive had given me his name. I pretended to be a go-between for someone who might make the film now Darlene was dead. This lawyer told me Darlene was supposed to pick him up from his office, then they'd go to Spark's. She never showed.'

'Did you believe him?'

I shrugged. 'Nice guy. Seemed genuine. He said he knew nothing about the storyline, that they hadn't even decided on a writer. Thing is, Olive had already mentioned one to me. Martell Grainger. He also said that Tatiana Spark was traumatized now, that it was all over. So I meet Martell Grainger. She was, well, kind of snooty about the lawyer, like she knew far more than him. She's excited, knows Tatiana Spark. She's got an ambition to write a different kind of movie from her usual...'

'..Garbage.' Beatty finished the sentence for me, refilling her glass. 'Who's the attorney?'

'Frederick Lyntner. He's got an office Downtown.'

Beatty just nodded. 'Go on.'

'Neither Lyntner or Martell gave me the feeling they think Darlene's death was suspicious. So maybe it's all been one big waste of time. Maybe Rhonda is out there somewhere. Maybe we should just wish her luck.'

Beatty now leant back, arms folded. I had to give it to her, calm in a crisis. She finally spoke.

'Where's the rest of your family? In England?'

'My mother was English. We spent the first six years of my life in California. Violet, my mother, was searching for my father, a GI in the First World War. Then she gave up. We moved back to England and then I was told she was dead. I grew up in children's homes. I ran away. I got in trouble with the law. Petty stuff, you know the stuff I mean. Then I was fostered by somebody nice, a decent woman. She educated me. Things were looking up until she died and I was stupid enough to hook up with a South London gangster.'

There was a long silence.

'You haven't told me how you know Caziel is dead.'

I stared at her. No, I hadn't. I took a sip of brandy.

'Clarence Johnson is trying to save his friend from death row. The guy was framed for killing Lauder's partner, Stan Perrin, by a bent cop who was working with Caziel, profiting from the porn pictures.'

Beatty glared at me. 'I read about Perrin's murder. Go on.'

I recounted Clarence's version of events and why they were watching Caziel in the first place; to get evidence to link Caziel and Fraser. I described how Lauder took me to the warehouse, where I discovered Caziel's dead body. 'Their plan was to get Caziel to rat on Fraser, using me somehow. Now he's dead, there's no chance for justice.'

I got Clarence's card out of my purse and slid it over the desk. Beatty picked it up. 'A school teacher. Working undercover with a cop? What are they – buddies?'

'I have no idea.' I pulled out the cream feather, handing it to Beatty. 'I found this at the warehouse. It's the same as the ones Reba T.'s got around her neck. She could be lying, or maybe she visited the place before he was killed.'

Beatty leant over the desk and took the feather. She examined it, pulling her glasses down her nose.

'There's something else.' Now for the punch line.

'More?' Beatty glared at me.

'Clarence made me feel guilty, said Caziel got away because I burned down the studio. So I've gotten involved with that, too.' I told her all about my appointment with Jim Fraser, and how I'd given him an ultimatum, tricking him into thinking Caziel had squealed.

'I could only get to Fraser because Lauder is away. He'd been watching him like a hawk.'

Beatty took another slug of booze and leant back. Her eyes were not exactly warm. 'Let me get this straight. The British police want you. The Italian Mob in London wants you. A bent cop wants you dead and another one controls you. A teacher has used you, and now a sleazy nightclub owner is suspicious about you.'

I nodded. I had no words.

'I figured you had a past, but jeez. You couldn't make this saga up. And you walk in here, dragging your crap into my business. Guess you thought I was an old fat sucker?'

We met each other's eyes. I looked away first. 'I just wanted a fresh start. Helping my friend after Caziel humiliated her was part of that, helping out someone who'd treated me nice. Later, with Shimmer and Rhonda, I felt just like them. Girls without a hope in hell. But I can't go on anymore. Not with Reba T. walking in and making threats.'

I stood up. I knew what I would do. Go. 'I'm done. Now that bitch is onto me, Lauder could find out in no time I'm working with you. You don't need the whole LAPD thinking you've been aiding and abetting a wanted felon. And Jim Fraser wants my blood, and he's the law until they bring him down, which, thanks to me, they can't. The longer you spend in my company, the worse it could be for you.'

I took out the car keys, the office keys and the box of cards from my purse, and pushed them across the desk. 'You're right. I duped you. You thought I had something to offer. I do, it's called a nightmare.'

I couldn't look her in the eye. I got up and headed for the door.

'And I thought you had gumption.'

I froze. Then I turned. Beatty shot me a look. 'Get back over here and sit your sorry ass back down.'

58

'True. I should let you walk out of here. That bitch is right. You got a pair on you. You should be lying low for the rest of your life, and here you are, running around, trying to make amends but just failing at that, right?'

I was sitting back down. I felt ashamed and nervous, an odd combination. I couldn't look her in the eye. Was she mad?

You can walk out of here any minute.

She went on. 'Let's say this Lauder gets wind of your secret business, and he pays me a visit. So I play the dupe. Not my style, but that's it. You just tricked me into thinking you were a do-gooder, helping an old lady. I had a vacancy, you said the right things, I offered you the job. You got a record for impersonation, so they'll believe you hoodwinked an old biddy like me. I don't have a clue about your past. We never had this conversation. That ease your conscience?'

'Yes, a lot.' I fiddled with the buckle on Violet's purse.

'Good. Because it saves my bacon. So that's how we'll play it from now.'

'But I'm trouble. Why don't you take the chance to be rid of me?'

'A good question. Selfish motives, I guess. You walk out and I find out you've been mown down or shipped back to hang...'

I shuddered, my hand instinctively going to my neck.

Breathe!

I grabbed my glass and knocked the dregs back. Beatty watched me. 'I'm looking forward to a nice retirement, and visions of your death ain't going to ruin it for me, young lady. Lesson number four. Two brains are better than one, and we got a whole bunch of problems to solve. Saving your sorry ass of a life is somewhere near the top of the list.'

She twisted the emotional knife. 'Now the slate's clean, no more surprises. That's an order. You mess up, conceal anything from me, I'll call up this Lauder guy myself.'

I nodded. I'd jumped off the cliff, and I could see the sea below. It could save me or drown me.

'You involved with anyone else, other than this stranglehold the Vice Squad cop has got you in? Lover or two stashed away? Male or female, I don't judge. I want whole story.'

'I slept with a film producer. A one-night thing. He knows nothing about me.'

And there was Lena. But she's gone, too, like everyone else.

A plume of smoke told me she was puffing on her pipe. 'Okay. That settles that. Back to business. First, Otto Heymann did not kill his daughter. He's hard as nails and old too, and in my experience age don't soften anybody, but him doing her in is crazy talk. Grief is making Olive screwy, like I said.'

I countered that Olive had said Heymann was ashamed of Darlene. That her success would embarrass the family. Beatty was irritated at my persistence.

'He could have controlled the movie anyway,' she countered. 'Studios have a habit of snapping up projects just to stop them in their tracks.'

I thought of Troy and his chums. Spending their lives hunched over typewriters, inventing stories that ended up in a filing cabinet, never to see the light of day. At least it seemed to pay well.

Beatty went on. 'Let's just leave Olive's screwy theory out for the moment. This Lauder guy and his pal Clarence? Jury's out. We'll get back to them as well. Thirdly, your girl, Rhonda, she could still be in trouble. What does your instinct say about Reba T.?'

'My hunch is she isn't involved, she just didn't like me snooping. Could be that she's paying Caziel off. He's got to have dirt on her. She's worried about something getting out.'

Beatty emptied her pipe before stuffing in fresh tobacco. 'My feeling, too. Now, as for the attorney, Frederick Lyntner. I know him. About twenty or so years ago, he was a hotshot executive at the Heymann Studio. Got into some funny business with a young starlet he dated for a while. She made some accusations, he did the same back. Blame game. It was an internal investigation, no cops were called and he was fired. He may have got a payout, but he was finished. Nobody would touch him. As for the starlet, her star rose, and fast. I had no idea Frederick Lyntner became an attorney. Maybe he used the payout to bankroll himself through law school. And somehow, he got himself Tatiana Spark as a client. Interesting. But Tatiana Spark always had a mind of her own. No blacklist would sway her.'

'So you know her personally?'

'Met her a few times back in the day. Did you give the lawyer my card?'

I shook my head. 'No. Not to Martell Grainger, either. Nobody can connect us.'

'Something you've done right, then.'

'Do you think Lyntner could be involved somehow?'

'Revenge on the studio after all these years? But he would want the movie to go ahead, a nice little earner for him.'

I said, 'He said as much. Seemed like a blow but he said he has other clients, too. Says he wants to focus on breeding racehorses. His office is crummy and he's got a nervous shake, something with his hands.'

Beatty absorbed this. She then started pulling off her rings, her bracelet. She unpinned her brooch. She placed them all down the table. She slid open a drawer and removed her cosmetics bag, and lifted out an assortment of gold-cased lipsticks and powder. 'Now. We have a lot of ingredients, but the cake isn't rising. Let's stir the mixture. We'll start with the facts, add the assumptions and instincts, then cook it all up and see what we got left over.'

She slid her turquoise ring to one corner of the desk, near the lamp. 'Over here is our missing girl. Rhonda.' Then she pushed a lipstick, two nail polishes and her brooch over to the ring. 'And here is Shimmer, Darlene, Olive and Frank. Rhonda, here, has no direct relationship to Darlene or Frank, as far as we know, so we'll put Shimmer nearer. Now, over here, on Darlene's side,' Beatty pushed her bracelet, a nail file and powder puff, 'are Lyntner, Martell Grainger, and Tatiana Spark. All with plans for a movie. Let's say this trio, Darlene, Frank and Shimmer, were murdered. Who gains? Not Otto Heymann. Probably in torment now for not helping her when he had the chance.'

Beatty went on. 'Now. Martell Grainger. A player, for sure. Could be talking herself up. But killing Darlene? I know her, got involved in her divorce. One of the most ambitious women I've ever met, but a killer? Hardly. And yes, she is friendly with Tatiana Spark, even if she didn't reveal it to you the other day. So we don't know what they've planned. But she's smart as they get.'

'Tatiana Spark. She's like a mystery. Is she rich?'

'She'll have more than enough. She wasn't as big a star as Clara Bow – Tatiana's niche was playing the tragic martyr who died for her man. Strong accent, made no difference to the silent movies, but later she was downgraded to supporting actress in the talkies. Let's come back to her.' Beatty plonked two lipsticks in the middle. 'Caziel and queen of scum Reba T.?'

Beatty pondered.

'Reba T. knows Caziel – though she maybe doesn't know he's dead – *and* she employed Shimmer and Rhonda. Caziel and Reba T., the common denominators. Reba T. could want Caziel dead and her little visit today is a bluff. She didn't like you sniffing around, but why? Caziel peddles porno. Like you said, he might have something on her.' She held up one of the lipsticks, narrowing her eyes. 'Fair to surmise he knew Shimmer from their time with Reba T. Maybe he killed the three of them, took pictures of the bodies. Snapshots of a few Hollywood names. Dead, as well. Another nice little earner. That's his game, right? Some perverted types would cough up for that.'

I blinked. That seemed plausible. I joined in, excited. 'If Shimmer trusted Caziel, he could have set up the job. Tricked her. Shimmer was going for a job, and she had to look good. He could have easily found out from her that Rhonda was home alone and visited her afterwards. Tricked her into going with him! But now he's dead. What can he have done with her?'

'Hold your horses! We don't know how they all ended up together in that hotel.' Beatty cautioned. 'Then again, maybe the killer is not on this table.'

We both stared at the pattern on the desk. The ticking of the brass clock suddenly became very loud.

'Lyntner said Frank Acker was trouble. But Olive said Darlene liked him.'

'Trouble with Frank, maybe? Sounds like a B movie. Well, let's assume he was in the wrong place at the wrong time. Note I said *assume*. We can get to him later, if need be.'

Beatty was clearly wasted on divorce work. She peered at the items. 'Oh. We're forgetting. Your cop and his pal.' She placed her brandy glass down. 'Multiple possible agendas, and this Lauder fella can use you as a scapegoat. Sure, if he's in bed with Reba T., he may very well know Rhonda's whereabouts. Let sleeping dogs lie for the moment. Let me know when he gets back in touch.'

I nodded. Then...

'Oh, my God!' The love letter I'd swiped from Lyntner's office. I plucked it from the purse and handed it to Beatty. It was slightly worse for wear. She scanned it. 'Lordy, how did you get this?'

'There was mail laying around on the front desk. I couldn't resist.'

Beatty finally looked impressed. She waved the floral note. 'This is the sort of simpering garbage a woman who doesn't think a whole lot of herself would write.'

'Yeah. She's head over heels and insecure.'

'Worth checking this Janice out. More engine grease. You should go there tomorrow, with a fresh mind.'

My mind had raced on. Out of the blue, an idea came to me. Obvious, but daring. The logical conclusion of my fixer role. I looked up.

329

'The only way I got anywhere with Lyntner and Martell was playing a go-between for an imaginary producer. But what if the producer becomes real? If the movie is a problem for somebody in this inner circle, then maybe we should get word out it's going ahead.'

Beatty leant back. 'Luring out the killers? Interesting move.'

'I can ask somebody to be the producer. But he'd have to think it's genuine.'

'Don't tell me. The guy you screwed?'

I felt myself blushing in response.

'So what's lover boy's name?'

'Lyle Vadnay.'

Lyle was starting out, he had money and he was hungry. Martell was hungry for artistic merit, or so she claimed.

A match made in heaven.

59

Barney Einhorn gave me a big smile with tired eyes. It was nearly the end of the day. We shook hands across the counter. He immediately asked, 'Something up?'

'Rush hour traffic. So, I got your message,' I said, distracting him from the fact I had overindulged on the brandy after opening up to Beatty and now was feeling it.

I asked, 'Any luck?'

Barney looked around, making sure nobody was near him. Most of the other clerks were on the telephone.

'Skill and patience, Miss Slate, not luck. I cracked your code. Your Nightshade Club meets every now and then. A very select group.' He handed me around five newspapers, each with a yellow marker within the pages. 'I've marked the pages. Nothing in the others. Want me to toss them?'

'Sure, thanks.' Was this the right call? I could always tell Lauder I had put them in the trash.

Barney grinned. 'Took a little time. Then, well, yes, I suppose I did get a lucky break. Look.'

I opened one page where the yellow marker was. Under the *In Memoriam* column, a small notice had been circled in pencil. Barney leant over and pointed to it. 'They sound like names. *Tinah D. Gesh*; *Dan. S. Height*; *Desi. H. Gnath*. They are all anagrams of *Nightshade*. See? I only just got it today, because yesterday a woman telephoned to place an entry, the one for *Desi. H. Gnath*. I recognized her voice. It bugged me all night. Then I remembered, she'd done exactly the same last month, another *In Memoriam*. So I narrowed the search and found it. *Dan. S. Height.'* Each time, the address is the same. A private address. *36, Briar Lane.* It's in Santa Monica.'

'You're a genius,' I said. I was impressed. He should be working for intelligence.

Barney blushed, all modesty. 'Just got a memory for voices.'

'Know when the next one is?'

'Tomorrow night. Eight pm.'

'The woman left a name?' Lauder was leaving me well alone, and I had strict instructions never to call him. Until he returned, he wouldn't know about the next event.

'Yes. Jane Smith. Has to be phony. And she paid cash, I already checked the receipt.'

'I wonder why it's such a big secret.'

'Sex shows, gambling joints, cock fights, necromancy. You name it, this town's got it. Not like they can publicly advertise.' Barney closed the file and passed it to me. 'It's all yours. Be careful. A lot of freaks out there.'

'I will. I can't thank you enough.'

Barney came out and we shook hands. It felt sad I wouldn't see him again, unless I was placing an announcement for a wedding or a funeral.

I didn't plan on doing either anytime soon.

60

The wind was up at the Veramonte Hotel, causing mayhem. Palms waved frenziedly like tropical dancing girls, waiters zoomed about closing canopies and umbrellas. I handed the keys to the valet and hurried inside.

I had resisted the temptation of putting on something too glamorous and now I was in the opulent dining room, I instantly regretted it. Buzzing with film industry movers and shakers, the men were dapper, and women were out of this world, dolled up in elegant dresses and ornate hats with feathers, fruit, and fur trimmings. Quite a few women diners wore turbans with elegant stones in the center, like a nosey third eye with which to spy on other diners.

But it was important for Lyle to see me in a completely new light and for Janice, who I'd go on to next, to open up to me. I'd gone for as bland as I could. As little make-up as possible, just a dusting of powder and a touch of mascara. I wore my pantsuit with a pale gray shirt and pearls.

I had to face my only reality. While I still lived and breathed, Elvira Slate was a career girl.

But maybe I had taken bland a little far. As the waiter ushered me towards a row of half-moon booths along the far wall, I was getting noticed. I looked like the office girl called in to take notes at a studio executives' lunch, not to eat the food.

Each table was positioned a discreet distance from the others. Low lamps with red shades matched the floral mural on the wall. Other waiters buzzed around, attentive and discreet.

Lyle had his head in a menu. He looked even better in daylight. His hair was shinier than I remembered and his bone structure more chiseled. Under a pale blue suit, he wore a cream silk shirt that flowed like liquid. His tie was alabaster silk with an abstract peacock design.

Of course he was born to eat in places like this. 'Hi,' I said, brightly.

He looked up, and gave a half-smile, as he stood up. He shook my hand. 'Good to see you again.' His eyes wandered over my clothes, a look of disappointment mixed with disbelief. Had he really bedded such a frump?

I sat down at the opposite end of the semicircle.

Lyle had a flute of champagne and a little dish of green olives. A vintage bottle poked out of a chiller. Interesting move, born of male pride. Ordering and opening a bottle of bubbly before my arrival? The message was clear. He didn't need to wait for me.

'Celebrating?' I queried.

He hesitated, deciding not to share anything with me. 'Good day for business.'

'Congratulations.' I said. 'Look, I left early the other night. Couldn't sleep. I didn't want to disturb you.'

Lyle signaled to a passing waiter for another flute. 'I'll just have some water,' I said. Booze could prove my undoing and I had work to do.

'It's a free world, the last time I checked. You missed out on my waffles.'

I changed the subject to our only mutual friend. 'How's Troy getting on?'

'Oh, please. Failed to meet my deadline. My fourth deadline.

I have a lot of pet causes; bankrolling alcoholics isn't one of them.' Lyle swigged some champagne and popped an olive in his mouth. Gone was the smitten boy with too much money, he had another hat on. A shrewd, hard-nosed movie producer hat. And he felt like a stranger. It was weird we'd been intimate. Sober and in the cold light of day, we could be at permanent loggerheads.

Lyle was just warming up. 'Sure, he's talented, but he's also a festering mass of self-pity. That's writers for you. Handle with care!'

'Maybe you should go easy. I think he's got wife trouble.'

'Some feat that he's even got one to have trouble with.'

He was already irritating me so it was time to get to the point. 'Forget I mentioned him.' I studied the menu, and closed it.

'You're mad?' His brown eyes twinkled.

'Not at all. Think what you like. Free world, as you say.'

'Anyway, you know what? Your words kind of left an impression on me. Maybe those wicked ladies are old hat. I'm looking for different stuff now.'

Troy's troubles could be my scheme's gain. I felt an odd pang of guilt.

The waiter returned with the glass, and asked if we were ready to order. Lyle looked up. 'We'll take the special. As it comes.' The waiter nodded, retreating.

I smiled falsely, hiding my outrage. 'Did you just order for me?'

'It'll be good.'

Irritation rose in me but I quelled it. This was his invitation, his territory. His wealth gave him a sense of entitlement to make others fall into line. I had to ignore it if I was going to reel him in. 'Well, I just don't eat meat.'

He rolled his eyes. 'What? I'll get the menu back.'

'Forget it. I'll pick at the salad. I really came to talk.'

'And I'm a little tight and happy you rang.' He took the empty champagne flute, filled it with an inch of bubbly, and refilled his own. '1935 vintage. You can't refuse.' He flashed me a patronizing smile, raising his glass.

I raised mine. 'To a happy lunch.'

'To a happier afternoon?' He winked. Sex wasn't going to happen but maybe it wouldn't hurt if Lyle thought it might.

We clinked our glasses, locking eyes.

To Shimmer, Rhonda, Frank and Darlene.

To Arnold Moss.

To everyone who will never sit in a place like this.

I ran my finger around the rim of my glass. 'I called you because I've got a project you might be interested in.'

'What do you mean, a project?'

'A movie project. After meeting you, it occurred to me you could be interested in getting involved. Thing is, it's top secret.'

'I don't understand. Are you in the business? Thought you didn't act?'

Not that kind of acting.

'I'm an investigator.'

Lyle somehow contained what could have been a big splutter of expensive champagne. 'What the hell?'

'I haven't been looking into you. I'm not working for your wife or anything. Meeting you the other night was as unexpected for me as it was for you. What I'm about to tell you, you can't tell anyone.' I lowered my eyes, glancing from side to side.

'Go ahead.' His body language was tense, arms folded. I'd lost him for the moment.

'It's a real-life story. A former star, with a secret past. The movie's going to tell the truth. You just need to express an interest, and I can fix you up with the writer and the star whose life story it is.'

'Who's the producer?'

'Nobody yet. That's the whole point. It could be you.'

'What?' Lyle folded his arms, looked puzzled.

'First, swear on your life not to breathe a word.'

'All right. I swear.'

'Tatiana Spark wants to make her true life story. A version of events that is apparently incredible. But she got cold feet when a bad thing happened.'

Lyle put his glass down. 'Tatiana Spark. Did you ever see *Saint Augustine*?'

I said I hadn't. 'I met the writer. Martell Grainger. I mentioned to Martell that I knew someone already interested. I had to jump in quick to reserve the space, if you see what I mean. I didn't name you, so you don't have to go any further, but the opportunity is there.'

'Martell Grainger, huh? Apparently she's a piece of work.'

'And very talented.' *According to Martell*, I could have said.

'How did you hear about it, anyway?'

I looked him directly in the eye and said Darlene Heymann had told me, before she died. Lyle absorbed this, giving nothing away. After a while, he said, 'I'm yet to meet the Heymann Brothers. I heard about the daughter dying.'

'It's tragic. Darlene was going to direct, but now I guess it's an open field.' I sipped my water, meeting his eyes over my glass.

337

'You sure hid your cards the other night.'

I looked at him. 'Don't be sore. If you're interested, I'll put you in touch with Martell and Spark's attorney. But hurry, the clock's ticking. Might have been snapped up already.'

'All right.' Lyle leant back, still studying me. 'Set the meeting up.'

'Okay. Remember, it's hush-hush. Wait to hear from me and don't go jumping any guns. Promise?'

I didn't want anyone drugging and killing Lyle Vadnay. They'd have to get past me first.

'Fine. I swear. I don't want any competition anyway. So what kind of fee are you looking at?'

What? I had no idea what to say. I blurted out the first words that came into my head. 'Ten...'

'Come on! Call it five, fair and square?'

'Er...' I stuttered, out of my depth.

Incredibly, Lyle took it as if I was negotiating. 'All right, meet you in the middle – seven! No more. Done?'

'Sure. Done.' I said.

Here I was, utterly clueless, brokering a movie deal for a star, a writer, and a producer. I didn't even own a bank account and probably never would.

Lyle slid around the booth to sit closer to me. He cupped his fingers gently over my hand, lying on the seat. I let him, liking the contact. Nobody could see our touch.

Careful. You need to keep a low profile.

I was on fire inside but this time I would resist him.

After lunch, I excused myself, telling Lyle I would get the ball rolling. On my way out, I went to an empty payphone booth in the long row in the hotel lobby. I quickly dialed the number for Falaise Investigations. Beatty came on the line.

'Where are you?'

'Veramonte Hotel.'

'Not bad.'

'The producer is game.'

'So you pulled it off. That's something.' I smiled to myself. 'I negotiated seven-something as a fee. I have no idea what that means.'

'Means you want this movie made, and fast,' chuckled Beatty. I reminded her I had no bank account. 'Mine's good.' she said.

She reminded me to tread carefully, that all communication had to be through me. 'If somebody in that circle killed to stop the project prematurely, this could put you in the line of fire.'

I said I'd make sure nobody else was at risk.

'You know, maybe I should pop by Martell first to keep her warm, now that Lyle's in. Then I'll head out to Janice. What do you think?'

'Okay. But could be the lover is small fry.'

It would be another long day.

61

The cold wind had died down to a warm and pleasant breeze.

A long line of expensive cars lined the side of *Perpetua*'s front drive. The cream of the motorcar crop.

I rang the bell and looked around, taking in the neighborhood's genteel vista.

Phyllis opened the door, wiping her hands on a cloth. She looked frazzled. 'You here for the pool party, too, Miss?' She shot my clothes a doubtful look.

'No. I've just got a quick message for Martell. Is she around?'

'Uh-huh. She's in the garden. Remember the way? I got some chicken in the pan. About to catch fire.' She let me in, grumbling. 'They were supposed to be going out for late lunch, but looks like they changed their minds. They're multiplying like fruit flies.'

'Maybe you should get out the bug spray,' I said, drily.

Phyllis glanced at me. *Yeah. Maybe, one day, I will.*

She showed me through a door leading to a sun lounge which I hadn't noticed before. Fashion magazines and nail polish lay scattered on the floor next to a wicker recliner. Pammie's clutter. The doors opened onto a covered patio, where fragrant blooms hung from the beams.

Some distance away, a large group of women lounged in expensive swimsuits like exotic parakeets around an oasis, cocktails in their perfectly manicured hands. Spirits were high. There had to be about twenty people already, and the doorbell was ringing again.

Frou-Frou scampered around with other perfectly groomed pedigree dogs – a blonde Afghan hound and an Irish setter. They fought and whined over a toy rabbit.

The canine version of a girl harmony trio.

Martell waved me over. She wore a pale silk sundress with peasant-style stitching over a purple satin swimsuit, and a wide-brimmed hat with a lilac chiffon scarf dangling over it like a veil. Her shades were a deep plum glass bordered by ivory rims.

As I approached, she rose from her sun lounger and met me halfway across a lawn that felt like bouncy green carpet. 'Well, look at you working hard. No rest for the wicked, huh?' This was a humorous dig at my work getup. 'Come meet the girls. We'll talk later.' She pulled her shades down her nose and rolled her eyes, a reminder not to reveal anything. Then she pushed them back up.

'I don't have long.' A lot of faces staring at me made me nervous. I didn't want to get too well known.

She put her arm in mine, which I found somewhat awkward. Suddenly bosom buddies? Either she was banking on good news or she was tipsier than she looked. She propelled me over to the gathering. 'Girls, this is Elvira Slate. Helping me with a few matters, business and personal. Somebody get her a goddamned drink.'

'I'm good, thanks. Working.'

'One won't hurt.' A hand with red talons plonked a glass of fizz in my hand. I looked up to say thanks and my heart jumped. A blonde in red shades, wearing a white satin swimming costume, smiled at me. She looked suspiciously like Lana Turner from a picture June had taken me to. Up close, all the women were extremely glamorous. Nobody else paid me much attention, too involved with their own conversations. Maybe one or two smiled and waved.

Martell gracefully slid back onto her lounger and gestured for me to take the one next to her. I sat awkwardly on the edge.

Martell raised her voice, to bring the focus back to her. 'So, girls, back to the Pammie situation. Who have we boiled it down to? Chazz Melton, Buster Brigson, Duane Flanagan.' She turned to me. 'I'm taking matters into my own hands and introducing my niece to some fellas that meet Auntie's approval. Oh, what's the name of that fighter pilot turned producer? Lyle Vadnay.'

Of course Lyle would be on the list. New to town, no spouse in sight. Pammie would make a perfect wife for Lyle – pretty, fun-loving and with great industry connections thanks to Auntie Martell. Their kids would be golden and never know a hard day's work in their gold-plated lives. He just had to get divorced.

Martell turned to me. 'I want them all vetted. That's where you come in.'

Someone called out. 'Anthony Goggins' family *is* Texan oil. Shame he's bug ugly.'

Martell frowned. 'And no grandchild of mine will have the surname Goggins.'

One woman said, 'Lyle Vadnay was canoodling with some gal at the Palms. Might be taken already.'

'Oh, he's too smooth. I like them rough around the edges.'

'Hardly a wimp. Bombed enough Nazis.'

'And pounded enough pussy.' They screamed with laughter.

And he's married, I could have added.

Martell's smile was fading by the second and then she

snapped. 'I'm not expecting a saint. God knows, Pammie isn't. I just can't have her dating any crazies!' She said this with some force. Everyone went silent. Martell laughed it off. 'Listen to me. I'm so overprotective!' She turned to me. 'You know what? Let's get away from this rabble!'

We got up and we headed towards the French doors at the back of the house. 'Well?'

'Want the good news or bad news?' I said.

Martell stopped by the patio and shook her head, momentarily frazzled. 'Both, whatever. Good news first. Optimism goes a long way.'

'Well, the good news is the producer is keen to meet you and hear more. He's looking for projects and has bucks to burn. The bad news? He's Lyle Vadnay and he's married.'

Martell's face fell for a second but she rebounded quickly. 'Oh, there's plenty more fish in the sea of hunk. I wouldn't call that bad news at all. This is all marvelous news!'

'I'm seeing him later, and we'll be in touch about meeting. He's very excited to hear all about the story.'

Martell widened her eyes. They were shining, the look of somebody dying to reveal something. I smelt the liquor on her breath. Could sun, fun and alcohol loosen her tongue?

She leant in, to whisper in my ear. 'Tatiana Spark has been reunited with her long-lost child. The kid recently arrived from Europe. All grown up now, of course. It's just too dramatic. You couldn't make it up!'

'Gee.' A kid. I noticed she pointedly wasn't saying what sex. 'Is this the new story?'

'Uh-uh. You got the bare bones. Lots more meat to come, but all in good time. I'm only telling you because I know you won't blab. There's something about you I trust, and I don't say that very often, believe me. I'm an excellent judge of character.'

'Have you met the kid?'

'Not yet. They needed time to get to know each other.'

Another lipstick to be slid around on Beatty's desk. How could a long-lost child be a factor Darlene and Shimmer's death? Maybe somebody didn't want the news of the kid to come out. Maybe the father didn't want that? Enough to kill?

I thought of my own absent father, so desperate to remain unknown he'd gone by a phony name. But the father of Spark's kid surely had to be European. The Heymann Studios wouldn't care, Tatiana Spark's contract had expired decades ago and they weren't interested in Darlene's pitch anyway.

I had to call Beatty. 'Who would benefit?' She would ask. 'Who gains from this?'

Then it hit me. Somebody could lose. Beatty and I didn't know how much Tatiana had stashed away since her glory days, but money, the great motivator, could be behind everything.

Martell was still cooing, excited. 'This picture is going to be big, so big. It's going to speak to every woman who's made an impossible choice. Which is most women, in my book! Now we just need some big boys to let us prove it!'

I wondered if that was her story, too. I assured Martell I would set up the meeting very soon.

62

The Laurels was a small apartment block on a junction with 18th Street in a leafy corner of Santa Monica. It was a squat Deco style building, nestling between large family houses. I liked the atmosphere in the area. The sky looked bigger down here, the air was fresher, and my mood more optimistic.

Perhaps I would go to the pier and get my fortune told. Validation on the cheap. Knowing my luck, I'd get a fortuneteller who took an instant dislike to me and predict disaster.

A tabby cat basked in the sunshine on the front steps, licking its fat white paws. The cat ignored me as I buzzed number seven. I held a bunch of peach-colored roses, intermingled with some kind of blue daisies. If Janice answered, I'd play it that I'd been sent to the wrong address and ask if she could help me. If she was as obsessed as her letter sounded, she'd be kind of disappointed she wasn't the intended recipient. If I played my cards right, she might even open up about any love troubles with Lyntner.

No answer, so I rang again and waited. For want of anything better to do, I stroked the cat, which rolled onto its back and swiped at the flowers. I grinned, remembering Kettle. I'd like to get another cat one day, if Lauder ever let me move out of the Astral.

'Calling for Janice? She ain't here!'

I turned. Damn! I hadn't even considered that possibility. A young mother with flushed cheeks and a hassled expression was staggering towards me. She lugged a toddler on one hip and shopping on the other. The kid had a runny nose and his arm wildly flailed at the flowers. The mother yelled 'Baxter! Quit that right now. Gee, ain't that a pretty bouquet.'

I gave Baxter's cheek a pinch, steering clear of the snot. He wriggled away, protesting. 'Oh, you big baby!' cried his mom. 'He's got a cold. Just leave them with me, I'll put 'em in water. Janice gets back real late.'

She put Baxter down. He lunged at the cat, which took off. Baxter whimpered in frustration and toddled off after it. The mother shrugged. 'Boys will be boys, huh?'

I had a choice to make, and fast. Either stick to my wrong address story, as I hadn't actually said the flowers were for Janice, and just walk away.

Or stick around and use the situation to get some gossip. But this was high risk. Janice would thank Lyntner for the flowers, he would then find out somebody had been pretending to be his assistant, brandishing bouquets, and even stealing his mail. The neighbor would be able to describe me.

Risk suddenly appealed.

'Thing is, my boss sent them. Strict instructions to give them straight to her.' I rolled conspiratorial eyes. 'Looks like a kiss and make up bouquet to me.'

She peered at the bouquet and shot me back a meaningful look. 'Could be. Never said nothing to me, just she was seeing someone. To be honest, thought she was a spinster for life. That cat is hers. I feed it if she don't come back at night.'

Funny how the world put cats and spinsters together. Was it my destiny? I could live with that.

I looked around, acting concerned. 'He's gonna be real mad

if she don't get them today. Maybe I should take them to her work? Know where that is?'

The woman frowned. 'Well, she's a nurse.'

'I can drop them there. Which hospital?'

'Private nurse, somewhere in the Palisades.' She leant closer, so precious Baxter didn't hear. 'Patient's not doing so well. Dying. An old lady. That's why Janice is staying over a lot. You didn't hear it from me, but the old lady, she's a retired movie star.' She rolled her eyes, clearly impressed.

'That's too bad. Who is it?'

'No idea, Janice doesn't gab.'

I stared into space. My instinct was waking up like a hungry baby. Janice had sent the letter to Frederick Lyntner, her lover and Tatiana's attorney. Janice was nursing a retired movie star who was dying. Lyntner had suggested a ticking clock...

Tatiana Spark was dying.

Did Martell know? If so, she wasn't giving it away.

Hadn't Janice written something to Lyntner about being more careful? And if Spark's child had shown up recently, was Janice worried about either Tatiana or the child knowing about the affair? It could look unprofessional, tactless even.

There had to be a motive in there somewhere.

I collected myself and looked down at the flowers. 'Such a waste.'

'Give them to me. I'll enjoy them till she comes back. Mind you, she does the night shift a lot nowadays.'

I might as well leave the flowers, she would tell Janice I'd come anyway. My first breakthrough was riddled with risk. But possibly I had a little time before any of this came out, particularly if Janice wasn't coming back home often.

'Okay, thanks.' I handed her the flowers and walked away.

The woman called out after me. 'Maybe it'll get my husband thinking I got an admirer!'

63

A heavy blanket of late afternoon sea mist had rolled in and settled Downtown, collecting at the foot of buildings. The gloom made Trenton Towers appear even more dingy. It reminded me of foggy London days.

I entered the building through the same revolving doors. No doorman, again. The elevator was still parked on some other floor.

I hurried up the stairs.

The corridor was deserted. I hurried along to Lyntner's office. The door swung open. No one around. I hovered on the threshold. 'Hello? Mr. Lyntner?'

The window in the antechamber was open, letting in cold air.

Silence. I stepped inside, gripping the pistol.

The place had been cleared out. Every book, every paper, every photograph of a docked nag. There wasn't even a telephone left from which I could call Beatty. Just a wire, dangling like a piece of string.

Somebody had left for good.

Lyntner had said he wasn't moving out anytime soon and now he'd packed up and gone. Had my first visit spooked him?

Could he be the one who didn't want the movie going ahead?

I rushed back down the stairs and into the street. There was a bar on the corner, packed with office workers letting off steam. Happy, ordinary people leading happy, ordinary lives. I headed for the payphone on the bar and called Beatty. Therese must have left already because Beatty picked up herself.

I spoke as low as possible. People were near me. 'Martell's keen. She told me Spark's long-lost child has arrived, from Europe. That's what the movie's about! But Lyntner's gone. Office totally cleaned out. So he lied, because he said he wasn't leaving anytime soon. And guess what – Janice, the lover, is a nurse, but to one single private patient. In the Palisades, a very sick patient. A movie star who is dying!'

'Good Lord. Tatiana Spark lives in the Palisades.'

'Right. And the love letter said something about being careful. There's a motive somewhere in all this. And I think Darlene was murdered because of it.'

'Jeez. I don't like this, Booby. Now I'm thinking it wouldn't be so farfetched if Caziel and Lyntner do know each other.'

'Lyntner could have paid him to do something, maybe? To do with Darlene? Maybe Lyntner and Janice are in cahoots, making Spark sick!' My mind raced.

Beatty spoke low. 'Poison? Or maybe the kid is in on it, too and he or she hired the nurse.'

'What if Lyntner has messed with the will? He's Tatiana's attorney, after all. He could have designs to get rid of the kid. I should go to Tatiana's now. Can you get her address?'

Beatty said she had it, in fact.

'But if they see you, you're in big trouble.'

'If it's what we think, Lyntner was shaken up by my first visit. He could have speeded up with his plans. I'll park at a distance and just watch the house.'

'All right. Go there, but make it quick, and see what's going down. Report back to me. You can't exactly call the cops, but I

350

can! See how many cars are there, any movement, that kind of thing. Park somewhere well out of sight of the house. You hear me? Do not approach the house. We still could've got it all wrong. All right?' Beatty sounded tense.

'And what about Olive Harjo?' I asked.

'What about her?'

We'd kept Olive out of the line of enquiry, but now it was open field. 'She could be pretending to be the nurse, in on it somehow.'

'You know I never suspected her. Why not drop by on your way? Tell her the good news about the movie going ahead. See how she reacts. As ever, proceed with caution.'

I said I would.

With that, Beatty finally gave me her home address and telephone number. Then she gave me Tatiana Spark's address. *Juniper House.* She didn't need to look it up, I noticed.

The cabin looked as if it had been shut up tight for winter. No rugs airing, no swinging hammocks, no spying parrot. The shutters were closed. The building had lost some of its romantic charm. It was now a shell.

Everyone is clearing out today.

The only sound was the wind rustling through the grasses. Even the grasshoppers had gone elsewhere. I suddenly wished I hadn't left my jacket in the car.

I made my way to the little hut. A half-dead creeper covered the building. The charcoal remains of a fire blackened the ground outside. The heavy door was padlocked. Could Rhonda have been locked in here? I shuddered to think of it. I edged around the side and peered in through the window.

Nothing. The place was empty.

Maybe Beatty's instincts had always been right. Olive Harjo, the mysterious artist, had just decided it was time to pack up and move on. Maybe she really was grieving her lost lover.

Maybe she was somehow in cahoots with Lyntner. His real lover?

Maybe she was on the run.

Whatever, she was gone and I couldn't waste any more time here. As I turned back on my path, something caught my eye.

A note, stuck with tape on the front door of the cabin. I walked up the steps and pulled it off. One word was scrawled on the envelope. *Elvira.*

I grabbed it and tore it open.

Dear Elvira, you will be the only person to come back. I hope you have given up your search. It is pointless. I have left Los Angeles. I am living now with Blandine Hundley, in New Mexico. The address is below. When you can, please visit our artistic community. By the way, your name means Truth.'

I stared at the writing.

My instinct now matched up with Beatty's.

Olive was innocent.

64

I was winding my way back through the Canyon towards Sunset when I realized I wasn't alone. The wheels were churning up a dust cloud, but as it subsided, a dark car came into view, a fair distance behind me. It was black or very dark gray. I could make out one driver, a shadowy figure. A tail? When had it picked me up? And more to the point, who was it? My stomach knotted up. Had Jim Fraser found me already?

I wasn't in the mood to die today, or to go to Tatiana Spark's house with someone tracking me. I put my foot down and picked up speed, careering down the hill, the car lurching as it bounced over potholes. I had no idea how lose a tail, but logic dictated to keep moving and fast. I was tempted to stop, and see what the car, or rather the driver, did. But the place was deserted and there was nowhere to run. I didn't fancy my chances.

I soon reached the more populated foothills with their manicured gardens and smoother road surface. Houses and humanity offered a greater sense of security; I could always pull up, ring a doorbell, and pretend I was lost.

The car kept a reasonable distance.

At last I blended into the traffic on Sunset. It was busy. The black car was still behind me. Was it a Plymouth? I had to lose it.

I weaved in and out of several cars, switching lanes jerkily. Somebody blasted a horn at me. Screw them. I glanced back. There was a big truck ahead. I overtook it, and caught sight of a right turn, a narrow lane. I dived down it, without indicating.

The alley was punctuated by the back doors of restaurants, overloaded garbage cans and hungry alley cats. I slowed down slightly. In my rear mirror, on the main road behind, the dark car charged straight on.

He hadn't seen me turn.

The sign for Juniper House was barely legible, eroded by years of salty air. It poked out from thick evergreen shrubs. The road climbed past the house, which was not visible from the road.

I drove on, finally pulling into a turnout before a major bend. I got out of the car. The turnout offered a good vantage spot over the hill. It was deadly quiet except for the distant roar of the ocean. Juniper House itself was in fact two single-story houses with pitched shingle roofs, set far back in grounds that reminded me of a fairy-tale forest. It was all the more atmospheric with the mist hovering between the pine trees and the house. The whole thing felt rural, as if the occupants had wanted to forget they were in a fast, modern American city and create a tranquil little corner of Europe.

Looking down, there was a long garage and I could only see the part of the drive that led to the forecourt, where two cars were parked. A large, black car and a smaller, mushroom-colored convertible. I couldn't make out the models. Was it the same black car as the one that had tailed me? No. Impossible. I'd have seen it.

There was no sign of life in the grounds of the house. I lit a cigarette and walked a little higher up, to view the ocean. A group of pelicans passed over me, magnificent shapes over a pink sky. I'd only ever seen them before in cartoons. They headed east and were soon lost in the gray haze.

I turned back to look at the house at exactly the right moment. A tall female figure in shades with a wide-brimmed hat headed towards the convertible. Janice? The long-lost kid, a daughter?

The woman jumped into the mushroom sports car with agility, and drove down the drive. Her movements – the elegant stride – had something familiar about them.

Soon the car disappeared from view, under the heavy trees. If she turned left, the woman would pass me on the hill and could easily spot me. I dashed back to the car and crouched down behind the bonnet on the nearside. I hoped my car would look it was abandoned.

Sure enough, a powerful engine soon surged up the hill. The coupe flew past. I peeked out. Up close, it was a very nice car. Immaculate, gleaming, and fast. The sort of car I'd buy in another life.

I was torn. Should I watch the comings and goings at the house? My desire to follow the woman was overwhelming and I jumped back in the car.

Beatty had said no sudden moves. I was to check in with her. But if I lost this opportunity, and it led to the truth, surely I'd regret it. I could equally imagine her telling me I was stupid for not acting on instinct.

I was soon cruising some fifty yards behind her. I happened to glance in my rear mirror. I jumped. A tiny black speck behind me. The tail?

Whatever or whoever it was, it was catching up.

My stomach lurched. I was following the woman, while being followed.

Dammit!

We drove for several miles. I kept a big enough distance. So did my tail. The woman was heading deeper inland, into agricultural land. The odd farmhouse was dotted here and there. Simple structures for simple lives. I recalled Lauder's words about me running and holing up in the sticks. He'd got me wrong. I'd go crazy out here.

A truck loaded with grain began to pull out from a country lane, turning right. The vehicle was so massive, the move took up the whole road. I had to wait, impatiently tapping my foot, cut off from the car ahead. My tail seemed to slow down, no doubt to avoid being obvious.

I let the truck pass, cursing inwardly. I reached down for the pistol out of the purse and put it in my lap, remembering I still hadn't stocked up on bullets.

As soon as the truck passed, I sped up. Finally I saw the coupe in the distance, just as it turned right down a drive. A second later and I'd have missed it altogether. I slowed down, to cruise past. My tail followed relentlessly behind me. I glanced down the drive. Behind some tall, rusting iron gates, now open, there was an old farmhouse nestling on the hillside. The grounds were full of well-established, bushy fruit trees. I decided to park as soon as I could and go over the hill on foot.

If the guy tailing me chose to join me on my hike, he'd have to find out it was a rather hazardous jaunt. But I only had one shot. I couldn't waste it.

I parked and jumped out, grabbing the gumshoes from the trunk. I slipped them on and clambered through a hole in the broken fence. I could hear the engine of the tail racing past. Was he slowing down? I kept looking back in case a figure appeared on the horizon. I scrambled over the scrubby land. Slow going

356

over the long furrows of tufts of straw, rigid remnants of the harvest. I looked back – nobody was in pursuit.

I almost laughed.

The car was being driven by somebody who had zero interest in me, someone just going about life.

In the distance, I could make out the fence around the farmhouse's large plot. As I got closer, I could see it was just chicken wire attached to posts. Easy enough to climb over, particularly in the pantsuit.

A dog started barking. Shit! I froze, rigid, then darted behind a large, pale shrub with a lot of bees buzzing around its orange flowers. I crouched down, out of view. The mutt was on high alert, and didn't shut up.

I heard a door open and a woman call out something. The voice was familiar, somehow. The dog whimpered and I heard a rustle.

I peered around the leaves.

The car was parked outside.

A tall blonde woman was bending over, stroking the dog.

Starlet blonde.

Lena?

Impossible!

It couldn't be. Not Lena. Tatiana Spark's long-lost daughter could not be Lena.

The wide-brimmed hat had gone but in every other respect it was the woman who had left Tatiana Spark's house. No, it must be a look-alike. Just another tall blonde in a city chock-full of them. I had to be seeing things, like the 'tail'. Turning into a crazy fool. That's what life on the edge does, right? I was just a wreck.

You never mourned your loss and this is what happens. You're seeing her because you want to.

The woman was standing still at the door, holding the dog's collar, both alert. It was a large, brown hunting dog. A killer with a strong nose.

I didn't move.

The dog began barking again. He knew I was there, and he was making damn sure she knew it.

The woman took a last look around and then she turned around and closed the door.

Should I knock on the door and quiz her? See for myself up close that this was somebody else? Stop my delusions, once and for all?

No. I should creep back up the hill quickly, quietly. Get in the car, fly back to Beatty's and let Beatty tip off the cops to check up on Tatiana. Avoid any mention of chasing the woman. Avoid revealing the one element of my past I'd neglected to tell her. That on the day of my release, my best friend in jail had killed herself. And now it turned out her look-alike was living in L.A.

Let the cops figure it out. Sweat broke out over my face. I had to get out of here.

Five minutes later I got back to my car, breathless. I fumbled for the key. Where the hell was it? Had I dropped it? Maybe it had fallen out when I crouched down by the orange-flowered shrub. Booby, indeed. I had no choice but to retrace my steps. I headed back the same way, creeping back down the field, an eye on the ground, trying to spot the key. I had to find it before the dog heard me again.

I reached the plant, and scrabbled around the base.

Crack!

An explosion of light, filling my eyes as my head seemed to spin into its own orbit. Then the pain, before the darkness.

358

65

Something or somebody was knocking a nail into my head. It pounded in time with my heart. I tried to feel my head, but couldn't move my hands, or my legs. My eyelids were too heavy to open. My tongue felt too big for my mouth, like a dried-out sponge. I must have sweated buckets in here before coming around. My clothes were drenched, glued to my body.

I was lying on my back. I lifted my head slightly and tried to look down at my body. Bound across the chest with thin nautical rope. Somebody had removed my jacket top. I seemed to be in some kind of shed, lying on a soft, sagging surface. I groped with the tips of my fingers and felt rough canvas. A cot? Striped deck chairs and recliners were propped against the walls. I had to be on some kind of camp bed or lounger.

A sharp, chemical smell hit me. Huge waves of nausea took over, making the pain in my head play second fiddle. I willed myself not to vomit.

Vomit, you'll choke.

Choke, you'll die.

Two pale blue eyes, staring into mine. Familiar eyes. The mouth was making shapes at me. I couldn't hear anything. The pounding in my skull made it impossible.

I felt wetness on my forehead – a damp washcloth? It did nothing to relieve the pain.

A face came into sharper focus.

Lena's face.

Was I hallucinating? I tried to open my mouth but couldn't move my lips. Her hand came towards my face and made a yanking gesture. My lips were ripped apart as tape was pulled off.

'Lena?' My voice was hoarse.

She hissed, 'Don't even twitch, if you know what's good for you.' The same Aussie twang. Unmistakably her.

I looked up at her as she peered into my face. She threw her head back, and burst out laughing. 'Imagine this, a Holloway reunion. Jemima fucking Day.'

I murmured, 'You died. I saw – inside. I thought...somebody killed you.'

'Aw, sad were you? You were a tough little thing. Sorry I couldn't kiss you goodbye. Did your hair up, though.'

I didn't know this woman. I had never known her. 'The suicide was a setup. They got you out. Why? Are you pretending to be Tatiana Spark's daughter? Or her nurse?'

'Nosey Parker, all of a sudden? Never asked a thing inside.'

'What's going on? You're a spy?'

'And you're some kind of sleuth?' She waved one of Beatty's cards over my face. 'You work for this Falaise Investigations?'

I stared at her in shock. Lena tossed the card on the ground and reached down for something. A bottle of lemonade came into view.

She held it to my mouth, sliding her hand behind my head. Fuck her. I twisted my head aside, feeling the liquid splash my face.

'Stupid cow, drink.'

'Damn you!' I spat out whatever fell into my mouth at her.

'Suit yourself.' She stood up again and downed the drink. 'We're going on a long hot drive.'

'I saw you. At a club, Seven Palms. What are you doing here?'

Lena rolled her eyes. 'Tell you what, you first.' She produced a menacing revolver and waved it in my face. 'You're in the wrong place at the wrong time, so you better have a bloody good reason.'

My brain couldn't think fast enough.

'I was released, same day as you...they...staged your death. I bolted, jumped probation. I managed to get here, to L.A. I just wanted to find my father.'

This lie could work.

'Your father?' Lena wasn't expecting this.

I nodded, turning my head to meet her eye. 'He's a Yank. Turns out the yearning for a reunion wasn't mutual.'

'Ah, poor little Jemima, Daddy didn't want to see her? Bullshit!' She knelt down and jabbed me with the gun, hard on the ribs. 'Try again.'

'That's the truth.'

Lena lit a cigarette. 'Want some more burn scars on that skinny little arm? Out with it!'

'I swear it's true. I'm on the run. I needed a job, so I'm working for an investigator on a missing person case. She doesn't know anything about my past.'

'So why are you spying on Tatiana Spark's house?'

'The missing person, she's got a connection with Darlene Heymann's death.'

Lena stood up. 'The director who snuffed it?'

I nodded. So she knew about the film. If there was a scheme, she could be in on it. Or she was there for entirely different reasons and she didn't know about Lyntner, Janice or Olive. Maybe there was a kid, somebody else in the house, and I'd got everything wrong. Everything – even Rhonda running, the overdoses, the lover, the daughter, Lena, Olive and Lyntner disappearing; maybe they all had no significance whatsoever. Maybe Beatty and I had just been blown along by the hot air of a canister full of assumption.

Lena finished the lemonade and tossed the bottle in an empty metal oil container. It ratted noisily before falling still.

'And here we are. What a mess.'

I looked at her. 'What's a mess?'

She guffawed, mimicking me. 'What's a mess, says the fascist.'

I tried to bolt up, straining against the rope pinning me down. 'What? I'm no fucking fascist!'

'What was your story inside again? That your boyfriend had dumped you in it? But here you are, on the run, snooping on me. Want to wreck my operation, is that it?'

Operation?

'What?'

She guffawed again. 'You really take the fucking biscuit.'

This conversation was going nowhere.

'I don't know anything about you or what you're up to. If you're in on the murders, you want Spark's money or whatever, I'm dead meat. Who cares? I'm on borrowed time anyway. If you're impersonating Spark's kid for some espionage-related reason, good for you. But Spark's lawyer is up to no fucking good.'

Lena studied me. 'Frederick Lyntner?'

'He's having an affair with the nurse, assuming that isn't you, and he's cleared out of his office. He could be after her money. Are you in on it? Is she dying?'

Lena burst out laughing. 'Oh, Jem. You silly cow. Did you always have an imagination like this? Wish I'd known. Would have made the clink far more bearable.'

Jem. That's what she used to call me; it felt weird to hear it again. I closed my eyes. If she was working with Lyntner, I could be dead any second.

'All right. For old times' sake, because I got fond of you and seeing you again is some party, I'll give it to you straight. Spark is dying. Janice is her nurse, and the lawyer is taking care of her affairs. That's all. No big murder plot, no shenanigans. And yes, I am impersonating Sophia Spark, as you guessed. Or as you bloody well already know.'

'Know? I don't know anything about you!'

Lena moved around. She now leant against the wall, right in my line of sight, long legs crossed.

'Enough with this whole P.I. rubbish. If somebody in Britain's a triple agent, and feeding you intelligence about my work, you've got time to make your own deal. But you name names, or this is where the conversation ends.'

Deal? Crazy! I almost laughed with sheer panic that she thought I had some credible agenda, that I was after her, some kind of fascist spy. It struck me she definitely seemed more perturbed by this than anything I'd said about Lyntner and the nurse.

If I didn't convince her otherwise, she would kill me.

Once again, there was only the truth card to play. But truth was a lame duck. I was against a master game-player, probably the best in town, trained to dig out duplicity. My mouth was sticky and dry. I tried to swallow, meeting her eye. 'I've got no names to give. I was just a dumb gangster's moll and my chap, Billy, set me up. He was a racketeer. I thought he was sending me out to collect a cargo of French brandy. But it was guns, and the Secret Service was onto it. I never had any interest in politics. The mass slaughter of Jews and Gypsies? Pure evil – I'm no fifth columnist. I'm no saint, either. The only reason I was dumb enough to keep my mouth shut all those years inside? It wasn't for love. It was just to secure a way out of Blighty. Money and a way out.'

Lena surveyed me, taking it all in. She waved Beatty's card. 'What about this?'

'Just a job, a means to survive. To give some point to my fucking existence.' Beatty could be getting worried. Not to mention very pissed. No word from me could push her to picking up the phone and tracking down Lauder. Even if I got away from Lena, I'd have more music to face. A whole symphony.

'Look, I have no idea what you are doing here, or who you are. I hope it's for the good of the world. All I care about is finding a girl who's gone missing, pathetic in comparison. Three people have been murdered. Maybe four. I'm sure of it. Just like I'm sure Lyntner is behind it. And if you haven't a clue about what him and this nurse could be up to, you could be in danger, too. They could be the ones to wreck whatever you are planning.'

Lena walked over in silence, holding the glowing cigarette. Burn time? Or was she going to shoot me?

Instead, she knelt down and stared at me. She put her hand up, and I flinched. Her hand stayed still in the air. Lena smiled.

364

Then calmly, softly, she stroked my brow. It was comforting and terrifying. She whispered. 'Poor Jem. What a to-do.'

Then she untied my bonds. Those brittle blue eyes remained unreadable.

I was freed, and sat up on the camp bed, rubbing my arms back to life. Lena stood back up. She said, 'We're going for a ride.'

Another realization hit me. In the blink of an eye, Lena could tell her superiors I was alive and in L.A.

Her British superiors. If her story was true, she had to be an Allied spy.

If she didn't kill me first, I'd have to kill her.

66

'I'm going to drive you near to the Mexican border. You can get on a bus there. I'll give you money and some clothes. Don't ever cross back over the border again. Start over. Get a boat all the way up to Canada if South America doesn't suit you. But I got here first. You being in town...well, as the Yanks would say, it cramps my style.'

Lena dragged me up onto my feet. I was unresisting, limp as a rag doll. We were face to face. Up close I could see those Holloway blood blisters all over again, the Cupid's bow curve of her top lip, and her glacial eyes. She gazed into my face for a while. Her expression was unreadable. She could kiss me or shoot me.

She left the shed, taking her gun.

A few minutes later, I heard an engine. Lena opened the door, and beckoned me out. I followed.

A different car purred outside, the doors open. This one was a shiny, large beast, in dark blue.

'Get in. The front,' Lena pointed with the gun to make it clear.

I sat down in the front passenger seat. The leather was cream, immaculate. I glanced around; there was a small leather suitcase on the back seat and a blue purse. One might contain a gun. How far would she take me before she shot my brains out?

Lena jumped in next to me. 'I don't know you, and you don't know me. We just have to trust each other. Let's start now.'

Sure. Best buddies, just like old times.

The wheels crunched the gravel. We reached the far corner of the plot. The gravel path wound back around to the front. The shadows of the cypress trees were long, dark talons against scorched earth; I must have been locked up for hours.

Beatty. She really would be freaking out.

Lena pulled out of the gates. She began to speak. 'My name is Nora Holst. Eva Holst was my twin sister. She was a Nazi, a real scumbag. She left Australia in '36 to live in the Fatherland, as she called it. She worked for Himmler. When it looked like the Jerries were losing, she made a plan to escape Germany and come here. She did not get out alive, but her friends here do not know that. They believe I am Eva. That I have found a safe haven with Tatiana Spark.'

'Tatiana knew Eva?' The actress was a fascist?

'Spark knows nothing. She just wanted to find her daughter. Sad and pathetic. She had the kid in Austria before she found stardom in America. So, an inconvenient love child. I guess she felt guilty in her old age. She is riddled with tumors, and she doesn't have much time left. Her lawyer, this Frederick Lyntner, was instructed to locate the daughter. He spoke to an agent, somebody with contacts in Europe. The agent put the word out that the Austrian daughter had a home waiting for her in America. The agent's partners in Europe were able sell this opportunity to the highest bidder. As you can imagine, many people would pay for a way out this good. And Eva was one of them, first in the queue to escape justice. But we were on to her. We made it look like she'd got away when, really, we caught her. She was eliminated. I had been lying low in Holloway waiting for exactly this chance to replace her. We made sure that the word got out that the fascist twin sister had topped herself.'

I turned to her. The land girl. The perfect model. The ruthless operative. Had she killed her own sister as well? *Eliminated.*

Lena went on. 'Spark believes I am her daughter, Sophia. So does everybody else. The lawyer, the nurse. Your theory is nuts.'

'Don't tell me, you're getting the dosh when she dies?' I asked.

Lena glanced at me. 'Spark had planned to leave the whole lot to Janice, the nurse. Been with her for years. Janice will still get something but now Sophia will get the vast bulk of the estate.'

Nice for Sophia. Lena glanced at me, knowing what I was thinking.

'It will go to a trust, for when the operation is over. Then we will try to locate the real daughter. We aren't thieves.'

The pieces suddenly came together. Lena was the missing item on Beatty's desk. 'That's it, can't you see? You've upset Lyntner's plans to get the money through his affair with Janice. You are in danger. So is Tatiana Spark.'

Lena shrugged. 'Maybe. She's dying, and now you've tipped me off, I can deal with them, *if* it's true. But others have to pay for their crimes. Crimes against humanity. They can't just run away and start new lives in paradise. And enough of them get away with it. I'm embedded with Eva's friends, and I can make sure they face justice, in due course. Look, I'm sorry if the movie director and her buddies were murdered, but there's need for a wider justice now.'

A wider justice? Or true justice? My hopes for justice felt pathetic next to her lofty ideals.

But it's kept me going. It's given me a sense of integrity when nothing else ever has.

368

I turned and looked at her. 'You killed your sister, didn't you?'
Lena didn't flinch. 'None of your business.'

That confirmed it. I didn't have to worry about Lena. It would be piece of cake for her to defend herself against Lyntner and Janice. And Lena could easily kill me, out here in the vast desert. Why bother with trust? Sentiment was not exactly her thing, if she could bump off her own flesh and blood. Surely she was telling me about her whole operation anyway because she had one thing in mind.

And what if Lena was lying? What if she'd been turned? Maybe getting justice was really an excuse to keep the money for herself and her European cronies? This didn't square with the fact she had been sent here, that she had been trusted enough to be released. The authorities had plotted her incarceration. Even virtuous Dr. Seldon had been complicit with Lena's fake suicide.

As it turned out Lena had been the one with friends in the high places.

'You know, starting again gets easier. Anyway, L.A.'s too dangerous for someone in your position. The Italian Mob's moving out here in droves from Europe now the war's over. So if they want your blood, they'll get it.' So she was keeping up the pretense she cared about me.

Trick your captives. Lull them into a false sense of security. Go easy on them in their last hours.

Lena passed me a pack of cigarettes from her jacket pocket. I hesitated, but took it. I put two in my mouth, lit them and passed her one. I would play it cool, for now.

'Thanks. Find some place off the beaten track.' Lena exhaled. 'Sounds like you could do with a quiet life.'

369

Sure. I'll get a cat, and read a book on a sunny porch.

It was ironic. If I disappeared, Lauder would assume I had run off. An outraged Beatty calling him up would confirm it. Lauder's plan for Jemima Day would kick in. He would claim that the woman's body in the desert was somebody else. Jemima Day/Ida Boyd, spy and murderess, would still be hunted, when I'd actually be a desiccated carcass, just in a different desert. Scotland Yard and God knows how many secret agencies and Mafiosi would all prick up their ears and start searching.

If I escaped Lena, I'd have to go far to really hide.

We drove on, cruising over the dried-out hills, somewhere south of the Los Angeles basin. It was not the main route out of the country. The landscape was barren and harsh and the car was jolted by bumps in the narrow road. I started to feel green.

'Stop the car. I'm going to puke up.' I held my hand to my mouth.

'What?'

I gagged, holding it back. Lena slammed the brakes. 'All right! We got ages, I don't want you stinking the car out.'

I jumped out and chucked my guts up. As I was spitting the last up, bent over, I could see her take the blue purse out of the car. The gun! She was going to do it now, shoot me, right here and now. I tensed up, ready to pounce.

'Got some water here,' she said. 'Get it all up, that's right.' Next thing, she'd be saying 'good girl'.

She got closer, pulling something out. This was it.

Now, my only chance!

I turned around and flung myself at Lena. She fell back hard, too surprised to react fast enough. I punched her head, as hard as I could. Her eyes rolled back, dazed. She groaned but managed to bring her knee up into my diaphragm. I gasped and punched her again and again. My knuckles hurt.

She was out cold. Should I throttle her? I didn't want to kill her. The desert would do that sure enough. Squatting on her to prevent her moving, I pulled the purse over towards me. It was open.

A bottle of water rolled out.

I rummaged inside for the gun. The only other item was a white handkerchief.

Water and a hanky.

No gun.

Lena was tending to me, not killing me?

The hanky looked familiar. Pretty violets were embroidered on the corner. Had Dr. Seldon also issued one to Lena when she left prison? It really was the Holloway souvenir. Crazy. I lifted it to my nostrils, expecting to smell lavender water.

So you meant it about the new start?

I put the hanky to good use, twisting it up diagonally. Just long enough to tie Lena's wrists behind her back. Using all my might, I somehow dragged her to a rock formation, which created a natural barrier with the road. There was some shade here. Before the sun moved, Lena would have time to say her prayers.

I drank from the bottle, then tossed it near her. If she could free herself, she had a chance of survival. Slim, but a chance.

Sorry, Lena.

I left her curled up, in fetal position. She was a pathetic sight, her hair encrusted with sand and grit. Dribble trickled out of her mouth.

She'll die here. This is Lena.

I went back to the car and lit a cigarette. Inside, it felt like a greenhouse in the Sahara. I left the door open, but it made no a difference. Above, high in the sky, a dark object circled. A vulture, spotting an imminent feast. Waiting for me to vacate the territory.

Ironic.

I was leaving her to die so I could run.

Lena, who might have good motives.

Lena, who wasn't going to kill me.

Lena, who some part of me still loved.

You're no killer!

What the hell could I do? It was too late. If I freed her now, Lena would change her mind about killing me. Especially now.

Unless I could spin this around, somehow.

I had a two-hour drive to work that one out.

Fuck.

I dragged Lena back to the car. Lugging five foot ten of unconscious blonde so soon was no mean feat. She began to groan. A long slur came out.

Somehow I got her onto the back seat. I opened the case and found some garments, including a couple of silk scarfs. Again, no weapon. I tied her legs together, and used one to gag her. She groaned again, coming around.

I jumped in the driving seat. I was about to turn on the engine when I saw a black shape on the horizon, hurtling along the track I was about to take.

The tail?

There was no other explanation.

Lena had to have a gun somewhere. The glove box. Sure enough, a heavy revolver lay inside. I grabbed it and checked the barrel. Fully loaded. Better than Dede's one-bullet wonder.

Time was running out. The black car rattled towards us. Lena's eyes flickered. She could hear it, too. She made a noise.

I spoke low. 'Shut the fuck up and lie down.'

Lena was silent, her eyes meeting mine. Her fate depended on me. On my prowess, on my training. The few lessons in sleepy Ashdown Forest a decade ago.

What a joke.

The car was browned by desert mud. It pulled up, about twenty feet in front of me.

'All right. Out you get,' I muttered, waiting. My fingers were wet with sweat and the gun slid around. I felt sick. This was a standoff and I wasn't going to move. The driver wouldn't shoot through his own windscreen, and he wouldn't sit parked up all day waiting.

Inevitably, the door opened.

A tall figure got out, a lanky figure. A man was silhouetted against the sun.

I recognized him immediately.

Randall Lauder.

67

We stood opposite each other, a few yards apart. Here we were, back in the desert. Only this time I was armed. I held the revolver tightly as my sweaty grip allowed, pointing it down.

'Going someplace?' Lauder snarled. 'Don't bother answering. I know you've been getting around town.'

'How long have you been tailing me?'

'Long enough.' So he hadn't gone away. He'd been watching my every move. But since when? And more to the point, why? What did he know?

'You alone?' He glanced at the car.

I nodded. 'Yes. I'm alone.' I said it loud enough for Lena to hear. She had better keep down. It would be better both of us if Lauder didn't find out.

'Taking a trip down South?'

He thought I was running.

'No. I'm heading to the Pacific Palisades, actually. I want to prevent a homicide. And you shouldn't stop me.' I sounded tougher than I felt. I definitely did not want to shoot him. What did I want? For him to just drive away and leave me alone? That wasn't going to happen. I had to make him believe me.

'Oh, yeah? Funny route. Who's gonna be killed?'

'Tatiana Spark. She's a...'

He interrupted. 'I know who she is. I want the gun, Day. Nice and slow. Drop it.'

'No!' Now I raised it, and pointed it at him. 'I want to find

Rhonda and you aren't getting in the way. Tatiana Spark's in danger and I've got a chance to do something. Shimmer, Darlene and the guy, all murdered. You cops don't give a damn!'

'What the hell?' Lauder stared at me, with disbelief.

'I've cracked it and you've got to let me go...'

Lauder's eyes shifted to something behind me. Then they narrowed as his arm suddenly rose up, gun in hand, firing.

Bang!

I froze, confused. Lauder was suddenly thrown back in the air. His body collapsed on the ground. I spun around.

Lena was half sprawled out of the car, her arm still aiming, holding a pistol. Somehow, she had managed to free her hands, but not her feet.

She had found Dede's gun, with its solitary bullet. From that distance, she had felled Lauder.

'What the fuck?' Without thinking, I fired back at her but missed. She quickly scrambled back into the car and slammed the door. She must have hidden Violet's bag the whole time.

I ran to Lauder. He was on his side, clutching his chest, groaning. His legs kicked out in pain. I knelt down. 'Let me see!' I opened his jacket. Blood surged through his white shirt, a red mass already staining his tie. His groan turned into a whimper. His breaths were shallow, tight rasps.

'Jesus Christ.' I didn't know what to do. Press on the wound? Why? Slow the inevitable? Warm blood pumped through my fingers, drenching my hand. Lauder went white, and his head lolled backwards. Was he dying? He couldn't die. I couldn't let that happen.

I raced back to the car. Lena lay back on the rear seat, arms bent back, her head in her hands. The bitch was relaxing! She raised her brows. 'Looks like a cop. Got something on you? Leave him here. You've got a chance. We both have. Think about it, Jem. I beg you. We can work something out.'

I stared at her. Another me, the old me, would have grabbed the chance. I could be really free now, free of them both. I'd drive south, the sole victor. Lena would fry under the sun, Lauder would bleed out, and soon the desert would claim whatever the birds of prey left.

I could claim my life for myself. No strings, no ties, no witnesses.

I looked up at the sky, and then into the horizon, where the border surely lay. I could run.

But I was no longer that person.

I leveled my eyes at her. 'I'm not leaving him. You're going to drive me to a hospital or else I'll shoot your brains out, right now.'

I hopped in the front seat and spun the car back towards Lauder. I slammed the brakes on, turned to Lena and pointed the gun at her. 'Untie your fucking legs and get out.'

She obeyed, a sly grin on her face. 'Jem. Are you stupidly sentimental? Think about it. Nobody will know if he dies here.'

I ignored her, jumping out. 'He's not going to die out here. Help me get him inside.'

Lena, unbound, followed. Her cold eyes dispassionately surveyed Lauder. I kept the gun on her, knowing if she had the gun, I'd be dead already.

Elimination.

'This is a bad idea. You aren't thinking straight. You're panicking.'

I pushed her towards him. 'You're trained. Stop the bleeding! Now!'

Lena looked at me. 'You want to save him? You really can't. I'm a very good shot.'

'If he dies, you die.' I raised the gun. 'So get moving.'

She glared at me back, then sighed. 'Give me your fucking jacket, then.'

I slipped it off and hurled it at her. Lena caught it. She used the side of the open car door to rip the jacket to long strips. In minutes, she bent over Lauder, feeling his pulse. 'This is a waste of time. He's definitely not going to make it.'

'Just help him!'

She applied her makeshift dressing to his wound. 'Someone will have to hold it down, hard. But it really isn't worth it. And if you're driving, why should I play nurse?'

'Just get him in the car.'

'Moving him will kill him. The pain alone could give him a heart attack. Just let him go. Be free.'

'Do it!'

We met eyes. 'All right. Have it your way.' Lena put her hands under his shoulders. 'Your fella's heavy. Help, will you?'

Lauder didn't look good. Motionless, his skin was now bluey gray. Slate gray. Getting him in that car was his only chance. I weighed it up, and slipped the gun into the top of my pants. I could grab it before she could.

Lena and I managed to drag Lauder onto the back seat. His face glistened with cold sweat. I snapped at Lena. 'Get in the front. You're driving. You better not do anything stupid or you're dead.'

I got in the back, carefully lifting Lauder's head onto my lap.

I pressed down on the wound. He whimpered, his eyes rolling. I caught a glimpse of turquoise.

As we drove away, I looked back. The large pool of Lauder's blood was already sepia.

The desert and the sun would work their magic and make it disappear.

68

A new life in L.A. had been a dream. Criminals like me didn't get fresh starts. I'd been born under an unlucky star. Recently, the star had been outshone by the glare of Los Angeles' neon lights and I finally thought I'd escaped its sick beam. Now it was back, all baleful glare. It brought bad luck to me and everything and everybody I touched.

Lauder could be dead. I had no idea. He was ashen, his lips almost blue. He wasn't making any noise and his eyes were closed. The dressing was a rigid dark brown crust, glued to my hand, and now smelt rotten.

I'd hand him over to the doctors, but I wouldn't ever learn his fate.

Dusk was falling by the time we pulled into the grounds of the County Hospital. The car crawled around to the signs to the ER. 'Now what?' Lena asked. 'Straight to the morgue?'

'After they take him you can go. I advise you not to go back to Tatiana Spark's. Ever.'

'If I don't, my mission is compromised. You'll have more blood on your hands. Sorry for the pun.' God, she was a bitch, even now.

'Make something up. Trained liar after all. Tell your Nazi friends Spark cottoned on you weren't her real daughter. Her baby had a birthmark. Something, anything. You had to run. I don't give a damn what you say.'

Lena met my eyes in the mirror. I said, 'Like you said just a little time ago, we have to trust each other. I won't mention I ever saw you. You won't mention me.'

Lauder's head rolled a little in my lap.

Where was the ER entrance?

'All right. One more thing, Jem. Something you should know. I got curious about my little chum inside. I asked my handler at the Secret Service about you. He didn't tell me much, just that somebody had done a deal to keep you inside.'

'What? You're lying. They didn't know a thing about me. I never squealed. There was no fucking deal.' My cheeks felt hot, flushed with frustration and a looming, irrational sense of dread.

'I'm serious. You being interred? Part of a deal, in return for information. You were kept inside for a reason.'

'Shut up.'

'I heard you went on the run, after you killed a few people. That pissed people off. Funny we ended up in the same city. But you know, I actually believe you. You're just a sweet fool, aren't you?'

She wanted to twist a knife, one I could never pull out. She would leave me with it, crippled.

It's the past. Let it go.

I looked down, at Lauder's face. It had never looked childlike, but it did now. Near to death, he had an innocence.

Yes. Just a fool.

Finally, the car pulled up. I jumped out and yelled for help. In seconds, orderlies swarmed the car, pulling Lauder onto a gurney. It was all a blur. A man's voice barked in my ear, 'You gotta wait inside, Miss.'

Lena looked up out of the car window at me, remarkably poised. I held the small case in one hand, and Violet's purse in the other. I looked down at her. 'I'm taking all that money and both the guns.'

She nodded. 'I'm sure we'll both survive. Well, have a nice life, Jem.'

With that, the car sped away, swallowed up by the big city.

69

The Emergency Room was crammed full. The exhausted receptionist listened as I explained that my friend and I had discovered a man lying on the street, with a gunshot wound. He had managed to give us his name, Randall Lauder from the Vice Squad, before he passed out.

That information would enable his friends and family to rally around. It was all I could do.

I somehow thought up a false name and address to give her. The woman instructed me to sit in the waiting area until the duty cop arrived. He wouldn't be long. I looked down at the bloodstains on my blouse, and waved my hands at her, and told her I wouldn't mind going to the ladies' room. She thought about it, then nodded and pointed down a corridor. In seconds, she was besieged by another disaster. A young boy was being carried in the arms of a distraught father amid a swathe of crying relatives.

Their tragedy, my lucky break.

I turned around and marched straight out of the hospital. A yellow taxi was about to pull away. I ran towards it and jumped in.

'Where to?' It was a female voice, somehow familiar. The taxi driver turned around. I recognized her bony face, hollowed out by too many night shifts. Sal, who had taken me to the Miracle Mile Hotel. It felt like a century ago.

She remembered me, too. 'Hey, still at the Miracle Mile?'

'Moved out.'

Damn!

'Didn't suit you?' Her eyes roved over my blood-stained blouse and my encrusted hands. 'You been in an accident or something?'

I snapped I was in a hurry, that I'd left my car in the Palisades. She said no more, putting her foot on the accelerator.

I slumped in the back seat. My past and present had collided like massive rocks. Lena's parting shot about the deal was cold retaliation. Just that. I'd messed up her business and she wanted to mess with my mind.

What deal, Billy? What did you do?

As the taxi wound along the road, I realized I was nothing to anybody, never had been, never would be. I could challenge Lyntner. I still wanted to find Rhonda, if it wasn't too late. I could make him talk.

And then I'd leave town. I was cashed up and well armed for a future on the run.

Finally, the gleam of the ocean appeared beyond the hills. Thin lines of streetlights formed an illuminated grid charting our path towards the Palisades.

Thirty minutes later, we found Beatty's car. I handed Sal ten dollars. 'I want you to deliver a note to this address.'

I took out my pad and wrote the following words down. '*I'm leaving town. Thanks for everything. E.*' I folded it up and handed it to Sal. I gave her Beatty's home address.

Beatty didn't know it yet, but she was rid of me.

Luckily, the moon was almost full, giving enough light to navigate the bumpy terrain.

I took Lena's gun and left the car. This time, I walked down the road towards the front gate. It was now pitch black.

I reached the courtyard, where two cars were parked. The only light came from a small metal lamp over the back entrance to the main house. I approached, silently. I turned the handle. It opened. Very quietly, I stepped into the gloomy passage.

It smelt of damp. A dusty coiled wall lamp gave a modicum of light. The wallpaper in the hall was ornate and old-fashioned. I crept along.

Wait! A woman's wail. Absolute distress.

It came from the door at the end of the passage, partially open. The room glowed with low lamplight. A man's voice growled, stern. Lyntner's? It was a repetitive sound, as if he was repeating himself, again and again. Reminiscent of a nun forcing a child to repeat a penance.

I peered through the crack. A middle-aged woman sat upright at a table. Lyntner leant over her.

Her skin was colorless. Her gray hair was pulled in a tight bun, and she wore a white nurse's uniform. Her shoulders sagged in despair. This had to be Janice. She set down a pen and pushed away a handwritten note. Her hands rested on the table, shaking. Lyntner held a pistol by the barrel, gesturing towards her.

'Now take the gun.' Lyntner growled at her.

'No. I beg you,' she whimpered. 'Let me go. I won't say anything, please. Please, Freddie. This is me, darling.'

He struck her around the face with the pistol grip. 'Get it in your dumb head. I'm not your darling and never was. Take the gun!'

Lyntner was planning on a fake suicide for Janice and then taking her money. Was Tatiana Spark still alive upstairs? Had he changed the will? Clearly, he had made up his mind to murder Lena the moment she got back. Nobody else knew about the daughter. Nobody except Martell. Did Lyntner know that, too?

Janice began to wail again, but he shoved the side of his free hand into her mouth.

Bite the bastard.

He hissed, 'Do it. Do it now.'

'No! I beg you...' Her eyes implored him. 'Oh, God, no! You love me!'

'Shut up.' He tried to force the gun into her hand.

I burst in, pointing Lena's revolver at Lyntner. 'Don't touch her!'

Lyntner spun around. He masked his shock quickly enough with a slimy smile. 'Well, Miss Slate. What a surprise.'

'Drop the gun! Now! Hands up.'

He dropped the weapon onto the desk. It clattered loudly. He raised his hands back up.

I trained my gun on him. 'Get away from him!' I spat at Janice. The poor woman was paralyzed.

'Hey!' I yelled at her. 'Wanna live? Get the hell out of here!'

Janice seemed to register, finally scrambling out of her chair. I turned to Lyntner. 'You killed Darlene and the others. You're after Tatiana's money. Where is she?'

'She's upstairs. She's all right!' Janice turned to me. 'He hasn't hurt her.'

He didn't need to. If his homicidal plan worked, could sit it out, until she died of natural causes. Lyntner pulled as sincere an expression as he could. 'Think about it. Wouldn't serious wealth give you the life you deserve? You could live how you want, where you want.'

Janice whimpered. I kept my aim on Lyntner. 'Shut up. Where's Rhonda?'

'Who?'

'Don't act dumb. Rhonda. Shimmer's girlfriend.' I turned to Janice. 'You know where?'

She shrugged, helpless. 'I don't know her.' She had no reason to lie now.

Lyntner laughed. 'You mean Slim Caziel's stooge? Don't tell me she had a girlfriend.'

Was this the truth? I stepped forward. 'You paid Caziel. You took Darlene to The Flamayon. You killed them.'

'Just paid him to drug them. I wanted sleazy pictures, that's all. It was easy to get them there. Slim knew Frank. He told him to meet him at The Flamayon, he had something on him. Something from the past. But after I left, guess Slim was greedy, went too far. Peddling pictures of dead people was too tempting. I just wanted Darlene disgraced, but there you go. People like value for money.'

'Why involve Shimmer?'

'From my perspective, she added the required degenerate factor.' He sounded patronizing.

I saw red. 'You're the degenerate. Get on the floor. On your front. Now!' Lyntner got down. I turned back to Janice. 'Check on Tatiana.' Did I want her to call the police? No, not now.

Janice was shaking. Her world had collapsed and shock was setting in. She was useless in this condition; I'd have to handle her later. Lyntner looked up at me. 'Elvira, let's talk. Think straight.' He wasn't giving up.

'Did you kill Slim Caziel?' I screamed.

'What? He's dead? Guess he had it coming. Look, we're talking over a million dollars at stake. You'll get half.'

I moved further into the room, positioning myself so nobody could come from the hallway. Janice had moved. Now she was hovering nearer to Lyntner. Was she hoping he'd say it was all a mistake? The fool. I turned slightly. 'What are you doing? He wants you dead! Get out!'

Lyntner grabbed his chance, suddenly kicking out, striking her shin with his heel. Janice stumbled and fell. I fired, missing his arm by a fraction. Shit! I pulled again, but he was fast, too fast, jumping to his feet. He grabbed his gun from the desk, grabbed Janice's hair, pulling her towards him. He immediately shot her through the temple. Blood sprayed out as she crumpled onto the floor.

I gasped, pulling the trigger and fired. He screamed. A hit? He was staggering towards me, the gun aimed at me. I rolled to the ground, aiming upwards, anywhere on his torso, firing again.

Suddenly he froze, staring at me, something like shock on his face. His knees buckled forward. I rolled back, gasping, to get out of the way of his falling body.

Panting, I got up. Jelly legs again, my heart pounding. Janice's body was inert. Lyntner's convulsed slightly before lying motionless. He was dead.

Now what? Now where? Back to the Astral, to collect my things? To Mexico? To Canada? The clock could be ticking, propelling unknown events my way. Would my note hold off Beatty's anger? Would Lauder somehow survive, quick enough to name me, to name my plan to go to Spark's? I wanted him to live, but living, he would hunt me down.

I had the cash, I had a gun, I had a car.

Get out, now!

I let out an involuntary sob.

I couldn't bear the fact a dying lady lay upstairs, probably terrified.

I had to see her.

70

Tatiana Spark was frail, sitting up in a four poster bed, a shawl around her shoulders, propped up by pillows. Her eyes were sunken, her cheekbones high, covered in papery skin. Bottles of medication were lined up on the large mantelpiece. The only light was moonlight, through the open window.

'Sophia?' Her voice was hoarse, barely above a whisper.

I entered the room. Could she even see me?

'Sophia's gone.' I walked towards the bed.

Her head adjusted, trying to follow the sound of my voice. 'I heard shooting. What is it? Who are you?'

'I'm a friend.'

'Where's Janice? What's happening down there? Where's Sophia?'

I sat on the bed. 'Miss Spark. I have something to tell you. You have to be very brave.'

There was a cough. 'Leave it to me, Booby.'

I turned. Beatty Falaise stood in the doorway, a gun in her hand. She couldn't have got my note yet, not if she was here. She summoned me back out of the room. I got up and went over to her. Beatty pulled the door shut after us.

She looked tired in the moonlight. Her voice was terse. 'I figured you might be here.' She eyed the revolver in my hands.

I met her eyes. 'You called the cops?'

'Not yet. Wanted to see the mess you were in first. Find out why you didn't call me.'

She didn't sound angry. Something else, I couldn't tell what exactly. I could tell her everything and leave. Or tell her nothing. Either way, she'd be a fool to stop me and the weapon reinforced the point. But she was here, and the cops weren't. I spoke low, and fast. 'I followed the phony Sophia Spark. Caught her. She's a spy, trying to catch war criminals, using Spark's as a base.' And then I had to drop the most unlikely bombshell. 'Turns out I know her.'

To give her credit, Beatty didn't bat an eyelid. I rapidly explained everything that had happened since we parted. She let out a sigh. 'So we were right about Lyntner.'

'Yeah. You should leave now. I don't want to drag you down.'

'So you're running?'

'No other choice, is there?' I glared at her.

Beatty put her finger under my chin, as if I was a child. 'There is. You are gonna let me fix this.'

Fix it? Two dead bodies and a dying witness who had heard a shoot out? A cop who might rally round and who wouldn't take too kindly to me doing my own thing?

'Go back to that motel and stay put. All right? You gotta trust me, which I guess is hard for you. So, will you? Say it.'

She had a plan and it wasn't turning me in. I felt weak, overcome. I was putting my life in her hands. If I could let go, it would be like finally ascending the peak of the mountain. The dreadful slow climb I'd been making my whole life, always getting nowhere. Prometheus on the rock, that had been the myth that spoke to me the most as a child. Same old shit.

Trusting Beatty, I'd be unbound. Maybe I'd reach somewhere I had never got to. Finally see new vistas.

I had nothing left to lose.

'I trust you.' My voice was hoarse, a lump in my throat.

Beatty took the revolver from my hand. 'Good. I'm going to need this. Now get the hell out of here.'

I let her take it, my hand limp. I moved towards the stairs, hearing her open Spark's door. Then her voice, surprisingly gentle.

'Tatiana, it's Beatty Falaise here. Do you remember me?'

71

I slept for what seemed an eternity. Maybe Malvin knocked and asked if I was okay. Maybe that was a dream. Sleep was the comforter and the healer. I surrendered myself completely to her grip.

I checked the clock. I'd been asleep for fifteen hours. I looked down. I was half undressed. Exhaustion still consumed me, and I surrendered back to sleep.

Day turned into night, and night into day.

And at some point, sun filled the room again. I roused, to a soft knocking at the door.

Groggy, I slipped on a dressing gown and opened the door. Beatty, surely?

No. Clarence, suave and immaculate. He looked me up and down. 'Bad time?'

I stared at him, trying to process the reason for this visit. 'Want to come in?' He declined. 'I got something to tell you. I'll make it real quick.'

My legs felt weak. I braced myself for the words I dreaded. 'Lauder?'

'He pulled through. Be right as rain in a few weeks. Bullet went in and out, punctured a lung. He's a fighter.'

I met his eyes, biting back what I wanted to say: 'You know he got shot because of me.' But I didn't speak. Until Beatty told me anything, I had to stay put and keep my mouth shut. I had to trust in her.

'I wanted you to know that Arnold Moss is going to be released.'

Now I met his eyes. 'Really?'

He nodded. 'New evidence, he's off the hook.' I had no idea what Clarence knew or guessed. Lauder would know. He could have told Clarence I'd been meddling with Fraser.

'That's swell.' I leant against the frame and gave a half-smile. Clarence had given me the chance to redeem myself, by telling me about Arnold Moss in the first place. To do that, he'd gone behind Lauder's back. He had forced me to take real responsibility. *Your mess, clean it up.* Maybe he had seen the good in me. If so, I had honored the call.

'Lauder wants to see you. Today. He's here.' He handed me a scrap of paper. I barely glanced at it.

I stiffened. 'Why?'

'Just the messenger, Goldilocks.'

'Scratched a rib, could've been worse.' Lauder's voice was croaky. Stiff white bandages swathed his chest. He was propped up, his skin sallow, even more tightly drawn over his bones.

He lay in his own private room, in a swish clinic. Huge bouquets of roses were stuffed in crystal vases. A whole gallery of ornate greetings cards decorated every conceivable ledge. So he was loved. Either that, or his high society circle was wide and this was the done thing. The fiancée was probably bankrolling the recovery process. It was odd, witnessing this other side of his life. And uncomfortable. If he hadn't made it, his death would have had huge reverberations in the lives of many other people.

'So I had a little talk with your colleague Mrs. Falaise.' He pointed to a chair, instructing me to sit down. I pulled one near to the bed.

Beatty had said she was going to fix it. Seeing Lauder had to be number one on her to-do list. So she'd already been here, but she'd so far avoided me. Why? Forcing me to trust the process, I bet.

'Nobody knows you were at Spark's. The official line is that Darlene, Frank and Shimmer were murdered by Elmore Caziel, as part of a wider blackmail scam involving the lawyer on Tatiana Spark, something about her past that she didn't want to get out. Story goes Lyntner got on the wrong side of the Mob, who mowed him down at Spark's. The innocent nurse was fallout. Tatiana heard the whole thing, and managed to make a statement to the police verifying she only heard a shootout.'

Beatty's master plan. A good one. I met his eye. 'What about you? How did you get shot? What's the line there?'

'Drive-by shooting. Got away. A few leads, nothing promising. I won't be able to identify anybody.'

He looked at me. I gulped.

'She is a spy. I was in prison with her.'

'Don't know what you're talking about.' Was that a wink? No. Lauder wasn't the winking type. The message was clear. Lena was not to be mentioned. She did not exist.

'Has Caziel's body been discovered? Reba T. put pressure on me and Beatty to find him.'

'Don't worry about that.' He didn't want to say more about that, either. I wouldn't push, his eyes were heavy. I wouldn't ask about Arnold Moss' release, either.

Lauder motioned me nearer with his finger. I could tell it hurt to speak. 'This stays between us. Shimmer was my informant on Reba T. Her leaving Reba's surprised me, and I was concerned for her. That's why I sent you over there. I knew she would never go back but it was a warning to be careful. She'd have known that. Then she died.'

This came as a shock. Shimmer had pulled the wool over my eyes completely about her connection with Lauder. She'd pretended the whole time, protecting their relationship. And she'd never got another chance to laugh about me with him. Was the fiancée made up? It didn't look like it, considering the luxury clinic now treating his wounds. As for his penchant for a certain stripper, I couldn't exactly ask him about that now.

Or ever, probably.

'Shimmer was some actress. Had me fooled.'

'That's why she came out here, originally. To make it in the movies. Ended up a bookkeeper.'

One question I couldn't hold back. 'So if she was loyal to you, why weren't you interested in the murder? Or Rhonda?'

'I was. But Murder Squad was solid; no evidence. Otto Heymann was broken up, he didn't want the world all over the case. Pressure from every which way to keep it closed. Turns out you beat us all to it.'

I looked down. 'I never found Rhonda. I tried.' The not knowing didn't rest easy with me.

'My guess is she's safe and sound.'

I looked at him. Did he *know*?

'And no, I don't know where she is.'

We sat in silence for a while. I suddenly remembered something. 'Oh, your homework. The code. I found out how the Nightshade Club communicates. You just missed one. They run every month.'

'Nice work.' He didn't sound very surprised. 'I know all about it. I just wanted to keep you out of trouble. Guess I failed at that. It's Reba T.'s new gig. Before she ran, Shimmer had found out Reba was using *The Chronicle* to spread the word. Who the members are and what they are doing in there is the information I'm after.'

Lauder pointed to a brown envelope on the side table. 'For you.'

Me? Maybe a note from Beatty, at last. I opened it. Inside, a folded document. It looked official. I carefully slid it out and opened it up.

A private investigator's license. Granted to Elvira Slate by the City of Los Angeles. Was he releasing me? 'What does this mean?'

'Means I don't need you.' Lauder looked exhausted, his eyelids dropping. 'You aren't exactly employable. Profession you dig, right?'

I nodded. He was freeing me, literally. The reward for saving his life, but he wouldn't make a big deal out of it.

Profession. The license gripped me. As close to legitimate as I could get. I could operate.

I had an identity.

There was one question I really wanted to ask. 'Why did you help me, really? In the beginning?'

Lauder thought about it for some time. 'Burning Caziel's place down was a blow but I guess I liked your style, helping a pal. Then you came out with the truth about your past, in the desert. Knew you wouldn't have got justice back home. Odds were stacked against you as soon as you jumped parole.' His voice was heavy, the words coming out with great difficulty.

He managed one more sentence. 'Guess I wanted you to prove me wrong.'

'How?'

He was already asleep.

72

Beatty summoned me into the office. A pile of squirming Dachshund puppies and their mother lay in a basket in the corner. The pups were blissfully sucking from their mother's teats. When I had got back from the plush clinic, Malvin let me know I should pay Beatty a visit.

Over a cognac, Beatty didn't beat about the bush. Now I was licensed, I could set up on my own if I wanted, or I could remain under her agency. In any event, she would be on hand to share tricks of the trade and advise me. I told her I remained a liability to her, I had to be a lone operator.

Beatty gave raises a brow and shrugged. 'Your call.' I think she appreciated it because she said I could continue to borrow the car.

It was clear her conversation with Lauder was not on the agenda.

'I'd take you to dinner but I got the babies here. Anyhow, Luigi's is shut for renovations.' She explained how a few gangsters had bumped each other off and shot the place up. 'Luigi didn't get hit but Jeez, poor fella. In broad daylight. The place I go to for my lunch!' I could imagine the bullet holes puncturing the idyllic murals.

But something else was still irking me. 'What about Martell Grainger?' Martell was the one loose end. She knew all about the daughter's return and Beatty would have had to deal with it. At a push, she might buy the party line as Lauder had explained it, but Tatiana's life story was Martell's *tour de force*.

'Relax. Martell thinks the daughter's return was pure delusion. Tatiana being high as a kite on all the morphine she was taking. Imagining things.'

Beatty had sewn it all up tight. She slid a letter across the desk. 'You better read this.'

The envelope was crisp. I opened it, my eyes widening as I read.

Dear Miss Slate,

By the time you get this letter, I will be dead. I understand the bravery you showed in finding out the truth and trying to save my life.

I will never know if Sophia is alive or dead. As her mother, I feel she is alive. Maybe I am a fool for believing this. Events have already proven I trust when I shouldn't. For this reason, I want you and you alone to find my daughter and bring her to America. My true Sophia. She will forgive me if she understands how much I tried. All the information about my past, and all my personal files are now with your associate, Mrs. Beatrice Falaise. She will entrust them to you.

I know you will succeed and this will let me rest in peace. I have instructed the Trustees of my estate to pay you a monthly stipend for your time and all your expenses. I hope you will find this acceptable.

With eternal gratitude
Tatiana Spark.

I gulped, lowering the letter. 'She's dead?'

'Last night. In her sleep.'

We exchanged a glance. She can't have died happy. No daughter, no beloved nurse to tend her.

'You can't say no.'

398

I nodded. 'I'll find Sophia. One day. Step by step.' Europe? I was in no hurry.

Beatty added that Spark had left it that Martell could still pen the film, but certain conditions would apply. Number one, the real Sophia first had to be located by me.

Tatiana Spark finally got her comeback. She had the biggest funeral Hollywood had seen that year. Beatty attended and described it in lavish detail over lunch. Otto Heymann apparently spoke fondly of a great star.

Someone else was on my mind. Thelma, Rhonda's neighbor, let down by a rookie private detective who had failed to crack her missing person case. I decided to visit her.

I got out the car, barely recognizing the blighted street. Most of the houses were empty and boarded up, awaiting demolition. Hollow, soulless prisoners waiting for the executioner's axe.

As I walked around to Thelma's front door my foot stumbled on something. A dark, hard object. I bent down and grabbed it. The black queen, from the chess set. She was a little scuffed but I slid her into my purse and rapped on the door.

The lace curtains were still hanging down. Two pints of milk had been delivered by the side gate.

The door opened a crack. Thelma's watery eyes blinked back at me.

'Thelma, it's me, Gina? Remember?'

'Sure took your time.'

'Can I come in?'

She nodded. I picked up the milk bottles.

Cautiously, Thelma opened the door and I stepped in. She was in a black crepe dress with a lacy bib and a small black tilt hat, at least a decade old, was perched on the front of her head. Her hair, out of curlers, fell around her shoulders in wispy waves. 'You on your way out?'

'No. Just got in.'

She led me through the passage to the kitchen. The doors were closed on either side, except one. I glanced through and saw the portrait of Rhonda as a child. Thelma must have moved it for safekeeping until her beloved Rhonda came back. I put the milk down on the table.

I wasn't looking forward to this one bit.

There was a pleasant smell. 'You been baking again?'

'Just my peanut cookies, for the few kids left on the block.'

'Planning to relocate?'

'Nobody's kicking me out, I told you so already. So, it's bad news, ain't it? I read about that Shimmer's death. Sure sounds like she with some rotten eggs.' She leant against the worktop, hands behind her back.

'The private investigator did her best. No sight, no sound of Rhonda. But she isn't back with those bad people. And the P.I. has links with the cops, and asked them to look out for her. They came up empty too.'

Thelma looked as if she was about to cry. 'Dear Lord.'

'She may show up yet. Remember she went without a fight, with her suitcase, you said?'

'I did.'

Thelma sniffed. She came over and squeezed my arm. 'You're a good girl for coming here. For letting me know. I appreciate it.'

Her forgiving tone made the licensed detective feel even worse.

73

Standing outside the Miracle Mile Hotel, it felt as if I was coming home.

I'd called Mrs. Loeb to see if she'd be open to renting a suite as an office and a place for me to flop. She passed me onto Dede who, it turned out, owned the entire joint. Dede summoned me over for tea. I entered the cool lobby. A new wave of career girls had taken over the hotel; some to make their mark in the big city, to scale the heights of their career, some to find husbands, and a few, like me, to have fresh starts.

Dede poured the tea. She was interested in the idea of having an in-house detective. 'I want a discount, though. Should the need arise for a P.I.'

I told her I could do that. And my new name was Elvira Slate.

'Girl's gotta do what a girl's gotta do.' Dede seemed relaxed enough about the change of name.

We sipped away. The door opened. Alberta breezed in, wearing a white dress and red shoes. She stopped as soon as she saw me. 'Oh. You're back.'

'She wants to rent a suite. Run her business here. Sleuthing. What do you think?'

'You asked her what she was doing at Joyce's?' So Alberta had seen me. And reported back to Dede. Maybe they thought I still snooping on them, even after I'd quit the hotel and proved myself helping June.

'Well? Both women looked at me.

401

'I was on a case. A missing person. I swear it was nothing to do with you.'

Dede put down her cup. She turned to Alberta. 'I believe her. Do you?'

'All things considered, sure.' *All things considered.* I wondered what that meant, but I wouldn't ask.

I turned to Alberta. 'I had no idea you were in a band.'

'And now you do.' Alberta still wasn't entirely sure about me. She left us, heading for the kitchen.

I asked about June.

'Moving back in January. Opening her own dress shop.' Dede smiled. 'She's doing fine.'

I took a suite with a couple rooms on the third floor, on the corner of the building with windows on two walls. It had recently been repainted and the furniture thrown away. Mrs. Loeb handed me the key and the contract. She didn't bat an eyelid as she said, 'These are for you, *Miss Slate.*' It was as if she'd never even met Connie Sharpe. Dede's instructions must have been iron-clad.

Mrs. Loeb hovered by the door. 'Want a brass plate on the door?'

A brass plate? It hadn't occurred to me.

'Sure. *Slate Investigations.* By appointment only.'

'A female shamus. Now I've seen it all.'

'There's a few of us around town.'

'I don't want any double-crossed wives blubbing their eyes out in the foyer,' she grumbled.

'I don't do divorce,' I said, rather quickly.

'So what's your specialty?'

'Missing persons, blackmail, extortion.'

She flashed a glance that verged on respectful. 'That'll pay,' she grunted.

I stood alone in the empty suite. I badly needed a desk. More than anything, I would need an assistant to sit in the front office, type up reports, or pretend to, and pacify emotional clients. I knew just the person.

'Your assistant! Oh, my God. You mean you're really saving me from this hellhole? You will not regret this, Boss.' Barney's eyes gleamed with amazement.

'Can you start in a month?'

'And how!' Any minute he'd be jumping on the counter and spinning his cane. Then I remembered his wooden leg.

I needed a month to sort out things with the Spark Trust. Tatiana's trust fund would bankroll the office, mine and Barney's salary and everything that goes along with running a P.I. business. I didn't want to take liberties with the account. I owed Tatiana Spark big-time. The job of tracing Sophia felt like a poisoned chalice, albeit one I couldn't avoid.

'Oh, it might get a little...hairy at times. Goes with the territory. But not too often, I hope.'

I would never know what happened to Lena. Sometimes my heart leapt when I glimpsed a certain shade of blonde. In time, that reaction would pass. Lena and I had saved each other's lives. Jailbird loyalty.

We had no choice but to trust each other.

74

'How's business?'

Lauder strolled into my back office, looking groomed and rather dashing in a snazzy gray suit.

The last time I'd seen him he had just escaped from death's door. Now, Lauder's normally pale skin had a touch of gold about it and he actually looked healthy. The fiancée had no doubt taken him off somewhere nice to heal properly in the sun. Up close, his eyes were more turquoise than ever; cold and glittery like a millionaire's swimming pool – like Martell's, Lyle's and all the others I got to admire in the gossip magazines lying around the lobby these days.

'Going well, if you've got a case for me.'

Lauder smirked and looked around my office. It consisted of a desk, a lamp and a telephone. I didn't even have a chair to offer him. I slept on a sofa in the interconnecting room but luckily, the door was now closed.

The one item of decoration was the chess piece; the black queen. She sat on my desk. For me she was Rhonda, and I wouldn't forget her.

He said, 'You busy now? Could you come someplace?'

'Right now?'

'Yeah. I want to show you something.'

'So long as we're not going on any jolly jaunts to the desert, guess I'm fine.' I joked. It was a little awkward. The etiquette between an ex-con and her ex-handler was unknown to both of us. We would have to make it up as we went along.

Lauder gave me a withering look. 'No. Even better. The city morgue.'

My heart did a very different kind of leap. 'Rhonda?'

'No. Somebody else.' He wasn't going to tell me before he was ready. One thing I did know was, with Randall Lauder, persistence got you nowhere.

We drove towards Downtown. Lauder explained a family had been walking the dog near Echo Park Lake. The dog had run for a ball in a shrubbery, the kid had followed. The kid had discovered a dead body. It hadn't been announced yet, but it was a cop. As we entered the parking lot of the city morgue, Lauder instructed me not to ask any questions inside.

The skull was shot through, close-range impact. A boiled egg with the top sliced off. The skin was like gray putty.

In death, Jim Fraser still looked like a mean piece of work. But like all corpses, the stillness lent him an innocent air. Perhaps death returned us to our unsullied selves. Purified us, so our bodies could return to the soil without taking the poison of our lives with them. I wondered if anyone loved him, and would mourn his death.

I looked away, shivering inwardly. For all its clinical efficiency, the morgue filled me with dread. I wanted to get out.

Why here? He could have told me all this in the office.

Lauder thanked the mortician who pushed Jim Fraser's body back in the chiller.

In the parking lot, I gulped the fresh air. Lauder offered me a cigarette. 'You okay?'

'One less enemy's always good news.' Was that what this trip was really about? To tell me today I was a little safer? I doubted

405

it. He pressed his lighter and I leant forward to catch the flame. I avoided his eyes, which I knew were studying my face.

We puffed away in silence. After a while Lauder spoke. 'Anything strike you about the body?'

'Other than his head's been blown off, like Slim Caziel's? Didn't need me here to tell you that.'

'It happened some days ago. Maybe we'll get a lead. Maybe not. Like I said, those two probably rubbed enough people up the wrong way.'

'You think it's the same killer?'

'Could be.' Elusive as ever.

We slowly walked towards his car. I wondered if Reba T. was behind it. Caziel had plenty of dirt on her and she could easily have found out Jim Fraser worked with him. Tying up loose ends, using a henchman or two.

'They'll be cold cases, won't they? Caziel and Fraser?'

Lauder looked at me, stopping by the passenger door. 'Murder Squad is throwing everything at it.' His voice sounded flat.

Had my blackmail of Fraser led to his demise somehow? I was still very sketchy on how exactly Arnold Moss had been released and what Fraser had come up with to tell his bosses. I had suggested to Fraser, more like instructed him, to say an informant had hinted that Moss was framed. Fraser would have had to name a real person to the Murder Squad, and get a plausible statement out of him. Surely just saying a C.I. had tipped him off wouldn't have been enough grounds to release Moss?

'Think it's anything to do with Arnold Moss?' I said, weakly. Lauder glanced at me. If he knew I was behind it, and I was certain he did, he would know I could be more than curious.

I suddenly felt queasy. I didn't want to finish my cigarette, stubbing it out on the ground. Lauder held the passenger door open for me. I slipped in, wishing we could be straight, put it all out in the open.

Lauder got in, beside me. 'Turns out Fraser had a C.I. who squealed, said a real nasty guy was Stan's real killer. A mobster. Stan had busted one of the guy's gambling rackets. The mobster framed Moss, an easy target. But guess the latest twist? The mobster's dead. Mown down by a rival mob days before. A stack of witnesses, too. Took place in some Italian restaurant.'

The shooting Beatty had mentioned to me. Now I could see Fraser had been very smart, using a known public showdown to conceal his lies. After my threat, he must have cooked the story up with one of his real C.I.s. Probably paid him, or gave him no choice. Now wouldn't it make the real C.I. a target, to badmouth a dead boss?

But Luigi's was an eerie co-incidence. If there were circles within circles, I was lost.

The bottom line was that Moss had got justice, at the expense of an informant's safety. Lauder must have read my mind.

'The C.I. is safe in witness protection. Solid enough information for the DA to release Arnold Moss. The mobster can't be charged with murder, he's already dead. Now Murder Squad like the same crew for putting Jim Fraser down. Treating it like a series of slaps in Vice Squad's face.'

What he seemed to be saying was, *we got it covered.*

He started the engine. 'Oh, yeah. Something else. The weapon that was used to kill Fraser was probably a rifle, older type, with a close-range hit like that.' Lauder put the car into reverse, his cigarette dangling from his mouth. 'Know anybody with a rifle?'

75

There was a chill in the air. Autumn was finally on its way.

I stood outside Thelma's house.

The curtains and nets were gone, and the place was dark. No milk deliveries. I peered in through a window. The front parlor was empty.

She had moved out.

I rapped on the door and waited. Pointless. I turned to leave, noticing a sack of garbage that the pigeons had been pecking at.

'Can I help you, ma'am?'

I spun around. A man and his dog stood on the sidewalk by the front gate. I said, 'I'm looking for Thelma, the old lady who used to live here?'

'Thelma? Don't know any Thelma. You mean Gladys? She just sold up.'

'Gladys?' My mouth fell open. Gladys? Wasn't Rhonda's granny called Gladys?

Yes. Yes, she was.

'Is Gladys about eighty? Skinny, bakes peanut cookies for kids?' I asked, already knowing the answer.

'That's Gladys,' the man smiled, affectionately.

'This place is sold?' I pointed to the house.

'Uh-huh. Wrecking crew coming next. I'm last to go, end of block. Gonna be a whole row of apartments here. How about that? City's changing too fast for my liking. You just missed her. Gone to Union Station. You a relative?'

I shook my head. 'Just an old friend.'

I like stations. News-sellers, candy stalls, tobacconists, flower shops, lost and found, they are tiny cities in themselves; the buzz, the excitement, the air filled with hope for endless possibilities; new ventures, sad goodbyes, and hidden escapes.

The end of the line for some, a place of rebirth for others.

Waterloo Station had made it possible for me and Union Station was doing the same for Rhonda and her grandma Gladys.

They were disappearing into thin air.

Staring at Rhonda was like watching my own past unfold. I stood a fair distance away, observing her through the crowds. She was sitting alone in a wheelchair. Her head was bowed slightly, her hands were resting on a small purse on her lap. She'd been pushed to one side, just like those soldiers had been at Waterloo, but I knew very well she hadn't been forgotten. Her hat had a veil, and underneath that, she wore gold-rimmed spectacles. A woven blanket covered her. Was it a disguise?

She and her granny had gotten away with it. They had played me. Perfectly.

Commuters came and went. Wait! Now Gladys approached, briskly walking through the station, tickets in her gloved hands. She looked the picture of health, with a mink around her neck and a jaunty hat. She was making her way back to Rhonda. I watched as she protectively patted Rhonda's hat and rearranged the veil. Then she leaned down and squeezed Rhonda's hand.

I stepped back, shielded by the side of the newsstand, a safe vantage point. Then my stomach flipped.

A fur-clad apparition, heading straight at me. Joyce! She was making for the stand, so I shot back around the side, and looked away. I heard Joyce's imperious tones asking for a

Chronicle. I didn't move, counting the seconds. Surely she'd have bought the damn thing by now.

'What a pleasant surprise, Miss Slate.' Joyce's dark gray eyes drilled into mine.

I turned, eyeballing her back. 'A big day for surprises. I just found out Rhonda's safe and well, that she has a granny who poses as a neighbor, and they're leaving town. You're here to see them off, I presume?'

Joyce raised her brows. 'Isn't it just wonderful news? Sorry I didn't get a chance to call your office and put you in the picture. Crazy busy as ever. Anyhow, I must dash. Good to see you.'

'Wait. I have a few questions.'

'Why? Case closed, surely. So long.'

She wasn't just going to leave me standing. My arm shot out and grabbed her arm. She shook it off as fast. I hissed, 'Rhonda knew Shimmer had met with Caziel, didn't she? She knew he was behind the murder.' It was a long shot, but one worth taking. Gladys had a rifle. Rhonda wanted justice.

Joyce deadpanned, stepping back. 'I have no idea what you are talking about, Miss Slate. Always such a fanciful imagination. I really must go, their train's about to leave.'

Her furs undulated like a furry caterpillar. I called out after her. 'Guess you can handle a rifle no problem, right?'

Joyce spun around, her eyes flashing. She charged back, like a bull. Then she stared me down, weighing it up.

'I gotta hand it to you. You're smart. And persistent as hell. Let me tell you this, and then we are done. You're looking at it the wrong way round. Elmore Caziel was a very nasty piece of work. How did Rhonda know? Because on the day, she went with Shimmer to the Flamayon! She sat in the lot. She waited. She got worried when things took longer than they should. Shimmer had said it was an in-out affair. Rhonda went to the bungalow and looked right in through the window. She saw Shimmer, obviously drugged, and that creep snapping away with his camera. And guess what. She sees him see her. So she drives away fast as she can, because she could be next. She was in mortal danger. We had to get her out before those bastards killed her as well.'

I stared at her. I stammered, 'Caziel and Jim Fraser?'

She stared at me. 'Same night, a cop comes around. Yes, a Detective Jim Fraser. To break the news that Shimmer is dead. He wants to take Rhonda away for questioning. We'd never have seen her again, and he'd have come up with some crock of shit excuse how she winded up dead. Luckily another cop's already beaten him to it and warned Gladys. But guess what else? I'd already taken Rhonda away, to safety. You know who the other cop is.'

I did. Lauder. That was the one visit Thelma/Gladys had told me about.

'Fraser was scum. His fingers were deep in the pie of perversion. That cop sure wasn't going to let it lie, and tracking down a girl having brain surgery wouldn't take so long.'

Caziel and Jim Fraser were hunting Rhonda down.

Her or them.

But who had pulled the trigger? Joyce or Gladys? I would never know. Only Joyce was strong enough to move a body as large as Jim Fraser's and bury it in the undergrowth of Echo Park. They hadn't killed for vengeance. These hits had been preventative, but did that make it right? In a perfect world, murderers Caziel and Fraser would have faced justice. But what kind of justice? A justice that turns a blind eye to the truth and is happy to pin any face to a crime?

And I'd killed like that, too. In a room, above a pub, I'd shot a man in cold blood. An expensive lawyer could have argued self-defense but I knew the truth. I simply hadn't let Billy's killer live. Heat of the moment, vengeance, rage, and self-preservation compounded in one pull of the trigger. If I'd let him run, and then sat there for the police, it would have just led to a longer incarceration, and I wouldn't be any safer from Mob retaliation inside. I was already on the run when Billy was shot, and no lawyer in the world could argue a way out of that. I'd already chosen my path, I had long been branded by society and maybe society was right. I'd been loyal to Billy, after all, a criminal who had few scruples.

I became aware of Joyce's face leaning into mine, her arms folded. 'Then lil' ol' you comes sniffing around. That's why Gladys pretended to be Thelma. Nobody knew Rhonda and Shimmer had family, and we needed it to stay that way.'

Gladys had simply reeled me in, sending me off on a wild goose chase to track down Rhonda, with her cover story that she'd let her best friend down. She'd got me out of the way easily. 'I don't understand why you told me about Olive Harjo. Did you want me to snoop?'

'Well, I figured it couldn't hurt. We knew you were reporting back to 'Thelma'. And it convinced me you cared about Rhonda. We had a good laugh when we figured out Gina had turned into Elvira Slate, the pain-in-the-butt snoop! Some gal.'

'You knew Lauder was a good guy the whole time.'

'Shimmer's been informing on Reba T. for Lauder for years. But a cop's a cop, I prefer to keep them all at arm's length. Yes, she was annoyed he tracked her down after they left with the money. But she knew by sending you it was just a warning from him to get out of town fast. Turns out the one thing he didn't know was that Caziel had approached her for a job.'

'What about Shimmer's body? Will she get a funeral?'

'She did already.'

'Wait. Did her family claim the body?'

'Don't concern yourself. She's resting in peace.'

Was that why Thelma had been in black? Had Lauder played a part in the funeral, too?

He mentioned the rifle to me. Did he *know*? Did he guess? Maybe he was content that his buddies in the Murder Squad were on their own wild goose chase hunting Fraser's killers.

Maybe that was the path of justice for Lauder.

The perfect crime.

Nobody suspects an eighty-year-old woman.

Don't judge a book by its cover.

There was nothing left to say. Joyce shot me a cross between a smirk and a smile. 'Now we've cleared all this up, why don't you pay the club a visit some time?'

Departure time. I was riveted to the spot, watching as the escape unfolded. Joyce suddenly embraced Gladys, and knelt down, kissing Rhonda's cheek. Rhonda said something to her, and Joyce laughed.

She watched them depart, waving for a while, as Gladys pushed Rhonda along the side of the train, accompanied by the porter wheeling the trolley of cases. Then she strode

413

through the vast station towards the exit, every inch a woman, one who could aim a rifle and lug a body.

A compassionate woman.

Shimmer's, Darlene's and Frank's deaths had been avenged. This felt like true justice.

Nobody except me knew, and nobody else would.

Acknowledgements

During the writing of *Jailbird Detective* numerous friends, allies, and mentors have magically appeared at the right time with support, input and encouragement along the way. You know who you are. Special thanks go to: Patrick Altes, for being my rock during the whole endeavor, particularly reading endless drafts, and collaborating on the cover design; Sheila Hyde, for editorial support, spot-on notes and awesomeness; Franky Kentish for being the perfect social media guru and being all round brilliant; Cassia Friello, for creative graphic design at the drop of hat; Humfrey Hunter of Silvertail Books, for infinite publishing guidance and being an oasis of calm in a storm; Elaine Sharples for typesetting with such flair.

Part of the book journey was making the characters of *Jailbird Detective* come to life in the trailer, and was all down to the generosity, talent and time of wonderful friends. I would particularly like to thank: Dirk Nel (Director of Photography) and Sjaan Gillings (Hair and Makeup Designer) for your vision, belief, and encouragement; it couldn't have happened without you guys; Judy Parkinson (Production Manager) for incredible drive, and organizational support; Eddie James Knight (DIT, Editor), partner in crime, going above and beyond always; Glorija Z. Viktus, Annabel Azura, Rosie McMinton and Jack Jacey (Cast) for immense talent as actors, each portraying Elvira, Jemima and Billy brilliantly; Oleg Poupko (Focus Fuller) for expertise and encouragement; Lisa

Harmer (Costume), for amazing help on the day and through life. I would also like to thank Tim Nathan (Set Photographer) and Mark French (Gaffer), for giving invaluable and warm assistance and use of Shoot on Site Studio; Maja Jensen (Grip) for joining us late in the day and being great; Mark Soye for giving so much help in post with the grade; Paul Mackie at 24/7 Drama, for generous support. For supplying some stunning vintage costume: Greyhound Vintage (that hat!), Liisa Rohumaa (that other hat!), Michelle Lester, and Gill Jenks at The Stables Theatre; Jan Archibald for the beautiful Jemima/Elvira wigs. For the soundtrack, deepest thanks and love to my BFF, Babs Savage for a unique and soulful vocal; Paul Taylor for a very special day at dsound and, with Sam McCormack, for a wonderful recording; Eric Meyers for a fantastic voice over; Julian Bentley for guidance and support.

Printed in Great Britain
by Amazon